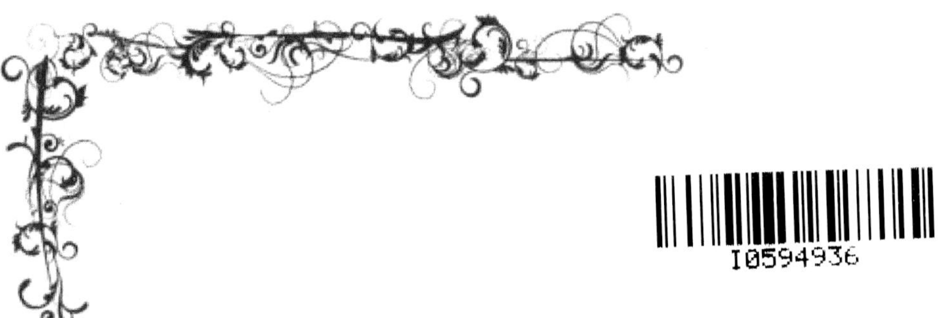

BOOK I:
"THE PLAGUE OF REBIRTH"

SERIES: RESURRECTION OF THE FORGOTTEN REALM

Book One: The Plague of Rebirth

Once, the realm of Luminara thrived, its skies ruled by dragons, its lands protected by elven kind, and its people bound by ancient magic and fragile unity. Peace is easily shattered. Betrayal came like a shadow, and with it, war. The dragons vanished. The elven kind fell, and what remained was a fractured world…forgotten by its gods and choking on the ashes of its own power.

Now, a plague rises from the ruins, not just of flesh, but of memory and magic. Whispers speak of rebirth, of a prophecy stirring after centuries of silence. Some seek salvation, others, domination, and amid the chaos, a girl destined for more than survival must decide whether to become the weapon fate demands… or the hope it forgot.

This is the beginning of a story woven with lost legacies, redemption, and the reckoning of a broken world. Those willing to rise must face the truth: the realm cannot be reborn without blood.

Book Two – Awakening of the Queen of Elves and Dragons
The battle for the throne begins. Elara's survival, and the future of the kingdoms, hinges on choices that may break her or crown her.

Book Three – Legacy of the Lost Kingdom
Darker paths await as the fight deepens. Secrets buried in ancient bloodlines threaten everything. The past demands its due.

Book Four – The Final Rebirth
Hope and darkness collide one final time. The soul of Luminara will either rise… or be lost forever.

Title: The Plague of Rebirth

Author: Sarah Jackson

Published in the United States by:

DragonShrimp Publishing LLC

Cape Coral, Florida

DragonshrimpPublishing.com

Cover design by: Anthony Martin

ISBN: 9798999734907

Printed in the United States of America

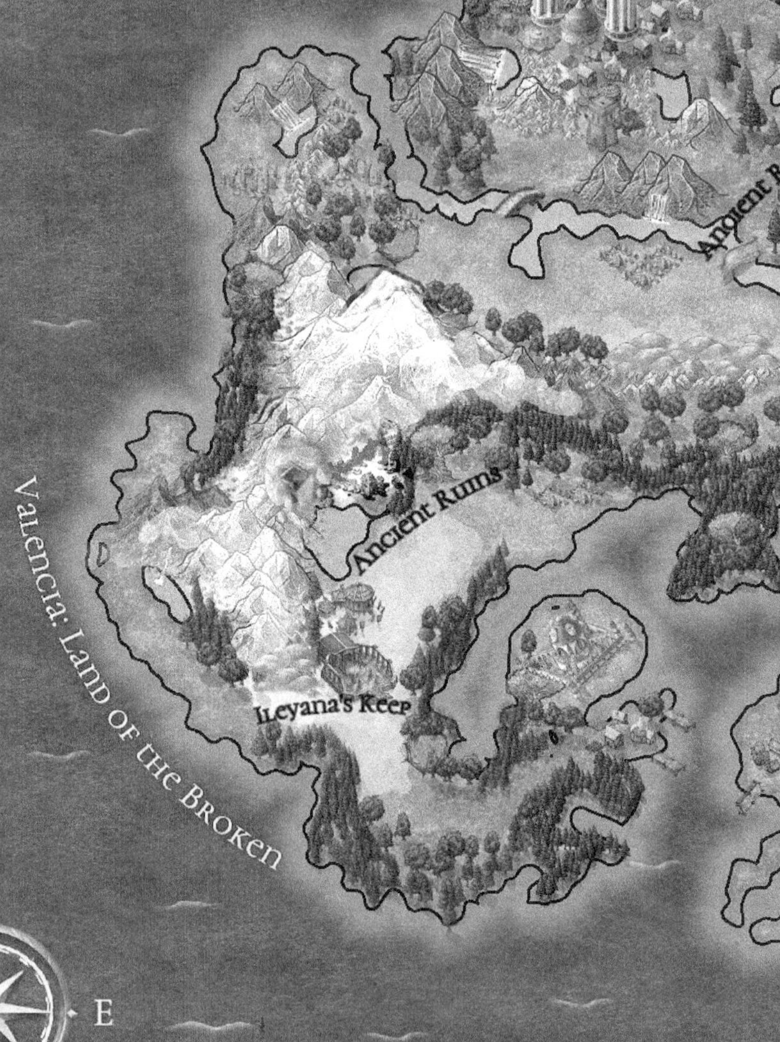

Sylvaris: Land of the Elven
Ael'thar
Ancient Ruins
Ancient Ruins
Valencia: Land of the Broken
Ileyana's Keep
N
W
E
S

Luminara
Aetheris: Land of Dragons

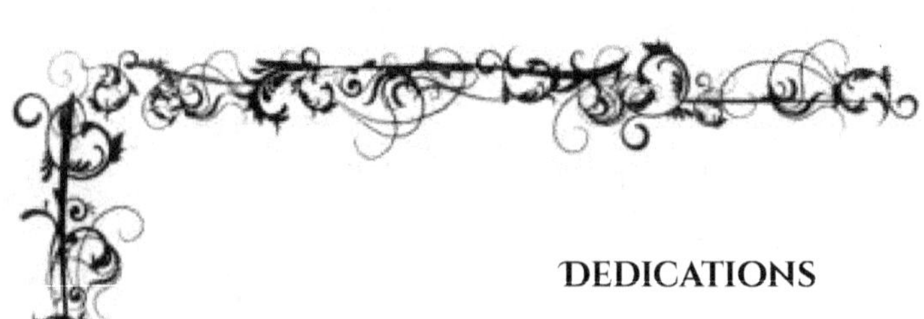

DEDICATIONS

To Laura Marangoni Gualdani:

The spark that lit the fire, the voice behind the veil, the soul who became my muse.

I never imagined the path to authorship would begin in the quiet corners of an online game, but fate has a way of writing its own stories.

There, amidst digital quests and scattered dialogue, I found you…unexpected, brilliant, unforgettable.

What began as passing laughter became a bond unshakable, a friendship woven with trust, passion, and the quiet magic of being understood.

I did not know I could write like this…not until you reminded me that I already had story telling embedded deep in my soul. You saw the stories before I dared give them breath. You believed in the embers when all I saw was ash.

Hajira, the heart of The Plague of Rebirth, carries your spirit in every step, every scar, every defiant breath in the face of a broken world. She is shaped by your wisdom, lit by your fire, and softened by the same grace you carry in every word you write.

This book is for you, because without you, there would be no Hajira, no story, and no me, brave enough to tell it.

To those holding this book:

When Supreme Noctis finds its way into the world, turn its pages slowly.

Laura's magic is not to be rushed.

DEDICATIONS

To Anthony Martin:

My artist, designer, and steadfast friend.

This is his first book cover…but you'd never know it.

I handed him a storm of half-formed visions, scattered thoughts, and impossible ideas… and somehow, he gave it shape, soul, and beauty.

The cover he created doesn't just represent The Plague of Rebirth…it captures the very essence of the book.

Every brushstroke carries the heart of the story, and I'm endlessly grateful for the way he brought my world to life.

Anthony has given me more than art.

He's been a constant source of encouragement, a creative partner in chaos, and a quiet force reminding me to keep going, even when the path felt too steep.

His belief in this book, and in me, never wavered.

Thank you, Anthony, for taking the leap with me. This story wears your work with pride.

DEDICATIONS

To my husband and partner in crime, Damian Jackson:

My heart's quiet anchor,

my fiercest protector,

my greatest champion.

For fifteen years, you've walked beside me through every storm and sunrise, never once letting me drift too far from who I am…or who I'm meant to become. When doubt whispered in my ear, you silenced it with belief. When the pressure felt crushing, you held my hand tighter. You've been the steady flame in every dark night, the laughter in my chaos, the strength when mine wavered.

You've read my wildest ideas without flinching…well, almost without flinching…and somehow embraced even the spiciest scenes with a raised brow and a grin. You never made me feel silly for dreaming too big or writing too bold. Instead, you stood behind me, always gently pushing me forward, always reminding me that I could.

You are my best friend, my loudest cheerleader, and the love that threads through every word I write…even the ones I can never quite find to describe you.

This may not be the last dedication I write…

but you will always be my final thought,

my constant muse,

my always and forever.

PRONUNCIATIONS

Hajira Valendor – Ha-Zhi-Ra Va-Len-Door

Elara Aelaron – E-La-Ra Ay-La-Ron

Kaelen Arathiel – Kay-Len A-Rath-Eal

Aeris'Kal Nyrathos – Air-Ris-Cal Ny-Wrath-Os

Seraphina Lirael – Seh-Ra-Fina Lie-Ra-El

Valorian Arathiel – Va-Lor-Ian A-Rath-Eal

Miraelen Arathiel – Mi-Ray-Len A-Rath-Eal

Orion Delacroix – Oh-Ryan De-La-Cruse

Ileyana Veloria – Ily-Ana Ve-Lor-Ia

Valencia – Va-Len-Sia

Sylvaris – Sil-Var-Is

Aetheris – A-Ether-Is

Arach'naara – A-Rak-Naa-Ra

TRIGGER WARNINGS

This book contains mature and potentially distressing content that may not be suitable for all readers.

Please be advised that the story includes:

Gruesome and graphic death scenes

Intense flashbacks and traumatic nightmares

Themes of emotional isolation and self-deprecation

Mentions of mental and emotional struggle

Explicit sexual content ("open door spice")

At its heart, this story is about more than war, magic, or monsters. It is about **facing the darkness within**…and choosing, again and again, to rise.

You will meet characters who are broken, grieving, haunted by past choices... and still, they fight. Still, they love. Still, they hope.

If you see yourself in their struggle, know this:
You are not alone.
Your story isn't over.
There is beauty in survival, strength in vulnerability, and power in rediscovering who you are.

So keep going…
Even when the world burns.
Even when it hurts.
Especially when it hurts.

You are worth the rebirth.

Table of Contents

CHAPTER 1: THREADS OF FATE

"We're losing him," I scream as the blood pools at my feet. Another victim of a senseless stabbing. I look at his grimacing face, crusted over with blood and dirt. We found him along the broken stone path on the outer bend of the village. I wonder if he has a family somewhere, maybe kids…a wife. I glance at his hand and see a tan line where a ring used to sit.

The scent of blood unfurled like a red ribbon through the small cottage, delicate at first, like crushed iron leaves, but deepening into a scent of sorrow and earth. It mingled with the perfume of night blossom poultices and the quiet magic woven into the gauze. Even here, in a place of healing, it reminded me how thin the line was between life and loss.

"HAJIRA, focus, we need you with us." Lyrian's voice snaps me back to reality. I wipe the sweat from my brow and continue to apply pressure to the wound. "He must have put up one hell of a fight," I glance across his chest, face, and arms. There's a slash down his right arm, not too deep, but enough to cause a great deal of pain. Plus, there are upwards of 30 cuts and bruises ranging from his legs to his head. I sigh and imagine the agony and fear he must have endured.

"Lyrian, hand me more cloth. I can't see where this wound ends…There is too much blood…" I say and trail off trying to stop the constant flow of blood from the worst of the wounds. Lyrian runs across the cottage, grabs more cloth, and rushes back with them and a glass medicine jar in his hands. "Will this help?" He shows me the last bit of powdered Hemorris Leaf. "What would I do without you?" I whine to him.

When dried and crushed into a powder, Hemorris Leaf acts as an antiseptic and accelerates the coagulation of blood. It has been known to create a numbing effect to slightly relieve pain. The Hemorris Leaf released a pungent, piney scent, like vinegar over dry herbs. I quickly direct Lyrian to sprinkle some across the slash on his arm, and the cuts across his chest and face.

When sprinkled onto the wounds, it brings a cooling sting and a bitter, earthy smell that mingled with the iron tang of blood, cleansing it with every breath. "It won't work on the stab wound, but if we can even take some of his pain, his survival rate will rise steeply!" I refocus back on his stomach.

There's a 2-inch stab wound that just will not stop bleeding…What am I missing? I must do it...he will die if I don't. "Everyone except Lyrian, leave, I can't focus," I instruct the room. The two girls' glance at one another with concern filling their eyes, but do not move. "LEAVE NOW!" Lyrian demands. The two apprentice healers jump and scurry at the booming voice.

As soon as they left, I peered across the wooden table at Lyrian. "Do it," he says, knowing that I am second guessing myself. I hold my hand over the stab wound and take a deep breath. A warm sensation travels down my arm and illuminates his belly, light pulsing over the wound. I am careful to focus my energy on the worst of the wounds. If he were to magically heal completely, it would bring unwanted attention to the skills I have worked my entire life to hide.

Before I can blink, the bleeding slows to a trickle. "I think that will do it," I exhale as I glance at Lyrian, his jaw loosens with relief. "You always amaze me," he says as he continues to sprinkle the Hemorris Leaf powder across the many scrapes and cuts. I dab the clean cloth around the patient's stomach, clearing away some of the blood. I reach for my needle and begin sealing the wound shut. "Save some of the powder for when I finish his stomach. The antiseptic properties will help him stay infection free."

I peek at Lyrian and see that he has his iconic mischievous smile plastered across his face. I pause; he truly is good-looking! Lyrian Dewbrook is almost 6 feet tall with a lean, athletic build that emphasizes agility over bulk. His black hair is short and slightly tousled, and his warm, honey-colored eyes sparkle with a playful mischief. His face is sharp, with high cheekbones and a strong jawline, marked by a faint scar from past scrapes.

As he stepped closer, his scent caught on the air…clean and warm, like sun-dried linen and wild herbs. Beneath it lingered a trace of leather and sweat, faint but grounding, like someone who'd just come in from a long ride through a pine-covered trail. There was a hint of spice too, something subtle and dry, like crushed cedar bark or peppered sandalwood. It was such a warm familiar smell that I have grown to love over the past few years.

We have traveled together for many years now; we met after a drunken night at a random tavern. I had a bet with one of the farmers of the villages that I was passing through. He bet that I couldn't beat him in a drinking game and I never back down from a challenge. After slamming back several glasses of ale, I realized that the farmer stopped drinking and looked completely unphased by the drinks. I groaned and slowly looked up, my head was spinning, something was wrong.

Before I knew what was happening, the farmer lurched forward and planted a wet, sloppy kiss right on my mouth. I froze for half a second, stunned, before recoiling like I'd been slapped. I glared at him, disgusted, scrubbing the trail of spit from my lips with my sleeve. "Mother Above," I hissed under my breath, stomach churning. He reeked.

The smell hit me in waves…thick and putrid, like a pigsty left to ferment in the summer sun. Manure clung to his clothes, soaked into the coarse fibers of his tunic like a second skin. There

was a sharp, eye-watering tang of ammonia beneath it, mixed with

the sour musk of unwashed skin and damp wool. His breath was

even worse: stale ale, old onions, and something faintly rotten, like

he'd chewed on spoiled turnips for lunch. I could practically taste

the filth in the air between us.

I staggered backward, gagging, nearly knocking over a

barstool as I stumbled into the tavern counter. Behind me, I heard a

few snorts of laughter, either at my reaction or at the farmer's

boldness, but I was too busy fighting the urge to vomit. When I

looked up, he had this animalistic look on his face. I felt someone

grab me and my heart sank. "Okay, enough drinking tonight sis, let's

go back home already." An unknown male emerged from the

shadows. Mother Above, he looked quite beautiful.

The farmer tried to sidestep him, "Boy, mind your manners,

we're busy," he growled. As he reached for my wrist, the mystery

man pulled me back toward him, causing my stomach to lurch.

Before I knew it, I vomited all over the farmer's boots, and he

kicked the mess off with a disgusted grunt. "This isn't worth it, get her out of here." He shouted. The mystery man apologized and directed me out of the tavern. "Okay, let's get you cleaned up," he said as we stumbled over the threshold. I can't believe that it was almost 8 years ago, so much has happened since then.

"You're gawking again!" He teases, realizing that I was still looking at him, my cheeks flush. I quickly glance back down and retort, "I am just trying to figure out why you are smiling at this man's body. You know…if he is your type, I can let him know when he wakes up." "I think you know my preferences, and my eye is on a little someone." He winks at me, and my heart starts thudding in my chest. Could it be one of the apprentices? They are both so beautiful with long flowing blond hair and crystal blue eyes that would make any man murder for them to just glance their way. They always look amazing, with form-fitting dresses that show their slender figure.

They are both breathtaking in a way that hardly seems fair…identical, radiant, and utterly magnetic. Their long, golden hair falls in perfect waves down their backs, catching the light like strands of spun sunlight. It sways when they walk, silky and untamed, as if even the wind can't resist touching them. Their eyes are a piercing, crystalline blue, the kind of gaze that can stop a conversation, or start a war. There's something ethereal about them, something almost too flawless, like a painting brought to life. They wear dresses that cling just enough to make heads turn…rich fabrics in jewel tones that shimmer as they move, tailored to highlight every graceful curve and the elegant lines of their slender frames.

They always look like they've stepped out of a storybook…untouched by dirt, by grief, by the weight the rest of us carry. Everyone calls them "the twin goddesses," and it's not just flattery. It's a truth people whisper, half in awe, half in envy. Then there's me. I'm of average height…five foot seven, neither willowy nor delicate. My chestnut-brown hair is long like theirs, but thicker, heavier, falling in soft waves that rarely behave. My eyes are a warm amber, not striking, but gentle…eyes meant to soothe, not seduce.

I wear the robes of a healer: plain, functional, and modest, dyed in soft earth tones and stitched for utility, not beauty. They drape over me in a way that hides the shape beneath, smoothing out every curve I've spent years trying not to notice. I've always felt more comfortable fading into the background, my body something to cover, not celebrate. Next to them, I've never stood a chance…not in the eyes of strangers, not in the eyes of men, but I've learned that beauty fades, while quiet strength endures.

The twins had been displaced from their home ever since Veilstone took their parents. They once told us the story of how hard the disease hit their household. It wasn't a quick death, but cruel and unraveling. The disease didn't just steal sight, it stripped away perception itself, layer by layer. At first, their mother had squinted at the morning light, brushing it off as fatigue. Their father had knocked over a pot of stew, claiming the ladle was missing when it was right in his hand. Then came the rest.

Sounds dulled or twisted into static; voices became echoes or vanished entirely. Smells faded or warped…fresh bread reeked of ash; lavender turned to rot. Their parents began to move strangely, reaching for things that weren't there, flinching from invisible threats. In time, they stopped responding to the world completely, their eyes glassy, their expressions blank. It was like watching them sink into a place no one else could follow, a silent void that neither cries nor touch could reach.

By the end, they had forgotten the warmth of the sun, the taste of food, even the feel of their daughters' hands. Their bodies wasted away, as if the soul had starved before the flesh. When they were gone, the girls were left alone…two mirrors of each other, sharpened by loss, bound together by grief and necessity. The twins learned to survive in a world that had turned hollow far too early. They carried Veilstone's shadow with them, not infected, but forever marked by what it had taken.

I still remember the first time Lyrian and I found them, or maybe it's more honest to say *stumbled* across them. It was near dusk, a thin gray fog creeping in from the marshes, and the forest was quieter than usual, like even the birds knew something had gone wrong. We saw the smoke first…just a thin, lazy thread rising from what looked like a half-collapsed cottage. Inside, we found them: two girls crouched in the corner like half-wild things, thin as reeds, covered in soot and dirt, with cracked lips, and hollow cheeks.

Their hair, once golden and bright, hung in tangled mats, streaked with ash, and dried blood. Their eyes…those haunting, ice-blue eyes…were wide and rimmed red from sleepless nights and tears that had long since run dry. They didn't speak at first, not a single word. One of them held a rusted kitchen knife like it was a sword, hands trembling but ready to fight, while the other kept her back pressed against the wall, shielding what little food they had hoarded in a torn cloth bundle.

There was a feral edge to them, a brittle defiance in the way they watched us…as if we might vanish like everything else they'd loved, and Mother Above, they were so young. Too young to look that hard. Too young to have eyes that knew what dying looked like. I remember Lyrian crouching low, slowly extending a hand like you might to a frightened animal. I said nothing…just took a step back and let the moment breathe, heart aching in my chest. They were fighting for life with nothing but bones, instinct, and a kind of silent, burning will, and I knew, without delay, that whatever came next, we weren't walking away from them.

When I snapped back from my memories, I realize that I could never have a man like Lyrian. My chest starts to tighten the more I think about it. I want to be happy for him, but it hurts my heart to know he likes someone else. I fake a chuckle, "The wanderer of hearts strikes again, I assume." He scoffs as if I missed something. "What?!" I exclaim. "You know, you can be as dense as an Elderwood tree at times." He begins to clear the bloodied rags from around the patient. I ignore his jab at me and finalize the last stitch of the wound. "There! Now, sprinkle some powder along the seam," I instruct him.

"You know, just because you have "*fancy powers*" does not mean I am inept. I study just as hard as you do!" He sighs again, and I begin to reply, when the twins burst through the door. "We brought more cloth…" Alina trails off as she sees us finishing up. "Do we really distract you that much that you cannot work with us near?" Belinda snaps and folds her arms across her chest like an angry teenager.

"You each serve your purpose well, and do not lose sight of my teachings. In time, you both will be great healers. I just need silence to think and cannot focus with your piercing blue eyes staring at me." I bluntly explain before Lyrian clears his throat, but I continue, "Healing is not just the restoration of the body, but the mending of the soul. Even in the deepest of wounds, kindness can take root."

Lyrian cuts in, "What she means is that she doesn't want anyone to see her if she fails. She cannot take the disappointment on your face when we lose a patient. You both have dealt with a great deal over the past years, and seeing too much death takes its toll on anyone." Belinda's body relaxes and tears begin to fill her eyes. "We are disappointed in life being lost, not that you couldn't save them."

Alina rushes over when she sees my shoulder drop, "I'm sorry, I shouldn't have sent you two away, I know you are strong enough... I just..." Tears begin to stream down my face. "I do not always have enough faith in myself, I try so hard, but we have lost so many patients this past year, it weighs on my soul. I do not want you two to see the horrors that plague my dreams."

I sniffle as Alina rubs my back and I continue, "In the act of healing, I find my true purpose. Not to simply cure, but to soothe

the heart that suffers in silence, which includes you two." "You know for such a great healer, you are such a crybaby." She mocks. Lyrian's husky laugh disperses through the cottage, breaking through the depressing moment.

"Okay, let's get cleaned up. It is almost dinner time, and they made stew at the tavern. I heard the village talking about how they caught a boar, so we can finally eat some meat!" Lyrian chimes in and glances my way. He nudges me as I wipe the last of my tears. "You heard the man! Let's get cleaned up!" I exclaim. The twins begin to chatter away as they begin to clean the cottage. We move the patient to the bed in one of the inner rooms.

It is not much, but this cottage serves as our home. An abandoned cottage at the edge of the village. We came here soon after we found the girls and felt the need to take root. This village does not have much to offer, but the people are welcoming, and the food is always warm. "I will be back; I have to retrieve more water from the village well to clean this mess on the floor before it dries."

I begin to leave the cottage when I feel a tug on my robe. "Do you mind if I walk with you?" It's Lyrian, and he seems to have something on his mind. "Sure, but you're carrying the water vases," I respond as I reach for the door. I pass over the threshold and take a deep breath in. Stretching, I catch a glimpse of the sun setting and enjoy the pink and blue horizon. "Beautiful, isn't it?" I peek at Lyrian and falter as I see that his honey eyes are focused on me. "Yes, it is," he says without breaking eye contact.

I stumble and he catches me by the arm. "Will you stop playing and help me?" I tease. His jaw clenches and he bends over to grab the two water vases, one in each hand. I watch him carefully and my eyes dart from his wrists, up his forearm, following the thick vein that travels the length of his arm. When I get to his face I see his half smile, and I immediately look away, forcing myself to begin walking along the path behind the back of the cottages toward the center of the village.

We hear clamor from the center of town as we round the last corner. Lyrian places the vases on the side of the well, as he begins to pull up the water bucket. After a long silence, he finally speaks. "What do I have to do for you to see me?" "It's hard to miss you when you are right in front of me," I respond matter-of-factly, the smell of fresh earth and damp hay filling the air as I lean against the wooden stable nearby. The scent of soil, warm from the afternoon sun, mixes with the faint tang of horses and the sharp freshness of growing grass just outside.

He snaps, "That is not what I mean, and you know it. It has *always* been you." His voice is sharp, but I can hear the underlying frustration, the way it rises and falls like a breeze rustling through the nearby trees. I sigh deeply, my breath mingling with the rich, grounding aroma of the stables, the scent of earth and life all around us. "What? Do you not believe me?" He asks, raising an eyebrow. He almost whispers, as if the words are carried by the wind itself.

In response, I scoff, letting the earthy smell settle around me. "I do not know what to believe… You are always facetious, so I never know what the truth is and what a joke is." In the span of three seconds, he strides to my side and places his hand on my chin, forcing me to look in his eyes. "I am being serious. I may joke around a lot, but I would never placate my feelings." His hand tremors, and he pulls it back to his side. I think for what feels like a lifetime, and reply, "You have all of the world to choose from, why me?"

He looks almost torn by my response. "The world can burn away for all I care!" He responds without thinking. "I just need you…" "You don't mean that…" I say and glance away as my cheeks begin to flush again. "You do not see what I see, you always help without ever taking. You always put others' needs before your own. I hate seeing you cry, so I try to stay lighthearted, but I just can't hold it in any longer…" He says so firmly.

Rocks crunch as footsteps near, and I take a step away from him. Belinda rushes around the corner, "He is awake, hurry up you two!" We rushed back to the cottage, a thousand words left unspoken. Is he serious? Could it be me that he was talking about? My head begins to spin as we reach the door. The first thing we hear is, "What happened to them? Please tell me, you have to tell me." Lyrian is the first to speak, "Sir, lay back down, your wound will open back up if you thrash around like that." "To hell with me, my daughter, they took her. I can't stay here," He argues.

He begins to panic, "How far are we from Andaria?" I rush to his side and try to push him back down to a lying position, "Let's start with your name, and then tell us what happened." Reluctantly, he lays back down on the bed and after a few silent moments, he begins again. "My name is Vin, my daughter, Lizabeth, and I were hanging out our clothes to dry on the line, when a group of bandits came and tried to force their way through our gate. I tried to yell at Liza to run into the cottage and bolt the door, but before I could finish my sentence, one of the guys grabbed her. Sheer rage is what I felt. She is all that I have left after my wife and eldest son caught the Veilstone Disease, after a year of struggling, I put them out of their misery."

"I ran toward the guy who grabbed my Liza. That's when I felt the knife at my back. She began crying for me to help her, but I couldn't get to her." Vin begins to cry, "I asked them what they wanted, and their response will haunt me for the rest of my life." He continued, "They said they came for a quick payday, but saw…"

He swallowed deeply, a look of disgust flashing across his face. "They saw how delicious Liza looked and wanted to have some fun. She is only 12 years old. I quickly threw my elbow back, catching the man with the knife to my back and dove for Liza. A third guy came from around the corner and kicked me in the ribs, knocking the breath out of me. I started crawling toward the man who threw my Liza over his shoulder, when he kicked me in my jaw, and I lost consciousness."

Silence surrounds him, as we all listen intently and he continues, "When I came to, I heard her screaming from the cottage… I jumped up and grabbed the door swinging it open…Those monsters…they were on top of her, and she was screaming for me to help her. I saw red when I saw her ripped shirt and grabbed one of their daggers… I jumped on the back of the man closest to me, plunging the dagger into the back of his neck."

"Normally, the sight of blood makes me queasy, but it didn't stop me this time. I yanked the dagger out of the first one and sliced at the second, but I didn't see the third one, maybe this is what went wrong. I felt a sharp pain erupting down my arm. When I realized what happened, another guy burst through the door and he grabbed me, slamming me on the ground. It knocked the very breath from my lungs and my head bounced off of a nearby wall and slammed into the floor."

"I heard one of the men growl that I would regret killing his brother. He kicked me over and I rolled to my back. His boot ground into my hand and I let out a bellow. That's when they saw Liza climbing through the back window and I sighed in relief. Then two of the guys began to rush after her, one to the window and one through the door."

"I panicked, I tried to stand up and the third man grabbed my shoulder and thrusted his dagger in my stomach. The pain…everything started to go black. It was then that I realized that I didn't have my boots on. I got so angry at myself for thinking about something so trivial amid what was unfolding. I tried to stand after the last two men rushed out of the cottage, but I couldn't stay up."

"I stumbled onto the dinner table, taking the plates from our breakfast down with me. When I woke back up… the cottage, it was empty. I pulled myself up and ran out the door. I am so weak, I don't even know how long I was out for. I stumbled out of the cottage, saw footsteps, and began following them. I walked what seemed for hours, I finally leaned against a broken wall along a path and woke up here. You have to help me…My Liza…" He began to sob and Lyrian gripped my shoulder. I looked at him and realized that I couldn't see clearly through the tears now streaming down my face.

"You are not weak; we have heard many stories like this," I began. "I think it could be the bandits from the forest. We started tracking them after our last patient, an elder woman who was gardening. They struck her head with a rock and pillaged her home, when they grabbed all that they could…they just left her there," I choked out.

Lyrian finished for me, "We couldn't save her, the damage was too bad. There is a mercenary group in the village about a day's ride from here. Once we find them, we were going to pay them to get rid of the bandits." I tried to catch my breath, and Lyrian grabbed my hand, he was shaking. I could not tell if it was from fear or anger, maybe a mix of both.

I looked back at Vin, still visibly upset, and I nudged Belinda. She scurried to the dresser and mixed a tonic with some tea. She brought it back and handed him a small cup. "Drink this, we do not want you to get an infection, we can't find Liza just to lose her father." He took a moment and glanced at us all, finally he grabbed the cup and downed the drink in one gulp.

We continued to clean up after he drifted back to sleep. I hate lying to people, but if he knew we gave him a sleeping tonic he would never have taken it. We all solemnly went to the tavern for dinner. After a few minutes poking around at my stew, the bar maiden approached and asked us if the food wasn't to our liking.

Lyrian smiled and said, "Marian, how could your food ever NOT be to our liking." He grabbed his bowl and finished it within a minute flat. Satisfied, Marian went back behind the bar to retrieve refills of our ale. I took a deep breath and told Lyrian, "You know what we have to do." He replied in a whisper, "We will leave after the twins fall asleep." We both nodded in agreement and tried to go back to the sliver of normalcy so that we could fake it until the time to leave came.

I woke up to a shake, it was Lyrian, I must have fallen asleep. "It is time, the girls will begin to wake up for their morning duties soon. I wrote a letter to them and left it on the table to explain what we were doing and how to tend to Vin," he said in a hushed tone, ensuring to not wake the girls. They would surely ask to come with us, but it is far too dangerous. I wiped the sleep from my eyes, pulling the blanket that magically appeared over me, swinging my legs off of the couch. I shivered as I realized that it would soon be Winter, and the temperature was already dropping fast.

Outside, the dusky sky was alive with the flutter of Echo Moths, delicate creatures with wings that mirrored the night sky, speckled with starlike patterns that shimmered in the fading light. As they flitted past, they emitted soft, melodic hums that seemed to harmonize with the wind itself. It was said that if you listened closely, their song could carry secrets whispered through the breeze. Lyrian handed me a thick coat, his gaze flicking upward briefly toward the murmuring moths, before he began gathering the rest of our supplies.

After a few quiet moments, we were ready to leave. I felt a strange chill creep down my spine as I glanced back at the cottage one last time. Trying to shake the unease, I tightened my grip on my sack and medical kit, then stepped out into the cold, echoing dusk. We strode past the villages well and began to saddle our horses. "We should start at Vin's cottage to see if we can find any clues," I began as I jumped on my horse. "Promise you won't do anything brash," Lyrian had a look of concern in his eyes.

"I promise, as long as you do not kill me with your stupid jokes the entire ride," I chuckled as he tripped over a rock before catching himself and jumped on the back of his horse. He shot a look at me, that suddenly stopped my laughing, and we began heading toward his village. I am sure it is only an hour ride from here, so I hoped for a silent journey.

No less than ten minutes later, Lyrian started, "Are we ever going to talk about it?" I asked, "About what?" Hoping it would aggravate him enough to not push the subject further. "Damn Hajira, I love you, is that what you want to hear?" My heart stopped at that moment, and I whipped my head to look at him. There was a soft look in his eyes, that I have only seen a few times, and asked him, "What did you just say?"

"…I love you," he replied almost instantly. My breath caught in my throat. Silence. For several minutes, neither of us spoke until I finally gained the courage to respond. "You don't mean that…" "You are infuriating, Hajira, I have loved you from the moment I met you. I tried to tell you so many times, but you kept shaking it off, so I stopped trying. I know that I am grasping at straws. You deserve so much more than I can offer…" He states.

I cut him off, "You do not get to tell me what I deserve!" "Then answer me," he pleaded, his horse evened out with mine and he looked at me, it made me feel like he could see straight to my soul. "Tell me you don't feel anything for me, and I will leave it alone. Just please… put me out of my misery…please," He whimpers. I looked at him, really looked at him, he wasn't lying… Lyrian loves me? How? When? Why? So many questions sped through my mind.

"I…I don't know what I feel…" I trailed off. "Don't lie to me, Hajira…" He grabbed my hand from the reins and stopped both of our horses. "Look at me and say that you don't know how you feel about me, if you are going to lie, tell me to my face," He said.

I took a deep breath and looked at him. Tears welling in my eyes, "I can't lose you; you are the only reason that I keep pushing, the only reason I haven't given up. Don't make me say it, I worry that when I do, you will tell me that it was just a joke, I can't take another joke." He took a deep breath. "Please…" was all that he said. I looked down at my hand, his hand was still gripping mine. He was shaking. "I … love you too." It all spilled out so quickly, "Lyrian, you stupid fool, how could you not know how I feel? You drive me insane, yet I can never leave your side."

Before I could finish speaking, Lyrian's hand shot to the back of my head, his fingers threading through my hair as he pulled me toward him. His lips crashed into mine, urgent but somehow tender. The taste of him hit me first…salt and something faintly bitter, like the air after a storm, mixed with the hint of a campfire that still clung to his skin.

The scent of him…wild, like pine and leather, wrapped around me, a familiar and intoxicating blend that made my pulse quicken. His breath was warm against my lips, sharp with the remnants of wine and something earthy, like the sweat of a long day's ride through the woods. I was so caught up in the sensation of him, his hands gentle but insistent, his lips soft yet demanding, that I didn't even realize I had stopped breathing until my horse shifted restlessly to the side, breaking the moment.

I gasped for air, blinking up at him, disoriented. His lips were still tingling on mine, and when I met his gaze, his smile was a mix of satisfaction and mischief, like he knew exactly what he had done to me. At the age of 24, I have been kissed by a man before, but this was different. This was with Lyrian, the man who I have sought after for 7 years... I could feel my heart throbbing in my ears.

My neck, face, and ears all flushed. I quickly looked away and Lyrian let out a sultry chuckle. "There is no going back now. You are mine. End of discussion." I began to retort when I saw Vin's village peaking over the hill. "We will talk about that later," I finally got out. He laughed again, "We will see about that." Five minutes of silence, it felt like days, I couldn't stop thinking about his lips.

Until something snapped me back to reality. A small body, right outside the village, was it Liza? I froze while Lyrian jumped off his horse and raced toward the tiny body lying in the snowy road. She had no shoes, a ripped shirt, and her pants… they were in tatters. My heart dropped as he reached her body. "It's Liza, HURRY, Haji come quick."

CHAPTER 2: THE CALL OF THE FOREST

I jumped down with my medical bag and raced toward the two. I reached out to her and felt a chill down my spine. I could feel that she didn't have much time left, she was in freezing temperatures all night, and her lips were blue. I threw my bag to the ground and placed my hand over her chest.

Once again, the warmth radiated from down my arm and to my palm. I do not care who sees me, I have to save her. A light brighter than any I have seen before burst from my chest and seemed to tunnel through her. With a gasp she shot up in a panic. "Daddy, help me," she screamed. I grabbed her and held her tight, "You are safe Liza, your father sent us, breathe, it is okay, you are safe."

After a few moments of rocking the small child, her sobs slowed, and her body finally relaxed in my arms. Her grip around me tightened, though. She glanced up at Lyrian, eyes wide and filled with a mixture of fear and uncertainty. Without warning, she shoved her face into my chest, her tiny body trembling as she whispered, "No, do not let him take me, please miss…please." Her voice cracked, and she began sobbing again, shaking uncontrollably in my arms.

The scent of her hit me then…a mix of dirt, sweat, and something far more tragic. Her hair was matted, the tang of the forest clinging to it, along with the faint odor of fear and fatigue that clung to her skin. It was as if she had been living in the shadows for far too long, her small body bearing the weight of more than any child should carry. The smell of the night's cold still clung to her clothes, mingling with the salt of her tears, a reminder of how much she had endured.

Lyrian, sensing the unspoken plea in her trembling frame, crouched down in front of us, his expression softening as he met her tear-filled eyes. "I bet you are hungry," he said gently, his voice low and soothing. "I promise I will find whoever did this to you. Eat this." He held out a stale piece of bread, its edges hard, and a small chunk of boar from the previous night's dinner, still wrapped in a bit of cloth. The food had cooled, but it was the first offer of comfort she'd had in days.

"Sweetie, can you tell us what happened?" I began as I grabbed the food and handed it to Liza, wrapping a small blanket from my bag around her. She remained silent for a few moments, until she finally spoke, "Where is my daddy?" "He is safe, he was in really bad shape, but he made it all the way to us to save you, he is a really brave man. He did all of that for you!" I whispered, brushing her hair with my hand.

She started sobbing, "There was so much blood, I was so scared…the men… they grabbed me." She started crying and rocking again, but continued, "They tried to take me, but daddy wouldn't let them. They kicked him and he fell asleep. I started screaming for him and one of the bad guys slapped me. I heard this loud bell in my ear and then everything went silent." I glanced toward her ear and gritted my jaw when I saw a streak of blood down the side of her face, stretching from her ear. How hard did these monsters hit this poor girl?

She took a bite of the bread and continued after swallowing it down. "I couldn't hear what they were saying, but they threw me on my bed. One of the bad men started pawing at my shirt and I

tried to fight back. My shirt ripped on the corner of the bed when I

tried to run away.

One of the men grabbed me and threw me back on the bed. That's when daddy came to try and save me again. I couldn't see what happened, but in a flash, there was blood everywhere and daddy was on the floor. I screamed for him, but I couldn't hear what I was saying. I kept screaming hoping he would hear me. I saw that no one was near me anymore and I ran out of the back window. I ran and ran. There is a tree that I always hide in when my daddy and I play hide-and-seek. I climbed in and waited for daddy to come get me. I fell asleep and woke up when I felt a cold chill.

I couldn't feel my feet, but I climbed out and tried to go back home. I was so tired, I think I tripped over something, and I couldn't get back up. I laid there for so long, but no one came to help me. I was so sleepy, I guess I fell asleep. I started to feel warm, but I couldn't wake up. I tried to scream for help, but my voice wasn't working.

I was so scared, then you came to save me. You looked like an angel, when the light shone above me, I thought The Mother came to take me to see mommy and my brother. Was that you? Did you save me?" she whispered. I took a deep breath in; my hands were shaking; they didn't violate her. I started sobbing with relief, "Yes, sweetie. My name is Hajira; you can call me Haji. This goofy looking guy is Lyrian, he helped me find you."

"So… he won't hurt me?" she almost whispered. "No, I will never hurt you, Liza. I promise you; you are safe now." Lyrian replied in the calmest voice. "Can you stand up? I am sure your daddy is worried sick. Let us go home and see him, you can ride on the horse with Haji. I will not do anything to scare or hurt you," Lyrian whispered. I placed my hand on my heart, as if I could will it to beat at a normal pace.

I stood up and held my hand out to Liza. She grabbed my hand, and we began walking toward the horse. "Can I help you on the horse?" Lyrian directed his question to Liza. She glanced at me, I smiled and nodded. She quietly replied, "Yes, please." I jumped on the back of my horse and Lyrian carefully picked up the little girl and placed her in front of me.

He gathered our supplies, mounted his horse, and we started back for our village. Outside of a little comment here and there, Liza was mostly quiet. We rounded the last bend when she started shifting on the horse. "We are nearly there," I explained to her. "Be careful when you see daddy, he is in a lot of pain." She silently nodded.

We arrived at the village and tied the horses up, giving them fresh water and food. We began walking back to the cottage. Liza gripped my hand harder the closer we got. When we opened the door, Belinda, and Alina both stopped what they were doing and froze in place. Their eyes grew as wide as dinner plates. "Is that...?" Alina started, when a shadow lurched past us. "Daddy! I was so scared," She started crying as he dropped to his knees and hugged her.

"I am so sorry honey; I couldn't save you… I tried… I promise… I tried everything I could to find you… I failed you… my sweet Liza…I am so sorry." She gently placed her palm on his cheek, "You didn't fail me, daddy, you sent me an angel. She fixed me, see I'm all better." Vin glanced at me, dumbfounded.

I smiled and shook my head, "…later, for now, let's have some lunch and you, sir, need to get back in bed." For the first time Vin smiled." I do not know what I can do to ever repay you." Again, I smiled and said, "Later." He seemed to understand me as he groaned, trying to get back to his feet. Lyrian rushed to his side and helped him back to bed.

"It will take a little while before you are back to your normal self, Vin. So, let Belinda or Alina know if you need anything." I said as I brushed through Liza's matted hair. We decided to go search for the bandits again tonight. We overheard folks warning people in the town center, talking about a group of scary guys around the edge of the next town over, at the forest opening.

Lyrian glanced over my way, as if trying to convey some unspoken message. He stood and walked into the kitchen. I placed Liza on the bed and followed him shortly after. Lyrian was at the wood burning stove, stirring a small pot of broth, the soft glow from the fire casting shadows across his face. He didn't turn as I entered, but his posture was rigid.

I leaned against the doorframe, arms crossed, watching the way the firelight danced on the walls, almost as if trying to avoid his gaze. "You're worried," I said quietly, breaking the silence that hung heavily between us. He didn't respond immediately, his fingers tightening around the wooden spoon in the pot. "It's not just that," he said, his voice low and strained. "We've been pushing too hard, Hajira. This... all of it. We can't keep rushing into these situations without considering the cost. We both know what could happen if we aren't careful."

I stepped forward, brushing a lock of hair behind my ear. "I know, but we have to do something. If we don't, more people will suffer. More families will lose loved ones." My voice faltered for a moment, but I quickly steadied myself. "We're the only ones who can stop them. No one else can afford the mercenaries." Lyrian finally turned, his dark eyes locking onto mine. The weight of unspoken fears and regrets lingered there, but so did the unshakable resolve.

He stepped closer, placing the spoon down, and wiping his hands on a rag. "I know you're right, but I still don't want to lose you," He murmured, his gaze softening. I reached out, placing a hand on his arm. "You won't lose me," I said, the words sounding more certain than I felt. "We'll do this together. Like we always do."

His lips twisted into a small, rueful smile, but it didn't quite reach his eyes. "Together," he repeated, as if tasting the word. He glanced back toward the bed where Vin and Liza were resting, the flickering firelight casting long shadows across the room. "We'll get them, Lyrian. We have to." The tension in the room was palpable, and for a moment, neither of us spoke, the weight of our choices hanging in the air.

The village is a little over a day's ride from here and the forest is on the far end of it. We need to be sure to travel light in case we run into problems, but also enough that we won't die. I have been having these strange dreams when I am in the forest. Almost like a familial, sense of longing. I am not looking forward to camping out in the woods. I always wake up in a panic, like I am missing out on something important. Yet my heart still yearns for the feel of the ground beneath my feet, the air in my lungs, the sounds of the animals around me. There is nothing that can compare.

Every time I step into the forest, a sense of peace washes over me, but it's also accompanied by an unsettling feeling, like I should know something I don't. The way the sunlight filters through the trees, the earthy scent of damp moss, the rustling of leaves, it's all so familiar, yet elusive. It's as if my soul recognizes the forest, but my mind is struggling to recall why. There's a quiet tug in my chest, something that whispers that I've been there before…long ago, in a different time, maybe another life.

When I walk beneath the thick canopy, the shadows seem to embrace me, wrapping around me like a cool, familiar cloak. The air is thick with the earthy scent of moss and damp soil; the tang of pine needles crushed beneath my boots. The soft rustle of the wind through the leaves carries with it the subtle sweetness of decaying wood and the fresh, sharp scent of wildflowers hidden in the underbrush. It feels like a lullaby from the past, a whispering memory I can't fully grasp. I can almost hear voices, distant yet comforting, drifting on the breeze, like echoes of a time long gone.

The smell of old leaves and wet earth grows stronger with each step, a grounding presence that makes the world feel both ancient and alive, but when I turn to listen, the voices fade, slipping away as if the wind itself had swallowed them. It's as though the forest is trying to remind me of something…something I once knew, a fleeting memory just out of reach.

Each step brings with it a greater sense of familiarity, but also an emptiness, a longing for something I can't place. The scent of pine and earth grows deeper, richer, and the cool dampness of the air clings to my skin like a forgotten touch. It is maddening, but at the same time, I don't want to leave. The forest, with all its smells, its sounds, and its shadows, calls to me like an old friend, one whose face I can no longer remember but whose presence still stirs something deep inside.

I snap myself back out of my thoughts to realize that hours have passed. I glance around the room and all is still. The sun has set, and I lean my head back to listen to the silence of the world. It is almost time. Right when I begin to stand up, the door opens, and a familiar smile embraces me. It's Lyrian, with food in hand. When the aroma hits me, my stomach rumbles. Lyrian chuckles, "I thought you would be hungry, it's nice to see that I am still always right."

He hands me the food from the tavern. It's still warm. "A bothersome wind in my ear, yet again," I say as I begin to gulp down the food. He smiles and walks toward the dinner table, "We should leave within the hour if we want to make it to the forest by the midnight veil." Why did you not get me sooner?" I ask as I finish off the last of the Sun Root Soup. He scoffs, "Well, you seemed a bit…preoccupied with something. I didn't want to interrupt you."

I look towards the bedroom. "Everyone is still at the tavern eating dinner. I missed you, so I came back early," Lyrian says in a soft tone. "I thought you said it was because you believed me to be hungry, and here I thought you were thinking of my wellbeing," I said with a mischievous smile. He approaches me, I look up, and our eyes meet. He is the first to break the silence: "What were you thinking about so deeply?"

I exhale deeply, "I am not so sure. I was thinking about the forest." Lyrian raises an eyebrow, his smile fading into something more thoughtful. "The forest?" he repeats, his voice soft, almost cautious. I hesitate, unsure of how to explain. It's a feeling, not something I can put into words easily. It's not just the trees or the land, but something deeper. Something I've been carrying for far longer than I can remember.

"It's hard to explain," I finally say, my voice barely above a whisper. "It's like the forest calls me. It feels familiar, like I should know it, but...but I don't." Lyrian watches me closely, his expression unreadable. "A call from the forest?" he murmurs, as though assessing the words. "Maybe the land itself has a way of drawing people in, but I can tell you've felt it before, something more than just curiosity." I nodded, swallowing the lump in my throat.

"Every time I go in, it's like... like something is trying to remind me of something, but I can't quite grasp it. It's maddening, Lyrian. I'm not sure what it is, but it feels important. Too important." I ran a hand through my hair, frustration creeping in, but I continued. "I think I've been there before, in another life or... or a time I can't recall, and each time I step into those woods, I feel like I'm losing a piece of myself, like I'm failing to remember something crucial."

He steps closer, his presence calming in a way that makes my heartbeat just a little slower. "You know, the forest has always been full of stories. Old ones, forgotten ones. It's not just the trees or the animals, it's the magic, the deep, ancient magic that lingers in every root and every leaf. Maybe there's something you're meant to find there." I shake my head slowly, still not understanding.

"I don't know. It feels like I should already know what it is, as if my very soul remembers...but my mind is a blank slate. I'm starting to believe that I'm supposed to remember something, and that the forest is holding the answer, but what if I never remember?" Lyrian reaches out, resting his hand on my shoulder.

His touch is firm, steady, like he's trying to anchor me to the present. "You will remember one day, I believe that, and I'll be there with you when you do." His voice is quiet, but his words are reassuring, as though he genuinely believes the answers lie ahead. I give him a small smile, appreciating the warmth in his voice. "I hope so," I whisper. "I really do."

The room is silent for a moment, the weight of our conversation hanging in the air before he pulls back with a slight grin. "Well, if we're going to reach the forest by the midnight veil, we'd better get moving." He moves toward the door with a small gesture. "Your thoughts might be pulling you in every direction, but the journey ahead will keep you grounded, I promise." I stand and nod, taking a deep breath. "Right. The forest waits for no one."

As we gather our things, the evening outside grows darker, and the air begins to chill, carrying the scent of the coming night. The forest calls, as it always has. I just hope that this time, I'll finally understand why. As we step out into the cool night air, the forest looms in the distance, its silhouette just visible against the fading light. The familiar tug at my chest pulls harder now, urging me forward, urging me to uncover what lies hidden within the depths of the trees.

With Lyrian by my side, I take a steady breath, knowing that whatever awaits us in the woods, I can no longer ignore the call. I remind myself of a time when I was learning to use a bow and arrow. I felt this feeling then too. I shake my head, I must be worried about leaving the girls, that's it!

We make our way to the tavern to say our goodbyes, and a gust of wind howls through. The wind stilled, and even the birds had gone silent, as if nature itself held its breath in fear. I glance around, trying to see if someone was following us. Perhaps that was a dark omen behind the unsettling weight in the air.

I hurried to catch up with Lyrian, he didn't seem to catch the air surrounding us, so I left it alone. After a short walk, we meet Liza, Vin, Belinda, and Alina leaving the tavern. "Is it time already?" Alina squeaks. I give a tight nod, trying to shake off the feeling that something isn't quite right. The air around us still feels charged, like a storm is brewing just out of sight.

Lyrian gives a small laugh, clapping Vin on the back. "Better late than never, right? We've got a journey ahead of us, and no time to waste." Liza's face is serious, though her voice betrays a hint of excitement. "The forest is scary. You have everything you need, right?" She gives me a pointed look, as if trying to gauge my readiness in a single glance.

I force a smile, trying to project confidence, though a part of me wonders if anyone can truly be ready for what lies in the woods. "We're as ready as we'll ever be," I say, my voice betraying only the slightest tremor. Alina steps forward then, adjusting the pack on my back with determination. "Let's get going," Lyrian says.

His words sound almost too bold in the heavy silence that has settled around us, but it's enough to break the tension. We all begin walking toward the mare's stalls. Soon we will begin down the broken stone path that leads into the forest, the sound of our footsteps oddly muffled.

We mount our horses, saying our final goodbyes and begin our travels. As we move closer to the edge of the trees, the night deepens, casting everything into an eerie shadow. The forest looks different now, darker, more ominous. The trees stand like silent sentinels, their twisted branches reaching toward the sky, as if they're waiting for something... or someone.

A low hum rises from somewhere deep within the woods, barely audible but unmistakable. It's a sound I've heard in my dreams, though I can never place its origin. A chill runs down my spine, and I can feel the pull growing stronger now, as though the forest is trying to reach into me, to take something from me. I glance at Lyrian, whose expression is unreadable. His eyes are scanning the darkened trees, alert and vigilant. He's heard it too.

The hum. It's a sound that's never quite left him, a constant reminder of the strange connection he, too, has with the forest, a connection that has always left me wondering just how much he knows about what awaits us in the depths. "Stay close," he says softly, his voice cutting through the night. "We don't know what we'll find tonight." I nod, my hand instinctively reaching for the bend of my bow.

With the bandits around, we can never be too careful. The horses begin to pull us down the path, broken rocks crunching under their hooves. I glance back one more time, and a strange feeling washes over me, like I will never see this place again. I swallow the lump that seems to have formed in my throat and follow close behind Lyrian. We travel for several moments in silence. Lyrian looks worried about something, so I try to leave him to his thoughts. Only a 4-hour ride until we reach where we will camp. I hope things remain quiet and uneventful.

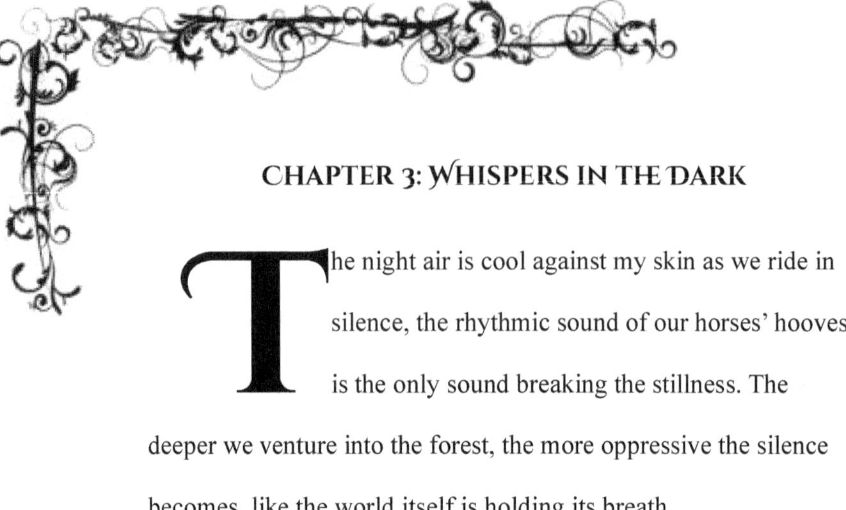

CHAPTER 3: WHISPERS IN THE DARK

The night air is cool against my skin as we ride in silence, the rhythmic sound of our horses' hooves is the only sound breaking the stillness. The deeper we venture into the forest, the more oppressive the silence becomes, like the world itself is holding its breath.

The shadows of the trees loom high above us, their twisted branches weaving together to create a canopy that barely lets the moonlight through. It's as if we're entering a world untouched by time, a world that has its own pulse, its own secrets. The pull I felt earlier in the tavern hasn't faded; if anything, it's grown stronger, more insistent. I try to shake it off, but it gnaws at the edges of my thoughts.

My chest tightens as the weight of it presses on me, and I can't help but wonder, what is it? What am I supposed to be feeling, to be learning, in these woods? Lyrian's presence beside me is comforting, though I can feel the tension in him too. He's more alert than usual, his eyes scanning the shadows, his posture rigid. His focus is unwavering, and for a moment, I almost envy that.

The sound of the horses' hooves crunching against the stone path is oddly muffled, and I find myself wishing for the familiar chatter of the tavern, for the noise of the world outside the forest. Instead, the air around us is thick with an unspoken anticipation, and I can feel the forest drawing closer, pulling at me, calling me. Okay, I take it back, this silence and overbearing feeling is killing me.

After what feels like hours, we reach a small clearing. Lyrian slows his horse and dismounts. Without a word, I follow suit, my muscles sore from the ride, but the discomfort barely registers. My thoughts are elsewhere tangled in the strange sensations coursing through me, the question of what I'm meant to find here growing increasingly urgent. As the camp is set up, the fire crackles in front of us, casting flickering shadows on the ground.

I help unpack the bags, my fingers moving almost mechanically, my mind far from the task at hand. I'm too distracted by the pull of the forest, by the sense of power that seems to be building inside me the longer we're here. The air feels charged, alive, and as I draw a breath, I swear I can taste the earth on my tongue, like the forest itself is inside me, breathing with me.

Every step I took seemed to draw me closer to something I couldn't explain. It was as if the earth beneath me was alive, shifting with an energy that thrummed through my veins, syncing with the beating of my heart. The sensation was strange and unsettling, like being both a part of this place and separate from it at once. The power growing inside me wasn't just mine, it was ancient, tied to the very land itself. My fingers tingled, as if the forest's secrets were waiting for me to unlock them…but the more I felt, the less I understood, and the more I wanted to flee from it all.

"Are you alright?" Lyrian's voice breaks through my thoughts, and I blink, surprised by how lost in my own mind I'd become. He's looking at me, his brow furrowed in concern. "You've been quiet for a while." I nod, but it feels like a lie. "Just tired," I say, forcing a smile that feels too thin to be convincing, but it's enough to satisfy him, at least for now. He turns back to the fire, and I sit down beside him, feeling the warmth of the flames on my skin.

Though the heat envelops my body, it's not enough to chase away the coldness creeping into my bones. I can't ignore it anymore…the deep, gnawing feeling that something is happening to me, something I'm not prepared for. "I don't understand," I murmur, more to myself than to Lyrian.

My voice is barely above a whisper, carried away by the wind as I sit with my legs drawn to my chest. "Why do I feel so connected to the earth all of a sudden? Why does it feel like… like something is growing inside me? Something I can't control?" Lyrian doesn't answer right away. Instead, he stokes the fire, his face unreadable in the dim light.

I noticed the way his jaw tightened as he scanned the trees, the flicker of unease in his eyes when the silence stretched too long. Lyrian wasn't just alert; he was on edge. I wondered if it was the forest, or if it was something deeper, something within him that he was fighting to keep hidden. His concern for me was palpable, as though the bond between us went beyond physical.

It wasn't just about protecting me, it was about something more, something unspoken that I was starting to feel too. The weight of his gaze made me realize that no matter how strong he appeared, he carried his own burdens. I wished I could help, but right now, I was lost in my own confusion. When he does speak, it's quiet with certainty. "What if, the more you use your powers, the stronger they will get, but it's not just about control, maybe it's about understanding. The forest has a way of amplifying what's already there, what's already inside of you. You've only just started to tap into it."

I let out a frustrated sigh, my fingers clenching around the fabric of my cloak. "But I don't even know what it is. I don't remember anything. How can I control something if I don't even understand it?" I retort. "You're not supposed to have all the answers yet," Lyrian says gently, his eyes meeting mine. "The forest doesn't work that way. It won't give you everything at once. You have to trust it. Trust yourself." I look down at the fire, watching the flames dance, feeling the pull of the earth beneath me as though it's calling me home. The warmth from the fire isn't enough to combat the unease settling in my stomach.

"What if it's too much?" I ask, my voice small, vulnerable. "What if I can't handle it?" Lyrian's hand rests on my shoulder again, firm but not possessive, grounding me. "You're not alone. Remember that. You're stronger than you think." I close my eyes for a moment, trying to steady my breathing, trying to make sense of everything.

The strange sensation in my chest, the growing power, the deep connection I feel to the earth, it's all so overwhelming. However, it is clearly undeniable. I am connected to this place. The forest calls to me, but why? Before I can voice my next thought, a noise from the trees catches my attention: a rustling, snapping branch.

My head jerks up, my hand automatically reaching for the bow on my back. Lyrian is already on his feet, his expression hardening. The silence presses in again, thick, and heavy. The forest doesn't want us here. Not yet, and I don't know if we're ready for whatever comes next.

We both freeze in place. I realize that I am holding my breath. I glance toward Lyrian, his face as hard as stone. I let out a sigh of relief when I see a stag cross our path. As if it sees us for the first time, it too freezes, before darting off into the darkness of the forest. We both sat back down around the fire and let off an uneasy laugh. "I thought we were as good as dead, before we even started our main journey." Lyrian sounds shaky when he says that, like he was deeply concerned about something.

I can no longer ignore his behavior. "Lyrian," I begin, "What has been on your mind? You seem…off." He looks my way as if he doesn't know how or where to start. "You have been different…since our kiss. I think I may have made you feel uncomfortable with my words. I don't want you to believe that I think of you as an object to possess. Yes, I love you, yes, I need you close, but I do not own you, you have the right to make your own decisions…" He says, trailing off.

I begin to smile as he rambles on, and it causes him to pause. "What?" He says incredulously. I scoot toward where he is sitting and placed my hand on his thigh. As I do, I can feel his entire body tense and slowly relax. I gently squeezed his leg, trying to reassure him. "Lyrian," I say softly, "You're overthinking this. You didn't make me uncomfortable. Honestly, it's the opposite."

His eyes met mine, searching, as if trying to read me. For a moment, the world felt smaller. It was just the two of us, the fire between us casting flickering shadows on our faces. I could feel his warmth, the steady beat of his heart through the gentle pressure of my hand against his thigh. It was a comforting feeling, one that steadied my erratic pulse.

As much as the forest made me feel untethered, in this moment, I felt grounded by him, by his presence. The weight of his gaze softened the storm inside me, but it didn't erase it. No, the storm was still there, brewing in the distance, just waiting to sweep us away. I take a deep breath, my heart racing a little.

"I'm not scared of you, or of us. I want this... all of it. Though, I think we both need to remember that we're still figuring things out. I don't have all the answers, and I know you don't either, but I don't want to push you away with my own fears." He blinks a few times, and then a small, relieved smile tugs at the corner of his lips.

He reaches out, taking my hand in his, and squeezes it. "I'm glad you said that," he murmurs, his voice low and warm. "Because the last thing I want is to make you feel trapped or uncertain. I just…" He pauses again, looking at me with more vulnerability than I've ever seen from him. "I care about you more than I've cared about anything or anyone, and that scares me, but not in the way I thought it would. I'm scared of losing you."

I take a deep breath thinking of how to best phrase my thoughts. "Is that why you didn't want to search for the bandits?" I question him softly. He begins, "You are just figuring that out? I saw the fear in Vin's eyes, he was helpless. I would do anything to not be in the same position. I could not imagine seeing you ripped from my grasp. I would do anything to keep you safe," he softens his tone, with a quiver in his voice, he continues, "Anything… I just got you; I can't lose you now." He glances back toward the fire.

A tear slips from the corner of his eye, as if the very air around us had turned heavy with sorrow. "Lyrian, I am not going anywhere, I am here. Look at me," I protest. He slowly drags his eyes toward me and pauses. His eyes meet mine, raw and

vulnerable, as if he's searching for something, reassurance, maybe, or a promise.

The flickering firelight dances in his gaze, casting shadows across his face, but the emotion behind his eyes is clear, unmistakable. My heart swells with a mixture of tenderness and longing as I lean closer to him. Without thinking, my hand gently cups his cheek, my thumb brushing over the dampness of the tear that had slipped from his eye.

He rests into my touch, his breath shaky, and I felt him let down a wall, he's built around himself. Then, slowly, his lips find mine in a kiss that is softer than the last, but infinitely more charged. It's a kiss that speaks of everything he's been holding inside; of all the fear and uncertainty he's been carrying. His lips are warm and insistent, and I respond in kind, my heart pounding in my chest, the world narrowing until there's nothing left but the two of us.

The kiss deepens, slow and aching, each of us pouring everything we've been holding back into this single, perfect moment. When we finally pull apart, breathless, his forehead rests against mine, and in the stillness between us, he whispers, "I never want to feel this afraid again, but I'd rather feel this, with you, than

not feel anything at all."

He pulls back and casts his arm around me, the faint scent

of earth and pine from his skin mixing with the smoke curling up

from the campfire. With the motion, I lean my head against his

shoulder, seeking comfort, trying to steady my erratic heartbeat. His

grip tightens, holding me firmly. If it weren't for his presence, I feel

like I might just drift away, lost in the gusts of wind that stir the air,

carrying the crisp, fresh scent of leaves and the dampness of the

forest floor.

The silence settles around us like a thick blanket, and for a

time, all that fills the space is the sound of the fire crackling, the

wood popping and hissing as it shifts. Above the flames, smoke

curls lazily into the air, its sharp, woody scent mingling with the

faint tang of pine and the earthy musk of the forest.

Just beyond the firelight, Moonlit Fireflies begin to appear,

drifting through the dark like tiny lanterns. They radiate a soft,

silvery glow, weaving luminous trails that shimmer with an almost

ethereal grace. Folklore says these trails are messages from the lunar

Mother Above herself…signs of guidance and protection for those brave enough to walk beneath the moon. I close my eyes for a moment, inhaling deeply, grounding myself in the scents of the wild, the warmth of the fire, and the quiet reassurance of his presence. For the next few moments, no words are spoken. The world seems to pause, the hush wrapping around us like the cool breath of night, and above us, the fireflies dance in silent reverence.

Finally, the silence is broken by the soft creak of the wood, the flames crackling louder in the stillness, and his voice, low and steady, cuts through the quiet: "It's moments like this, that I wish time would freeze. The calm, the warmth, you, me, all of it." I sigh knowing we will have to retire for the night, but just for now, I want to stay with him.

My heart aches for the time that we missed. A few moments pass, and Lyrian looks at me, "We need to get some sleep if we want to get anything done tomorrow." I let out a sigh and pull from his arms. "You are right, it is just so warm," I lie. Lyrian lets out a low chuckle, "The fire? That's why you don't want to go to sleep?" I smile at him. He always catches my lies. "Fine," I begin, "I don't want tonight to end. I know what tomorrow brings, and I do not think I am ready for what is to come."

He leans in for another kiss, and my heart stops beating. When we part, he stands, "Me neither, but remember, you are not going anywhere. I will be here when you wake up tomorrow and for eternity." I laugh, "Well, don't you have quite the silver tongue!" He laughs and begins to stand.

He ushers me to a small tent, made from tanned leather and rough-spun cloth, which was pitched against the rising chill of the evening. It was little more than a refuge from the elements, but its warmth and protection would be welcome when the night grew colder. A thin layer of woven moss and soft furs lined the ground beneath him, cushioning the earth's hard bite and offering us some comfort amidst the cold stone floor. "Let me clean up to keep animals out and I will be right back." He states leaving the tent.

I settled beneath a night-covering, a heavy, soft weave that seemed to hum with the deep pull of slumber. Lyrian snuffs the fire and returns. I keep my back turned toward him as he crawls onto the makeshift bedding behind me. Before I can blink, a warm embrace covers my body. He is so warm.

For a fleeting moment, I wonder if we are meant to have this, if we deserve this kind of peace. I turn and shift into his chest, the weight of the world beyond our little campfire seems distant, almost like a dream fading away as I hold onto him. My heart no longer just beats for survival but for something more. Something fragile.

I close my eyes, savoring the quiet, knowing that nothing lasts forever. There is a truth in the quiet between us, a truth that settles deep in my chest, a truth I can't deny. In this moment, I feel as though I belong. As though the universe has somehow aligned for us, just for this instant. I close my eyes, sinking into the warmth of his embrace, knowing that nothing lasts forever. Not even now. Before long, the darkness of sleep claims me, and the world fades away.

CHAPTER 4: THE ENCHANTED REST

The first light of dawn filters through the small opening of the tent, casting a soft glow over the world outside. I blink slowly, reluctant to leave the warmth of sleep, the peace of the night still lingering in my chest. The weight of the day ahead presses on me, pulling me from the comfort of the blankets and into a reality we can no longer escape.

Lyrian stirs beside me, his arm tightening around me instinctively, a silent protest to the new day. For a moment, I wonder if he too feels the weight of what's to come, the uncertainty that clings to the very air around us. I turn to face him, studying the calm on his sleeping face, a stark contrast to the turmoil building in my own heart. His features, usually so guarded, are relaxed in sleep, the lines of worry momentarily erased.

I envy him for that peace, wishing I could share it. There is no room for rest now, no time for hesitation. With a deep breath, I gently pull away, careful not to wake him. The wintry morning air wraps around me, sharp and biting as I step outside the tent, my feet meeting the rough ground. The world is still, quiet in its early hours,

but I know that won't last. The day calls to us, and though every part of me wants to ignore it, to hold on to this fragile moment forever, I know that soon, we will have to face whatever lies ahead.

I stride toward last night's fire, looking for any remnants that are still able to be used for a fire. My teeth begin to chatter, and if it was not clear before, I know now, the cold months have arrived. I look toward the sunrise, light barely peeking through the treetops. It is moments like this that I forget about the horrors of the world.

There is a silence that blankets the world, outside of the random chirps from the birds perched on the branches above me, and a faint sound from the other side of our camp. I realize the horses are awake, and they are probably hungry. So, before I start my day, I grab their bag of food, some fresh water, and approach them.

As I walk toward the horses, their soft whinnies and snorts reach my ears. The familiar sound brings me comfort, grounding me in this small, simple moment. I glance at the bag of feed slung over my shoulder, and as I draw closer, the horses perk up, their ears twitching in my direction. The gray mare, her coat speckled with

white flecks, nuzzles my hand gently, as if to say, hurry, I'm
starving.

I smile despite the cold, the soft rhythm of their breath making me feel just a little warmer. Kneeling, I scatter a handful of feed on the ground between them. The chestnut stallion, always a little more aloof, steps forward first, eagerly munching the food. The mare, however, nudges her companion aside, desperate for her share. They nicker at each other, a silent conversation in the language of their kind, before settling into a quiet rhythm of eating. I take a moment to watch them, their movements so graceful, so full of life.

It's easy to forget, in the chaos of everything else, how peaceful these creatures can be. After a few minutes, I stand and refill their water trough, watching as they drink deeply. Their big eyes, warm and trusting, glance up at me occasionally, acknowledging my presence. Satisfied they are taken care of, I turn to head back to begin the fire. Before I leave, I pause, watching the sunrise fully break through the trees now, casting soft golden light on the horses' backs. For a brief moment, I allow myself to breathe deeply, appreciating the quiet serenity of the morning. It won't last long, but for now, it's enough.

In the pale light of dawn, with the air crisp and biting, I kneel beside remnants of last night's campfire. My fingers, stiff from the cold, fumble with the flint and steel, striking them together with practiced precision. A shower of sparks danced briefly before the tinder caught, sending a wisp of smoke into the frosty morning air.

As the flames flickered to life, their warmth seeped into my chilled bones, offering a fleeting comfort against the relentless cold. I stand and walk toward the tent, I hear Lyrian rustling, he must be awake now. I pull the opening back and give him a warm smile, "It's about time you woke up." He looks up at me, sleep still crusting his eyes, and replies, "I would have slept much longer, but someone decided to leave me to the elements." I roll my eyes at his jest and enter the tent. "Are you hungry," I say calmly, not sure what else to say after remembering last night's events. "Starving," was his only reply.

After spending an hour eating and packing up, we set off toward the next town. The horses seem to enjoy this weather; they have a spring in their step, and I feel that we're covering more ground than usual. The sun is nearly overhead now, and I finally feel its warmth. I lift my face and hands to the sky, embracing the much-needed heat.

I think Lyrian mentioned that we're only half a day's ride from the town's edge, so we should arrive just in time to find lodging, clean up, and rest a bit before dinner. "How long did you want to stay in town?" I ask as his horse catches up to mine. He smiles at me and replies, "Well, how long would you like to stay?" I catch a mischievous look in his eye before he turns his head back to the path we are on. Ignoring his implications, I reply, "I think we need at least a day to speak to the townsfolk for information." He chuckles, "A day it is, then!"

The rhythmic sound of hooves on the dirt path is calming as we continue our journey. The landscape around us is gradually changing, the green hills giving way to more rugged terrain as we approach the town. A cool breeze rustles through the trees lining the road, carrying with it the faint scent of pine and earth.

The closer we get to the town, the more I can feel the shift in the air, people, life, activity. It's all so different from the quiet solitude of the open road. My mind starts to wander, thinking about what we might learn from the townsfolk, and I can't help but wonder if there will be any unexpected surprises waiting for us when we arrive. The thought of new faces and fresh leads gives me a sense of anticipation, mixed with the excitement of knowing that we're one step closer to uncovering what we've been searching for. I have not been to this town before, so the excitement of the unknown grows as we near the town.

My expectations are shattered when we round the final bend into the town. No children running around, no housewives in the garden or going to the local shops, no men plowing the fields. The town was almost eerie with how quiet it was. "Maybe the people here are late risers?"

I mumble more to myself than to Lyrian, but he catches what I say and responds quickly, "I don't think so, something is off about this place." We continue with more unease when we come across an inn called the "Enchanted Rest." The exterior of the inn is a tapestry of ivy-clad stone walls, with turrets that reach toward the sky and windows framed by flowering vines.

A cobblestone path, lined with softly glowing lanterns, leads guests through an arched wooden door into a foyer adorned with tapestries depicting legendary creatures and heroes. We dismount our horses and tie them to a nearby hitching post. Lyrian seems to be scoping out the area as we near the door to the inn.

Inside, the common room boasts a grand opening where a fire perpetually crackles in the hearth, its warmth filling the space with a comforting embrace. The air is thick with the rich, earthy scent of pine and cedar, mingling with the faint, spicy aroma of burning wood, creating a cozy, welcoming atmosphere.

The hand-carved wooden furniture, polished smooth with age, emits a subtle scent of oak and honeyed wood, while plush velvet cushions on the chairs offer both comfort and softness. Shelves filled with ancient books release the faint, musty smell of old parchment, inviting both relaxation and exploration.

The dining area is a feast for the senses, the sweet scent of freshly baked bread and the savory aroma of sizzling meats drifting from the kitchen. Stained glass windows filter sunlight, casting colorful patterns onto the rustic wooden tables, where guests would be served hearty breakfasts made from local, organic ingredients…eggs, cheese, and fruits still warm with the sun's touch.

The smell of warm, earthy coffee mingles with the fragrance of fresh herbs hanging from the rafters, adding another layer to the homey atmosphere. Though the inn appears large enough to accommodate half the population of the town, there are only two people, their presence felt in the quiet, almost still air of the room.

One man draped in a worn robe near the bar and an older woman sitting behind a large wooden table. She glances up and catches our stare, "Well, it has been some time since I have seen fresh faces. How can we help you?" We approach the table and Lyrian is the first to speak, "I am Lyrian and this is Haji, where is everyone?" The inn keeper looks shyly down at her hands and begins, "Most people have been scared to leave their homes the past few weeks…" she trails off. "Why is that?" I ask almost abruptly. Lyrian shoots a look my way as if to let me know that I shouldn't ask that.

She ignores the question and continues to write on a worn parchment, "Do you plan to stay here for the night?" She begins, quite coldly for an innkeeper and Lyrian is the one to answer, "Yes, we will only be here a night as we are just traveling through." The innkeeper's eyes widen, and she clears her throat, "Mind your steps beyond these walls, dear travelers. The roads are no longer safe, with bandits lurking at every turn, ready to relieve you of your possessions. It's best to stay vigilant and travel in groups when you can. There has been an unruly group around these parts."

I glance at Lyrian when he asks, "Who are you speaking of?" A gravelly voice from behind us jumps into the conversation, "These bandits, they call themselves the Nightshade Brotherhood. They're a sundry crew, not bound by any single race or creed, you'll find them all among their ranks. They're known for their stealth and cunning, often striking under the cloak of darkness, making it difficult for the local guards to mount an effective defense. Some say they are former soldiers who turned rogue, others believe they're

led by a shadowy figure with a personal vendetta against the crown.

Whatever the truth, they've become a serious threat, and it's best to

stay vigilant when traveling these roads."

It's the man who was sitting at the bar, now standing

nearby, he continues, "I do not say this to scare you, but please heed

warning. I am Sylvin and this is my wife Miffy. We run what is left

of the inn, though as Miffy mentioned earlier, we do not get many

customers due to the dark cloud the bandits have left over our once

lively town." I adjust my footing and Miffy catches the movement,

"I am so sorry love, would you like to have a seat while I prepare

your room?"

She peeks at her husband, as I walk to her side and sit next

to her on the bench. Lyrian and Sylvin continue to talk. I look at

Miffy and ask, "Your husband mentioned that this town used to be

lively, what happened?" She sighs loudly, straightens her dress

across her lap, and begins, "Our town sits on a main trade route, we

used to have many visitors that would stay for days at a time."

"We hosted several new people each night. Our town wasn't wealthy by any means, but we made do. Soon after the bandits arrived, people's belongings began to go missing. When we townsfolk finally had enough, we sent a group of our strongest to speak with the head of the brotherhood. It was silent for many days after. Then we woke to one of the men's home blazing in the night."

"We left the inn when we heard the chattering and screams of the other people in town. When the flames finally dispersed, we finally saw the group of men that were sent to the bandits' keep. I couldn't believe what was happening; we had never faced such turmoil in our peaceful town. Our eyes fell upon the grim display outside the tavern."

"There, hanging from the gallows, were the lifeless bodies of the men who had ventured to the bandits' keep. Their faces, once filled with determination, were now pale and contorted in death. Their hands were bound, and crude signs identifying them as weak were nailed above their heads. The townspeople gathered, some weeping, others whispering prayers, as the local guards stood watch, ensuring the display remained undisturbed."

"The sight was a stark reminder of the dangers lurking beyond our borders and the heavy price of defiance. It sent a chilling message to any who might consider challenging the bandits' rule: resistance would be met with swift and unforgiving retribution. Since then, people have been scared to leave their homes." She finished, her hands trembling and a single tear dropped from her eye. Without thinking, I placed my hands on hers and began to feel a slow rage coming over me.

I sit silently, my hands gently resting over Miffy's, offering a silent comfort as she gathers herself. After a moment, she takes a shaky breath and continues, her voice steadier now. "After that dreadful night, our town was never the same. The once-bustling streets grew eerily quiet, with shutters remaining closed and doors bolted shut."

"Trade dwindled, and travelers ceased their visits, fearful of the bandits' wrath. Sylvin and I did our best to keep the inn running, but without guests, it became more of a shelter than a business." She pauses; her gaze distant as if reliving those dark days. "The bandits' grip tightened, and our people's spirits withered."

"We became shadows of our former selves, haunted by the memories of that gruesome display and the ever-present threat lurking beyond our gates." Sylvin, who had been conversing with Lyrian, turns toward us, his expression somber. "It's a hard truth to swallow," he says, his voice rough, "but it's our reality. We share this not to burden you but to warn you."

Miffy nods, her eyes meeting mine with a mixture of gratitude and sorrow. "Please," she implores, "Be cautious on your journey. The roads are perilous, and not all who wander return." I squeeze her hands reassuringly, offering a silent vow to heed her warning. As I rise to join Lyrian and Sylvin, I feel the weight of our shared humanity, bound by stories of struggle and survival, and the unspoken hope that one day, peace will return to this troubled land.

I stand next to Lyrian, and I grab his hand, intertwining our fingers. I can sense his breathing quicken. It is the first time we held hands, though we are not children, I still feel a giddy sensation calming the anger I once felt. "Thank you for the warning, I am sorry your town has faced such destruction in recent days. To hear the stories, my heart breaks for those who now have to live in fear."

I trail off and feel Lyrian's hand grip mine firmer. "Well," Miffy cuts in, "Let me get your room ready with fresh linen, we will serve dinner in a few hours. There is a horse stall around the back if you wanted to settle in your horses. We lock the doors at nightfall and my nephew tends to the animals overnight."

We bring the horses to the back, we go back inside the inn, and the room is ready for us to turn in. After a few hours of resting and washing the smell of our travels off of us, we returned to the main room of the inn to see Miffy and Sylvin already seated for dinner. "It is not much but Miffy is a wonderful cook, and we felt this to be perfect for a cold night," Sylvin says and ushers us to sit. Before us lay a sumptuous dish: a stuffed shoulder of lamb accompanied by fragrant rice. The rich scents teased our senses, making our mouths water in anticipation.

Miffy, her cheeks tinged with modesty, explained, "It's a recipe from my late aunt, who once ran a small eatery in town. The stuffing includes saffron, apricots, almonds, sultanas, and a hint of lemon juice." The air was filled with the rich, fragrant scent of the dish, a blend of spices and sweetness.

The warm, earthy aroma of saffron danced through the air, mingling with the sweet fragrance of apricots and the nutty scent of toasted almonds. The subtle citrus note of lemon lingered just beneath the surface, cutting through the sweetness and adding brightness to the savory aroma. "It smells incredible!" I exclaimed, unable to hide my enthusiasm as I settled into my seat, eager to indulge.

The moment I took a bite, the tender lamb melted in my mouth, its smoky, savory flavor enriched by the spices that clung to the meat. The fragrant rice, infused with the delicate spices, carried the warmth of cinnamon and the hint of cardamom, enveloping me in a sense of distant, sun-kissed lands.

We dug in, savoring each bite as the aromatic blend of spices swirled around us, and I felt transported…each mouthful a journey to faraway places. Between bites, the comforting scent of cooked herbs lingered on the air, and we engaged in lighthearted conversation. We shared tales of our travels, the sounds of laughter blending with the earthy, woody undertones of the room.

Sylvin and Miffy told stories of the town's history, its challenges, and the way it had weathered time. The rich, lingering warmth of the meal and the hospitality filled the air, and soon, our bellies full and content, we retired to our rooms. The day's events faded into peaceful slumber, the scent of the meal still lingering in our memories, and our dreams filled with the promise of new adventures awaiting on the morrow. The night passed quietly, the soft rustle of the wind against the inn's wooden walls lulling me into a deep sleep.

Morning came with the first rays of light filtering through the small window of our room, casting a warm glow across the floor. I stretched, the previous day's exhaustion still lingering in my bones, but there was a renewed sense of purpose now that we were here. Lyrian was already awake, standing by the window, his figure silhouetted against the light. I watched him for a moment before walking over to join him.

"Morning," I whispered, my voice still thick with sleep. He turned, offering a small smile, though his eyes seemed distant. "Good morning. Did you sleep well?" I nodded, my hands still tingling from the warmth of his touch from the night before. "Better than I have in days." I hesitated, then added, "I feel like we're not just passing through here. Something about this place… it feels different." Lyrian's expression softened, and he nodded slowly.

"I know what you mean. It's almost like the town holds onto its history in ways it can't escape." He paused for a moment, then added, "We should be careful. There's more to this place than it seems." I agreed, though part of me felt reluctant to dwell on the unease that seemed to hang in the air. We had come seeking answers, but perhaps the questions were bigger than we'd anticipated.

After a quick breakfast, Miffy and Sylvin joined us in the common room, their faces marked by quiet determination. Sylvin, as usual, was the first to speak. "We've arranged for some supplies to help you on your journey. A merchant is heading west, and he's due to pass through here in a few days. We thought you might want to speak with him."

I met Sylvin's gaze, grateful for their help. "Thank you. We'll certainly make use of that," I respond. The mention of the merchant reminded me of the wider world beyond the confines of this town, of the dangers and opportunities that awaited us as we pressed forward. Miffy added, "Be cautious, especially when the sun begins to set. The roads can be… unpredictable." She glanced over at Sylvin, who gave a subtle nod, confirming her words. "I promise," I said, squeezing Lyrian's hand once more. "We'll take care."

After a few more moments of quiet conversation, we stood to leave, the weight of the journey ahead pressing on us. The road would be long, but with Miffy and Sylvin's kindness in our hearts, we felt better prepared than before. As we stepped out of the inn, the crisp morning air met us with the scent of fresh earth, a reminder of the life still thriving in this corner of the world despite the hardships. We mounted our horses, ready to face whatever lay ahead. With one last look at the inn, at the place that had offered us solace for the night, we set off toward the unknown, bound by the stories we carried and the ones still waiting to be told.

CHAPTER 5: WHISPERS OF ESCAPE

The morning air was crisp as we departed the warmth of the inn, our horses' hooves clicking against the cobblestones. Miffy and Sylvin's warnings echoed in our minds: "Be cautious, especially when the sun begins to set. The roads can be... unpredictable."

Their concern added weight to our mission; the bandits had to be found before nightfall. We began by visiting the local market, hoping to gather information from the townsfolk. The market lacked the typical activity, a single vendor calling out their wares, only two children darting between stalls.

Approaching the weathered merchant, I inquired, "Have you heard any rumors about bandit activity on the roads?" His eyes darted nervously before he leaned in, whispering, "Travelers have spoken of a group operating near the old mill to the east, about a two-hour ride from here." Thanking him, we set our sights in that direction, deciding Vin's cottage would uncover no more than what we already knew.

As we rode along the overgrown path leading to the mill, the dense forest closed in around us. The canopy above filtered the sunlight, casting dappled shadows on the forest floor. Suddenly, Lyrian held up his hand, signaling us to halt. He dismounted, crouching to examine the ground. "Fresh tracks," he murmured, pointing to the faint impressions in the soft earth. "They're recent."

Following the trail, we moved with caution, every rustle in the underbrush heightening our senses. The path led us to a clearing where the remnants of the old mill stood, its timber weathered by time. Behind the structure, a narrow ravine cut through the land, its steep banks offering a natural defense.

Lyrian motioned for us to approach quietly, his eyes scanning the area for any signs of movement. Suddenly, a twig snapped underfoot. We froze, hearts racing, as shadows shifted among the trees. Figures emerged, their faces obscured by masks, weapons glinting in the dim light. The bandits had found us first.

A tense silence enveloped the clearing, each side assessing the other. Then, with a swift motion, one bandit lunged forward, and the standoff erupted into chaos. Before we could react, the bandits surrounded us, their movements swift and practiced. Rough hands

seized our arms, pulling us from our horses and binding our wrists

with coarse ropes. A burlap sack was thrust over my head, plunging

me into darkness, and I was propelled forward, stumbling over

uneven terrain.

After what felt like an eternity, the sack was removed, and I

found myself in a clearing illuminated by the flickering light of a

campfire. Around the fire sat several figures, their faces obscured by

shadow. The leader, I assume, a tall man with a scar running down

his cheek, rose and approached us.

His voice was low and menacing as he spoke. "Who are

you, and what business do you have in these parts?" he demanded,

his gaze piercing. Lyrian, the diplomat, met his gaze steadily. "We

mean no harm," he began, "Simply travelers passing through,

seeking information about recent disturbances on the roads."

The leader's eyes narrowed, clearly skeptical.

"Disturbances, you say?" He turned to his companions, exchanging

looks laden with unspoken understanding. "Take them to Soult," he

ordered, his tone brooking no argument. Two bandits grasped our arms, guiding us through the camp. The area was a modest encampment, with a circle of tents surrounding a central fire pit. Scattered among the tents were various stolen goods: chests, barrels, and bundles, evidence of their recent exploits.

A small pond lay further into the forest, its surface reflecting the moonlight. We were led to a larger tent at the far end of the camp. Inside, a figure sat at a makeshift desk cluttered with maps and papers. The bandits shoved us to our knees before the desk, and the figure looked up, a woman, her eyes sharp and calculating. "Soult," one of the bandits announced, "These travelers claim to be mere passersby, seeking information about disturbances."

Soult studied us for a long moment, her gaze assessing. "Is that so?" She leaned forward, folding her hands. "Perhaps you'd care to explain why you've ventured into our territory, uninvited and armed?" The weight of her scrutiny was palpable, and I could feel the tension in the air, thick with suspicion and unspoken threats. Our next words would determine whether we left this camp with our lives or not.

I began to speak before Lyrian cut me off. He began first, "We have been warned of dangers on this side of town, so we thought it best to protect ourselves. We mean no harm. I am looking for my brother. Information led us to this town and soon to the old mill." She glanced between the two of us, seemingly unbothered. She scoffed, "No harm, you say? Peons like yourselves couldn't harm us even if we were greatly unprepared. Now, let's say I believe you. Who is this brother that you speak of? Only she is to answer me."

I swallow deeply, my mind racing to pull a name from anywhere in my memory that would make sense in this situation. I tensed and replied, "His name is Vin, he went missing a few weeks ago. He had a daughter who found us. Crying, she explained that their home had been ransacked."

Her brow furrowed, and she whispered to one of the men standing near her. He rushed out from behind the desk and left. When he reemerged, he had three savagely beaten men with him. Their eyes widened as they dropped to their knees in front of her. "Where was the house from your last expedition, and what was the man's name?" she barked at the men. The two bandits exchanged uneasy glances, their earlier bravado now replaced by palpable fear.

They hesitated, fumbling for words, clearly intimidated by Soult's unwavering gaze. One of them, a burly man with a scarred face, finally stammered, "We... we don't know, Soult." Soult's eyes narrowed, her patience wearing thin. She leaned forward, her voice cold and commanding. "I asked you a question."

The second bandit, a younger man with trembling hands, spoke up, "It was near Andaria, Soult." Soult's expression darkened, and she turned her attention back to us. "You mentioned a brother named Vin." She glanced at the bandits; her tone laced with menace. "Perhaps you can explain why these men were involved in ransacking his home." Lyrian and I exchanged confused glances, our minds racing to piece together the fragments of information. Before we could respond, Soult raised a hand, silencing us. "Enough."

She turned to the bandits, her voice dripping with authority. "Bring them to the captive tent." The bandits nodded hastily, their fear evident as they dragged us toward a nearby tent, the weight of the situation settling heavily upon us. As we were shoved inside, the tent flap fell shut, plunging us into darkness. We could hear the muffled voices of the bandits outside, their words indistinct but filled with urgency. The air was thick with tension, and the uncertainty of our fate gnawed at our resolve.

Time seemed to stretch endlessly in the oppressive silence, each passing moment deepening our sense of unease. The air was thick with tension, heavy with the scent of damp earth and the faint, lingering smoke of the campfire outside, which mingled with the musty, stale odor of the tent. It felt suffocating, waiting for something to break the stillness.

Suddenly, the tent flap lifted, and a figure entered, silhouetted against the campfire's glow. The sharp, acrid scent of the smoke that clung to her clothes hit me before I could see her clearly. It was Soult, her presence commanding and unyielding, her movements as deliberate as the slow, steady burn of the fire outside.

Lyrian winced as the bandits dragged him into the back of a dimly lit tent, his body aching from their rough handling. The air inside was thick, not just with the dampness of the ground beneath us but also with the heavy, oppressive smell of wet canvas and burnt wood from the fire that had barely made it through the night. The only light came from a flickering lantern in the corner, casting uneven shadows that seemed to stretch unnaturally across the walls. The smell of old leather and sweat filled the space, adding a sharp edge to the already suffocating atmosphere.

He glanced at me, his eyes clouded with pain and confusion. I could only offer a helpless shrug in return. Moments later, Soult left and then reentered, her presence commanding the attention of everyone in the room. She surveyed us with a calculating gaze, her eyes gleaming with an unsettling intensity. "You will answer my questions truthfully," she began, her voice low and dangerous. "Failure to do so will not be tolerated."

I swallowed hard, my throat dry, as I prepared to face whatever interrogation awaited us under Soult's unrelenting scrutiny. Before I could speak, Soult raised a hand, signaling for silence. She turned to the bandits who had brought us in, her tone icy. "Prepare them for questioning."

The bandits nodded hastily and began to bind our hands, their movements practiced but betraying a hint of nervousness. As they worked, one of them, a lanky youth with a nervous twitch,

dared to speak. "Soult, we've heard rumors about the woman and the

child. Is it true they're alive?" Soult's expression darkened, her eyes

narrowing dangerously. "Silence!" she barked, causing the bandit to

flinch and lower his gaze. She turned back to us, her voice cold.

"You will answer my questions, and perhaps you will learn more

about your precious Vin."

The mention of Vin's name sent a jolt through me. Could it

be? Was there a connection between Soult and Liza? I had to tread

carefully, every word weighing heavily on my conscience. As the

bandits finished securing our restraints, Soult stepped closer, her

gaze never leaving us. "Now," she said, her voice dripping with

authority, "Tell me everything you know about Vin, his wife, and

their involvement with the Empty Manor."

Lyrian and I exchanged a glance, our minds racing to piece

together the fragments of information we had. Vin, the wife, and

their connection to the bandit group, and the mysterious Empty

Manor. It was all starting to come together, but the full picture

remained elusive. Taking a deep breath, I began, my voice steady despite the fear gnawing at my insides. "Vin was a farmer and his wife, a healer, tended to the wounded with a gentle touch and a kind heart. Together, they raised Liza until the wife lost her life to the Veilstone disease."

Soult's eyes remained fixed on me, her expression unreadable. "And the child?" she prompted, her tone laced with impatience. I hesitated, the weight of the truth pressing down on me. "They had a daughter, Liza. We met her when they came for refuge from something dangerous, but they did not go into detail."

I swallowed, the guilt of our inaction weighing heavily on me. "We... we didn't know what they did nor where they came from before seeking our aid." Soult's laugh was cold and mirthless. "Pathetic, and here I thought he was your brother," she spat. I froze, realizing how badly I messed up. She glanced at the beaten bandits in the corner, "You had one job, and you failed." She turned to the other bandits, her orders swift and decisive.

"Prepare them for the next phase." As the bandits moved to carry out her orders, I couldn't help but wonder what 'the next phase' entailed, and more importantly, what it meant for Liza. What role did Soult play in all of this? The questions swirled in my mind, each one more urgent than the last.

Soult's eyes narrowed dangerously as she processed our words, her patience wearing thin. She stepped closer, her gaze never leaving us. "Vin and his wife betrayed me. We know Vin did not have any living relatives," she hissed, her voice laced with venom. "They stole my daughter, Liza, when she was just a child, and I've been searching for her ever since."

The revelation hit me like a thunderclap. Liza, the innocent girl we had met weeks ago, is Soult's daughter? The pieces of the puzzle began to fall into place, but the picture they formed was unsettling. Soult continued, her voice trembling with suppressed fury. "The truth was that Vin was a *mercenary*, skilled in combat and known for his unwavering loyalty until he met his wife. He was my right-hand man."

"His wife, a healer, joined our troops' ranks when she tended to the wounded of our brotherhood," I recalled the stories of Vin's wife and the Veilstone disease, a devastating illness that had claimed many lives, but the real shock came next. "When Liza was three," Soult's voice dropped to a whisper, "They took her from the Empty Manor and disappeared." The weight of her words hung heavily in the air. Soult's daughter, taken by the very person we had sheltered?

The betrayal was profound, and the consequences far-reaching. I nervously shifted, which caught Lyrian's notice. We knew not to speak unless there was a question that was directed at us. "Now, you will tell me the truth, one more lie and I will kill you both." I tried to swallow, but it felt like a rock was lodged in my throat. Lyrian began to explain how we found Vin, then found Liza. We explained the story, missing no detail.

When he finished, rage grew on Soult's face. With a swift movement, she snatched up one of the smaller beaten bandits. "You dare violate my daughter?" She growled. The front of the bandits' pants grew wet and darker. "We didn't know who she was. We would have never tried anything if we knew she was your lost daughter," the bandit pleaded. She dropped the weight of him and kicked him in his chest, drawing her sword and aiming at the underside of his jaw.

"Your death will not be swift. Soon, you will be begging me to grant you the reprieve of death. Take them away." The three men were drug away, screaming and pleading. Lyrian scooted back toward me, as if he were trying to shield me from her wrath.

The air was thick with the tension of the moment, every breath feeling suffocating. Soult's voice cut through the silence like a sharp blade, commanding. "You, stand!" Lyrian's body jerked slightly as though he didn't fully register the command. Despite the pain searing through him, he obeyed.

Slowly, he pushed himself to his feet, the grimace on his face impossible to hide. I could see how his breath caught, his body injured from earlier blows and rough handling, but his resolve remained firm. His eyes, though clouded with pain, never wavered. He would protect us, protect the village, at any cost.

Soult moved toward him, a predator stalking its prey. There was something animalistic in the way she moved, each step measured, precise, and filled with menace. She was a woman who thrived on control, who reveled in the power she had over others.

Her cold gaze flicked briefly toward me, as if to remind me that no one was safe in this game.

Her voice was laced with icy venom when she spoke again. "Where is your village?" she demanded. Lyrian's jaw clenched, and I saw his shoulders tense. He knew what she was capable of, yet he stood tall, unwavering. "We can't tell you," He said, his voice rough but firm. "We know what will happen to the town if we do."

For a heartbeat, there was silence. The kind of silence that presses against your chest and makes it hard to breathe. Then, that silence was shattered with the sudden flare of rage on Soult's face. She moved swiftly, too swiftly. One of the bandits behind us kicked Lyrian, his boot connecting with Lyrian's ribs with a sickening crack.

The sound rang through the room like splintering tree, and Lyrian crumpled to the ground in a heap, gasping for air. His breath was shallow, ragged, the pain unmistakable in his eyes. I couldn't think. My body moved before my mind could catch up. I rushed toward him, but before I could reach him, Soult was there. She stepped into my path, blocking me with a single, unyielding motion.

Her towering form loomed over me, an insurmountable wall of cold fury.

"As long as you tell me what I need to hear," Soult commanded, her voice unnervingly calm. "No harm will come to you." Lyrian, despite his suffering, shook his head toward me. It was the slightest of movements, barely noticeable to the woman standing over us, but I saw it.

He was warning me. He was telling me not to give in. His gaze was filled with such raw love and desperation that I felt the air leave my lungs. I turned my eyes to Soult, my defiance clear. I would not betray the village. I would not betray everything we had fought for. Soult's eyes narrowed, lips curling into a cruel smile that made my blood run cold. Without another word, she snapped her fingers.

Two bandits immediately grabbed Lyrian, forcing him toward the desk in the corner of the room. They slammed him against it, his breath hitching in pain as they pinned him there. I opened my mouth to beg, to plead for his safety, for our lives, but my words tangled in my throat, coming out in a frantic rush.

"Please…please…just let us go! The twins, the village…they took us in! They sheltered us, they saved us! Don't do this!" My voice cracked on the last words, but Soult didn't flinch. She crouched down in front of me, her face inches from mine. Her fingers were cold as they wrapped around my chin, jerking my head up to face her.

Her breath smelled of iron, of blood, of violence. "You dare stand between me and my child?" she hissed, her voice low and dangerous. "You will understand how serious I am very quickly, and we'll see if your tone changes." Before I could react, she unsheathed her sword in one fluid motion, the sound of steel sliding from the scabbard ringing in the quiet room. The blade gleamed like death itself as she turned toward Lyrian, her eyes gleaming with malice. "No! Please!" I cried, my voice breaking with the weight of my desperation. "Don't hurt him, please don't!"

I sank to my knees, the tears falling freely now, my body shaking as sobs racked through me. The only sound I could hear was the thunderous pounding of my own heart, and then the sickening thud of the sword hitting flesh. The scream that followed was not human. It was a primal, gut-wrenching wail of pain, one that twisted my insides and shattered my soul.

I opened my eyes, my vision swimming through the veil of tears. I couldn't move, couldn't breathe…but then, something wet and warm brushed against my lap. I looked down through blurred vision, my mind refusing to comprehend what I was looking at. I felt bile creep up my throat. It was Lyrian's hand. The hand I had once held so tightly in moments of peace, the hand that had comforted me in our darkest times, now severed. Its warmth fading as the blood soaked through the fabric of my clothes.

My heart stopped, and the world around me seemed to blur. I didn't know how long I sat there, paralyzed by the sight of the bloodied hand in my lap. The room was spinning, but all I could focus on was the gruesome evidence of what Soult had done to him. I snapped back, "Please, let me stop the bleeding," I begged, my voice raw, trembling. "Please, I will do anything…just let me help him."

Soult's smile widened, an almost predatory satisfaction filling her eyes. "I gave you a chance," she purred, her voice as cold as the steel of her sword. "Now you will see pain. If I find your answers to be truthful, perhaps I will let you live, but you only have yourself to blame for him." Desperation flared within me, a burning need to save him, to protect him from the abyss of death that was so close now. I glanced at Lyrian, his face pale and contorted with pain, his body trembling.

With the precision of someone who had killed countless times before, Soult struck. Lyrian's voice, rough and raw, reached me before he was silenced forever. "Haji..." he whispered, his voice full of an undeniable love, even in the face of death. "Don't, nothing will change our outcome..."

Lyrian's body was thrown at my feet like a discarded thing. Even in those final moments, he managed to smile, a small, painful smile that broke me completely. "I love you, Haji," he whispered, his voice barely audible. "Nothing will change that. You must live... remember the twins... find a way..." His words, soaked in blood and pain, echoed in my ears long after he fell silent.

His body, cold and lifeless, lay before me, and in the crushing silence, all that was left of him was his love and my shattered heart. Then, before I could fully grasp the enormity of what had just happened, his body crumpled, lifeless, and the world fell away from me. I could only stare at him, numb with disbelief. His eyes, once bright with love, were now dull, lifeless.

The sound of the sword sinking through his stomach was almost drowned out by the deafening rush of blood in my ears. His body went limp, his gaze unfocused, as his blood spilled across the floor. A final, rattling breath left him, and then, nothing. His once-strong presence was gone. "No!" I screamed, my voice breaking in a way I never thought possible. "No, no, no, no…" but it was too late.

The air was thick with the sharp, metallic scent of blood, its coppery tang cutting through the stagnant atmosphere. It soaked the floor, stained the walls, and clung to the air, heavy and suffocating. The sickly scent of spilled blood lingered, mixing with the acrid undertones of sweat, a reminder of the fear and violence that had unfolded in the space.

Every breath seemed to taste like fire and ash, the heat and smoke lingering on the tongue. I am suffocating in a room full of air, and no one seemed to care or realize. As the room grew colder, a

faint death smell began to creep in, mingling with the rotting

undertones of flesh and the slow, inevitable breakdown of the body.

The silence, it was deafening. If you listened close enough, you

could almost hear my heart strings…snapping…one by one.

The once-familiar scents of the room were drowned out by

the thick, sour odor of death, a scent that seemed to saturate

everything. The air felt oppressive, as though the very walls were

suffused with the earthy scent of mortality, making it almost

impossible to breathe without tasting the heavy weight of what had

transpired.

Even the distant smell of burning wood from outside

couldn't mask the suffocating presence of the death that hung in the

air, thick and nauseating. The oppressive scent of blood and death

had a way of creeping into my skin, lingering far longer than

anything else could.

Lyrian was gone, and I was left in the horror of his loss,

alone with the crushing weight of betrayal and grief. The world

around me collapsed, and the darkness of despair swallowed me

whole. Soult stood before me, the sword still dripping with Lyrians' blood that she plunged through his back, her eyes gleaming callously as she began to speak, her voice icy.

"Liza… she was *my* daughter," she said, the words hanging heavily in the air. "She was barely more than a toddler when she was taken from me. I had no idea where she had gone, but I knew one thing: my enemies had stolen her away." Her tone was filled with bitterness, but there was something darker beneath it.

My breath hitched. Soult's voice grew colder as she continued. "Vin's wife saw the ruthlessness of the group I ran with. She understood just how dangerous they were, and she knew, without a doubt, that Liza could never be raised in such a place. So, she took her, kidnapped her with Vin's help. They fled, took the child with them, and disappeared into the night, leaving me to believe that she was lost forever."

My mind spun. I had always known that Liza's past was complicated, but this? This was something else entirely. Liza was a child, stolen from her mother in an attempt to save her from a world of violence and cruelty. Soult's face twisted with rage. "They thought they could protect her. They thought they could shield her from the evil I had built around myself. However, what they didn't understand was that blood runs deep. I would find her. I would make her remember who she truly was."

Her voice dropped to a dangerous whisper. "I will make them pay for the betrayal." My chest tightened as I tried to grasp the magnitude of what she was saying. Liza was a victim, just like her. She had been torn from the arms of her mother, thrown into a new life far from the cruelty of Soult's world. Yet now, that same world had come crashing back into her life.

My thoughts swirled as I thought of Vin and his wife. How had they lived with the weight of that decision? They had known what Soult was capable of. They had known that by taking Liza, they were condemning themselves. Yet, they had done it anyway, in hopes that they could give her a chance at life. Soult's eyes narrowed as she watched me.

"And now, you see, Haji. This is the price of their choice…and yours. No one escapes this world unscathed." My mind buzzed with questions, confusion, and horror. The betrayal, the lies…it all made sense now. Liza had been torn between two worlds, her innocence stolen before she could even understand what had been done to her, and now, Soult wanted her to embrace that darkness. To become the very thing she had raised her to be.

I couldn't let that happen. Not now, not after everything I had already lost. Despite the crushing grief that filled me, something inside me began to stir, a sense of resolve, faint but undeniable. If I had learned anything from Lyrian's final words, it was this: I had to live. For him. For the twins. For myself. Soult's words continued to echo in my mind, but I was no longer listening. I had made a choice, and I would not let the darkness swallow me whole. I began to think of a plan to get away.

I glanced around the tent I was being held in, and my eyes fell onto Lyrian's body again. I have never been so disappointed in myself. I could do nothing; I was helpless to save the man that I had grown to love. Before I could realize it, I began sobbing again. Soult stepped near me, almost as if she could feel my sorrow, and began brushing her hand over my head.

Her voice cracked when she said, "I have a weakness for girls, I do not want to hurt you. Please tell me where Liza is! Do not make this harder than it has to be." Her voice had softened, and for a moment, I felt her pain. It was brief, but with the contact, I felt the anguish.

"I cannot tell you, but I can show you. We are only a few days' ride from my village. I will think of something, but I must have your word that nothing will happen to our home." I struggled out. Soult's voice cracked, "You have my word." Though Soult had once been a looming figure of control and authority, her gaze softened as she looked upon me.

There felt like here was an unspoken understanding between us, a bond that had begun to shift the nature of our relationship. It seemed, despite the years of tense interactions, Soult's heart could no longer ignore the flicker of compassion she felt for me. The harshness that had once defined her every command now wavered, giving way to a quieter, more calculating kindness. "I'm not sending you alone," Soult said, her voice less commanding, wearier. "I'll have myself, Taryn, and a few others accompany you on your journey."

I was surprised, my eyes narrowing in disbelief. "Taryn?" I

asked, my voice betraying confusion. I had never expected such an

offer from Soult, let alone one that came with such a personal

commitment. Soult began, "Taryn is known as one of the most loyal

and capable guards in my service, often tasked with the most

delicate and dangerous assignments."

To think that the woman would be assigned to me seemed

almost too much. Soult met my gaze with a knowing look. "Taryn is

trusted. She will ensure your safety, and I trust she will keep you

from straying too far from the path." My mind raced with the

implications of Soult's decision. On the one hand, the guard's

presence was a welcome assurance, if only for the protection it

promised.

On the other hand, it also meant that Soult still held the

strings of control. I wasn't entirely free. Not yet. As I prepared for

the journey, my thoughts turned inward. There was something

undeniably calculating in my demeanor as I glanced at Taryn, who

had already begun to gather her things for the journey. A part of me

felt a deep sense of responsibility for the girl stolen from this life

and the promise I had made to find her, but another part felt trapped under Soult's watchful eye.

I knew I had to plan, to move with the caution of a woman caught in the web of a much larger game. As much as I respected Taryn's capabilities, the presence of an ever-watchful guard meant that my every move would be scrutinized. It wouldn't be easy to escape, not with a group of guards at my side, but I was resourceful. My mind raced with ways that I could turn the situation to my advantage.

That night, I was left alone with my own thoughts. When Lyrian died, it felt like something out of a dream, a nightmare, one I couldn't wake up from. I couldn't believe he was gone. It didn't make sense. It couldn't. I sat there, on the edge of the cot set in a tent, shackled to a wooden post. Staring at the space where he should be lying beside me, cold and empty but still warm with the memory of him.

His absence was suffocating, but even then, I refused to let it in. Denial, I think they call it. I kept telling myself that any minute, he'd walk through the door. His familiar scent would fill the

room. His deep, steady voice would echo through the silence, but it
didn't. I touched the sheets, the way his body would shape them,
and it felt like a cruel joke.

My fingers traced the edge of my pillow like somehow…if
I held it long enough, the reality of what had happened would
disappear. That this was just some twisted dream, but it wasn't. I
could feel it in the pit of my stomach, that heavy weight I couldn't
shake. The air around me felt thicker, pressing against my chest, but
I couldn't bring myself to move. I just sat there. Numb. Empty.

It was like I was outside my own body, watching it all
happen, but not truly *feeling* it. I should have been screaming,
tearing at my clothes, anything…anything but this quiet nothing…I
couldn't. I don't know how long I stayed there. Minutes? Hours?
Time had no meaning. I didn't want to face it, but I knew I had to.
That night, alone in the dark, the truth started to settle in, bit by bit. I
tried to fight it, tried to push it back into the corners of my mind, but
it crept in anyway. He was gone, and I was still here…somehow,
that felt like the cruelest part.

In the quiet moments of preparation, I considered my options. Perhaps there was a way to use Taryn's loyalty against Soult. If I could gain the guard's trust, make her believe in the cause of my journey, perhaps Taryn would be the one to help me, without even realizing it. Until then, patience would be my most valuable ally. The plan would need to be subtle. Taryn wasn't someone who could easily be fooled, but I knew that if I bided my time, I might just find a way to break free of Soult's grasp without anyone realizing until it was too late.

The journey began under a quiet, tense sky. Taryn rode next to the cart that I was being transported in, the rhythmic clip-clop of hooves the only sound between us, as the small party made their way toward the distant village. Though Soult had not joined them in the immediate moments after their departure, her presence loomed over them. The guards were ever watchful, though none so close as Taryn. I couldn't help but feel a small sense of comfort from the guard's steady presence, but it also reminded me of the fine line I walked. On one side, the promise of safety, and on the other, the ever-present shadow of control. As we neared the outskirts of the town, I knew we were only a few days' ride from the village I had called home.

The familiarity of the land should have been a source of peace, but instead, it only served to tighten the knot in my chest. I had to act soon, or the chance would slip away. It was time to gain Taryn's trust. "I still cannot tell you," I said softly, glancing at Taryn as we rode, "But I can show you. We are only a few days' ride from my village. I will get the child out, but I must have your word that nothing will happen to my family." Taryn's brow furrowed in confusion, but she nodded after a moment's hesitation. "You have my word." There was sincerity in her voice, but also a hint of wariness. She probably didn't know why she was being drawn into this, but the promise lingered between us.

I struggled to hold my composure, my mind whirling with possibilities. I knew the risk I was taking, involving Taryn in my plans, but I had no other choice. If I could get Taryn to see things my way, I might find a way out of the cage Soult had built around me. The plan was far from foolproof, and time was running out, but it was the only option left. Taryn glanced over at me, catching the flicker of unease in my eyes. "What's really going on, Haji?" she asked, her voice lower now, more intimate. "What are you planning?" I met her gaze, offering the smallest of smiles.

"You'll see soon enough. Trust me, Taryn. I'll make sure you understand, but it has to be in my own time." For a moment, Taryn said nothing. Her hand tightened on the reins of her horse, but she said nothing further, as though considering my words. The guard's loyalty was evident, but it was also clear that the walls she had built around herself were not easily breached.

As the night settled, we made camp near the town, the fire crackling softly between them. It was then, as the shadows of the evening grew long, that I began to weave my next steps into action. It was subtle, a mere suggestion in the way I spoke, a quiet invitation for Taryn to let down her guard. I spoke of the village, of the daughter Soult had lost, and the deep need to reunite with her, painting the picture of a woman desperate to reclaim something she had lost. Taryn listened quietly, but I knew the guard was absorbing every word, every nuance. I made sure to speak of the village with such emotion that it seemed impossible for Taryn to ignore. She had to see humanity beneath the hardened surface of my facade. Though that was only part of it.

As much as I needed Taryn to trust me, I also needed to be careful. If Taryn felt too much suspicion, the guard's loyalty could turn into a trap. I had to balance being vulnerable enough to win Taryn over, without letting her guard down entirely. Every word was measured. Every glance was calculated. The night was quiet, but my mind worked quickly. There was still so much to consider.

I needed to make sure that if Taryn truly began to trust me, the plan would work without Soult noticing until it was too late. Time was slipping by, but for now, patience would be my greatest weapon. I could feel the weight of the next few days pressing down on me, and though the road ahead was uncertain, one thing was clear: this journey was about far more than just finding Soult's daughter. It was about securing my freedom.

CHAPTER 6: THE WEIGHT OF CHOICES

In the stillness of the night, with the fire flickering between them, I let my thoughts drift. There would be more to gain Taryn's trust, more to maneuver around Soult's watchful eye. However, for now, we were allies, at least for a time, and that was all I needed to begin making my move. The next days blurred together. By day, I casually made conversation with the guards; by night, I mourned for Lyrian, sobbing as if no one could hear me.

I realized that my body was here, moving through the motions. My soul…that was gone…cursed to walk forever alone. When we got closer, I told the caravan to stop and tried to let them know that we were too close to continue. Soult, who finally caught up to the troop, stopped her horse next to my cage and began, "If you dare betray me, you and everyone in your beloved village will perish." Taryn tensed next to me, and it was then that I realized that I had cracked her impenetrable wall.

"I will take only one guard; everyone else will wait here, or you can just kill me now and never find your daughter." I threatened the ruthless leader. Soult, caught off guard by my threat, reared back with a deafening laugh. "You know," she began, "You would fit in great in our brotherhood. Fine, Taryn will go with you, return in two days, or I will hunt you to the end of the world, nothing and no one will be able to save you from my wrath." My heart started pounding at the very real threat she made to me. The village is still a day's ride from here, which leaves me less than a few hours to enact my plan.

The night was oppressive, thick with silence and the crackling of the fire. The embers burned low, but my thoughts… they burned far hotter. I couldn't sleep. I haven't slept in days. The image of Lyrian, lying lifeless, his body still warm but his soul already long gone, those were memories I couldn't shake. I had made a choice. A mistake. I let the mask fall from my face, the one I wore so carefully for Soult, for Taryn, for anyone who might be watching.

Though here, in the dark, away from prying eyes, I was nothing but a broken woman. I hadn't meant for Lyrian to die. The words I had spoken to him were the last he heard from me. Why didn't I let him know how much I loved him or needed him? I hadn't wanted his death. The pain of what happened to him, what I had done to him, was far worse than anything the physical world could bring. He had been innocent, caught in the wrong place at the wrong time. My fatal mistake speaking to Soult, and now... now I would carry his death with me. I would wear it like a weight around my neck, dragging me down until I could no longer breathe.

My chest ached as though his spirit was pressing against it, pushing me to remember what I had done. What I had allowed to happen. If only I could turn back time, I thought bitterly. I couldn't. It was done. Lyrian was gone. The moment I had buried him beneath that unforgiving silence, a part of me died with him. I clenched my fists, feeling the sharp sting of pain. "Focus," I whispered to myself, my voice trembling, but with purpose. Focus on the twins. Focus on Liza. They're the reason you're still breathing. They're the reason you have to keep going.

The reason you can't let this go. I looked across the fire at Taryn, who was still awake, her posture stiff. She hadn't seen my tears. She hadn't seen the vulnerability in my eyes that night, the pain I tried to hide. I would make sure she didn't. Not yet. Not until the time was right. I couldn't afford to let Taryn see me break. Not yet. Not while we were still so close to Soult. Not when the plan was so fragile, so delicate, teetering on the edge of disaster.

My heart raced again. This was about more than just saving them. This was my redemption. My reckoning. I needed to make sure the twins survived. I needed to make sure Liza was safe. I had already lost one person I loved. I couldn't let that happen again. I squeezed my eyes shut, taking a shaky breath in, trying to calm the storm inside me.

I needed to silence the guilt, to push it down far enough so that I could continue on this path, this dangerous game, without being overwhelmed by the memories of what I had already lost. The twins. They were still out there, waiting for me. Liza, too. I had to hold onto that, onto the promise of their safety. They had to come first. Lyrian was gone, but they were still alive.

I pushed those thoughts away for the moment, turning my attention to the present. The fire crackled in front of me, casting long shadows across the dark ground. I needed to finish this and when it was all over, when the last of this was done, I would have to live with the choices I had made. For now, I have to focus. Focus on the plan. Focus on what would save them. By the time the first light of dawn bled across the sky, my resolve had solidified. I would do what needed to be done.

I would play this game to the bitter end, and no matter the cost, I would make sure Taryn, Soult, and all of them would feel the weight of my revenge. I could still hear her laughter, the mockery in Soult's voice, her taunts about joining her brotherhood. I could feel the anger building within me, pushing up from the deepest part of my soul, threatening to burst free and consume me. Revenge, I thought, my hands trembling with the desire to make her pay.

Let her think she's won. Let her believe I'm weak, that I can be manipulated by her threats. I wasn't weak, and I wouldn't be manipulated. I would take down everything she had built. The chaos I would create, the fear I would strike into her heart, she would have no idea what would hit her. She thought she had the upper hand, that I was a pawn in her game.

She didn't realize that I had already made my move. I turned toward Taryn. She was watching me again, her eyes sharp, unreadable. She would never understand why I had done what I did. She would never understand the sacrifices I had made, the pain I had endured. She might see me as ruthless, even as a traitor, but in my heart, I knew the truth. I lost. I had lost Lyrian, I had lost my innocence, but I had not lost myself, and that was what Soult would regret most.

Before long, I drifted into a deep sleep. I was transported back to the horrific scene, days prior. *She scoffed, "No harm, you say? Peons like yourselves couldn't harm us even if we were greatly unprepared. Now, let's say I believe you. Who is this brother that you speak of? Only she is to answer me."* I saw myself struggle for the next words. I began, *"His name is Vin, he went missing a few weeks ago. He had a daughter who found us. Crying, she explained that their home had been ransacked."* No, any other name, not Vin.

Please… The world began spinning. *"Now," she said, "Tell me everything you know about Vin, his wife, and their involvement with the Empty Manor."* I watched my mistake go deeper. No matter what I did, I couldn't stop myself from continuing. *"Vin was a farmer and his wife, a healer, tended to the wounded with a gentle touch and a kind heart. Together, they raised Liza until the wife lost*

her life to the Veilstone disease." No, just stop. Keep your mouth

shut. I lunged for myself, as I reached me, I vanished into a

whispering illusion. I turned when I heard more speaking.

The room started to spin. *"You will answer my questions*

truthfully," it was Soult again, *"Failure to do so will not be*

tolerated." Lyrian glanced at me. I only shrugged as a response.

Why didn't I say more, do more? Lyrian, please. I watched the next

moments play out, unable to move, as if my feet were stuck deep in

the mud. The room spun again. *He looked at me and smiled as if he*

knew his fate. "I love you Haji, nothing will change that. You must

live, remember the twins, find a way..." No, no, no, no, no. Not

again. Please. DON'T! I awoke from my nightmare.

My hair plastered across my forehead, slick with sweat. I

tried to slow my breathing so as not to wake Taryn. I gripped the dirt

beside me, trying to find anything to ground me. I lay back down,

my heart beating through my chest, tears streaming from my eyes.

My fault. It was all my fault. I did this. Oh, Mother Above. How

could I be so dense? I lay there for another hour trying to regain my bearings when I heard Taryn stir. It is truly suffocating to choke on your own thoughts. I shook the images away and straightened my face back to steel. It must be time to leave. I sit up and force a friendly smile toward her and ask, "What is for breakfast?"

Soon after, we both mounted horses, mine tethered to hers to prevent escape. The hours blurred into each other as we continued our trek toward the village. Time was slipping away. I was running on borrowed seconds, each one stolen from the inevitable reckoning that would come. It was all a delicate dance, one where every misstep could lead to ruin.

I felt like a ghost. The mask of pain I had worn for so long was slipping away, leaving me exposed. My emotions, raw and uncensored, had no place here. I had to push them down, lock them away in the recesses of my mind, or they would tear me apart. I felt like I was watching myself from the outside. A disconnected, hollow shell of a woman. There were moments when I couldn't feel my heartbeat, when my thoughts seemed to be moving at a distance. Everything felt too surreal, too distant.

In the quiet of the morning, I couldn't remember who I had been before this. Before the betrayal, before Lyrian's death, before this twisted journey. It was as though I was playing a role in a story I couldn't control, trapped inside a script I hadn't written. Still, there was only one thing that kept me going: the twins. They were my anchor. My purpose. Without them, I had no reason to fight, no reason to survive.

The anger, the resentment, the pain, they could all be washed away if I could just get to them. If I could save them, save Liza. I closed my eyes, my chest tightening as I felt the weight of what I had to do. Save them. Whatever it takes. That was the only thought that remained. The rest was a blur, a cacophony of noise that could not reach me, because I had no time for it.

The ride to the village was long and quiet, the rhythmic clop of hooves against the dirt road the only sound between us. The hours blurred into one another as we made our way through the dense forest, the canopy above muting the sun's light and casting the world in a shadowed gloom. I could feel the weight of the coming confrontation pressing on me with every mile, but I kept my focus on the present, on the task at hand.

Taryn rode beside me, her horse tethered to mine, but there was a tension in the air that made it feel like we were miles apart. She hadn't spoken much since we left camp, her eyes scanning the road ahead, her brow furrowed in thought. I could see the gears turning in her mind as she tried to piece together the things I'd been holding back.

Finally, she broke the silence, her voice steady but laced with curiosity. "You never did tell me much about your past, Haji." I stiffened but didn't let it show. "Not much to tell." She glanced at me, raising an eyebrow. "It's just... I don't know much about you. Why are you doing this? I know you're not just doing it for the twins. You don't owe them anything. So why?" I didn't want to tell her. The truth was too much, too raw, too dangerous. I could tell that she wasn't going to let this go, not now, not with the way her gaze lingered on me.

She had always been observant, sharp. I couldn't let her see how fragile I was beneath the mask. "It was just me and Lyrian when we found the twins," I said quietly. "Fighting for something, for someone. They were alone, and we became a family. You may not understand, but I would do anything for those two girls." My thoughts drifted, but I quickly pushed them aside. "Our once-happy family had plans to heal the world, but that was before. Before things went to hell." Taryn stayed silent, watching me, waiting for more.

"I had a family," She began, and I glanced at her, swallowing the anger forming a lump in my throat. "A brother. His name was Mikahael. We were close once, before all of this... before the betrayal. Before I found Soult, I lost him. After that... after he died... it became about the brotherhood. About Soult. They needed to be saved, and so did I."

I could see the flicker of understanding in her eyes. She knew loss, knew what it was like to have someone ripped away from you. I could feel her eyes on me as we spoke, but I kept focusing on the road ahead. I couldn't afford to be distracted now. Taryn was quiet for a long while, but eventually I broke the silence.

I began again, "You never said what happened to him. To Mikahael. How did he…" She cut me off, the pain of it written across her face. "It doesn't matter. What matters is getting to the village. We'll deal with it later." I didn't press her any further, but I could feel the weight of her gaze, the memories that she was holding back. I could tell she was trying to understand, trying to piece together the details of our intertwined stories.

The landscape began to change as we neared the village, the trees thinning out and giving way to open fields. The air was thick with tension, and the quietness of the road felt wrong. As we drew closer to the village, I could see the faint outlines of the houses in the distance, the smoke from chimneys curling into the sky, but there was no sound. No laughter. No children playing. The place felt... empty. It sent a chill through me, a feeling I couldn't shake.

"Something's wrong," Taryn murmured beside me, her voice barely above a whisper. I nodded, eyes scanning the horizon. "Keep your guard up." We rode in silence the rest of the way, the village drawing nearer with each passing moment. I could feel the knot tightening in my chest, the realization settling in that we were walking into a trap. There was no turning back now. Not when Liza and the twins were still out there, waiting to be freed. As we entered the village, the air grew heavier, thick with the scent of damp earth and smoke.

The streets were deserted, the buildings quiet and still. It felt like we were intruding on a place that had been abandoned, like we were walking through a ghost town. Taryn's hand brushed mine as we dismounted, and I could feel her unease. She was starting to see it, starting to realize that this wasn't going to be a simple rescue mission. I couldn't explain it to her, but not yet. Not until everything was in place. I had to stay focused, keep my plan in motion. There was too much at stake.

We walked toward the center of the village, the sounds of our footsteps the only noise that cut through the heavy silence. I kept my eyes on the buildings around us, my hand resting on my satchel. I could feel the eyes of unseen watchers on us. Someone, or something, was waiting.

Ahead of us, a figure stepped into view, tall, broad-shouldered, and cold. His eyes were dark, empty, and he looked at us with the same detached stare I had seen from Soult's men. The predator's gaze. "Stay close," I whispered to Taryn, my hand tightening around my dagger. This was it. This was where the plan began. The man didn't speak, didn't move to stop us, but I could feel the tension in the air. He was watching us, waiting for us to make a mistake, but we didn't.

We kept moving, every step bringing us closer to the village's heart, and to the answers we sought. Taryn's voice was barely a whisper when she spoke again. "What now?" I met her gaze, forcing my expression to remain neutral. "We find Liza. Then the twins. After that, we deal with the village. Everything depends on this. We can't afford to fail." I quicky responded. She didn't argue, just nodded, her jaw clenched tight.

I could feel her doubts, her questions, but for now, they didn't matter. I had one goal: to get to them, to save them. Whatever it took. The rest, everything else, could wait. As we moved deeper into the village, the shadows grew longer, and the weight of what was to come settled on my shoulders like a suffocating cloak. I couldn't afford to hesitate now. The twins were counting on me.

Nothing, not even my past, could get in the way.

Taryn groaned, "What is wrong?" I asked. She responded, and that gave me my opening. "I have been sore for days, before this I was on a week's journey and have had no real rest." She stated. The village square came into view as we walked toward the well at the center, its old stone walls weathered by time. The air around it felt heavy, as though something ancient and forgotten had settled there, watching us.

The well itself was a quiet, eerie presence, the kind of place people passed without a second thought, until you needed it. However, for me, it wasn't just a well. It was a signal. I paused for a moment, scanning the surroundings. Taryn was still beside me, but I could feel her unease growing, seeing the flicker of suspicion in her eyes. She didn't know what I was planning, but she could sense it. The problem was, she would never understand, not the way I needed her to. Not until it was too late. "Stay here," I said to her quietly, my voice low, but enough to be heard above the distant hum of the village.

Taryn gave me a sharp look but didn't question me. She
knew enough by now to trust me, or at least to follow my lead. She
stepped back and leaned against the stone rim of the well, watching
me with those eyes that saw far too much. I needed time, a moment
to act.

I crouched by the edge of the well, reaching into my pouch
and pulling out a small bundle of dried herbs, plants I'd gathered
along the way, plants I knew like the back of my hand. My
knowledge of the land, the medicinal properties of plants had always
been something that set me apart from others. It was a skill I never
genuinely appreciated until now, when it became a tool for my
escape.

The herbs I selected were potent, quick-acting. They would
knock Taryn out before she could even realize what had happened. I
crushed them in my hands, mixing them with a small vial of water I
kept for emergencies. The pungent smell of the concoction made my
stomach turn, but I ignored it.

There was no time for hesitation. I stood, turning to Taryn
with a faint smile. "I need to check something," I said casually,

holding the vial in my palm. "Please, I need you to drink this. It's a pain remedy. You've been riding for days. This should help. I have a bad feeling and will need you ready for anything that may happen."

She eyed the vial with suspicion but shrugged. "Alright, but I don't usually..." Before she could finish, I was already close enough to tilt the vial to her lips. She hesitated for a split second, but the exhaustion in her eyes, the weight of the journey, made her accept it without protest. The liquid was bitter, too bitter to hide its true nature, but she swallowed it down.

Her eyes fluttered for a moment, and then her gaze softened, her stance loosening as the herbal mix began to take effect. I watched carefully, waiting for the moment when her body would betray her. Her eyelids drooped, and within seconds, she was slumped against the well, fast asleep, her breath shallow and steady.

I didn't feel guilty. Not this time. I had to do this, *had to*. It was the only way I could make sure the twins were safe. Quietly, I moved around the well, making sure not to disturb her. I had to leave before she woke before she had a chance to stop me. I glanced back at her one last time, feeling a pang of something, guilt, perhaps, or maybe regret, but I pushed it down. There wasn't room

for weakness now.

The village behind me was silent, and as I moved through

the streets, I couldn't help but feel the weight of the moment

pressing in on me. Taryn would never know what I was doing until

it was too late, but by then it wouldn't matter. I arrived at the small,

modest house on the outskirts of the village, the one I knew Vin and

Liza had made their home.

It was tucked away, hidden from the main road, as though

the world had forgotten it. I hadn't forgotten. I hadn't forgotten

anything. I knocked lightly on the door, a code, a simple knock, one

only they would recognize. It took a moment, but soon the door

cracked open, and Liza's face appeared, her tired eyes blinking in

surprise.

She looked older than the last time I saw her, but her

strength was still there, buried beneath the exhaustion. "Liza, it's

me. Haji," I whispered, glancing over my shoulder to make sure no

one had followed me. Liza's eyes widened. "Haji? What are you

doing here? Where's Lyrian?" I swallowed hard. The question hit

me like a punch in the gut. It wasn't that I didn't want to tell her the truth, it was that I *couldn't*. Not now. "Lyrian... he's gone," I said, my voice trembling. "But right now, you and Vin need to leave. Soult is coming. She's found us."

Liza's face faltered for a moment, confusion and disbelief flashing in her eyes. She glanced back inside the house, her hand tightening around the doorframe. "Soult?" she murmured. Vin emerged from the shadows. "How do you know that name?" I shook my head urgently in response. "It doesn't matter how I know. All that matters is that you leave. Now."

Liza opened the door wider, and I could see Vin in the background, standing with a tense posture, his hands on his hips, eyes narrowing at me. "Is it true?" Vin asked, stepping forward. "Are we in danger?" I nodded, my eyes scanning the street behind me. "Yes. I came here to warn you. Take the twins and go. Get out of the village now."

Vin's eyes flickered toward the back door, and a moment of silent understanding passed between us. He turned to Liza and whispered something I couldn't catch, but it was enough for her to nod, pulling him toward the back exit. They slipped out the back door quickly, just as the twins came running into the house, their faces painted with concern.

"Where's Lyrian?" one of them asked, wide-eyed, their innocent voices filling the room with an eerie sense of calm, but I couldn't answer. I couldn't even look at them. The truth would break them, break me. "You need to leave now," I warned them. I turned my gaze toward the door, listening for any sound, any sign of danger.

That was when I heard it, the unmistakable sound of boots crunching on the gravel outside. I spun, my heart racing, but it was too late. The door to the house creaked open slowly, and Soult stepped inside, her cold smile cutting through the tension like a blade. "Well, well, well," she purred, her voice smooth as silk. "I knew you'd come here, Haji. I never trusted you. I never trust *anyone* who thinks they could escape me."

I lunged for the twins, but before I could take a step, their bodies dropped, arrows in the back of both of them. I shrieked in horror. "No, no, not again," I screamed. I felt a sharp rip at the base of my skull. Soult gripped my hair and snapped my head back at her.

"I told you, if you betray me, everyone in this village would perish.

Now you will see the full extent of my fury. Where is my daughter?"

Her words, spitting like acid against my ear.

"You will never find them." I yelled back in protest,

evoking a spine-chilling laugh and response, "I won't, looks like

you are too late." The door kicked in, and Vin's body slammed to

the ground with a nasty crack. The guard from near the well was the

one who dropped Vin. He caught my eye and gave me an evil smile.

My head spins as I realize I never had the upper hand. She

continued, "Now you will see despair. There is nothing that you can

do."

I glanced up to look out of the window, and Liza was tied

up on the horse. My heart dropped. "Don't hurt her!" I yelled. Soult

responded, "Stupid girl, I would never hurt my daughter. She was

knocked out before she knew what was happening. I wouldn't worry

about her, though, not when you are in my grasp." I glanced up, and

my heart plummeted as I saw the bodies of the twins lying still,

arrows embedded deep in their backs.

The sight of them crumpled to the ground sent a cold wave of horror crashing over me. Belinda had died instantly, struck in the back by the arrows. Her body lay limp, motionless on the cold stone floor. Alina, though still alive for a fleeting moment, was fading fast. Blood poured from her wounds as she struggled for breath, the life draining from her with every second.

I heard a gurgle coming from one of the twins, and a smile was plastered across Soult's face. With a quick snap of her wrist, she throws me to the bodies of the twins, my head slamming into the stone floor. "Oh no, save them if you can." She spits out with a wicked laugh. Though blood stains my vision, I crawled toward Alina, my limbs trembling, my heart pounding with desperate hope.

As I reached out, my hand barely inches from hers, the final blow was struck. A sword was driven through the back of her neck, the steel cutting through flesh and bone with brutal finality. Alina's body jerked once, violently, and then went still, her life extinguished in an instant. Soult's maniacal laughter echoed in the room, but all I could hear was the blood rushing in my ears, the deafening roar of rage that surged through me, consuming everything else.

My body grew hot, and I let out a screech. I try to stand when I feel the boot of the perpetrator dig into my back. "You monster! You are vile, a vile creature. I will never forget this." I scream as I am being held down by a heavy foot. Soult laughs out and says, "Tell me more, tell me how you want to destroy everything that I hold dear to me. Give me all of your rage."

CRACK!

My head slams against the hard floor again. "Yell for help! Scream to the Mother Above. No one will help you. You did all of this. You killed Lyrian, you killed the twins. It was all you. Now, soak in despair. I warned you and you didn't believe me. You betrayed me. You did this Haji." She snarled.

SNAP!

She slammed her boot into my arm, snapping it. I let out a scream. "You knew they stole my daughter," she continued.

CRACK!

My ankle snapped under the pressure of fury. Pain, fiery pain, was all that I could feel. "You had a choice, and you made it," She began again.

CRUNCH!

My fingers were ground under her boot. "You almost made me lose Liza twice! Who is the monster?! Tell me." She screamed.

THWACK!

A steel pole to my back. "I said, tell me who is the monster?!" She repeated.

THUMP, THUMP, THUMP.

Three hits to my thighs with the same pole. I muster all my strength and say, "You, you are the monster!"

CRACK!

My shin cracked under the next swing of the pole. As I lie there, my mind is rushing, and dread fills me. I scream, "Me, it's

me, I am the monster!" The hits stop. Soult smiles and teases,
"There we go, now who killed Lyrian?" I groan, rolling myself over,
and whimper, "I did…" She continues, "Who killed your beloved
twins?"

Tears now streaming down my face, I squeeze out, "…I
did." She continues, "Who caused all of this?" I begin to weep, "…I
did." With my final words, a sharp pain erupts from my chest.
"Good!" Soult almost sings, a look of lust and hate in her eyes.
"Now, be a good little bug and die." She exclaims as she pulls the
sword from my chest. I gasp for air, but no reprieve comes.

The edges of my vision start to blur as I begin choking on
my blood. I must be close, because Lyrian appears from the shadows
and grabs my hand. With a gentle tone, he says, "It's okay, let's go
home!" I smile weakly as everything goes black. Once the searing
pain slips away, Lyrian's love is circling me in a warm embrace.

The darkness tightens around me, but it doesn't scare me.
It's strangely quiet, like the world has finally exhaled and let
everything fall still. My chest aches with a heaviness that I know too
well, but there's something else now, something almost... peaceful.

The last thing I hear isn't the screams or the chaos. It's laughter, clear, sharp, and full of malice. Soults' laugh. I try to grasp it, to pull it closer, but it's already fading, slipping away with the last breath I'll ever take. The sound is so hollow now, like it never really mattered, and just like that, I was gone.

CHAPTER 7: VALENCIA: LAND OF THE BROKEN

The last thing I remembered was the weight of exhaustion pulling me into darkness. A fleeting thought whispered in my mind. Is this it? Before everything faded away. The sensation of my body giving way, of my breath slowing, of my heartbeat gradually fading into silence... it had felt like the end.

I had thought I passed, but now, as my eyelids fluttered open, I found myself in a place I could never have imagined. The air was cool, damp with the fragrance of earth and moss, and the soft rustle of leaves filled my ears. I blinked, disoriented, and for a moment, I thought that perhaps it was all just a strange dream, but as I sat up, the world around me was too vivid, too... real.

The ground beneath my feet was soft, blanketed in a thick layer of fallen leaves that gave slightly with each step. Above me, the trees loomed…tall, ancient sentinels cloaked in heavy ivy, their trunks gnarled with time. They stood still and silent, as if watching me. The air was heavy with scents, and I breathed it in deeply: the sharp tang of wet earth, the crisp bite of pine, and something else…sweet and fleeting, like crushed wildflowers on the wind. It wrapped around me, familiar and strange all at once.

There was no trace of the world I'd known. No market stalls bursting with voices, no clang of iron or clatter of hooves, no townsfolk brushing past. Only the quiet murmur of the forest and the soft gurgle of a stream nearby, its water catching glints of a light from a sky that made no sense to me. Where… where am I? My chest tightened, and my heart began to pound, the thrum of it growing louder than the stream. Panic stirred, slow at first, then building like a tide.

This couldn't be right. I remembered the end. I *felt* the end…sharp and final…so why was I here? Was this death? If it were, why could I feel the sun pressing warmth into my skin, hear the wind weaving through the trees, smell the forest's breath…damp soil, pine needles, and blossoms so sweet they clung to the back of my throat? I could feel every breath, each pulse of blood through my body.

The water near me…it shimmered with life. Tiny fish darted through the shallows like flickers of flame, their bodies

streaked in glowing reds and oranges that danced as they leapt over
pebbles and leaves. Others drifted more slowly, their silvery bodies
catching the light like bits of moon, and as they moved, I heard it…a
soft melody, as if the water itself were humming. It wasn't loud, but
it was purposeful, like the stream carried secrets only they could
sing. This place, wherever I was, pulsed with life. It was too vivid,
too real…and that terrified me.

I clutched at the ground, trying to steady myself, my
fingers digging into the soft earth. My limbs were stiff and
unresponsive, as though they belonged to someone else. For a brief,
terrifying moment, I feared I might be dreaming, trapped in some
nightmare. However, as my hand brushed over my forehead, I
realized it wasn't just my limbs that had changed. My fingers came
away from my skin, and I recoiled slightly, not recognizing the
strange sensation that had swept through me.

My hand was... different. My nails were longer, more
delicate, and there was an odd, faint glow emanating from my skin.
Confused, I looked down at my body. The clothes I had been
wearing, simple and worn, were gone, replaced by a flowing, silver-

white gown I had never seen before. My heart pounded in my chest as I took in my surroundings again, but something else... something deeper felt off.

This isn't my body. I stood unsteadily, my hands trembling. My breath caught as I glimpsed something in the corner of my eye, and I hurried over to the stream, desperate for any sign of familiarity, something to anchor me. The moment my reflection appeared in the glistening waters; all thoughts of reassurance vanished. The woman staring back at me was not the one I had known.

My face, delicate and impossibly beautiful, was framed by long, silver hair that cascaded down my back, glowing faintly. It shimmered with an almost supernatural light, far beyond anything natural. I reached up, my fingers trembling, and touched the strands. Half-expecting them to disappear at the slightest touch, but they were real, soft, and warm.

The glow was subtle, like the soft shimmer of stars in the night sky. My heart skipped a beat as I studied my face. My features were delicate, yet there was an undeniable strength in them, a

nobility I had never seen in myself. My lips, now fuller than before, were painted with a wraithlike shade of pale pink. However, it was my eyes that truly stole my breath away.

Violet. Brilliant violet. The color was so intense, it seemed to glisten, like two gemstones set in my face. The kind of violet I had only ever seen in ancient texts, in stories of dragons and elves, stories I had long believed to be nothing more than myths. Are these my eyes? I looked at them, unable to tear my gaze away, as if they held secrets buried in my very soul. This... this wasn't just some bizarre trick of the light. This wasn't just the result of a strange dream. I was different.

My heart pounded in my chest as I reached up to touch my face, half-expecting to feel my old self, my tired skin, the weariness that had always settled into my features after years of struggle, but there was none of that. My skin was smooth, flawless, and it radiated a subtle, almost imperceptible glow, like moonlight on the surface of water.

My entire body felt lighter, as though I was no longer bound by the same weight I had carried in my previous life. It was as if I was made of something otherworldly, something more. I saw my ears were no longer the same either, sharp to a point, poking through my hair.

My hand trailed down my body, feeling the cool fabric of the gown, I now wore. The gown elegant, flowing, and impossibly perfect seemed to belong to another time, another world. It clung to my form, its fabric so fine it almost seemed weightless. This isn't me, I thought again, my heart racing, but there was a gnawing deep in my chest that it was me, in a way, a version of myself that I had never known.

As I stood there, frozen, the air around me seemed to pulse, humming with a quiet power. A strange energy flowed within me, something ancient, something that felt deeply connected to the land, to the very essence of the forest around me. A chill ran down my spine as I realized that this was no dream. I'm alive, but this is not the life I knew. My thoughts were interrupted by a faint whisper in the wind, a voice that seemed to echo through my mind, ancient and knowing. "You are no longer the person you were."

My breath hitched, my mind struggling to process the words. No longer? The voice faded, but the strange awareness lingered, sharpening every sense within me. I could hear the rustle of leaves on the trees, the distant hum of insects weaving through the air, the faint splash of water as a small fish darted in the stream.

Every tiny sound was now clear, vivid, as though I could hear the very heartbeat of the world around me. My hearing had transformed, where once I would have missed the softest whisper, now the smallest movement, the gentlest breath, stood out like thunder. I could also see better…so much better.

The sunlight filtering through the trees glimmered with more clarity than I had ever seen before, and the details of the forest, the veins on each leaf, the intricate patterns of bark on the trunks, the delicate dance of light across the stream, were all etched in my mind with a sharpness that left me breathless. Every color was richer, more vivid, and the shadows seemed to move with a life of their own.

It was then that I felt it, a subtle shift in the air. The very presence of myself, my aura, seemed to have transformed. I was not just standing there in this strange forest; I commanded attention. The forest seemed to react to my presence, the trees a little taller, the stream a little clearer, the sky a little brighter.

The hum of power was growing stronger, more intense, and I felt it thrumming through my veins. A faint smile tugged at the corner of my lips, though I didn't understand it yet, I knew, deep down, that this was my true form and that I was alive. The form I had always been destined for. As I gazed at my reflection in the stream, a new, terrifying realization settled into my heart. I am no longer who I once was.

I closed my eyes, trying to steady my breath. The air around me was too sharp, too vibrant, and my senses seemed overloaded, each noise, each detail crashing into me with an intensity that made my head swim. I reached up, pressing my palm against my forehead, trying to gather my thoughts, trying to piece together the memories that felt like they were slipping through my fingers like water. Where am I? What happened? The questions swirled in my mind, but no answers came.

All I had were fragments, glimpses of a life that felt so distant now. I could remember the weight of exhaustion, the ache in my bones, the sense of something finally giving way. I had been so tired, so drained. Had I not... died? My fingers trembled as I touched my neck, feeling the unfamiliar smoothness of my skin. I had once been worn by the struggles of life, but now, my body was as flawless as porcelain. Nothing like the tired, worn-out version of myself that I had known. Was this a second chance? My chest tightened, and a soft breath escaped me.

The panic, the disbelief, that growing sense of unease... it all swirled together. The world felt too bright, too overwhelming, and every sound seemed to magnify, pressing in on me from all sides. I could hear the soft rustle of the leaves around me, the steady flow of the stream, but even more distinctly, I could hear the scurry of small animals, the soft flutter of wings above me, the quiet breath of the earth itself.

Focus. Calm down, I told myself, trying to steady my mind. I closed my eyes once more, searching for that place of quiet in the chaos of my thoughts. I needed to think, to make sense of this. I remembered fragments of my past, the life I had lived, the struggles I had faced, but they were distant, like a fading dream.

The memories felt hazy, as though they belonged to someone else. I inhaled deeply, the cool forest air filling my lungs, and exhaled slowly, trying to ground myself again. The sharpness of my senses began to dull just slightly, and my thoughts began to slow. "Okay, focus. You're alive, somehow. You're not dead…" but why was I here, in this strange place, with this new form? What was the purpose of it all? Suddenly, just as I thought I might have a moment to myself, a faint sound interrupted my thoughts.

At first, it was nothing more than faint rustling, distant, almost imperceptible. Then, it grew louder and closer. I could hear the steady rhythm of hooves hitting the ground, the sound of horses approaching. My sharp hearing picked up the creak of saddles, the faint murmur of voices, four, perhaps five people. My heart skipped a beat as the sound grew louder, and before I could react, they were right in front of me.

A group of riders appeared from the dense trees, their horses moving with practiced precision through the forest. There

were five of them, clad in armor, each one radiating a sense of authority. They reined in their horses, halting just a few feet from me, the air now thick with the tension of their arrival. I stiffened, my eyes instinctively scanning for any sign of threat, but there was something in the way they held themselves that made me pause.

My gaze shifted to the man who stood at the front, slightly apart from the others. He was tall, his presence commanding the very air around him. His long silver hair was pulled back in a tight braid, the intricate weave making him look like someone of royal status. His armor was meticulously crafted, though worn with the marks of many battles, a regal black and silver that seemed to shift and shimmer with the faintest movement. His face was a study of quiet intensity, his sharp violet eyes observing me with a detached, almost icy indifference.

His expression was unreadable, but it carried a weight of experience, of loss, and something deeper, something hardened by years of hardship. The mystery man's gaze lingered on me for a moment, as though assessing my every move, his lips pressing into a thin line. There was an air of elegance about him, but also strength…an unspoken power that radiated from him like a storm just waiting to break.

His body was sculpted with the lean muscle of someone who had trained for battle, his every movement controlled, efficient. The others around him were clearly his subordinates, more alert, but their focus was not as intense as his. The wind stirred, sending a few strands of his silver hair fluttering, and I felt the shift in the atmosphere. His presence was like a storm…quiet, but undeniably powerful.

"Who are you?" His voice was low, commanding, and yet there was something almost distant about it. He wasn't speaking to me with the urgency one might expect in an unfamiliar situation. It was as though he had already made his judgment, already placed me in some unseen category. I opened my mouth to respond, but my voice faltered. Who am I? The question echoed in my mind as I stood before him, realizing I had no answers, only more questions.

Though, there was something in his gaze, in the way he studied me, that made me feel as though I was standing on the edge of something much larger than myself. I instinctively took a step back, unsure of how to react, but then his eyes softened just slightly, though his stance remained as rigid as ever. "Are you...?" he trailed off, his voice still laced with that same cold indifference, though there was a flicker of something else behind it...something like recognition, or maybe suspicion.

My heart raced. Am I who? What did that mean? Why did it feel like the weight of centuries of history was pressing down on me all at once? Before I could answer, the others dismounted, forming a semi-circle around me, their eyes all turning to me in varying degrees of curiosity and wariness. However, it was the man, the one with the silver hair and the sharp violet eyes, who remained the center of attention, his presence too magnetic to ignore.

I was alive, but I was no longer the person I had been. Now, standing before these strangers, I realized with chilling clarity that whatever had brought me here, whatever transformation I had undergone, had led me straight into the heart of something far greater than myself. I had no idea what role I was supposed to play in it.

I stood frozen, my heart hammering in my chest, every muscle in my body tense with fear. The riders around me were too close, too intimidating. I could feel their eyes on me, their silent judgment, and the pressure in the air grew thicker with every second that passed. My mind was in turmoil, swirling with confusion and panic. What do they want from me?

My hands trembled slightly as I clenched them at my sides, trying to suppress the fear that was creeping up my throat. I wanted to scream, to run, to escape this strange reality, but my body refused to cooperate. I had no idea who these people were, and something deep within me told me it was safer to say nothing at all.

If I said too much, if I revealed too much, I feared I might lose control of the situation. The man with the silver hair was the only one whose gaze never wavered. His violet eyes studied me with a chilling intensity. My breath hitched, my throat tightening. I wanted to look away, but his gaze was like a pull, an invisible force keeping me rooted in place.

His cold voice broke the silence, and though his words were calm, there was an undercurrent of authority in them that made me feel small and insignificant. "She is not speaking. Perhaps she fears us," he murmured, more to himself than anyone else. His lips thinned slightly, his eyes flicking toward one of the other riders.

"Check her," he ordered, his tone leaving no room for argument. "See if she's truly well." My heart skipped in my chest. Check me? The idea of someone touching me, examining me like I was some fragile thing to be studied, only made me more anxious. I instinctively took a step back, my gaze darting to the others who had dismounted, now slowly approaching me with a cautious, measured pace. I flinched. The rider that the mystery man had called to stepped forward, a young woman with short dark hair, eyes warm and sympathetic, though filled with a sense of duty.

I saw her move toward me with slow, deliberate steps, and something inside me recoiled. I opened my mouth to protest, to tell them to stay away, but the words never left my lips. I felt my knees give way beneath me, the world around me blurring, my body betraying me. The rider's hands reached for me, but before she could even touch my shoulder, the world around me spun into darkness.

The last thing I saw before passing out was a woman, standing quietly behind the rider. The woman's presence was like the gentle calm of a forest at dusk, the kind of peace that only nature itself could bestow. Her blonde hair shimmered in the dim light like moonlight, woven with tiny wildflowers that gave by an almost ethereal quality. Her eyes were enchanting green, deep, and wise, reflecting the ancient spirit of the earth itself. Is she... another one like me? I thought, my last coherent thought before everything faded away.

When I woke again, I was lying down, the weight of blankets over my body, the soothing scent of herbs in the air. I felt warmth, but also an odd stillness. My eyelids fluttered open, and I found myself in a small, simple shelter. The soft light filtering through the trees outside was golden and warm, and the air was filled with the rustle of leaves.

What truly caught my attention was the woman sitting beside me, her hand resting lightly on the edge of the bed. The woman, with deep golden hair that shimmered like the last rays of the setting sun, was watching me with a calm, almost knowing

expression. Her emerald eyes met mine, and for a moment, there was nothing but a shared understanding between us, like two souls recognizing one another across time.

Her hair cascaded down her back in long, silken curls, a striking deep blonde that shimmered with hints of copper when the light caught it. It seemed to carry an inner warmth, the rich color almost glowing with the radiance of a setting sun. The gentle curls danced with each movement, framing her face with a softness that only added to her delicate presence.

Her eyes were both penetrating and tender, glowing with an innate kindness, yet holding a spark of curiosity that hinted at the secrets of distant places and forgotten tales. Her build was slender, nimble, with an effortless grace to her movements. Despite the occasional stumble, she moved with quiet elegance, like a breeze that flowed around obstacles rather than rushing through them.

Her skin, fair and almost luminous, was as smooth as polished ivory, untouched by time, as though her very essence held the secret to immortality. It radiated a soft, otherworldly glow, a subtle reminder of Elven stories, that I read as a child. Her attire was simple but exquisite, a tunic of deep emerald green and gold. The fabric shimmered faintly, enchanted to reflect the natural beauty around her, and embroidered with intricate patterns that spoke of her connection to the earth.

"You're awake," the woman said softly, her voice gentle, like the whisper of wind through the branches. Her tone was both soothing and filled with purpose. She stood with graceful ease, her movements fluid, as though she were an extension of the natural world itself.

I tried to sit up, but my body still felt weak. My vision swam for a moment, the faintest dizziness overtaking me. I blinked rapidly, but the woman, with a soft yet firm hand on my shoulder, gently coaxed me back to lie down. "Don't rush," the woman said, a smile playing on her lips that was kind but knowing. "You've been through quite a bit. Your body needs rest."

My gaze flickered around the small room. It was made of wood and simple cloth, but the warmth that emanated from it made it feel like a sanctuary. The bed I lay on was soft, filled with herbs that smelled sweet and calming. Yet, despite the peaceful surroundings, there was still a sense of unease, the weight of the unknown pressing against my chest.

I tried to speak, but my throat felt dry, my words barely more than a whisper. "Where am I? What's happening?" My voice was shaky, as much from fear as from exhaustion. The woman's eyes softened further, and she leaned down slightly, as if to give me some space but to also offer comfort. "You are safe, for now. You're in the Forest of Valencia." Her lips tightened slightly, though her gaze remained unwaveringly kind. "As for what's happening..." She paused, her expression growing more serious. "That's a question only you can answer."

I stared at her, feeling the weight of the woman's words. I could sense there was something more to this, much bigger than my personal confusion and fear. Though…for the moment, the woman didn't push me. She simply sat quietly, offering the warmth of her presence, the kind of quiet support that I hadn't realized I needed.

The door to the small shelter creaked open, and my gaze flickered toward the figure standing in the doorway. It was the mystery man, his posture was still as regal and intimidating as before, though his expression now seemed slightly less harsh, less cold.

"Sera," he said with a nod toward the woman by my side, his voice low but carrying an undeniable authority. "How is she?" The woman turned to him, my expression unreadable for a moment, before she nodded gently. "She's recovering. She will be fine." My heart thudded in my chest at the sound of his voice, the mystery man's eyes locking onto mine for the briefest of moments before he turned back to her.

There was no warmth in his gaze, no hint of comfort or reassurance. "We need to know who she is," he said flatly. "We have no time to waste." My breath caught in my throat at the coldness of his words, but her gaze softened, and she placed a hand on my arm. Offering me a silent wordless promise that I was safe, at least for now. The tension in the air was palpable, but I had no strength left to resist, no energy to fight. I simply closed my eyes again, exhaustion sweeping over me as the world around me became a blur once more.

I woke up to an unfamiliar quiet. The kind of quiet that settles around you like a heavy blanket, thick and all-encompassing.

The kind that makes the heart race in the absence of sound. My eyes fluttered open, and for a moment, I didn't recognize where I was. The soft light of the forest filtered in through the cracks of the makeshift shelter I found myself in. I was lying in a small bed, it was warm, surprisingly soft, and the smell of fresh herbs filled the air, calming my nerves. The slight pressure on my chest, the weight of the blankets, felt familiar, but I couldn't quite place why.

I tried to sit up, but my body felt... different. Not weaker, per se, but like something had changed inside me. I had the sensation of having been here longer than I had, a strange comfort in the oddity. There was no one around. The bed beside me was empty, and the soft clink of armor, the sound of voices, was gone. The mystery man and woman …gone.

I didn't know whether to be relieved or disappointed, and the uncertainty gnawed at me, curling around my thoughts like the vines outside the shelter. I pushed myself into a sitting position, my legs dangling over the side of the bed, my feet brushing against the soft, cool wood beneath me.

There was a small wooden table in the corner, a single chair, a few scattered herbs. The room felt untouched, as though no one had come in or out for hours. Still, the weight of the world felt heavier now, as if something were pressing down on me, reminding me that I was not home, not anywhere I recognized.

I ran my fingers through my silver hair, still silver, still glowing. My ears still pointed; I sighed. The full weight of my confusion crashing down on me again. Where am I? What are you, Haji? I took a deep breath, trying to steady myself. The air was thick with the scent of pine and earth, a cool, calming scent that made me feel grounded.

Though it wasn't enough to clear the weight in my chest. The mystery man's cold, unreadable gaze flashed in my mind again, and I shook my head, trying to rid myself of the thoughts. No. Focus. My stomach growled, reminding me that I had not eaten since…since... what? It felt like it was years ago.

Slowly, I stood, wobbling at first but managing to steady myself against the wooden wall. I walked to the window of the shelter and peered outside, my heart rate increasing slightly. The

forest was still and calm, the trees stretching high above me, their leaves rustling gently in the breeze. Everything seemed peaceful, untouched by the chaos that churned inside me.

However, there was a sense of isolation that clung to me, and the unanswered questions twisted in my gut like a knot I couldn't untie. I sighed again and turned away from the window. Glancing around the room again, not sure what else to do. There was no one to talk to. I was alone in this strange place with a body I didn't understand, an identity I was still struggling to comprehend.

I wasn't sure how much time passed, but after what felt like hours, though it could have been mere minutes, I heard the faint sound. Hooves, the soft thud of horses' hooves on the earth, carried through the air. The hair on the back of my neck stood on end, and I froze. I couldn't help it. My instincts flared up immediately, my heart quickening as my body tensed in response to the sudden unease.

The scent of fresh bread, herbs, and something sweet, like honeyed fruit, wafted through the air, pulling me back for a moment, but the fear didn't fade. I told myself it was probably just that woman, probably just a small group of travelers passing through, but that primal anxiety still lingered deep in my chest…an old, gnawing thing that resurfaced every time I thought of the mystery man. The fear twisted in my gut, like it always did when I couldn't make sense of the unknown. I quickly moved back to bed, unsure why I felt the need to hide, to retreat. Just as I was about to crouch low, the door creaked open, and she stepped in.

Her blonde hair gleamed softly in the dim light, like moonlight caught in the stillness of night. She carried a bundle wrapped carefully in leaves, the edges of the fragrant herbs poking out, releasing a sharp, pungent scent that mixed with the warmth of the room. Her expression was soft, her eyes always warm, yet today there was something more beneath them…a glimmer of quiet understanding.

I could smell the lingering sweetness of the food she carried, something rich and earthy, but it was the subtle, comforting scent of her own presence that drew me in…the light musk of lavender, the delicate trace of something floral, maybe from the flowers she wove into her hair. It was a scent that calmed, that eased the tension in my shoulders, even if only for a moment.

She looked at me with a slight smile, the faintest laugh in her eyes. "I'm sorry to startle you," she said gently, noticing how tense I had become, "I brought you food." My stomach growled again, louder this time, betraying me. I glanced at her with a slight frown, uncertain, but the moment the smell of the food hit me, my hesitation vanished. It smelled unlike anything I had ever encountered, warm, savory, with an undercurrent of sweetness.

It was rich, earthy, and thick in a way that made my mouth water instantly. She set the bundle down on the table and unfurled the leaves, revealing what looked like a stew of sorts, with chunks of meat and bright orange vegetables I didn't recognize. The scent was intoxicating, heavy with spices that burned my nostrils in the best way possible. She smiled as she handed me a wooden bowl, a spoon resting atop it. "It's not much, but it's what we have. I hope you like it. My name is Seraphina. Seraphina Lirael."

Without waiting for her to finish, I immediately grabbed the bowl, lifting it to my lips and taking a greedy spoonful. The warmth of the broth hit me like a wave, rich and comforting, and I didn't even notice how quickly I was eating. The meat was tender, the vegetables sweet yet earthy, and the spices... Oh, the spices were like nothing I had ever tasted before. It was like I could feel every flavor in my soul. I continued eating, barely pausing for breath, my hunger overwhelming me.

As I took another spoonful, I felt something catch in my throat. I coughed, the liquid and food suddenly choking me, a bitter, sharp pain shooting up from my chest as I gasped for air. My eyes watered, and I choked again, the stew spilling from my mouth and staining the floor. Seraphina's hand was on my back in an instant, steadying me with surprising strength. Her touch was cool and comforting, and I looked up at her, mortified.

"Easy, easy," she murmured with a soft laugh, her voice light. "It's not going anywhere. Here." She reached for a small, wooden cup beside the stew and handed it to me, her gaze still kind. "Drink. It'll help." I took the cup, but my hands were shaking, still unsure whether to trust it. Seraphina gave me an understanding smile, her lips curling up at the corners. "I think it's safe. You're going to need to drink something if you keep eating like that," she teased gently.

I hesitated, but my throat was still dry, and I could feel the tension in my body. I brought the cup to my lips and drank. The liquid was cool, refreshing, and slightly sweet. It soothed my throat, but there was a flavor to it I didn't quite understand, a strange herbal aftertaste that made my head swim. I lowered the cup, and Seraphina chuckled softly at the look on my face. "I know it's unfamiliar," she said, her voice calm and reassuring. "But it's meant to help you regain your strength." I placed the cup down, the strange liquid still lingering on my tongue.

My stomach had quieted, but my mind was still racing. My gaze shifted back to her, and I finally found the courage to speak. "My name is Hajira, I go by Haji," I said quietly, my voice still hoarse. "And... who was that man? The one with the silver hair... his eyes, they... they were so intense." Seraphina's smile faltered for just a moment, and her eyes softened with something I couldn't quite read.

"Ah," she murmured. "You mean Kaelen." "Kaelen?" I repeated, trying the name on my tongue. It felt strange, almost foreign. "Yes," she said, her gaze thoughtful. "He is... complicated. Powerful…and yes, his presence can be overwhelming. Don't worry, Haji. He means no harm." I wasn't sure whether I believed her, but something in the way she said it, her calm, her understanding, eased a bit of the tension that had coiled tight within me. "I don't trust him," I said quietly, though I didn't know why the words felt true. "Or anyone, really. Not yet."

Seraphina's gaze softened even further, and she gave me a reassuring smile. "You don't have to trust him right away. I promise you, he will not hurt you. Not while I'm here." The warmth of her words washed over me, and for the first time since I woke, I allowed myself to believe in the possibility of safety. The hours passed in silence, the kind of quiet that lingers after a storm has passed…heavy, expectant.

I had eaten, drank, and even managed to sleep a little, though my mind was never truly at rest. The strange, unfamiliar food and the surrealness of the entire situation kept swirling around

in my head. What happened to me? Why did it feel like something

was shifting inside me, something I didn't understand? Why had I

been chosen to wake up here, in this strange world, with no

answers?

Seraphina had been kind and patient, offering little snippets

of information about the world I now found myself in, but nothing

that really explained what had happened to me, or why I felt so... out

of place. Before long, I found myself drifting back to sleep after

Seraphina left again. For the first time I felt light, like the troubles of

my past life vanished.

CHAPTER 8: A GLIMMER OF HOPE

It wasn't until later in the day, when the forest began to soften with the fading light that Seraphina finally entered the room again, waking me up. I quickly sat up in bed, almost embarrassed by how much I had slept.

She began to speak, her voice carrying an edge of something heavier beneath her calm exterior. "We've been on a journey, Haji," she said softly, her eyes distant for a moment, as if something beyond the trees was calling to her. "A journey to find help." I looked at her with furrowed brows. "Help for what? What's happening?" Her gaze softened as she met my eyes. "The Curse of Ashen Rebirth."

The name sent a shiver down my spine. "Curse?" I repeated, voice barely a whisper. Seraphina nodded slowly, her expression serious, almost sad. "It affects both dragons and elves. Those who tamper with the natural order, who dabble in necromancy or dark resurrection rituals. It corrupts them, twists them into something else. Something... dangerous."

I blinked, trying to piece together the disjointed thoughts forming in my mind. "Necromancy? Dark rituals? That sounds like something from myth, not real life. Like stories told by old bards to frighten children." Seraphina didn't flinch at my disbelief. Instead, she watched me closely, her lips pressed together as if weighing her next words carefully.

"It's real, Haji," she said softly, but with undeniable conviction. "The curse is real, and it's spreading. There are still those who believe they can control it…elites, dragons, elves, but none have succeeded. The curse twists their bodies, their minds, and it feeds on their strength. It makes them aggressive and volatile... It's the reason we need help." I felt a growing sense of unease. "And you're telling me this because... I'm cursed?" The words felt strange coming from my lips, like they weren't even my words. Seraphina's expression didn't falter, though there was a touch of sorrow in her gaze as she spoke.

"No. We believe the curse is what brought you here, Haji. It's why you felt... different. We think it is why you were awakened in that forest. We haven't had hope in many years, but for the first time, we have hope. Kaelen seems to believe that you are the answer." My mind reeled, the pieces of the puzzle falling into place one by one, though the picture was nothing like what I had expected. "I... I don't understand. Dragons? Elves? I thought they were myths…stories from another time."

"They are not myths," Seraphina replied, her voice low but firm. Her eyes showing a look of confusion. "You are one of them." I stared at her, my heart pounding in my chest. Me? One of them? A dragon? An elf? I shook my head in disbelief. "I'm not. I'm not any of those things." My voice was shaky, and the words sounded like they belonged to someone else. "I'm just... just a girl. A human."

Seraphina's gaze softened, and she took a step closer, her hand resting lightly on my arm. "Haji, you're not just a girl. You're an elf, though the kind of elf, we're not entirely sure of yet. What we do know is that your appearance, your magic... it's different. It's more. We were riding for days, when we felt a surge of power, that led us straight to you…" She paused, her eyes locking with mine.

"We think that is why you're here. To stop it from consuming all of Luminara." The air around me felt thick, oppressive. How does she know about my gift? My heart started to thrum in my chest. I haven't shown anyone here. I opened my mouth to protest, but the words caught in my throat. Another fact hit me. Elf? Me? The very idea felt impossible, but the deeper I thought about it, the more the pieces seemed to line up.

My silver hair, my radiant eyes, the inexplicable glow that had pulsed through my veins when I first woke. Could it really be true? Was I some kind of mythical creature, the stuff of legends? How could that be? I had been human. I knew I was human…didn't I? I looked down at my hands. My skin still glowed faintly in the dim light of the shelter, and when I flexed my fingers, I felt a strange power on the tips of my hands, like a current of energy pulsing just below the surface.

I rubbed my palms together, unsure of how to control it, unsure of what I was supposed to do with this new feeling. Seraphina's voice broke through my thoughts, gentle yet resolute. "The curse is linked to dragons and elves who tamper with life and death. It forces them into a half-death state. A hollow state. Their bodies remain alive, but their souls are lost, and they become slaves to the curse. They become aggressive, but they still have power. Enough power to destroy everything around them." She paused, looking at me with a mixture of sadness and hope. "We need to find a way to stop the curse before it consumes us all! With your power…"

I snapped, "How do you know of my gift, no one knows…" She smiled and began, "We can feel it radiate off of you." Feel it? What did she mean? The room seemed to grow colder as I processed her words. She held her hand above a cut on my arm, a warm pulse radiated through her hand and through me. It was gone.

She too has a gift. "How…?" I murmur to her; she smiles in response. She straightens her back in an act of pride and said, "Everyone with the Elven blood has magic. Though our magic varies through each bloodline, we all have a gift from the Mother Above. You are an Elf, so it would be odd if you did not, however few can heal."

She continued, "When I was treating you, some of your cuts and bruises healed on their own. That is when we knew that you were one of us." Elven bloodline? I wasn't sure if I could trust this.

The idea of being part of some ancient lineage, of being a creature from legends... it sounded too far-fetched, too impossible to believe. However, the way she spoke, the way her eyes held nothing but sincerity, made something inside me wonder if there was truth in her words. I looked up at her, my throat tight, "So... what happens to me now? Do I just... assume you do not lie?"

Seraphina's expression softened, and she moved toward the door, the last rays of sunlight filtering through the trees and casting an ethereal glow on her face. "No. We will find help. There is a place far from here where you can get the answers you seek. First, you must trust us. Trust that we're doing this to help you."

My mind was a whirlwind of doubt and fear, but something in me, the part of me that wasn't ready to die, the part of me that had awakened in this strange new world, told me that perhaps Seraphina was right. I didn't know what was ahead, but for the first time since waking up in this world, I didn't feel entirely alone. Maybe that was enough to hold onto.

My breath faltered and my brows furrowed. I feel like I am forgetting something. What could it be? I try to brush off this ache in my heart, not wanting to feel the growing dread. I glanced at Seraphina wondering if she felt the shift in the room. She stood and walked toward a nearby table and said, "Though you can heal yourself, your mind may be weak from everything that has happened."

"Please be sure to drink your tonic." I shifted in my seat on the bed and grabbed the wooden cup she handed to me. I took a drink; it was the same sweet drink. There was a faint knock at the door, and Seraphina glided to the door. I glanced to who stood beyond the door as she ushered the female in.

She introduced Tamsin Valeria. The female moved with quiet purpose, her presence calming yet unwavering, a stark contrast to the tense energy that surrounded Kaelen. With short black hair loosely tied back, she held an air of simplicity, her warm amber eyes reflecting a depth of empathy and understanding. Her gaze never lingered on the surface, always seeking the heart of what needed healing.

Though of average height, there was an unassuming grace to her movements, a quiet strength that emerged most clearly when her hands worked their quiet magic, mending the broken or easing the weary. It was then that I remembered her, she was one of the riders who had first approached me before I succumbed to darkness, Tamsin's expression had been soft yet attentive, her instincts immediately guiding her toward compassion. Beneath her calm exterior lay the kind of quiet resilience that could not be ignored, a force shaped by years of learning to heal not just the body, but the soul.

She began speaking to Seraphina, explaining that Sylas wanted to leave soon, but that Kaelen had sent her to see if the guest was able to travel. It was odd how they spoke about me like I wasn't in the room. Seraphina looked toward me and explained that we would be leaving in the morning, to get good sleep tonight. "Where are we going?" I asked. "Who is Sylas?" Seraphina laughed and said, "That is for tomorrow. I do not want to overwhelm you too quickly."

Tamsin cut in, "Don't worry, he is insufferable, and you will get sick of him quickly. There is no rush to meet him." Seraphina began laughing and I felt like I missed the unspoken joke.

"Are they elven too?" I asked. "Sylas…is not, but the rest of us are. No worries, though, you will meet everyone else in the morning." Seraphina stated.

I was confused, was Sylas a human? Is that why Tamsin is not fond of him? I cleared the many questions from my head but realized that one was missed. "You never answered my question," I began again, "Where are we going." "To get answers for you…" A deep growl cut in from the hallway. As Kaelen stepped into the room, the air shifted…before I even saw him, I *felt* him.

His scent arrived first, curling around me like smoke: warm cedar, worn leather, and something darker, like the charge in the air before a storm. It hit me low in my gut and spread like wildfire through my veins. I hated how much I craved it…how every time he was near, that scent made something in me unravel, slow and helpless. It was addictive, grounding and overwhelming all at once, and I breathed it in without meaning to, like it could fill some hollow place inside me.

Tamsin and Seraphina stood at attention, fists crossed against their chests in a respectful bow, but Kaelen shot them a sharp look…just a flick of his eyes…and they straightened immediately, arms falling away like they'd been caught doing something foolish. Then his gaze found mine. My entire body locked up. The heat in my stomach surged, raw and sudden, and my breath caught in my throat. I couldn't speak. Couldn't move.

Kaelen stepped closer, slow, careful, like he was approaching something fragile…or dangerous. The room narrowed until it was only him and me, and that scent…*his* scent…curling tight around my ribs. He looked at me like he could see everything. Like the layers I tried to hide behind meant nothing. His jaw tightened, a muscle ticking in his cheek, and for a heartbeat, I swore he was about to speak, but he didn't. He just stood there, eyes burning into mine, and I couldn't tell if the ache in my chest was fear or want.

His body stiffened and looked toward the women on the other end of the room near the table. I moved slightly, ruffling the blankets on the bed. His eyes snapped back to me and our eyes locked. A shiver ran down my spine, prickling my skin like the very air around me had thickened with a sudden chill. My hair stood on end, each strand vibrating with strange, unspoken energy, while tiny bumps rose on my arms like the presence of Kaelen had woken something in me. It was a sensation I could not ignore, a silent whisper from the earth or the stars, a warning, or a promise... I wasn't sure.

"My name is Kaelen." He finally spoke, "I can see that I still make you feel uneasy." He walked to a chair near my bed and my body tensed as he sat down. With this motion, the two women left the room in quick movements. I began to panic. Why would they leave me alone... with him. He began again, "Will you share your name with me?" His eyes softened.

"Ha...Hajira," I squeaked out in a voice so low, that even I couldn't hear myself. He smiled and my heart exploded. What was this sensation? His aura circled me like the world blanketed me in a soothing embrace. "Thank you," he began again, "Tomorrow we will leave, it will be a long journey, but the people we will go see always seem to have all the answers that we are looking for. They are the ones who told us where to look for you. *The fallen star,* is what they called you."

My voice cracked when I finally responded, "Who are they." Embarrassed by the crack in my voice, my cheeks blushed. Kaelen's eye shimmered at my reaction, something deep within made my breath snag on his stare. "Orion Delacroix and Ileyana Vaeloria," he began again after a moment of silence. "They are trusted elders; their insight has saved my life more time than I would like to admit."

I looked at him for several minutes. I couldn't quite pinpoint what it was about Kaelen. There was something in the way his eyes locked onto mine, as if there was a language between us, unspoken, yet undeniable. Every time our gazes met, a strange heat surged through me, coiling deep in my chest, making my heart pound in a way I couldn't explain. My breath hitched, and I could feel the air around us grow thick, heavy with tension.

It wasn't just his presence, though that in itself was enough to unsettle me. It was something deeper, something beneath the surface. When he spoke again, I noticed how his voice carried a weight, it reverberated in my very bones. The words seemed to resonate within me, leaving a lingering echo. Orion Delacroix,

Ileyana Vaeloria…the names felt unfamiliar, but not entirely. There was something about them, something that tugged at the edges of my memory, like a forgotten dream I couldn't quite grasp.

I swallowed hard, trying to steady myself, but Kaelen's attention was unwavering, and my pulse quickened under the intensity of his stare. "I... I don't know them," I stammered, though I felt the truth in my voice was a bit of a lie. My words felt hollow as they left my lips.

I glanced down at my hands, gripping the blanket tightly as my heart hammered in my chest. Kaelen didn't speak immediately, but his eyes softened again. There was a flicker of something in them, a flicker I couldn't name, and it sent another jolt of inexplicable energy through me. It was as though he was waiting for me to understand something, to reach out to him in some way I couldn't quite bring myself to do.

The silence stretched, and I felt like I was standing on the edge of something…something vast and unknown. Then, almost imperceptibly, he shifted in his chair, the movement so subtle, yet it seemed to draw the room closer to us, the air thicker, heavier. I felt a strange pull toward him, like some invisible thread was weaving its way between us, tightening with each passing moment. It wasn't the kind of connection I had ever experienced before, not the bond of friendship or familiarity, but something deeper, something primal and raw.

"You're not the only one with questions, Hajira," Kaelen said quietly, his voice laced with an almost imperceptible hint of something softer, a vulnerability that I hadn't expected from him. My name on his lips, stirred something deep within me. He continued, "But I think we both know there's more to this than what's been told. More than I can explain. More than you can understand just yet." I didn't know how to respond.

His words left me unsettled, stirring a mix of dread and anticipation within me. I wanted to ask him what he meant, to push for answers, but something in the way he spoke made me hesitate. It was as though pushing for those answers would be like pulling at a thread, unraveling something neither of us was ready to face. Instead, I simply nodded, the words caught in my throat, unable to leave.

The air between us buzzed with unspoken understanding, a silent recognition that whatever bond was forming, it was something neither of us could control. Kaelen leaned back in his chair, but his eyes never left me. I could feel the weight of his gaze, not just on my skin but deep inside, as if he were waiting for me to make some kind of move, some kind of decision I wasn't sure I was ready for.

The tension in the room was palpable, thickening with every passing second. I could feel it pressing against me. Yet, despite the discomfort, there was something else too…something that tugged me toward him, drawing me closer without me even knowing why. I shifted in the bed, the blankets rustling beneath me, but Kaelen didn't break eye contact.

His presence felt magnetic, like a force pulling at my very core. I didn't understand it, but I could feel it, as if this unspoken bond between us was becoming something undeniable. A connection forged by fate, perhaps, or something darker…something dangerous. The weight of the silence between us deepened. I could feel it pressing into me, thick and suffocating, and I had to force myself to look away. The sensation of being tethered to him, bound by something unseen, was almost too much to bear. When I turned my gaze away, I could still feel his presence like a shadow hanging over me, a whisper at the edge of my consciousness. Why couldn't I shake the feeling that somehow, at that moment, this strange connection, was something I would never be able to escape?

He was the first to break the silence, "Please, for now sleep well. Seraphina will come back in the morning to prepare you for the ride. Would you prefer to ride with her?" Without thinking I blurted out, "Much more than with you!" His body tensed and his jaw clenched. "Very well." He growled as he rose from the chair, muscles tensing. Before walking through the doorway, he looked back at me, for a split second, his eyes showed a hint of hurt and sorrow. My chest ached as he turned back toward the door, and he left. The silence still resonating through the air. "Haji…you are so stupid." I murmured to myself.

I know he would not hurt me. I am not sure how I knew, but something deep told me that he wouldn't let any harm come to me. I lay back on the bed, my mind racing. What was that? Who is he? The questions swirled in my mind. I had barely closed my eyes before I was pulled into a deep, restless sleep, haunted by images of Kaelen, his violet icy eyes, his unwavering determination. I couldn't help but feel a distance, a divide that was too wide to bridge. Though, there was something between us that I couldn't quite understand, something almost feral.

The sun was still low in the sky when I awoke, its pale light spilling through the cracks in the wooden shutters, casting soft golden beams across the room. The air felt cool and fresh, carrying the scent of dew-covered earth and the promise of a new day. I stretched out, feeling the stiffness in my limbs, remnants of the tension that had plagued me in the night. The memory of Kaelen, his presence, lingered in the back of my mind.

His face, the intensity of his gaze, and the way his words had cut through the air like an edge of steel. It was all so fresh, too fresh, and I could still feel the weight of his words hanging in the air like an unfinished melody. Why does it feel like he's still here? I wondered, shivering despite the warmth of the morning sun. What was that?

A soft knock on the door broke through my thoughts, pulling me back to the present. I took a breath, pushed my confusion aside, and called out. "Come in." The door creaked open, and Seraphina stepped in, her long blonde curls catching the light as she moved gracefully toward me. Her presence was as soothing as ever, her steady warmth a balm to the chaotic thoughts swirling in my mind. She gave me a smile that was both gentle and knowing, the kind that said she understood without needing to ask.

"Good morning, Hajira," she said, her voice soft yet firm. "The day is upon us, and the journey begins soon." I blinked, still caught between the remnants of my dreams and the reality of the moment. "I suppose so," I said, forcing myself to focus. "What's the plan?" Seraphina's smile faltered just a bit, a shadow crossing her face as she set to work gathering herbs and oils.

There was something in her expression, something unreadable, and I couldn't shake the feeling that she knew more than she was letting on. "We leave shortly after breakfast," she said, her hands moving swiftly, though there was a slight hesitation in her voice. "Kaelen made all the arrangements for the journey. He will be accompanying us." At the mention of Kaelen, my chest tightened.

Even after everything, I couldn't deny that something about him had gotten under my skin, something that made my heartbeat just a little faster, my breath caught in my throat. There was no denying the tension between us…the magnetic pull that both unsettled and intrigued me. Nonetheless, even as I stood there, trying to push aside my feelings, I couldn't help but wonder if I was making a mistake.

Seraphina continued, oblivious to my inner turmoil. "He left most of the planning to me, though. He's... preoccupied."

"Preoccupied?" I echoed, raising my eyebrows. "With what?" Seraphina paused for a moment, her fingers stilling over the small vial of herbs she had been holding. She met my gaze, her expression becoming more serious.

"Kaelen has been protecting the elves for years now…but lately, there's been... something darker approaching. He's been preparing for it, though he hasn't shared much about what he believes is coming. The tension is growing, and Kaelen feels the weight of it on his shoulders. More than ever, he is determined to

protect us all."

A chill ran down my spine at her words. Kaelen…this man

who had appeared in my life so suddenly, so intensely…was a

warrior. A protector. Nevertheless, to hear Seraphina speak of him

with such gravity, as if the fate of all the elves rested on his

shoulders, made my heart race. "Do you think we're ready?" I

asked, my voice almost a whisper.

Seraphina gave me a reassuring smile, but there was a glint

of worry in her eyes that she didn't try to hide. "We have no choice

but to be. You, Hajira, are the key to this journey. Whatever Kaelen

is preparing for, we must face it together." The words echoed in my

mind, the weight of them settling heavily in my chest.

I'm the key? I didn't feel like any sort of key. I felt like I

was barely hanging on to the unraveling threads of my own

existence. "Let's get ready then," I said, my voice steadier than I

felt. Seraphina nodded, "We don't have much time," her hands

moving swiftly as she finished preparing everything we'd need for

the journey ahead. After a few moments, we left the room, stepping out into the cool morning air. The courtyard was peaceful, the early light casting long shadows across the stone paths.

Even in the serenity of the moment, there was an undercurrent of tension…an unspoken awareness of what was to come. As we walked through the courtyard, my eyes fell upon him. Kaelen. He was standing by the stables, his posture straight and strong. His silver, windswept hair caught the morning light, shimmering like a moonlit sky, while his strikingly sharp features were set in a hard, unreadable expression.

He was wearing his armor, a mixture of practical leather and elven design I assumed, each piece fitted to his powerful frame. He seemed like a force of nature. Even from a distance, I could feel the difference. The change. There was a stillness about him, a quiet intensity that set him apart from everyone else.

He wasn't just a protector. He was something more…a presence, a being whose very essence seemed to hold the weight of centuries of responsibility. I couldn't explain it, but I felt drawn to him, to the way he carried himself, to the air of command that surrounded him. He froze and glanced at me, our eyes connecting.

My breath caught in my chest, but I quickly looked away, unwilling

to let him see the effect he had on me. Focus, Haji. Focus on the task

ahead. Seraphina spoke first, approaching Kaelen with quiet

familiarity. Their conversation was low and indistinct, but the air

around them seemed to hum with something unspoken.

Kaelen's voice was calm, controlled, as always, but I could

see the flicker of something darker in his eyes as he glanced at me.

His gaze held for a moment longer than necessary, and the weight of

it settled into my bones. It was as though he was silently measuring

me, assessing something hidden beneath the surface. Finally, he

spoke, his tone more clipped than usual. "I trust you're prepared?"

His gaze flickered over to me again, and I felt a strange

knot tighten in my chest. "I am," I replied, my voice steady despite

the storm brewing within me. Kaelen nodded, though I could see the

trace of something in his eyes, something that made the air feel

heavy between us. He turned and motioned for us to follow, leading

the way to the horses.

As the first light of dawn painted the sky in soft gold and

violet hues, I stood in the clearing, preparing for the long journey ahead. The horses stood calm, their coats gleaming in the early light, their breath forming soft clouds in the cool morning air. Though, in the peacefulness of the moment, an oppressive silence hung over the group, as if the land itself understood the burden we were about to carry.

I glanced around at the company, each of us standing on the brink of the unknown, drawn together by the weight of a curse that threatened to consume all of Luminara. My attention was pulled to one figure, standing slightly apart from the others. His presence was impossible to ignore, even in the stillness of dawn. He was tall and lean, with a powerful aura that spoke without words, he commanded attention without even trying. His electric blue eyes, sharp and unwavering, were fixed on the horizon, and the air around him hummed with quiet yet intense energy.

His dark hue hair, almost black in early light, rippled like storm clouds in the breeze, an extension of the storm that always seemed to follow him. His armor, a mix of elven craftsmanship and battle-hardened practicality, shimmered faintly in the fading

darkness, a subtle hint of the power he carried beneath his composed exterior.

My gaze was fixed on him, full of unspoken questions. "That's Sylas," Seraphina said, her words carrying a blend of reverence and respect. "He's a dragon shifter. His connection to the dragons is unlike anything I've ever seen. He's not just a warrior; he's the guardian of our kind. He's dedicated his life to protecting the elves and ensuring that the ancient alliance with the dragons endures." My eyes widened in awe, and my disbelief clear on my face. "A dragon shifter?" I asked, my voice full of wonder. "But I thought…"

She nodded, her expression growing serious. "Yes, the dragons are not as prominent as they once were, and the bond between them and our people has weakened over the centuries. Sylas... he believes that restoring that bond, reviving the power of the dragons, is the key to breaking the curse that's slowly consuming Luminara. For him, it's not just about power. It's about understanding the ancient magic that binds us all." I could feel

Seraphina's gaze flick back to Sylas, who stood motionless, his eyes distant but filled with purpose.

Seraphina began again, "Sylas is a dragon shifter. When he shifts, his form becomes massive, his scales shimmering like the deepest ocean waters, his wings crackling with the raw energy of lightning. Though he rarely fully shifts." I felt a tug of curiosity toward him. The healer, who stood nearby, explained every detail. She knew that understanding Sylas, and the bond he shared with the dragons, was vital for what we were about to face.

Sylas turned towards us, for a moment, our gazes met, and I knew he had already assessed me, perhaps even sensed something about me that I hadn't yet discovered. It was the way he was…so composed, calculating, but in tune with the world around him in a way few others were. "His strength…it was a quality that made him both a natural leader and a solitary figure. His power…" she continued softly, "…Is unlike anything we've ever seen. When he shifts, he becomes a living legend. He can call the winds and bring storms to life. It's not just his power that makes him invaluable. It's his wisdom, his deep understanding of our history, and his ability to see the bigger picture." She paused, glancing back at Sylas.

He had yet to move, standing like a statue, his quiet presence both calming and unnerving. "He's lived for over a hundred years, and in all that time, he has never wavered in his loyalty to the elves. His mission, his purpose, is to guide us through this dark time. He believes that reviving the bond between dragons and elves is our only hope."

"That's why he's here, why he's part of this journey," she finished. I was silent, still staring at Sylas with wide eyes, as though trying to comprehend the enormity of what she had just told me. There was no arrogance in him, no overt display of power. He simply existed, and in that simple existence, there was a weight few could carry without breaking.

I gave a small nod toward Sylas, who had turned his attention back to the path ahead, his eyes scanning the trees with a focus that seemed to anticipate something none of us could see. "Whatever this curse is, whatever it will take to break it, Sylas will be at the forefront. He believes, no, he knows that restoring the bond with the dragons is the key. In that belief, we may find our salvation."

As Seraphina spoke, a deep stir of something strange and foreign flickered within me. Hope. For the first time in a long while, I felt something like hope. We were about to face a darkness that could consume us all, but with Sylas and Kaelen by our side, I no longer felt like it was a battle we would lose. With them, we were not just fighting for survival, we were fighting for something greater than ourselves.

We mounted, and I could feel the tension in my limbs, the anticipation building in my chest. The horses were magnificent, strong, and proud, their coats gleaming in the early light, but it was the way Kaelen moved, the way he carried himself, that captivated me. There was a quiet strength in him, a power that could not be ignored. It was both terrifying and mesmerizing. As the horses began to shift around, the journey ahead stretched out before us like an endless horizon.

I didn't know where it would lead, but I knew one thing for sure: Kaelen was no longer just a warrior I had encountered in passing. He was a constant now, a figure whose fate seemed intertwined with mine. Whether I wanted it or not, I was bound to him. I couldn't help but wonder if that was a blessing, or a curse. The road ahead was uncertain, the shadows growing longer by the minute. Though as we journeyed into the unknown, I realized there was no turning back. Whatever Kaelen had planned, whatever he was preparing for, it was now my fight too. I had no idea how I was supposed to face it.

CHAPTER 9: THE ONES WE LOST

As the morning mist began to lift, revealing the path ahead, Sera nudged our horse a bit away from the group to see the nearby scenery. Her voice was low, tinged with a mix of excitement and apprehension. "Haji," she began, her voice thoughtful, "Our group is more than just companions; we're a family forged through shared trials and unwavering trust."

"Tell me about them," I prompted, eager to understand the dynamics that bound them so closely. Sera smiled, her gaze distant as if she were dying to tell me about the group. She began recalling each member. "Kaelen leads us with a strength that's both inspiring and humbling. His decisions are guided by a deep sense of responsibility, always considering the well-being of the group."

"Tamsin," she continued, "Is a healer, like me. With this rowdy bunch we need to have two just to keep the group going. Her knowledge of herbs and healing arts has saved us more times than I can count. Though, it's her empathy that truly sets her apart; she feels our pain as her own."

"And Sylas?" I inquired, curious about the dragon who was more than just a mythical creature. Sera's eyes lit up with a mischievous gleam. "Sylas is a force of nature, both literally and figuratively. His fiery breath and formidable presence are matched only by his playful spirit. He keeps us grounded, reminding us not to take ourselves too seriously."

"Ah, and not to forget Bennick," Sera continues, her voice soft with a mix of fondness and reverence, "There's no one like him, you know. Tall, broad-shouldered, and built like the very oak trees we protect. He stands like a mountain, unyielding, unshaken. You haven't officially met him yet, but I am sure you have seen him several times. He's the kind of man who could give a soldier pause simply with the weight of his presence. I've seen it. You might think someone like that would be all harsh edges, all about strength, but there's something more underneath. A warmth that sneaks up on you when you least expect it."

She pauses for a moment, looking out across the landscape. "I remember when he first joined our group. A younger man, just starting out, still had that fire in his eyes, you know? But even then, you could see he was cautious, always calculating. He wasn't quick to trust, not even back then. That's just how Bennick is. He's a man who's seen enough of the world to know that not everything is as it seems."

Sera leans forward; her eyes gleaming with a quiet understanding. "He's a Sylvan Elf, of course, and you can see it in the way he carries himself. There's something about him, something in his very bones, that connects him to the earth. It's not something he flaunts, mind you. He doesn't parade around with glowing hands or mystical powers, but he has this... presence."

"It's like he can feel the land in ways others can't. He can talk to the spirits of nature: plants, trees, even the earth itself. It's subtle. He doesn't often use his powers, but I've seen him stand in a forest, his hand resting on the trunk of an ancient oak, and you can almost hear the whispers of the spirits in the wind."

She smiles, shaking her head as if recalling some distant memory. "And the healing... Bennick doesn't boast about it, but his touch can mend more than just a broken limb. It's not just the body he heals, it's the soul, too. The pain people carry, the weight of grief or fear, fades, even if just for a moment. That's something no one else can do, not the way he does. His magic isn't flashy, it doesn't demand attention, but it's there, woven into his very being."

Sera's gaze softens, her voice quieter now. "Bennick's a man of contradictions. He can be stern, almost cold at times, yet there's a deep well of kindness in him. He's a protector, but he also knows the value of keeping the peace between worlds, between the living and the spirits. I think... I think that's why he never lets anyone get too close."

"He doesn't want anyone to see the parts of him that he's afraid to show. However, I've seen them. The way his eyes soften when he speaks of the old groves, the way he pauses when the wind carries the voice of a long-lost friend. He's a soldier, yes, but he's also something more. Something ancient…that's why Kaelen trusts him."

She finishes with a deep breath, settling back in her chair. "Bennick's not a man to be underestimated, Haji. His loyalty runs deeper than blood, and his bond with the earth itself? Well, that's something few can ever truly understand." She paused, her expression turning contemplative.

"Each of us brings something unique to the table, creating a balance that's hard to describe. We've faced countless challenges, but it's our unity that has always seen us through." I listened intently, beginning to grasp the depth of their bond. Before I could respond, a rustling from the trees caught our attention.

Emerging from the shadows was a tall, broad-shouldered figure, his presence commanding yet calm. His mahogany brown hair was neatly trimmed, and his warm brown eyes met mine with a cautious yet inviting look. Sera halted our horse, her face lighting up with a warm smile.

"Ah, speak of the devil," she murmured, more to herself than to me. "Haji, there's someone else I'd like you to meet." Following her gaze, I saw a figure approaching on a dark stallion, a tall, broad-shouldered man whose presence seemed to command the very air around him. His mahogany brown hair was neatly trimmed, and his warm brown eyes met mine with a cautious yet inviting look.

He wore simple armor marked with the insignia of his kingdom, and despite its simplicity, there was an undeniable strength in his demeanor. Sera smiled warmly, her eyes reflecting a deep respect. "Haji, this is Bennick Ashford, our protector. Bennick, this is Haji, a trusted companion on our journey." Bennick inclined his head slightly, his gaze assessing yet kind. "A pleasure to meet you, Haji," he said, his voice carrying the weight of authority tempered with genuine warmth. I nodded in return, intrigued by this new acquaintance. "The pleasure is mine, Bennick. I've heard much about your unwavering dedication."

As we continued our journey, I couldn't help but notice Bennick's attentive nature. He moved with purpose, his every action deliberate, yet there was a quiet humility about him. Occasionally, he would catch my eye, his gaze lingering for a moment longer than necessary, as if measuring something unspoken between us. That evening, as we sat around the campfire, Sera leaned toward me, her voice barely above a whisper. "Bennick is more than he appears. He's not just a warrior; he's a protector at heart...but there's a burden he carries, a past he's reluctant to share."

I glanced over at Bennick, who was engaged in a quiet conversation with Sylas, his expression serious yet approachable. "What kind of burden?" I asked, genuinely curious. Sera sighed, her gaze distant. "He's lost many comrades in battle, and the weight of their memories often haunts him. It's why he guards his heart so fiercely."

The revelation added layers to Bennick's character, transforming him from a mere protector into a man shaped by loss and duty. It made me wonder about the stories he held close, the experiences that had forged him into the person he was. Through the night, my interactions with Bennick remained cordial yet tinged with an unspoken distance.

He was always polite, always present, but there was a part of him that remained veiled, a mystery I felt compelled to unravel. A few days pass on our journey, and as we rested by a tranquil stream, I found myself beside him, the silence between us comfortable yet laden with unasked questions. "You've seen much in your years," I began, choosing my words carefully. "The world must hold countless stories for someone like you."

Bennick's gaze shifted to the flowing water, his expression unreadable. "Stories are like the wind," he replied softly. "They pass through, leaving traces but never staying." His cryptic response only deepened my intrigue. There was a sadness in his eyes, a longing for something lost, that resonated with my own unspoken sorrows. As our journey continued, I began to see glimpses of the man beneath the protector's armor. In quiet moments, he would share tales of his homeland, of traditions and customs that spoke of a rich heritage.

He spoke of the Sylvan Elves' deep connection to nature, their ability to commune with spirits, and their reverence for the natural world. His words painted vivid images of ancient groves and sacred rituals, of a people whose lives were intertwined with the very essence of the earth. It was a world so different from my own, yet there was a kinship in our shared understanding of loss and the search for meaning.

That evening, as the sun dipped below the horizon, casting a golden glow over the landscape, Bennick turned to me, his expression earnest. "Haji, there's a tradition among my people," he began, his voice steady. "When we find someone who understands our burdens, we share a token, a symbol of trust and kinship."

From beneath his armor, he produced a small, intricately carved pendant, a leaf intertwined with a spiral. "This is the Sylvan symbol for renewal," he explained. "May it remind you that even in the darkest times, there's always a chance for rebirth." Touched by the gesture, I accepted the pendant, feeling its weight settle against my chest. It was a tangible connection to a world I was only beginning to understand, a reminder that amidst our struggles, there was always hope for renewal.

The following night, the crackling of the campfire was the only sound between us, the embers dancing in the night as I took a seat beside Sera. I'd been carrying this weight all day, questions burning in my mind, and now, in the quiet of the night, I decided it was time to unload. I turned to her, the flickering firelight casting shadows over her face as I cleared my throat. "You mentioned Bennick is a Sylvan Elf, and Sylas... well, he's a dragon," I said, unsure of how to keep the conversation going, but the curiosity had been gnawing at me. "Can you explain what these are, and the different bloodlines?"

Sera glanced at me, her expression softening as she noticed the earnestness in my voice. After a brief pause, she nodded. "Of course, Haji. It's a lot to take in, but I'll try to explain what I can." She settled back a little, eyes glinting in the firelight as she began, her voice calm but rich with knowledge.

"Bennick's bloodline, the Sylvan Elves, they're among the most spiritually connected of our kind. They're known for their communication with the spirits of the land, and their bond with nature runs deeper than most. At six years of age, they come into their full power, awakening a connection to the spirit world that lets them communicate with ancestors, animals, and even the great dragons. Sylvan Elves like Bennick can call on the wisdom of those who've passed, guiding others through grim times."

She let out a soft sigh, as if lost in thought for a moment, before continuing. "But not all elves are like Bennick. There are several types, each with their own connection to the world around them. Let's start with the Verdant Elves. They're bloodline is more common, but their powers are rooted deeply in the natural world. They can heal not just people, but entire ecosystems: plants, animals, even the land itself. Their magic allows them to mend the earth when it's sick, and if you ever find yourself in a forest where the trees seem to sing in the wind, it might just be a Verdant Elf at work." I nodded, feeling like I was beginning to understand, but Sera wasn't finished.

"Then, there are the Tempest Elves, like myself and Tamsin. These are linked to the weather: the wind, the storms, the rain. They've got the power to summon storms and change the weather itself, a gift they fully manifest only once they reach maturity. They're not as common as the Verdant Elves, but still, their powers are potent. If you've ever seen a sudden thunderstorm roll in, it might have been a Tempest Elf at work, either calming or stirring the skies. They, too, can heal, but their magic is more about restoring balance than curing wounds." I leaned forward, eager for more, and Sera continued without missing a beat.

"Sylvan Elves, like Bennick, they're different again. They're not about storms or the earth's cycles. They're the keepers of the spiritual world, able to call on spirits for guidance, to commune with nature's ancient wisdom. They can heal minds as well as bodies, their magic focused on the heart and soul, rather than just the physical. It's a rare gift, and many of them are revered as sages or spiritual leaders."

She paused again, her gaze thoughtful. "And then, there's Kaelen's bloodline… Luminara Elves. These... these are the most powerful of them all. They are able to control the elements, heal with the earth's energy, manipulate nature, and even call on spirits. Their powers are vast…like a combination of all the other types but taken to a higher level. Luminara Elves are said to be born from the earth itself, and their magic is the most ancient and sacred. There are few left in the world, and those who remain are often seen as the very embodiment of nature's will."

I felt a little dizzy from the weight of it all, but Sera was just getting started. "And then, we come to dragons. You mentioned Sylas, and yes, he is a dragon, though not of the common sort." She smiled softly. "Dragons are rare…each one with its own unique bloodline and gifts. The Black Dragons, for instance, are cursed.

Their once-fiery breath fades into a toxic mist, a curse that twists their very souls."

"They are creatures of ash and ruin, but not by choice. It's the price they pay for dabbling in dark magic, in necromancy. If you ever cross paths with one…avoid it at all costs." She shook her head. "Then, there are White Dragons. They're common among the chromatic dragons, fierce and aggressive, but not as intelligent as others. They thrive in cold climates, their primal nature making them dangerous, though not the brightest of the dragon kind." Sera's voice grew quieter as she continued, her eyes reflecting the depth of what she was about to share.

She continues, "Green Dragons are uncommon, their intelligence making them more dangerous. They live in forests, using their wits and surroundings to outsmart their foes. They are cunning, manipulative creatures, and their sharp minds make them less predictable than the Black or White Dragons." Her gaze darkened a little, but the firelight flickered, casting long shadows around us. "Blue Dragons, though, those are rare. Proud and territorial, they live in deserts and thrive on lightning. Their breath

isn't fire, but a crackling storm. They are solitary creatures, but their intelligence and control over the weather make them the most unpredictable of the dragon blood lines." I was hanging on every word, and Sera's voice softened further, almost reverently.

"Then, there's the Red Dragons. The numbers are unknown, but they are most powerful of all. These creatures are the pinnacle of chromatic dragon kind, their fiery breath capable of melting anything in its path. They live in volcanic regions, often as kings or queens of their territories. Their rarity and strength make them legends."

She looked at me, a knowing smile playing on her lips. "And then there's something almost unheard of…Black Dragons with a gold shimmer. Born every 500 years, these are the things of myths. At first, they look like ordinary Black Dragons, cursed and dangerous, but as they mature, they develop a golden sheen on their scales, marking them as one of the rarest, most powerful creatures to ever exist." I sat there in awe, trying to absorb all that she had told me. The world was so much bigger, so much more complex than I'd ever imagined. I realized just how little I truly understood. Sera met my gaze, her eyes kind, but there was a depth there, as if she knew the journey ahead would be even more complicated than I could foresee.

As the days passed, my bond with Bennick deepened. We shared stories of our homelands, our dreams, and our fears. Through these exchanges, I came to see him not just as a protector but as a man who had faced trials and tribulations, who had loved and lost, and who continued to move forward with unwavering resolve.

In Bennick's presence, I found a reflection of my own journey, a path marked by challenges, yes, but also by moments of profound connection and understanding. Together, we navigated the complexities of our world, each step bringing us closer to the truths we sought and the healing we both desperately needed.

The fire had burned low that night, its embers glowing like the last heartbeat of a dying star. The others were long asleep, scattered beneath canvas and stars, but rest evaded me. The quiet was thick…too thick…with thoughts that wouldn't stop circling in my mind. I sat on a stone near the edge of camp, wrapped in my cloak, my gaze lost somewhere between the flames and the endless dark beyond them. That strange, pulsing awareness tugged at me again. Kaelen was watching. It had become a pattern, one I pretended not to notice. In stolen glances during travel, across the fire at night, always with that quiet intensity.

Each time our eyes met, it was like something deep in me stirred…a spark, a pulse, a current. It wasn't desire, not exactly. It was deeper, and older. A thread I couldn't trace back to anything tangible. Just a sense that something unfinished tethered us across time, but this night was different. He didn't just watch. He approached. His boots were nearly silent in the grass, but I heard them. Felt them.

Kaelen stepped into the firelight, his silver-trimmed cloak catching the glow like moonlight on water. "You're awake," he said, his voice rough with sleep, but calm. "So are you," I replied, offering a tired smile. He hesitated for a moment, then sat beside me, keeping a respectful distance. Still, I could feel the heat of him.

"Couldn't sleep?" he asked. I shook my head.

"Memories…or something like them…won't leave me alone."

Kaelen tilted his head, watching me closely. "Something in

particular?" I looked down at my hands, folding and unfolding my fingers. "Not anything solid. Just... flashes. Faces. Laughter. A voice."

I paused, then glanced at him. "Do you believe it's possible to love someone so deeply in one life that their presence lingers into the next?" Kaelen's jaw tensed slightly. "Yes," he said carefully. "I believe that." I let out a slow breath. "His name was Lyrian. Or at least... I think it was. I'm not sure anymore…but I remember how he smiled when he looked at me."

"I remember the way his voice sounded when he said my name. There were two girls. We took them in together…twins. Their faces come to me in dreams sometimes, one always with her hair in braids, the other with a lopsided grin. They were ours. Not by blood, but by heart." Kaelen didn't respond right away. His expression remained unreadable, but something flickered behind his eyes. Something sharp…possessive. "You loved him," he said finally, his voice quieter now. I nodded slowly. "He was my first love. Maybe my only love, back then." Kaelen looked away, into the fire. "And he's dead?"

The question was blunt, and it made my chest tighten. I nodded again. "I think... yes. The memories end in pain… so much pain and screaming. I see him fall. I see them taken from me. Every time I try to hold onto the moment, it slips through my fingers like ash." The silence that followed was heavier now, tinged with something tense, almost bitter.

Kaelen's jaw was clenched, his hands curled slightly at his sides. I didn't need to ask to know what it was. Jealousy. He didn't even know me when I was with Lyrian. He never met him, but still, I could feel the weight of it in the way he avoided my eyes, the way his voice dropped to a distant chill. "I know it's stupid," I said gently, trying to bridge the strange tension that had risen. "He's gone. I don't even know if I remember him right…but it doesn't feel like a story I read in a book. It feels like something I lived."

"It's not stupid," Kaelen said, finally meeting my eyes. "I have seen enough death to fill a thousand lifetimes, but the worst kind of death is the one that strips you of your humanity, leaving only a machine who obeys, but never feels. Some bonds echo across time. Some don't fade, even when they should." That last part hung in the air longer than it should've.

I looked at him, frowning slightly. "Kaelen," I said softly, "Why does it hurt you to hear about him?" His gaze dropped to the fire again, his shoulders stiff. "I don't know. Maybe because I didn't get the chance he did. Maybe because I've been watching you for weeks, feeling something, I can't explain, and now I have to picture you giving that part of yourself to someone else. Someone I can't compete with. A ghost." His honesty hit me like a gust of wind.

I didn't know what to say. I hadn't expected that kind of rawness from him. Not so soon. I reached out toward him but stopped, second guessing what I was feeling in that moment. I placed a hand gently on his arm, and something like an electric current shot between us. Our eyes met. "You don't have to compete with anyone, Kaelen. Lyrian is gone…and whatever I had with him... it lives in another life, but this? Right now? It's something else. I just don't know what it is yet."

He looked down at my hand on his arm, and then his eyes met mine again, that electric feeling sparking between us, but he

said nothing. I laid back not long after, exhaustion finally pressing down like a wave. Kaelen remained nearby, his silhouette still and quiet against the firelight. I closed my eyes, the weight of memory heavy in my chest, and then the dream came.

Everything came in blinding flashes, each one sharper than the last. Vin and Liza…first. Their laughter. Their fall. Their *story*. It struck like a blade straight to the chest, and still, I didn't wake. Then came *Lyrian*. The brush of his fingers, the kiss we swore the stars would remember. The way he looked at me like I was *his world*. Another flash…his death. A crimson blur. His final breath.

The silence that followed. The air thickened, choking, crushing. I couldn't breathe. Soult's fury came next…a storm of rage, molten, and wild. Her face twisted in betrayal, a flash of violent light, then darkness again. Then…*the twins*. Mother Above, the *twins*. Their names caught in my throat, but I couldn't scream. I couldn't move. I couldn't *look away*. What came next shattered me. The pain was not memory. It was *real*. My bones breaking beneath the weight of fate. My soul fracturing into a thousand screaming pieces. Through it all, I was still there…trapped in it. Living it.

Dying in it.

"Lyrian…" I gasped, my hand clutching my chest trying to ease the pain and tightness that had taken over my very being. "The girls…no…no…" I felt as though I was screaming, but my voice came out in a raspy whisper. I began rocking and sobbing uncontrollably. "Hey…hey, Haji, I'm here." Kaelen. He was kneeling at my side, hands on my shoulders, grounding me.

His voice was soft but firm, yet still gravely from the sleep that I woke him from. "It was a dream. You're safe. You're not there anymore." I trembled, trying to breathe, trying to separate the memory from the present. "I saw them," I whispered. "They all died, Lyrian…the girls... they were so confused. I failed them…their ghosts stay with me. They haunt me…refusing to let me sleep… it should be me rotting beneath the dirt…not them." My mind rushed from the forgotten information, and I struggled to catch my breath. The pain fresh like it had just happened…How could I forget…The shame washed over every inch of my body. My face flushed and I sobbed harder.

Kaelen's hands steadied me, one moving to gently wipe a tear from my cheek. "You remember more now," he said, "And that memory, it's a piece of your truth, but it doesn't have to own you." I nodded, barely holding it together. "It will hurt. Even if it was another life." Kaelen stayed close, holding me there as the panic ebbed. Though the fire had nearly died, and dawn lingered just beyond the horizon, I knew sleep wouldn't return.

Not now. Not with so many ghosts coming back to life. For hours, Kaelen sat there as I told him my once forgotten story. He didn't speak, but when I began breaking again, he would place his hand on my back to show that he was there…I was not alone. There was a part of me that wanted to stop speaking…to shove the memories back into the dark where they'd been buried for so long.

However, once the dam broke, I couldn't hold them in. The story spilled from me in broken pieces: the way Lyrian used to laugh like it would keep the stars in the sky, how the girls would sneak wildflowers into my hair when I napped in the garden. I told Kaelen how I had promised them we'd always be safe, how I swore we'd build a life beyond the disease that broke our world, away from the blood and ash.

Then…how I failed them. My voice cracked. "I left them. I let go." "No," Kaelen said quietly, his voice low and steady. "You were *ripped* from them. That wasn't your fault." I shook my head, tears blinding me again. "I should've held on harder." Kaelen didn't argue. He didn't try to fill the silence with reassurances I wasn't ready to believe. He just stayed beside me, his hand never leaving my back, his presence a lighthouse in the storm of my grief.

I didn't realize I was clinging to his tunic until I felt his breath catch slightly, his arms wrapping around me like he could shield me from a past already written in blood. "I can't breathe when I think of them," I whispered into his shoulder. "Their eyes… they looked for me, Kaelen. They thought I'd save them." He rested his chin gently against the top of my head. "And maybe... a part of you still will."

His words weren't loud or poetic…but they rooted into me like something ancient and true. He wasn't trying to fix me. He was simply *there*, bearing the weight with me. For a long time, we stayed like that. The fire faded into embers. The stars shifted above us.

Still, Kaelen didn't move…not once. When my sobs turned to silent

tears, and my words faded into silence, he just sat there with me in

the quiet.

At one point, I looked up at him through red-rimmed eyes.

"Why are you being so kind to me?" His expression was unreadable,

eyes cast in soft shadow, but his voice was barely a breath. "Because

when someone carries that kind of pain... they shouldn't have to

carry it alone." It broke me all over again…how easily he saw me.

How gently he held me without ever reaching for what

wasn't his. He wasn't Lyrian. He didn't try to be, but he was *here*,

and somehow, that mattered more than I knew how to say. I rested

my head against his shoulder, finally quiet. The grief still burned in

my chest, but I wasn't drowning anymore. "I don't remember

everything," I said after a while, voice raw. "But what I do… it feels

like it's unraveling me." Kaelen's fingers brushed a lock of hair

from my face. "Then let it unravel. I'll help you piece it back

together." Though dawn broke slowly on the horizon, casting its

pale gold across the trees, it felt like the first light I'd seen in years.

CHAPTER 10: THE CURSED ONES

The first day after the dream felt like moving through smoke. Every breath was shallow, every step heavy. I went through the motions, packing my satchel, helping tend the fire, even sharing a few words with the others…but inside, I was hollow. Like grief had scooped me out and left only the shell behind.

Kaelen stayed close, never hovering but always within reach. When I paused too long, staring into the trees or gripping my wrist like it might ground me, he'd glance my way. No words, just the same quiet presence from the night before. I both hated and needed it…hated it because it stirred something unfamiliar, something dangerous, and needed it because I didn't know how to be alone with my memories anymore.

We didn't speak of the dream. We didn't need to. It lingered between us, a shadow draped over the path we walked, stitched into every silence. Sometimes his hand would graze mine when we walked too close, and I'd flinch…not because I didn't want it, but because part of me still belonged to a ghost.

Lyrian. Saying his name in my mind still felt like slicing open a wound that had never healed. By the second evening, the others began to notice. Sera's eyes lingered a little longer than usual when Kaelen offered me a water flask. Bennick's brow furrowed as he watched Kaelen instinctively reach to steady me as I stumbled on a root.

Tamsin, bless her sharp little heart, didn't even try to hide her smirk when she caught me staring too long at Kaelen's back for a second as he moved ahead on the trail. Even Sylas, usually uninterested in anything besides riddles and the weather, arched a silver brow when Kaelen gave up his cloak for me without hesitation. It was Sera who finally broke the silence. That night, after camp was settled and Kaelen had wandered off to speak with Bennick, she slipped beside me near the fire, her expression unreadable.

"He's different when you're around," she said, stirring the embers lazily. "Softer. Like he's afraid he'll break something that matters." I didn't answer at first. My gaze stayed locked on the flame, watching it sway in the wind like it could burn away the ache in my chest. "He's kind," I said finally. "And I don't know what to do with that."

Tamsin appeared before I could say more, flopping down with a huff and plucking a piece of bread from her pocket. "Let me guess. Sera's trying to make you admit you're falling for the leader." She grinned as she bit into the bread, crumbs falling into her lap. "About time someone did, the tension between you two is thicker than dragonhide." "I'm not…" I began, too quickly.

Sera's smile was gentler than Tamsin's but no less persistent. "You don't have to be anything right now, Haji, but you should ask yourself something. When you think of Kaelen… does it hurt because he's not Lyrian?" Her eyes searched mine, quiet and knowing. "Or does it hurt because you wish he had been?"

The question hit like a punch to the ribs, and though I didn't speak the answer aloud, I felt it cracked in my chest like lightning waiting to fall. I didn't stay by the fire long after that. My chest was too tight, my hands too restless. I murmured something about needing air and slipped away into the trees, past the flickering reach of firelight, until the others' voices faded into a distant hum.

The forest was still. Just the whisper of wind through branches and the faint crunch of leaves beneath my boots. I sat at the base of a tree, hugging my knees to my chest, letting the cold settle in as if it might numb everything I couldn't explain. *Lyrian...* The name was a bruise I kept pressing, even though I knew it would ache. How could someone like Kaelen exist in the same world breathe the same air, when the person I loved had been taken from me so violently?

It felt wrong to be seen by someone else. To be *held* by someone else, and yet…his hands were so steady. His silence so soft, and when Sera asked me if I wished Kaelen had been Lyrian…Mother Above, I hated that part of me whispered *yes*. Not because I wanted Lyrian replaced, but because I wanted that love back. The kind that made the world feel like it was worth fighting for. I don't know how long I sat there, trying to pull myself apart and make sense of the pieces, but the quiet snapped when I heard footsteps…measured, slow, familiar.

Kaelen didn't speak at first. Just stood there in the shadows between two trees, watching me with that quiet sort of sadness that made me want to scream and collapse all at once. "Should've known you'd find me," I said hoarsely, not looking at him. "I wasn't looking." His voice was gentle. "I just knew where I'd be if I were you." That pulled my eyes to his. His expression wasn't pity, it never was. Just that quiet intensity he always carried, like he could see storms forming before they ever touched the ground.

"I don't know what you want from me," I whispered. "I can't give you what I gave him. I don't even know if I have anything left to give…" Kaelen stepped closer, kneeling in front of me so we were eye to eye, but he didn't reach for me. "I don't want what you gave him," he said softly. "I just want *you*. Whatever that looks like. Even if it's just your silence right now." Tears slipped down before I could stop them. "Why are you doing this?" I asked. He smiled…barely there, but real. "Because you keep trying to walk through fire alone, and I can't watch you burn."

Something in me cracked, quietly, without sound, and though I didn't fall into his arms this time, I didn't run either. I just sat there beside him, the two of us in the quiet of the woods, not quite touching, but close enough to feel the heat of something starting to stir. Not love. Not yet, but the *possibility* of it.

Nevertheless, for now, that was enough. The morning came gentler than I expected. No nightmares clawing at the back of my mind, no ghosts rising from the ashes of memory…just the filtered gold of early sunlight spilling through the canopy above and the crisp scent of dew on moss. I was still tired, soul-deep tired, but I no longer felt like I was drowning in the weight of everything I'd lost. Something had shifted.

Maybe it was Kaelen's quiet company the night before. Maybe it was hearing his voice cut through my guilt like he was unafraid of the broken pieces I carried. Whatever it was, I opened my eyes to a world that didn't feel quite so heavy. Kaelen was gone from where he'd been sitting, but his cloak still lay draped over my shoulders. The fabric smelled faintly of cedar and steel and something uniquely him.

I folded it slowly, carefully, my fingers lingering a beat too long before I tucked it under my arm. I barely made it back to camp before Sera was on me. She caught my wrist like a wraith made of silk and shadow, her brow arched in full interrogation mode. "You disappear into the trees with the Brooding King and come back with his cloak. Do not think I won't be asking questions."

Tamsin practically leapt out from behind her like she'd been *waiting* to pounce. "Did he kiss you?" she asked, eyes sparkling with wicked delight. "Did he confess his undying love while a moonbeam hit your face just right?" She jested. "I swear," I muttered, rubbing my temple, "Do you two sleep?" "Not when there's emotional tension thick enough to cut with a dagger," Sera said, utterly unbothered. "Come on. Out with it. What happened?" I hesitated, and Sera's expression softened just enough to nudge the wall inside me.

"We talked," I said finally. "That's all. I… remembered more of my past life. It wasn't pretty." Tamsin's grin faded, and she sat beside me, her tone unusually quiet. "And he stayed?" She asked, and I responded with a nod. "Then that says more than any kiss ever could," Sera murmured. I didn't respond. Not because I disagreed, but because I didn't trust my voice not to tremble.

They were right. Kaelen had stayed, not out of obligation

or strategy, but simply because I needed someone, and he had

become someone I didn't know how to stop needing. Though, I also

knew the truth. I could not give him the whole of my heart, not yet,

because somewhere in the deepest cracks of it, Lyrian still lived, and

letting go of that love would be another kind of death. Still, I

allowed myself to smile…just a little…at the way Sera looked so

proud, like she'd single-handedly orchestrated our entire emotional

journey. Maybe I was allowed small joys. Even if my soul bled, it

could still breathe.

The fire crackled low, glowing embers dancing like

whispers in the dusk. I sat a little way from the others, wrapped in

Kaelen's cloak again, though I hadn't meant to bring it with me.

Somehow it had become… comforting. Familiar. Like him. I wasn't

sure when his presence had started to feel like gravity, pulling me

back to myself every time I drifted too far…Maybe it had been this

way since we met.

I could still feel the echo of his hand on my back from the

night before, could still hear his voice reminding me that I didn't have to face the darkness alone. It terrified me, since I had loved once before, and the world had torn it from me. I was still staring into the fire, lost in the rhythm of my thoughts, when I caught faint murmurs from just beyond the circle of light. Not close enough to make out every word, but I knew the tones. Sylas and Bennick, deep in conversation. I didn't move. I didn't mean to listen, but some truths want to be found, even when whispered.

Elsewhere by the river, moments earlier...

Kaelen stood near the water, silent, tossing small stones into the current. Each one vanished without a sound. "He's brooding again," Sylas said, dropping beside Bennick with a dramatic sigh. "Should we be concerned, or has he just fallen helplessly in love with the girl who dropped into our world like a comet and shook everything loose?" Bennick didn't smirk.

He simply watched Kaelen with that quiet soldier's gaze. He all but whispered, "He hasn't been the same since that night by the fire." "Mm," Sylas hummed. "Well, he's been a lovesick idiot since before then, but sure, let's go with that." Kaelen turned sharply, clearly having heard them, but didn't walk away.

"Speak of the shadowed prince," Sylas teased. "Have a seat, or are you afraid we'll talk about your feelings?" Kaelen dropped down beside them, rubbing the back of his neck. He looked like he was trying to choose between staying silent or bleeding out. "I've never learned to let my guard down," he said finally, voice low. "Maybe it's because I fear what might happen if I do…Or maybe I fear what others might see if I let them too close." Sylas blinked. Even he didn't have a quip for that. Kaelen stared at the water, his expression unreadable.

"But with her, it's different. It's not something I let happen. It's just… happening." Kaelen continued and Bennick leaned forward. After a short silence, he asked, "Do you think she's your mate?" Kaelen didn't answer right away, but his back stiffened with the question. Then, in the softest breath, he admitted, "I think I've known since the first time she looked at me. There's this… pull. Not just in the magic in me. Like something ancient has been waiting to wake up."

Sylas whistled, low and long. "Well. That explains the way you look at her like she's made of starlight and tragedy." Kaelen's mouth lifted in a faint, pained smile. "Every time I look at her, I want to speak the words that claw at my chest, but I can't. Not yet. Not until I know if she could ever feel the same…or if I'm merely a fool standing in the shadow of a dream."

Back by the fire…

I didn't hear the words, but I felt something shift when Kaelen returned. His eyes found mine across the flames…and there was something burning in them I wasn't ready to name, but Mother Above, it made my heart skip. He didn't sit beside me right away. He kept a careful distance, like he was afraid one wrong move would undo the fragile balance we'd built.

Still, the silence between us wasn't empty. It was waiting. The fire had burned low again. Sera and Sylas had wandered off somewhere, probably trading secrets and sarcasm. Tamsin had tucked herself into her blankets with an exaggerated sigh about how "romance never seems to bloom when I'm around." Bennick was sharpening his blade on a stone, rhythmically, silently.

Only Kaelen remained near me, but not close…not quite. He stood by the edge of the trees, back turned, like he was deciding whether to stay or vanish into shadow. I don't know what made me say it. Maybe I was tired of pretending the air between us wasn't thick with unsaid things. "You don't have to keep doing that." His head turned, just slightly. "Keep doing what?" he asked, not moving.

"Keeping your distance like you'll burn me if you get too close," I responded. He stilled. The quiet that followed felt longer than it was. Then slowly, Kaelen returned to the fire, sitting across from me. Not beside me, but close enough that I could see the flicker of doubt in his eyes, the weight he carried like it had been hammered into his bones. "I'm not afraid of burning you," he said quietly. "I'm afraid of what you'll see if you get too close."

I didn't look away. "Try me." He studied me for a long breath before speaking again, slower this time. Each word dragged up from somewhere deeper than he usually let people near. "I wasn't sure how to tell you the truth. I know now that I cannot move forward without telling you…" He paused. "Tell me what?" I asked, now terrified of his untold truth. He took in a sharp breath and began, "…To tell you my story… I was never born to be heir of the throne." My eyes widened and my breath caught in my throat.

He continued, "My brother, he was the light. The future. Everyone saw him and felt hope." He paused, eyes distant. "They saw me and expected a blade." I didn't interrupt. I didn't have to. "I was trained to protect him. To fight for Sylvaris. To serve in the shadows while he stood in the sun. Discipline. Tactics. Obedience. That's what my childhood was. There were no lullabies or stories at night. Just lessons. Pain. Orders." My chest tightened.

"When the war came…" Kaelen's voice faltered for the first time. "He died in the first wave, and I…I couldn't stop it. My father was never the same. The court turned to me. *Me*, the weapon. The afterthought. They expected me to fix what was already broken." A tremor laced through his words, though he never raised his voice.

I felt the fracture line running through every syllable. "And now…" He finally looked at me. "Now I wear a crown I never wanted, carry a name that doesn't feel like mine. Every time someone looks at me, they see what's left…not what was lost." I

reached out without thinking, my fingers brushing against the back of his hand. "You're not what was left, Kaelen. You're what survived."

His breath caught…so soft I wouldn't have heard it if I weren't listening for it. He turned his hand slightly, letting his fingers graze mine in return. "I've never learned to let my guard down," he said again, voice barely a whisper. "Maybe it's because I fear what might happen if I do…Loyalty is the only thread that binds me to this world. It's not love, not ambition, but a vow made long ago to a kingdom that doesn't even remember my sacrifices…"

He trailed off. "And yet you're here," I murmured. Kaelen's eyes dropped to the fire. My heart cracked open in a slow, painful way, because I *did* feel something. Something dangerous, beautiful, and new. Though, Lyrian's ghost still lingered at the edge of every breath I took. "I don't know what I feel yet," I said softly, honestly. "But I don't think you're a fool." Kaelen gave me a faint, haunted smile. "That's the kindest thing anyone's said to me in a long time." We didn't say anything else for a while. We just sat there in the dark, letting silence do what words couldn't.

The following night, we sat with the others near the fire. Something charged the air and everyone seemed to be on edge, but I had no idea what was to come. I felt it before I heard it, an unnatural shift in the air, like the world itself inhaled sharply and forgot how to exhale. The fire snapped violently in the pit.

Bennick stood first, a hand already on the hilt of his blade. Sera stilled, her eyes narrowing. A ripple of energy crept along the back of my neck; the kind that made instincts sharpen like knives. Then came the sound. Low. Guttural. Choking and snarling, like creatures crawling out of their own graves. A scream tore through the trees. "Get ready!" Bennick roared. They came from all directions…Cursed Ones.

The cursed elves came without warning, at least 10 of them spilling from the line of trees like living nightmares. My eyes widened as I looked at the cursed group now circling us. Twisted elves, bloated with unnatural strength, vines of black veins bulging across their limbs. Their magic crackled and flickered, unstable and violent, and their eyes glowing violet through twisted helms. Their movements were sharp, jerky, like marionettes yanked by something unseen. Blades glinted with corruption. The air shifted. Sylas was already moving.

He stepped in front of me, his body tense, the change already taking hold. His spine arched unnaturally, jaw clenched as claws pushed through his skin and his irises blazed gold. His voice came out rough, barely human. "Stay behind me, Haji." He growled, no longer speaking in his usual cadence.

The first clashed against Sylas's scales now covering his arms from his partial shift, sparks flying as steel scraped down them. He twisted, parried, claws slashing across one elf's chest. Another came at his side. Sylas turned, part man, part dragon now, using his growing strength to shove two back with a savage grunt. Kaelen burst through chaos, roaring as he swung his sword.

It cracked through a cursed elf's shoulder, splattering dark blood onto the grass. His strikes weren't elegant…they were brutal, forceful. He fought like a shield wall come to life, bashing through opponents with desperation carved deep into his face. "Sylas, there's too many!" Tamsin yelled. We were surrounded now. The cursed elves fought like they couldn't die, pressing in tight with crooked swords and teeth bared. The forest echoed with clanging steel, snarls, and screams.

A deafening roar pierced through the sky. A screech that I had never heard before. It chilled me straight to my bones. We all froze and looked toward the darkened sky. Wind shifted. A sudden beat of massive wings stirred the treetops, and then it was there…descending like a storm. A cursed dragon. Its wingspan blotted out the moon. The smell hit first…acrid and suffocating, like burnt flesh soaked in rot, thick with iron and something older, fouler, that made the back of my throat close.

It was the scent of death, not fresh, but *ancient*, lingering like a curse in the air itself. Then came the sound…a screech that split the sky, not just loud but *wrong*, a jagged, echoing cry twisted with rage and agony. When the dragon landed, the ground shuddered beneath its weight, the force of it cracking stone and flattening the air around us with a gust of searing wind that reeked of char and decay. What once might have been a magnificent beast, noble and terrifying in equal measure, now looked like a desecrated shadow of itself.

Its scales were blackened, dulled like obsidian left to rot in ash, matte and flaking as if poisoned from the inside. Smoke dripped from between its teeth…not the vibrant blaze of a living fire, but a sickly, gray vapor, like the last breath of something long dead. Its eyes glowed with a pale, soul-hollowing light, unblinking and empty, as though whatever spirit had once lived inside it had been bled dry.

It moved like a titan in its death throes…massive, grotesque, and agonizingly slow, each motion cracking with the weight of something trying to remember what it once was. The smell clung to everything, infected everything. It wasn't just in the air, it was in my lungs, on my skin, under my nails. I could *taste* the curse on my tongue, bitter and thick, like ash that would never wash clean.

"SYLAS!" Kaelen shouted, but it was too late. The dragon struck. It slammed into Sylas from his left side, claws tearing into his back. He roared, dropped to one knee as blood burst from deep gouges across his shoulders. The ground cracked beneath him. His shift faltered, bones grinding, muscles twitching between human and beast.

"Haji, Sera…RUN!" Bennick bellowed over the chaos. Tamsin rushed a nearby cursed elf, as she reached out her hand toward them a crack of lightning struck through them. The smell of rotten, charred flesh invaded my senses. I stumbled back; my feet barely moved before a cursed elf lunged toward me.

Their blades arching down toward me. Before I knew what happened, I slammed into something hard. The elf's blade sliced into Sera's side as she shoved me clear from the strike, my body tumbling through the air and crashing into a tree with a horrible crack. "SERA!" Kaelen's shout was raw, broken.

He charged, eyes wide, shoving through cursed elves with a roar. One tried to grab him, Bennick snapped its arm like a twig before the elf had a chance. Kaelen kept running, sword cleaving through another's gut. His eyes were searching, glancing through the clashing of metal and the spray of black blood.

All I could do was crawl behind a tree, my heart racing, eyes wide, fingers clenched in dirt. Kaelen finally reached Sera and dropped beside her, shielding her with his body, teeth clenched in rage and fear. "SERA?!?! Are you okay?" He screamed, "Where is she? Where is Haji?"

There was sheer panic in his voice. Sera groaned, barely able to speak, but still muttered, "I…I am fine…I don't know…where she is…I shoved her out of the way and lost sight of her." Hearing her speak, I peeked out from behind the tree as an attempt to get their attention. I saw Sylas, injured but still fighting, clawing his way back to his feet, golden eyes wild with fury. Kaelen rose to his feet as another group charged at them. He stood over Sera, raised a sword, bellowing as he held off three cursed elves at once. Bennick slashed at the remaining 4 elves.

Sera wasn't moving away. She must be hurt badly, all I want to do is run toward her and heal her, but the fear and memories past have me stuck in place. Tears begin to stream down my cheeks as I begin to realize that I am too weak and again will watch the people that I have grown to love, die in front of me. It was then that

I saw Tamsin rush to Sera's side trying to heal her in the midst of battle. I let out a jagged breath, thanking the Mother Above that she made it on time.

Then everything slowed and a massive shadow caught my eye. The cursed dragon circled again, the ground thudding with every step. Its glowing eyes swept the battlefield. It appeared to be looking for something and then my heart dropped as its eyes locked onto mine. A shiver sliced through my spine. I froze.

Its gaze burned into me…cold, ancient, malevolent. A predator's stare. My legs moved, finally releasing me from the still of death. Before my mind caught up, I turned and ran into the woods, breath ragged, branches tearing at my face and arms. Behind me, trees cracked as the cursed dragon followed wings flattened.

Its wings were torn, ragged, bones jutting through torn membranes like rusted blades. I barely had time to react before one of the cursed elves slammed into the ground just beside me, sending up a shower of debris. "Scatter!" Sylas shouted, releasing a flare of radiant flame that turned two of the cursed elves to ash. I spun, searching for Kaelen…only to see a wave of the creatures surging toward him.

He was shouting something, my name? I couldn't hear it over the chaos. Then the cursed dragon shifter locked its eyes on me again. It snarled, low and primal, smoke curling from its maw. It moved…fast. I turned and ran. Branches clawed at my skin as I sprinted into the forest, away from the shrieks, the magic, the fire. I could still hear the others fighting, but they sounded farther and farther away. Then I was alone.

The cursed dragon followed. I heard its heavy breathing behind me, saw the faint, glowing shimmer of its ruined wings tearing through the trees. I tripped. The ground rushed up to meet me, and I slammed into it hard, my breath ripped from my chest. I crawled back, scraping my hands against roots and rocks as the beast stalked toward me, smoke rising from its nostrils, its body hunched and trembling.

It had once been something beautiful, I could see that even now. Hints of deep emerald scales glimmered faintly beneath the black rot. Its horns were broken, one eye clouded. Its rage burned bright…wild and unreasoning. I braced myself. Then…everything shook. A roar, far more human than a beast, split the night.

Kaelen. He crashed through the trees like a war god summoned from flame and fury. His eyes were wide, wild, afraid. He didn't hesitate…didn't slow. He hit the cursed dragon with the full weight of his rage, blade slamming into its chest. The dragon shrieked, smoke billowing from its mouth as it staggered.

Kaelen moved like a storm. He didn't speak. He didn't stop. His blade sang through the air, and with every strike, his grief poured out…his fear, his fury, the desperation I hadn't dared believe lived in him. It wasn't a fight. It was annihilation. He drove the cursed dragon to the ground, pinned it there with a knee to its neck, and raised his sword, but stopped. Just for a second. It looked up at him, this dying, cursed creature, smoke leaking from its broken mouth. Something human still lingered behind its ruined eyes and for a heartbeat, Kaelen hesitated. That's when it struck.

It lunged, mouth open, and Kaelen twisted his body to shield me from the blast of cursed smoke that hissed out…but it was weak. Dying. With a final cry, Kaelen plunged his blade through its skull. Silence fell, thick and shuddering. He turned to me, breathing hard. I was still on the ground, my hands shaking, a gash across my arm burning like fire.

He dropped beside me, pulling me into his arms like he wasn't sure if I was real. "Haji," he whispered, his voice breaking for the first time since I'd known him. "You're here. You're safe." I nodded against his chest, trembling. "I couldn't feel you," he said, his hands cupping my face, checking for blood, for breath. "I thought…I thought I was too late." I tried to answer, but all I could do was nod.

He pulled me close again, holding me like I was the only thing tethering him to the world. "I would've torn the entire forest down," he whispered into my hair. "I would've burned every cursed thing that touched you." …I believed him, the possessiveness in his word shook me to my core. It frightened me just a little. We didn't speak as Kaelen guided me back to what remained of the camp. His grip was gentle, but I could still feel the tremble in his fingers, the barely contained rage that had spilled out of him minutes before. Ash clung to his skin like a second layer, and his breath, though calmer now, came in shallow bursts like each one cost him. The others had begun regrouping in the distance. I heard Bennick shouting calls, Sera's sharp commands echoing through the trees. Kaelen didn't go to them.

He led me toward the edge of the clearing, away from the others, away from the blood and broken bodies. He finally stopped beneath the twisted arms of an old tree, half-charred and smoldering from the cursed magic. The firelight flickered across his face, highlighting the deep cuts on his cheek, the bruise blooming along his jaw. He looked… wrecked. Not just tired…*torn open.* "I shouldn't have lost control," he said suddenly, voice low. "Not like that."

I turned to him and said his name in something quieter than a whisper, "Kaelen…" "I was trained to be better than that," he continued, as if I hadn't spoken. "To keep a level head no matter the chaos. My entire life has been one lesson after another on restraint. Control. Precision." His jaw clenched. "And I threw it all away the second I couldn't feel you near me." There was something raw in his eyes…guilt, yes, but something else too. "I don't even remember

some of it," he admitted. "Just fire. Rage. You were gone and all I could think was that if I didn't get to you, I'd…" He stopped, shaking his head. "I would've burned this whole forest down."

I reached for his hand, and though he flinched at first, he didn't pull away. A deep warming sensation bubbled from my stomach. A light glow filtered through my body and out of my hand. Kaelen's eyes finally met mine as a wave of healing magic rushed through both of us. "You protected me," I said quietly. He gave a short, bitter laugh. "I destroyed everything. I lost myself." He said as he glanced away, toward the forest. "But you found me," I whispered. "You came back." His eyes met mine again…haunted, uncertain.

"That part of me… the one that surfaced tonight… it's always been there, waiting." The wind stirred around us, carrying the scent of ash and damp earth. "I saw you," I said gently. "All of you, and I'm still here." His throat bobbed as he swallowed hard, and for a moment, he didn't answer. He looked away, toward the charred tree line, the remnants of his rampage painted in blackened earth and crumpled bodies.

Then softly, almost like a confession, he said, "I can't lose you…I thought you were gone. I didn't realize…I need you with me…Here…with me…" He trailed off again but grabbed my hand and held it to his chest. I could feel his heart pounding through his skin. It was unmistakable. There was something in his eyes and as our skin touched, I felt it again. That electric shock to my senses.

My heart cracked open. He wasn't asking for promises or declarations. He was offering truth. Raw and unpolished. So, I stepped closer, rested my head gently against his chest, and let the silence speak for me. His arms wrapped around me without hesitation, holding me tightly…like he didn't quite believe I was real. For a while, we stayed that way. The chaos faded, the fire dimmed, and in the fragile stillness that followed destruction, I felt the stirring of something both terrifying and beautiful. Hope.

CHAPTER II: A NEW BLOOM

After a long stretch of silence, Kaelen suddenly springs to his feet, as if jolted by the memory that we weren't alone, that others were waiting. Without a word, we begin making our way back to camp. That's when I truly see the devastation the battle left behind. The cursed elves lie scattered along the path, their twisted bodies lifeless.

Pools of thick black blood darken the earth and stain the trees and underbrush we pass. The weight of it settles on my chest. When we finally reach camp Tamsin and Sera are tending to the others, healing them with swift, practiced movements. As soon as they see us, Sera's face changes. It looks like she wants to run to me, but can't, Sylas is collapsed in front of her, lying in a puddle of blood.

Kaelen's voice is firm but clipped. "Report." Sera speaks first. "Bennick isn't seriously injured. Just a few bad cuts. He'll be fine." Bennick scoffs, clearly annoyed she isn't taking his wounds more seriously. Tamsin is already crouched beside him, hands glowing faintly as she works. Then Sera's voice drops, almost trembling. "Sylas is far worse…"

"The cursed dragon did more damage than we thought. He's stubborn…kept fighting through pure will…" Her words trailed off as tears began to roll down her cheeks. Her hands are trembling now. I follow her gaze. Sylas is lying motionless on the ground, his eyes closed, his chest barely rising. Something is wrong. I look at Sera, silently urging her to say he'll be alright, but her voice breaks when she tries. "Kaelen, I've tried… I can't…he won't heal. What do I do?"

Kaelen goes rigid. For a moment, it's like the air has left his lungs. My heart sinks. This happened… because he was protecting me. Without hesitation, I move to Sylas and drop to my knees beside him. I place a hand on his chest…his pulse is faint. So… faint. Panic rises in my throat, and my breathing quickens. The others freeze, eyes on me. I press my palm more firmly against him and begin to pray to the Mother Above. Heat rushes through my body. I start to shiver.

Then, without warning, a brilliant light bursts from my chest. My head snaps back, but my hand never leaves Sylas's chest. The light pours into him, and he lets out a strained, painful groan. The others stared in stunned silence. Power flows freely from me, through Sylas, then begins radiating outward, touching everyone nearby. His back arches as I channel the last of my strength into him. Then the light fractures, shimmers, and vanishes. Darkness claims me, and I hit the ground hard.

When I wake, I'm surrounded by five familiar faces, but it's not relief in their eyes…it's fear. "Sylas…" I whisper, forcing the name past my dry lips. A hand grips mine gently. "I'm here, Haji," he says, voice rough and tight with emotion. I turn my head and see him…whole, healed. I blink, trying to focus through the haze of exhaustion. Something feels wrong. Off.

"Why are you all looking at me like that?" I ask. No one answers. I prop myself up on my elbows, looking around. That's when I see it…everyone is healed. Fully. As if the battle never happened. Kaelen is the first to speak. "Haji… you healed us. All of us. How did you…? I've never seen anything like it." He trails off, waiting for an answer I don't have. I say nothing. I don't know what I did.

Sera breaks the silence, a small, almost amused smile tugging at her lips. "I think she's of Luminara bloodline. No one else has that kind of power…not even the strongest in our history." As I try to sit up further, Tamsin reaches for me. At the same time, both Kaelen and Bennick move toward me. Startled, I swat their hands away. "I'm only tired. Don't treat me like a child."

My tone comes out sharper than I intended, but it has the desired effect. They back off, letting me rise. My legs buckle. Kaelen catches me, steadying me with an arm around my waist. Our eyes meet. "Are you okay?" he asks gently. I nod slowly, only now realizing how close we are. I try to straighten, glancing around.

The camp is spotless…no blood, no bodies. "How long… was I out?" I ask, my voice cracking. Everyone exchanges a glance, their faces grim. Sylas finally answers, "A week. We thought you'd never wake up. I thought you gave your life for me." His voice falters. His hands tremble. "Why would you do that?" I look at him, offering a soft smile. "I couldn't let you die."

His response is immediate…sharp. "You could have died. That was reckless." I lower my eyes, still smiling. "I couldn't lose anyone else." My voice drops to a whisper. "I don't fully understand what I am… or what I can do, but healing has always been a part of me. This was something I could do. I couldn't stand by and lose anyone else…" My voice quivers, fading into silence. Silence settles over the camp once more…thick, reverent, unspoken.

Then Sera breaks it gently, her tone thoughtful. "If you *are* of Luminara blood… you need to train, Haji. We need to know the full extent of what you can do. That kind of power doesn't just... *happen*." Tamsin nods slowly. "Power without control is dangerous. Even if it's meant for good." Bennick, still looking a little pale beneath his usual bravado, mutters, "She nearly burned herself out saving us. What happens next time… if there's no one left to catch her?" Their voices blend into the wind, but it's Kaelen's gaze I feel the most. He hasn't moved from my side. His arm still supports me, his body tense, like he's afraid I'll collapse again. However, it's his eyes…fierce and full of something deeper than admiration…and that steals my breath.

He speaks softly, almost like he's speaking to himself. "I've read the prophecies since I was a boy. Heard the stories. The world torn apart by the curse… and one would rise. A light in the dark." His fingers tighten around my waist, grounding me. "I thought they were just myths, old words to comfort people when there was no comfort to be had." He pauses, then looks directly into me. "But now… I think they were real. I think *you're* real."

I shake my head and respond, "I don't know what I am, Kaelen. I didn't ask for this. I didn't ask to be anyone's answer." "I know," he says gently. "But the world doesn't always ask. Sometimes it just chooses." The wind picks up, rustling the trees and tugging at the loose strands of my hair. For a moment, I feel the weight of his belief settle onto my shoulders…and I don't collapse beneath it. Not yet.

"Then I need to be ready," I say, straightening slowly. "I need to learn what this power is… and how to control it. Before it controls me." Kaelen's eyes light with quiet pride. "Then we train." Sera claps once, a smile breaking across her face despite the lingering exhaustion. "About time something around here gave us a little hope." Tamsin rises, brushing dirt from her knees. "We'll find someone to guide you. Or, if no one can… we'll figure it out together." Bennick gives a half-hearted groan. "Great. Now I get to be the guy who trains with a living legend. No pressure."

Everyone laughs, just a little, but it's the first real laughter we've shared since the battle. As the sun begins to rise over the horizon, casting gold over the remnants of the world we're still trying to save, I realize something… I might be afraid of what's inside me, but I'm not alone, and maybe…just maybe…I really *was* chosen. Not because I'm strong, but because I have something worth fighting for.

The next morning, the camp is quiet. Still. The others move softly around me, watching with careful eyes…concern, curiosity, and something like reverence in their gazes. No one says it aloud, but I can feel the shift in how they see me. Not just a healer. Not just Haji. Kaelen waits for me at the edge of the clearing, where the tree line breaks, and the earth feels open and vast.

He's dressed simply, no armor, no weapons, only a leather-wrapped staff in his hand and a calm expression on his face. The sun is barely rising, golden light just brushing his jaw, and for a moment, I forget to breathe. "You came," He said with a small smile. "I said I would," I reply, stepping into the field with him. "I meant it." He nods, then motions for me to stand opposite him.

"We'll start simple. Breathing, balance, focus. If your power is tied to emotion, we need to learn how to channel it, not just release it." I frown. "What if it won't come? What if I can't call it on my own?" His eyes soften. "Then we keep trying until you can." He begins by showing me how to ground myself, barefoot on the cool grass, eyes closed, palms open to the sky.

It's awkward at first…too quiet, too still. My thoughts race, memories flash behind my eyes, and my heart beats too loud to concentrate, but Kaelen's voice is steady, always so steady. "Breathe through it. Power doesn't need to be forced. It's already in you. You're not calling it, you're remembering it."

I listen. I breathe. Again, and again…and then, slowly, I *feel* it. A warmth in my chest. A flicker under my skin. Not burning, not blinding just *present*. Waiting. "Good," he says, as if he can sense the shift. "Now, try to move it. Just a little. Guide it, don't command it." I raise my hand slowly. Energy flickers to life at my fingertips…soft, pulsing light. It doesn't burst out or overwhelm me this time. It simply… *responds*. I laugh, breathless and wide-eyed. "Did you see that?" I ask, full of awe. Kaelen grins, "I saw it, and I think that was just the beginning."

Later, when the sun dips low and the others drift into their own routines, I sit at the edge of the camp, legs curled beneath me, staring into the trees. My muscles ache from the training, and my mind is still buzzing from the energy I touched earlier. It wasn't much…but it was *mine*. Controlled. Guided. Kaelen approaches quietly, a water flask in his hand. He offers it to me without a word, and I take it, gratefully.

We sit in silence for a while, the kind that doesn't need filling. Crickets hum in the brush. The fire crackles softly behind us. "You were incredible today," he says eventually. I shake my head. "I barely did anything." "You *barely tried*," he counters, smiling. "And already, you're doing what no one else can. That power…it didn't just heal us, Haji. It *changed* us. I feel… different. Stronger." I glance at him, studying his profile. He's not trying to flatter me. He means it, and I don't know what to do with that kind of faith. After a short while, I finally ask, "Do you really think I'm the one the prophecy spoke of?"

He turns to face me fully, and there's no hesitation in his voice. "I *know* you are. I've fought my whole life thinking the world was past saving…but now, when I look at you… I see the turning point." The words hit something tender in me. I look down at my hands, the same ones that just a week ago barely knew what they held inside. I whisper, "I'm scared, Kaelen." "I know," he says. "But you don't have to do this alone."

A quiet falls between us again, but it's warmer now. Closer. When I lean against his shoulder, he doesn't move…just lets me rest there, like it's the most natural thing in the world. Like he's been waiting for this moment just as much as I have. For the first time since the battle, since the burst of light and the darkness that followed, I let myself believe it, too. That maybe I *am* the answer. That maybe, with them beside me… I can save this world.

Three days pass. Every sunrise, Kaelen meets me at the edge of the woods, and every time I arrive, I feel a little stronger. A

little more sure of the power thrumming beneath my skin, but today… something is off. The air feels charged, tense. The sky is bruised with storm clouds, and Kaelen's expression is unreadable as I approach. "Today's different," he says. "We're going to push further. You've felt the light. Now you need to learn what it does when fear, anger, or pain fuels it."

I blink. "You want me to get *emotional* on purpose?" Kaelen's smile is brief. "No. I want you to learn how to *feel without losing control*." He tosses me a wooden staff…lightweight, but solid. "What is this for?" I ask. "To focus. To defend, and if you can manage it, to *channel*." I raise a brow. "So... no pressure, then?" His grin widens. "None at all."

We begin with breathwork again, but this time he circles around me, poking at my balance, testing my reactions. His movements grow quicker, more deliberate. The game becomes sparring, and soon my blood is racing. Then he says something that flips the switch. "You're holding back. Still afraid of what's inside you." I glare at him. "Of course I'm afraid. You've *seen* what happens when I lose control." "And if that fear controls you, the curse will win," he snaps. His voice is harder than I've ever heard.

I shove forward instinctively, slamming my staff against his with a loud *crack*. Power flickers through me. Sparks leap from my fingers. Kaelen doesn't move. I strike again. This time, the glow flares. A crack of light splits the ground beneath us. Kaelen holds his stance. "Don't run from it. *Use* it!" I scream…not in anger, but in release. All the fear, the weight, the pressure pours out of me. The staff lights up, fully engulfed in shimmering gold. I twist, strike downward, and the ground pulses beneath my feet. Then, silence. Breathless, I fall to my knees.

Sweat beads across my brow, heart thundering. Kaelen kneels beside me slowly. "That's it," he says, voice quiet again. "You felt it." "I nearly shattered the ground," I whisper. "You *shaped* it," he corrects. "That power didn't lash out. You *guided* it. You're not a weapon, Haji. You're becoming a force." The storm breaks that evening. Rain patters softly over the canopy, the scent of wet earth heavy in the air. The others are asleep or tucked away, but I find Kaelen standing at the edge of the cliffs beyond camp, gazing into the misty dark. I join him, still aching from training, my heart still humming with the energy I unleashed.

"Didn't think you'd still be awake," I murmur. He smiles without looking. "Didn't think I'd still be breathing after that blast." I laugh quietly, then fall silent beside him. The moment stretches between us…comfortable, fragile. "You scared me today," he says softly. "I scared *myself*." Kaelen turns to me then, eyes dark under the fading moonlight. "But you came back from it. You always do. That's what sets you apart."

A raindrop slides down my cheek, and I realize I'm shaking…not from cold, but from everything I've been holding inside. I open my mouth to speak, but Kaelen steps closer. "Haji," he says, his voice lower now, barely above the rain. "When I said I believed you were the answer… I didn't just mean for the world." My breath catches. "What do you mean?" His gaze searches mine. "I mean for me. You woke something up in all of us…but in me… it was more than hope. It was *wanting*. To fight again. To feel. To *live*." The space between us shrinks.

My mind races as he steps closer to me. Something tells me to take a step back away from him, but with the way his eyes peer into me, it keeps me from moving. He takes another step towards me. His violet eyes never waiver but slowly lowers from my eyes down to my lips and back up to my eyes.

His hand reaches for my cheek and once our skin connects an electric charge runs through the both of us. He raises his other hand, now cupping both of my cheeks. My heart quickens and the hair on the back of my neck stands. "Haji…" He whispers as he leans in. Our lips meet and another spark seers through my body. My hands that were once by my side are now gripping both of his wrists.

He pulls back just slightly, his breath brushing against my lips, his forehead resting softly against mine. His eyes find mine again, darker now…like the weight of everything he's ever felt is resting behind them. I feel like I can't breathe, like the world has gone quiet except for the roaring pulse in my ears. He's searching me, not for words, but for something deeper, something neither of us can name, and Mother Above… I feel it too…this aching, desperate bond between us that doesn't need to be spoken. It screams in the silence; it thrums in the space between our skin.

Before I can even form a thought, he leans in again and this time, it's not soft or tentative. This kiss is deeper, hungrier, like he's afraid that if he doesn't have me now, he'll shatter, and I let him. Mother Above, I *need* him. His scent is already flooding my senses, thick and warm…cedar, leather, and the raw, electric edge of something untamed. It sinks into my skin, clings to the back of my throat, and I breathe him in like he's the only thing keeping me tethered to this world.

I'm addicted to it…*to him*…and the taste of him on my tongue is just as dangerous: smoke, heat, something dark and bitter I can't name, but crave like a starving thing. Every inch of me is lighting up, alive in a way I've never known, like my body has been waiting for this exact moment, for *him*, my whole life. My fingers tighten around his wrists as the kiss deepens, and I know with startling clarity…I'm already his. Completely.

His tongue brushes the inside of my mouth, teasing, coaxing, and I answer without hesitation, lips parting to let him in.

He growls low in his throat, the sound vibrating through both of us, and suddenly his hands are everywhere…one sliding to the back of my neck, fingers threading through my hair, the other firm at the base of my spine, anchoring me to him, pulling me closer, *deeper*. There's nothing cautious in the way he touches me now.

It's possessive, primal, and it doesn't scare me…it ignites something in me, something wild and molten that's been sleeping until now. My hands find his face, trace the line of his jaw, the stubble along his cheek, then dive into his hair, pulling him even closer like I could somehow crawl inside him and never leave. Our lips moved with a growing urgency, mouths parting to drink in more…more heat, more of each other. Fingers tangled in hair; bodies pressed tighter as the world blurred at the edges.

The kiss deepened, fierce now, like we were trying to speak through it, to tell all the things words never could. It was hunger, yes…but something else too. A desperation, like letting go would mean forgetting how to breathe. When we finally broke apart, breathless, lips tingling, we didn't move far. Just close enough to rest our foreheads together, eyes closed, chests rising and falling in

sync, trying to catch up. The silence buzzed with everything we didn't need to say. It was understood. He was mine, and I was his. Wholly, and truly.

"You have no idea how long I have wanted to do that…" Kaelen says, our foreheads still touching. This causes me to open my eyes and look at him. His eyes were already on me. "…How long…?" I managed to squeak out. He lets out a low sultry laugh, pulling away. My body reacting to the loss of his warmth. "I don't want to scare you…" His tone lowered; his eyes locked on to me again. "…from the moment I saw you."

I gasped, "You're lying…" I let out a nervous laugh expecting him to change his story to the truth. He didn't budge; eyes didn't move from mine. "I would never lie to you…I know you feel what is between us. This force, this unrelenting pull. Every moment of every day, my soul craves you…needs you…" He finishes. I know exactly what he is talking about. From the moment I saw him. It was like my body, mind, and soul yearned for him.

"What is it…Why do we feel this way?" I almost whispered. With this question his body tenses and that's when I realize he knows something. "What is it?" I ask again, this time firmer. He finally breaks eye contact and turns away from me, taking a few steps away. "That scares me, don't turn away from me, Kaelen." My voice quivers when I say his name. He freezes and looks back to me. He finally responds, "I don't know…but I think…" He stops talking again, glancing around our surroundings.

I stood frozen, watching Kaelen with a mixture of confusion and something I couldn't quite name. He had that same quiet intensity in his eyes again…like the weight of the world was caught behind them, pressing down on him, urging him to speak. "Haji," he said, his voice softer than I'd ever heard it, almost reverent, "I believe we're mates."

The word hung between us, thick with meaning I didn't yet understand. I laughed, uncertain, trying to brush away the tightness that had taken hold of my chest. "What do you mean, mates?" I asked, tilting my head. "Like… friends?" The smile Kaelen gave me then was sad and warm all at once, like he pitied my innocence. "No. Not friends. Not like that at all."

He stepped closer, so close I could see the slight tremble in his fingers, the way he clenched them into fists like he was trying to hold something inside. "Among elves, a mate is… something sacred. It's a bond deeper than anything else we know. We don't fall in love often. We don't have many partners, but when we meet the one, the only one, we just… know. Our souls recognize each other before our minds do."

I felt my heart begin to race, his words soaking into me like icy rain. He wasn't just saying he cared. He wasn't saying he wanted to try something and see where it went. He was saying we were meant. That something beyond us had already decided we belonged to one another. "Mates aren't chosen. They're found. Like two halves of something broken, finally made whole again."

I couldn't speak. I could barely breathe. My chest was tight, and my hands felt cold despite the warmth of the sun filtering through the trees. "Kaelen…" I managed, but he kept going, his voice filled with something I wasn't sure I'd ever been worthy of. "When one of us is in pain, the other feels it. Not just emotionally…physically. If you were hurt, I would feel it in my skin."

"If you were scared, I'd feel it like a storm inside my own chest. That's how deeply the bond runs, and if a mate dies…" He paused, his throat working around the next words. "Some don't survive it. It's like living without air, like walking through a world where color has vanished. Most elves never find their mate. When they do…when they do…it becomes everything."

I looked at him then, really looked at him. The way he was holding himself so tightly, like he was afraid I might run. The way his eyes were soft but desperate, pleading for me to understand. Beneath all of that, the unspoken truth: he'd known before I did. Maybe for a long time and he'd carried that weight alone, unsure if I'd ever feel the same. Something cracked open in me. I didn't know if I believed in destiny, or fate, or soul-deep magic that tied one person to another across lifetimes…but standing there, with Kaelen's heart in his hands and mine suddenly beating louder than it ever had before, I couldn't deny what I felt. Not anymore.

"During the attack, you said you couldn't feel me…was that the Mate Pull?" I finally got out. He looks almost heartbroken. His brows furrow with his response, "Yes." I continue again, "That electric feeling I get when I am near you…" He takes a step closer, "Yes." I take a deep breath, "The pull I feel toward you?" He takes another step closer, "Yes." My heart begins beating faster again, "The feeling when…we kissed?" He finally closes the remaining gap between us and says, "Yes… all of it. It is the Mate Pull."

Silence falls between us before I speak up again, "If all of this is true, why do you only *think* we are?" His jaw clenches and pauses before he answers me again. "You can only confirm a mate bond, when two become one." I begin to ask, "What do you…" I stop as soon as I realize what he means. My face flushes and my hands tremble. Kaelen grabs my hands and kisses them.

"Haji, when two join as one, the Mother Above blesses them with a mate mark. This is the final joining, one that is lifelong, one that is never ending. There is no breaking that bond. Greater than any love, greater than any hate." He pauses and brushes my hair from my face. "When we are ready and not a day sooner, we will know for sure. Until then, I can only hope that we are." He finishes and leans in to kiss my forehead.

My head is spinning from all of this information, but I don't pull away. What he says makes sense. All of these feelings and emotions that I haven't been able to place. Could we truly be mates? "Haji…say something," He pleads. I look into his violet eyes and my breath catches from how vulnerable they are right now. Before I can say anything, I pull him close, our lips touch one more time catching him off guard. There is a rush of power that flows between the two of us, as if the Mother Above was confirming everything that we are feeling. When we part, he looks deeply at me, "Are you not scared?"

I slowly begin, whispering, "I am terrified…" Kaelen's back stiffens, and he holds his breath waiting for my next words. "I am terrified of these unknown powers I am finding within myself. I am terrified of the cursed ones. I am terrified of what is to come…But I know whatever this is…It doesn't scare me." I finish and he seems to finally breathe again. Kaelen smiles and pulls me

into a tight hug. His heart is thudding against my chest. He was scared.

This realization causes me to grip him tighter. After what seems like forever, we finally part. My stomach growls loudly, like a bear coming out of hibernation. We both burst out in a fit of laughter, the moment now long gone. "Let's head back, we have been out long enough. Maybe they have made dinner by now." He says, reaching out his hand for mine. I placed my hand in his and intertwine our fingers as we head back to camp.

I didn't realize how late it had gotten…The sun now hangs low in the sky, swollen and heavy, like an ember smoldering at the edge of the world. Its golden light stretches long across the landscape, turning the dirt path into a ribbon of fire and casting shadows that seem to sway gently with the breeze. The trees around us glow with an almost otherworldly warmth, their leaves catching the light like stained glass.

The air is softer now, cooler, tinged with the faint scent of pine and smoke…perhaps from the campfire already lit in the distance. As we walk, the hush of evening settles around us, broken only by the crunch of gravel under our boots and the far-off call of a bird heading home. It feels like the world is exhaling, slowly folding itself into night. As we approach the camp, everyone is waiting outside by an already lit fire. Their eyes fell onto us and then immediately down to our connected hands. The girls let out a high-pitched squeal and rush over to us and I know that this will be an exceptionally long night.

CHAPTER 12: A BURNING EMBER IGNITES

Tamsin gets to me first, her fingers wrapping around my wrist like a vise as Sera grabs my other arm, their excitement crackling louder than the fire behind them. "Oh, my stars, Haji! Finally!" Tamsin gasps, practically dragging me toward the circle of logs around the flames. Sera is already talking over her, her words tumbling out so fast they trip over each other.

"What happened? You two were gone forever. Did he tell you? Did *you* say anything? Did you kiss? Was it…wait…did the Mother Above give you a sign? Oh, my stars, did you *glow*?" Sera blurts out. I can't help it, I start laughing. A real laugh, the kind that comes from somewhere deep in my chest. Maybe it's the adrenaline still working itself out of my system, or maybe it's just them, these two wild, persistent, brilliant lights in my life.

"Slow down," I plead, letting them steer me to the fire like a prisoner to her fate. "One question at a time. Maybe." Tamsin plops down beside me and leans in so close I can smell the pine sap in her hair. "You did, didn't you? You kissed. I *knew* it! I told Sera it would happen." "And I told *you* she'd look exactly like this afterward," Sera says, settling in on my other side and gesturing at my face. "All starry-eyed and flushed. You're practically *glowing*, Haji." "I am *not*," I say quickly, though the way my skin still tingles, and my lips still remember the feel of his… maybe I am.

Meanwhile, across the fire, Sylas claps a heavy hand on Kaelen's shoulder, steering him away from the main circle. "Alright, lover boy, you're coming with us," he says with a grin. Bennick raises an eyebrow but follows, always the quieter shadow to Sylas's storm. The three of them drift toward the edge of camp, voices low and already teasing. Kaelen glances over his shoulder just once, his eyes catching mine, and something silent passes between us…steady, warm, terrifying in its certainty.

Back at the fire, Tamsin nudges me. "So… are you going to tell us *everything*? Or do we have to start guessing again?" I sigh and hug my knees to my chest, staring into the fire as it dances in gold and orange. I want to tell them. I want to spill every word Kaelen said, every look, every heartbeat. However, the truth is still so new, so raw. It doesn't feel like mine to give away just yet. Not all of it.

"I… I don't know what we are," I begin quietly, but even as I say it, I know that's no longer true. They both lean in, ready for more. "And maybe that's okay," I say, more to myself than to them. "Maybe some things take time to grow into." They go quiet, which is rare and almost unsettling. For a moment, it's just the fire between us, crackling and alive. Then Sera grins. "That's code for 'we're probably mates, but I'm going to pretend I'm still figuring it out, so I don't panic.'" I roll my eyes, but I'm smiling too. Maybe she's not entirely wrong.

By the time we've all settled down around the fire, the sky has slipped into twilight, the stars just beginning to peek through the darkening blue above us. The air hums with leftover warmth from the day, laced with smoke and roasting meat. Bennick returns from wherever they'd been cooking, balancing a wide, battered tray full of food. It smells like heaven…roasted root vegetables, seasoned strips of wild game, and something sweet and sticky tucked in leaves that Tamsin immediately reaches for. As plates are passed around and conversation bubbles up again, it almost feels normal.

Like we're just travelers, sharing a meal beneath the stars. Kaelen returns to sit beside me, his leg brushing mine in quiet reassurance. He doesn't say anything, but he doesn't have to. His presence alone calms the flicker of nerves still dancing through my chest. Sylas is cracking some half-serious joke across the fire at Bennick's expense, and even Sera's snark softens into something more playful as the night wears on. There's laughter, light flickering from the fire, full bellies, and for once, no shadows chasing us. I feel something building, even in the comfort of it. Not dread, not exactly, but anticipation. A storm circling the edge of my awareness.

Over the next two weeks, my training became relentless. Every morning without fail, Kaelen, Sylas, Bennick, and I hit the trail for our daily run. After that, I rotated sparring partners, facing new challenges each day. Once the sparring was done, I turned to honing my elven powers. It was a grueling cycle…day in, day out…with no room for excuses. In the beginning, I could barely make it half a mile before my legs gave out beneath me.

The others joked about my lack of stamina, but their laughter lit a fire in me. I wasn't going to stay the weak one…not anymore. I pushed myself harder than I ever had before. Morning, afternoon, night…I ran, even when my body begged me to stop. When I should've been resting, I slipped away to train alone, refusing to let fatigue or failure define me. I was done feeling powerless. Every drop of sweat, every aching muscle, every bruise was proof that I was getting stronger. Finally, I could keep up, with no more screaming calves, no more collapsing. Just me, pushing forward.

One morning felt heavier than most. I was sparring with Kaelen, my body already straining under the weight of exhaustion I refused to acknowledge. As we moved, the world tilted slightly beneath me…dizziness creeping in, vision dimming at the edges. Kaelen noticed immediately and halted, concern flashing in his eyes. "Please, let's continue…" I muttered, barely able to hold my stance. He didn't move. His expression shifted, darkened. "Enough, Haji. You don't think I know that you sneak out to train? You're pushing yourself too hard," he growled his voice thick with anger, but I couldn't stop. I *wouldn't.*

"Don't tell me what to do," I snapped, voice rising. "Haji, you don't have to push yourself this hard. You have to stop." Kaelen demands sternly. This unravels all of my frustration, and I begin to yell at him, "You haven't felt what I've felt. You didn't have to watch everyone you love die. You weren't there, helpless, pleading, *crying* while everything you cared about was ripped away. It almost happened again, Kaelen. We almost lost Sylas…and I did nothing but cower behind a fucking tree."

My voice broke. My chest heaved as the storm in me spilled over. "Do you understand now? Do you see why I'm doing this? I *have* to get stronger. I can't lose you too. I can't lose Sera. I can't lose *anyone.* I won't survive it again." Kaelen's anger faded. He took a cautious step toward me, his eyes softening, but I recoiled like he'd struck me. "DON'T!" I barked. "I don't need pity. I need to fight. I need to *burn.* There's something inside me…building, boiling…and I can't stop it."

Kaelen froze. Even he looked uncertain now, as if he saw something in me he didn't recognize. I felt my voice rise, booming, trembling with more than grief. "No one understands why I can't stop. Why I *won't*. It's not just training…it's survival." My skin pulsed with heat. My blood felt like liquid fire. I staggered, chest tight, flames licking at the edge of my control. Then the sky cracked open.

Rain came pouring down, heavy, and sudden. From the tree line, figures began to emerge, drawn by the chaos. Kaelen's voice rang out, "STOP…stay away!" The others froze at his command. He turned back to me, pleading now. "Haji, breathe. You're going to burn out. Please, stop this." Something in his eyes…fear, pain, love…hit me harder than any strike ever could. In that moment, I broke. I screamed, a sound so loud and raw it felt like it could tear the sky apart.

Lightning struck all around me, fire exploded from my hands, untamed and wild. I couldn't hold it back anymore. The power surged and I was lost in it…spiraling, drowning. Kaelen's voice was a distant echo now, his words reaching through the storm.

"Don't make me do this… Please, come back to me, Haji…" But I couldn't hear him. I was too far gone. My skin sparked with electricity, the burning unbearable. Then, like the crack of thunder…sharp pain pierced my neck. My body went cold. Numb. The fire flickered out, and then everything went black.

When I opened my eyes again, everything was quiet. The storm had passed. The sky above was a dull gray, weeping softly through the broken canopy. I was on the ground, my body aching, drained beyond anything I had ever felt. Kaelen was beside me, crouched low, soaked through and staring at nothing. There was no relief in his face.

Just exhaustion, and something deeper, something fractured. "You forced me to stop you," he said, his voice hoarse, hollow. "You gave me no choice." He didn't look at me when he spoke. "Do you know what it felt like, Haji? Watching you tear yourself apart? Watching the person, I care about more than anyone spiral into something I didn't even recognize?"

His hands were trembling, clenched tightly. "I couldn't reach you. I couldn't protect you. Mother Above help me, I almost lost you." His words hit harder than any blow. There was so much grief behind them, and fury…directed not just at me, but at himself. He finally turned his eyes toward me, and the storm was still there, just quieter.

"You want strength? Fine. Then when you've healed, when your body and mind are steady again, you'll start training with Sylas. Not tomorrow, not tonight…when you're ready. I don't care how stubborn you are, you will rest until then. That's not up for debate." His tone left no room for argument.

This wasn't a suggestion. It was a line drawn in stone. I wanted to protest. I wanted to fight him on it, but the truth was, I'd gone too far. The remnants of fire still coiled in my blood, simmering low, waiting. I had lost control. If he hadn't stopped me... I don't know what would've happened. I remember his story, the people he has lost. I made this about myself, my loss. My guilt settled heavy in my chest, dull and suffocating. "I'm sorry,"

I whispered, eyes stinging. "I thought I could handle it. I thought I had to." Kaelen sighed, finally letting the tension in his shoulders ease just a little. "I know," he said, and for the first time in a long time, I believed he understood. He reached out, resting a hand over mine. "But you don't have to carry this alone anymore, Haji. Not ever again."

The next few mornings drifted by as I rested. Kaelen did not allow me to run with them. He barely let me leave my bedding. Finally, after I was fully healed, he agreed my training would start again the following day. The morning came swiftly, golden light pouring through the canopy overhead and spilling across the clearing. The sounds of camp stirring woke me gently, and after a quick bite of fruit and bread, I find myself standing across from Sylas in the same practice field as before.

"Alright," he says, cracking his neck and stepping forward with a cocky grin. "Let's see what Kaelen's been hiding." I snort, rolling my shoulders. "Pretty sure this is more about what *I've* been hiding." He shrugs. "Fair enough. Just don't melt my face off, alright?" I pause…did he say melt?!? I shake the question away. Though the next training session, my movements are sharper, faster, like something old is waking in my limbs. Sylas frowns as he parries one of my strikes, something unreadable flashing in his eyes.

"You're different today," he mutters. "It's like... your energy's humming." Then it happens, Sylas lunges just a bit too close, and instinct kicks in. My body reacts on its own, my hand shoots out and suddenly a wave of fire bursts from my palm, arcing around us in a controlled ring that sears the air without burning him. The flames spiral upward before dissolving into sparks that drift down like golden snow. Silence slams into the clearing. Sylas steps back, wide-eyed. "What in the hells, Haji…" The others are running toward us now, drawn by the explosion of power.

Kaelen is the first to reach me, his eyes filled with awe, not fear. "You've awakened it," he breathes. I'm panting, my skin is glowing faintly with heat. "I don't know what that was. I didn't mean to…" But Kaelen is already shaking his head, stepping close. "You didn't just summon fire. You controlled it. That's dragon fire." "…What?" Sera's voice cracks as she skids to a stop beside Sylas. "That's impossible. Only dragons can…" "Exactly," Kaelen says. He places a hand over my heart, and I can feel it, that molten core of something ancient and wild pulsing inside me.

"Haji… you're not just bonded to dragons. You *are* one. At least… in part." Kaelen mutters. The words hit like a thunderclap. My knees nearly give out, and I stagger back. "No, that can't be right. I…I'm just…" "Just what?" Kaelen says gently. "Just a girl with buried memories and powers she can't explain? You *felt* it, didn't you? That fire didn't want to destroy. It wanted to *protect*." The world tilts as realization sinks in. I see flashes…dreams I'd chalked up to nonsense.

Soaring skies, scales gleaming in the sun, the roar of something powerful and proud echoing in my bones. Tamsin steps forward slowly, awe in her voice. "Haji… you didn't just summon that fire. You *commanded* it." "I…" I close my eyes. Deep inside me, something ancient shifts. Wakes. Maybe I've never been just one thing. Maybe I've always been something more. This…this is only the beginning.

We stay in the clearing long after the others drift away, their murmurs fading into the trees as Kaelen guides them back to camp with a promise that I'll be alright. The shock still clings to me, hot and electric beneath my skin, but Sylas just stands there, arms crossed, staring at me with an expression I can't quite read. For a long time, he says nothing. Then, finally, he speaks, his voice lower than usual, rough around the edges. "It makes sense now. The way you move. The instincts. You've always fought like one of us… a dragon. You just didn't know it."

I turn to face him, breath still coming hard. "You knew?" "I suspected," he admits, walking a slow circle around me, like he's seeing me with new eyes. "Kaelen's not the only one who's bonded. I come from an extensive line of dragonkind. That fire you just summoned… that wasn't a fluke. That was blood-deep. You don't just *have* dragon power, Haji. You *are* dragon." I swallow, my mouth suddenly dry. "Then teach me. I don't want to lose control like that again. I want to understand it."

A slow grin spreads across his face. "Now you're speaking my language." We begin with the fire. Sylas stands a few feet away, arms raised, fingers forming ancient sigils in the air. "Flame is emotion," he explains. "Dragons don't breathe fire because of magic spells. They *are* magic. Their breath is fury. Their flame is protection, rage, love, and sorrow. If you want to control it, you have to control yourself."

Easier said than done. He has me stand in the center of the ring he drew with ash, asking me to summon the fire again. At first, nothing comes. I close my eyes, trying to focus, but everything inside me feels tangled. Sylas watches for a while before stepping closer. "You're thinking too hard. Feel it. Where does it live?" I press my palm to my chest. "Here," I whisper. "Then bring it forward." He states firmly.

I reach for the warmth buried inside me, and this time it answers…slowly, cautiously. A flicker of gold dances across my fingertips, faint but alive. I open my eyes and stare at the flame, watching as it curls and coils around my hand like a living thing. Sylas grins again, pride flashing in his eyes. "Good. Now hold it. Breathe with it."

Over the next few hours, he pushes me harder. I learn to shape the fire into streams, into blades, into bursts of raw energy. I scorch lines into the earth, send bursts high into the air like signal flares. Sylas shows me how to build barriers of flame, how to call it back just as easily as I send it out. He teaches me how to burn *without* destruction, how to harness it for light, for heat, even healing in some strange, ancient way.

Though, it's more than just fire. My senses begin to sharpen. I hear more, smell more…the flutter of a sparrow's wings in the trees, the shift in the wind before a leaf even falls. My strength increases, my balance improves. When Sylas challenges me to a round of combat with my fire held in check, I move with speed I didn't know I had. He grunts, landing on his back in the dirt after I flip him with a strike I didn't even think through.

"You're fast," he says, coughing out a laugh. "Like a hatchling who's just discovered their wings." The mention of wings makes something stir inside me…an ache, a yearning. I glance up at the sky, the clouds drifting lazily above the treetops, and a question forms. "Have you ever shifted?" Sylas nods, more serious now.

"Only a few times. When I shift the majority of the time it is only partially. Few of us can take full form whenever we want to. It takes immense power and control. Most dragonkind only get flashes, a scaled arm, wings in a moment of desperation...but you…" He steps closer, eyes narrowing. "You have something in you. Something pure. I wouldn't be surprised if you're capable of more than any of us."

I'm not sure whether that terrifies or excites me more. As the sun begins to dip behind the trees, painting the sky in molten reds and purples, I find myself standing alone at the edge of the clearing. The ground around me is scorched in places, but not wild. Controlled. My hands are still warm, my heartbeat steady. I raise one hand, and with a single breath, summon a small, dancing flame.

It spins above my palm like a curious bird, responding to my thoughts. I am fire. I am dragon. For the first time, I'm beginning to believe it. The next few days blur together between my elf side, dragon side, and all of the training, I am so exhausted that I sleep for an entire day. When I wake up, I am refreshed and ready to jump back into training.

The morning sun arrives, but it is still cold and quiet, the mist still clinging to the treetops as I step barefoot into the clearing. The earth beneath my feet is damp, grounding, but it does little to settle the turmoil churning in my chest. Sylas is already waiting,

standing with his arms crossed, gaze steady and unreadable. His usual sarcasm is absent…he knows what today is. Today, we try shifting again. Fully. Not just fire, not just fragments, but the true transformation. The dragon within. He nods once in greeting and gestures for me to begin. I take a deep breath, closing my eyes, reaching inward like he taught me. I try to find that molten center…that place where the fire and the power live.

However, as I call to it, the shift answers with only a whisper. My arms tingle, my spine prickles, but my body remains painfully elven. I grit my teeth and try again. This time, a ripple rolls beneath my skin…my fingers elongate, bones stretch, black scales push through the surface…but it collapses before it can fully form, snapping back like a rubber band stretched too far. My knees hit the ground, hard.

"Take it slow, Haji," Sylas says from behind me, voice calm. "You're not failing. You're learning." Nonetheless, it *feels* like failure. Every attempt ends the same. The third time, I manage to half-shift, arms scaled, back arched with the weight of wings that refuse to fully emerge. I feel the power there, pulsing, *waiting*, but it's locked behind some invisible wall I don't know how to break through. It leaves me breathless, trembling, and angry. On the fourth attempt, I scream as my spine contorts, wings bursting forth only halfway before my body convulses and the pain snaps me back.

I collapse again, gasping for air, my palms digging into the dirt. Sylas moves in immediately, faster than I expect, and crouches beside me. He grabs my wrist, not harshly, but firmly, and holds it as I try to rise again. "Enough," he says, tone brooking no argument. "You need to stop. You're going to tear yourself apart." I shake my head, furious, blinking away the sting in my eyes. "I can't stop. I *have* to do this." His expression softens, but the grip on my wrist tightens slightly. "And you will, but not by sheer force of will. You're not fighting a battle, you are unlocking a memory. That takes patience and much power."

He drags me, reluctantly, toward the flat rock at the edge of the clearing, where he forces me to sit and drink from the flask he tosses into my lap. The water is cool and sharp, but it does little to wash away the frustration burning in my chest. "You don't get to hate yourself because it's not easy," Sylas says as he leans against a tree nearby, arms folded. "This isn't about earning your power. It's about remembering who you already are. You're trying to *control* something you were never meant to hold in a cage." I stare down at my hands, still faintly trembling. "Then why does it feel like I'm doing everything wrong?"

He exhales, then walks toward me again, crouching at eye level. "Because you are…but only because you keep trying to *be* the power instead of letting it *become* you." His words sit with me as the sky shifts overhead, the sun climbing higher. We sit in silence for a while. I hate resting. I hate stillness. Though, as my body begins to cool and my breath evens out, I can feel something subtle shifting in my mind…like the embers I've been stoking are finally beginning to catch. When I stand again, Sylas only nods.

I try again. A fifth attempt, then a sixth. My body contorts painfully, ribs expanding, legs shifting, my skin rippling with heat and scales, but it always stops *just* short. I roar in frustration, the sound barely human, barely contained. "Why won't it *stay*?!" I scream, standing in the center of the clearing, fists clenched, heart pounding. The ground trembles beneath me.

My fire lashes out without command, spiraling up from my feet in wild, uncontrolled arcs. "Why can't I be *enough*?!" Finally, something happens. The world seems to *crack*. Something inside me breaks wide open…no longer a whisper, but a *flood*. My breath catches, and the shift surges through me, not like before, not fragmented, or forced, but total. My bones stretch and realign with thunderous pops. Heat bursts beneath my skin as it hardens, darkens, transforms. My body grows, taller, longer, the earth buckling beneath me as massive wings unfurl from my back with a snap like lightning through the sky.

I feel my face elongate, jaw reshaping, my vision sharpening to impossible clarity. My scales are black, sleek as obsidian and just as reflective, but as I move, as the light filters through the canopy and strikes me, a golden shimmer rolls across my form…iridescent, shifting like sunlit water. It dances over my wings, down my spine, glimmering with every breath I take.

A gold sheen, subtle and blinding all at once. Familiar and *impossible.* Somewhere, buried in the whirlwind of transformation, a memory rises, Sera's voice, soft and reverent, telling a story beside a fire. *Black Dragons with a gold shimmer. Born every 500 years, these are the things of myths. At first, they look like ordinary Black Dragons, cursed and dangerous, but as they mature, they develop a golden sheen on their scales, marking them as one of the rarest, most powerful creatures to ever exist.* I never believed it. Not then. Not until now. When I land…if I even felt myself leave the ground…I am no longer the girl who stepped into the clearing. I am something *else*. Something *ancient*. Something *feared*.

The others appear at the edge of the clearing slowly, drawn by the roar that shook the sky. Sera is the first to step into view, her lips parted in disbelief, her eyes wide and glassy. Tamsin follows, stumbling as she takes in my form, one hand over her chest. Bennick draws his blade but does not raise it, awe locked into every line of his face. Kaelen walks forward last, quiet, reverent. He doesn't look afraid…he looks like he has found *home*. No one speaks. The golden shimmer curls around me like a second fire, glowing in places no light touches, and for the first time in my life, I feel *whole*. No longer a girl pretending to be strong. No longer power in hiding. I am dragon and the world will never see me the same again.

CHAPTER 13: THE BLAZE OF FORGOTTEN FIRE

There's something strange about silence after a storm. It hums. Not as emptiness, but as aftermath…as breath held tight in the lungs, waiting for what comes next. That's what it feels like here, in the clearing.

The trees still lean inward, branches bent from the force of what I unleashed... I shifted…I still can't believe that I am a dragon. My fire was much stronger in my dragon form. I let out a tunnel of flame before shifting back and almost burnt down the entire forest. Smoke still curls from the grass where the dragon fire licked the earth. Ash hangs in the air like fog.

The ground is still warm beneath my boots, and though the others are beginning to emerge from the shadows, no one dares speak. Not about me, because I'm not sure what I've become. I'm still catching my breath, trying to steady hands that aren't shaking from fear, but from the raw aftershock of change. Real change. Not the kind that flickers and dies before it takes root. Not the kind you fake so people believe you've made progress.

No. This was something else. I shifted. Fully. Cleanly. No fractures. No resistance. I don't know how long I stood there, surrounded by the golden shimmer of scales I never believed were mine. Maybe minutes. Maybe seconds. Though at that time, I felt everything I've ever doubted fall away. The weight of expectation, the pressure of fear, the voice that always told me I'd never be enough…all of it burned. When I shift back to Elven form, I am fully clothed, like a mythical power keeps them intact. I do not quite understand fully, but something tells me that in time, I will.

The fire didn't hurt me. It carried me. Wrapped me in heat, shadow, and light, and for the first time, I didn't fight it. However, now, standing in the smoking quiet, I feel like a ghost of the girl who screamed in frustration just moments ago. Not broken. Reborn. I don't know how to exist in this skin yet.

Kaelen moves first. Of course he does. He always moves first when everyone else is stuck. His steps are quiet, steady, eyes locked on me…not afraid, not even in awe, just steady, like he sees something worth standing with. "You know now," he says, voice soft enough that maybe only I hear it. "Not everything, but enough."

He's right. I do know something now. It's not clean or clear. It's not a list of facts I can repeat back to them, but something inside me cracked open, something old and vast, and it remembers what I don't. Still, the words don't come. My throat is dry. My body aches. The shift didn't just burn through the air…it carved through me. Yet, even with the pain, even with the exhaustion, I feel intact.

More than intact. Rooted. Whole. Kaelen glances toward the flat stone at the edge of the clearing, the one Sylas calls the 'seat of truth.' I hate it, and he knows I hate it, but he gestures to it anyway, like he's offering me a throne I didn't ask for. I groan and drag my feet, too tired to argue, too raw to pretend. "Seriously?" I mutter. "Sit," he says, and tosses a flask into my lap. "Drink." I sit. I drink.

The water is cold and sharp, and it cuts through the leftover fire still crackling inside me. My fingers tighten around the metal, knuckles pale. It's a tether. A link to something real. Something grounding. Sylas leans against a tree nearby, his arms crossed, shadow slicing across his boots like he belongs to the forest more than the sky.

"You don't get to hate yourself because it's not easy," he says. "This isn't about earning your power. It's about remembering who you already are. You're trying to control something you were never meant to hold in a cage." I stare down at my hands. They're still warm. Still trembling. Still changed. "Then why does it feel like I'm doing everything wrong?" I snap, though it comes out quieter than I intend. I sound tired. Small.

"Why does it feel like I'm failing even when I'm not?" I question. Sylas pushes off the tree and crouches in front of me, face level with mine. "Because you are," he says bluntly. "You are doing it wrong, still. Because you keep trying to be the power instead of letting it become you." The words slam into me, quiet and precise, and I hate how much they make sense. They settle deep, like stones dropped in water, like roots pushing through fire-scorched soil, and as we sit in that quiet, in that not-quite-peace, I start to understand something I didn't before…maybe the fire isn't here to destroy me. Maybe it's here to remake me.

Eventually, I rise. Not because I want to, but because I have to. The fire doesn't want stillness anymore. It wants motion. It wants purpose. "I can't stay here," I say aloud, mostly to myself. "You won't," Kaelen replies, stepping close again. "Because we're going forward." His voice steadies me. He waits for me to meet his eyes before he speaks again.

"You've felt what's inside you, but you don't know what it means yet. You need answers, Haji. Real ones. Not from me. Not from Sylas. From the people who remember what the world tried to forget. We need to go to Orion and Ileyana. They're the only ones who can help you understand what you've become." I look at him, the words catching behind my ribs. "I thought I was a dragon," I say, and my voice cracks. "You are," he answers without hesitation. "And something more. You're not just the shimmer on your scales. You're not just a Black Dragon who lived. You're a myth waking up, and they're the ones who can tell us why."

I haven't said anything for a while. I just breathe. Deep. Grounding. The fire is still there, under my skin, but it isn't roaring. It's listening. Waiting. For the first time, it's not a stranger. The power is mine, and I am it. I nod. Not a dramatic gesture. Just enough, and when I turn, the others are closer now. No longer frozen at the edge of the clearing. Sera, with tear-bright eyes. Tamsin, with her hands over her heart like she's trying to hold it in place.

Bennick, sword still in hand, but lowered now, like it's a question he doesn't need to ask anymore. They're watching me, yes…but it's not the way they used to. It's not fear. It's not pity. It's something closer to awe, maybe even belief. For the first time in my life, I don't feel like I have to prove anything to them, or to myself. We're not safe. We're not even close, but we're moving. The thought alone, for now, is enough.

We leave the clearing before the ash settles. No one says goodbye to the place that changed me. Maybe because we all know that change wasn't something we left behind, it came with us. It walks beside me now, just beneath my skin. The days blur as we move. Forest turns to highland, then to cracked stone trails worn thin by forgotten paths.

Kaelen leads most of the time. He doesn't say much unless he has to, but when he looks at me, it's with a quiet that anchors me. Like he sees the storm beneath my skin but doesn't flinch from it. Tamsin hums sometimes as we walk. She doesn't know I can hear it, soft and uneven like she's trying to calm herself more than us. Bennick brings up the rear, his sword always in reach, but his gaze is far off, like he's trying to figure out what I've become and whether it changes everything or nothing at all.

Sera walks closest to me. She keeps glancing at me, like she wants to say something but doesn't know where to start. I don't make it easy. I haven't said much since the clearing. Not because I'm avoiding them…but because I'm still sorting through the echoes of what happened. The shift wasn't just physical. It reached back in time, pulled on threads I didn't know were mine. It left something wide open inside me, something raw and ancient.

I dream more now. I don't always remember the details when I wake, but I carry the weight of them like smoke clinging to my clothes. Fire. Wings. A name not yet spoken. I see flashes…gold light on black scales, a voice like stone cracking open, a woman with eyes like starlight. None of it makes sense, and yet… it does. Like these pieces belong to me, like they've always belonged to me, and only now are they finding their way back.

The land shifts beneath our feet, slow and steady, as if the world is exhaling. The pine forests that once cloaked the hills fall away behind us, replaced by a harsher, drier beauty. Green fades to gold, then to pale gray and sunbaked ochre. Hills roll into jagged spines of rock that rise like the ribs of a long-dead beast, and the air grows thinner, sharper, edged with cold that cuts through even the warmest cloak. The scent changes, too…no longer the heavy green of moss and pine, but dry earth, sun-warmed stone, and something faintly metallic, like distant lightning.

This is Ileyana's country. That's what Sylas tells us as we crest a ridge, and the wind slaps hard against our faces. Below, a cluster of stone towers pushes out of the land like broken teeth, half-consumed by the drifting clouds. It doesn't look like a city. It looks like bones jutting from the earth. As we begin our descent, the silence of the high desert is broken only by the crunch of gravel beneath our boots and the occasional whistle of the wind. My lungs burn with every breath, but it's not fear tightening my chest…it's something else. Anticipation.

A restless, rising flame that flickers in my core. Then, just off the trail, movement catches my eye, something pale and quick. I turn and spot them, almost hidden against the sand: a small creature with enormous ears, its fur the color of bleached stone. It blinks at me, and I realize it's not alone. Three…no, four…tiny ones scurry around its feet, their ears too large for their heads, their bodies twitchy and curious. My breath catches.

"They're called fennec foxes," Sera says softly beside me, following my gaze. "Desert dwellers. They only come out in the cooler hours. Smart, quiet. Their ears can pick up the sound of beetles crawling underground." The mother fox watches us for a moment longer before turning, leading her pups away toward a cluster of rocks. Their soft paws make no sound, but their scent lingers briefly in the air…dry fur, sun, and something faintly sweet, like crushed herbs.

I watch them disappear, and that fire inside me flares again, brighter, hotter. Not fear. Never fear. Something older than that. Something like belonging. I don't know what they'll tell me…Orion, the lore keeper who remembers too much, and Ileyana, who was old when the first dragons vanished…but something waits there. Answers, maybe…or truths I'm not ready for. I don't know which I fear more.

As the towers rise higher and we cross the broken threshold of their domain, I feel the shimmer beneath my skin stir. The dragon part of me remembers this place. Even if I don't. That night, I lay awake staring at the exposed beams overhead, the sky bleeding into the cracks between stones. The others sleep or pretend to. I don't bother trying.

My heart won't quiet. My bones ache…not from travel, but from change. Like they're still catching up to what I've become. I keep thinking about the moment it finally happened. That roar. That shift. The way the fire surged through me, not as something I summoned, but something I finally stopped resisting. I keep replaying the words Sylas said: You're trying to be the power instead of letting it become you.

I wonder…how long have I been fighting myself? How many times did I mistake control for strength? I was so sure power meant force. Mastery. Precision. However, the moment I let go…truly let go…something ancient found me. Something mine, and now that I've touched it, I'm terrified of losing it. Of getting it wrong again. Of slipping back into the shape of a girl who pretended to be fire instead of admitting she already was. There's something else that keeps circling in my mind…Kaelen's voice, steady in the clearing: You're a myth waking up. I want to believe him, but myths don't bleed. Myths don't shake when they wake up in strange places. Myths don't need help to survive, but I do.

I want to ask him what he meant. I want to scream at the sky until I get an answer, but I stay quiet. Because deep down, I know the truth isn't in the asking. It's in the remembering, and I'm remembering more every day. Little things. Fragments. Gold light on water. Firelight reflected in eyes that weren't human. Names spoken in reverence. Not Haji. Something older. Something more. My name is a question I'm only beginning to ask, and when I find the answer, I don't think anything in this world…or the next…will be able to unmake me again.

That night, the dream comes before I even close my eyes. It doesn't creep. It arrives. Like stepping through a door that I don't remember opening. *I'm standing in a vast clearing bathed in soft twilight. The air is thick with the scent of lavender and something sweeter...wild nectar, maybe, or some forgotten flower that only blooms in dreams. The sky above glows violet and gold, not quite dusk, not quite dawn, and the stars shimmer faintly, like they're listening.*

The trees here are taller than towers, their bark silver-veined and humming softly, leaves whispering in a tongue I almost understand. The wind carries voices. Laughter. Music. It winds around me like a memory wearing new skin, and even though I know I've never been here before...not in this life...something in my chest aches with recognition.

I step forward, my feet bare against the cool moss, and the scene opens before me like a story unfolding in motion. Elves. Dozens of them. Maybe hundreds. Long-limbed, ageless, dressed in robes that flow like water and shimmer like starlight. Their ears are pointed, faces luminous in the half-light, but their eyes... their eyes are fire.

Not cruel. Not wild. Just bright, and full of knowing. They're not afraid of the dragons. They walk among them. Tall, sleek beasts of every color…emerald, sapphire, crimson, white, but only one, a deep, endless black. I see it pass through the trees, wings folded, its scales shining like onyx glass, and I know that form. My form.

The black with the golden shimmer that dances like sunlight across still water. The myth. The truth. They don't bow to the dragons, and the dragons don't bow to them. They exist together, woven like threads in the same cloth. I watch an elf child climb onto a dragon's back, laughing, braiding wildflowers into the ridges of its neck.

I watch another dragon shift mid-stride, her massive form shrinking into that of a woman with silver hair braided in rings around her horns, smiling as she joins the others at a long table carved from crystal wood. The table is set beneath a willow whose branches fall like liquid light, and I feel drawn to it. My feet move on their own.

The ground beneath me is soft and humming. Not just alive…but aware. As I move through the crowd, no one stops me. No one stares. I get a feeling that no one can see me. A few touch their chests in greeting as they pass each other but simply look through me. It isn't until I reach the edge of the table that I see her. The woman. Is that me? I get an odd feeling and scoff.

More like someone I once was. She's tall…taller than I am now…with braids woven with gold threads and fire in her eyes. She wears armor gilded in obsidian and a flowing mantle the color of storm clouds. Her hand rests on the curve of a beautiful bow and arrow, though she isn't tense. She's laughing. Leaning into whispering something to the elf beside her, who has skin like moonlight and a crown of woven antlers, and I know, somehow, that this elf was someone that I held dearly.

Before the breaking. Before the silence. My dream-self doesn't acknowledge me, but I can feel her. I can feel the echo of her in my bones. She doesn't burn the way I do now…she radiates. Calm. Power. Grace. The way the others glance at her, the way the dragons settle when she speaks, tells me everything I need to know.

She was a bridge. A balance. Not just between dragons and elves…but between something greater. Between fire and sky. Between memory and magic. Between life and the deep unknowable. I want to speak. I want to reach out, ask her…ask myself…what I'm supposed to do, who I'm becoming?

Though as I step forward, the air shifts. The light dims. A shadow passes across the clearing, subtle at first, then heavier, like clouds swallowing a sun. The music fades. The laughter stills. Heads turn toward the horizon. My dream-self stands slowly, her expression hardening into something sharp. She looks at the sky, and so do I. That's when I see it.

A crack, like lightning held still, running down the heavens. Not natural. Not right. The shimmer of the stars begins to flicker. Dragons rise into the air. Elves draw blades of light and shadow. My other self says a name under her breath, a name I don't recognize but it feels like a dagger in my chest.

I take another step forward. My pulse roars in my ears…but before I can reach her, before I can ask anything, she turns. She looks directly at me. Really looks. Her eyes widen…not in surprise, but in recognition. "You're not ready yet," she says. Her voice is a thunderclap wrapped in velvet. "But you will be." I try to speak, to ask what's coming, what that crack in the sky means, but the world is already unraveling. The moss beneath my feet falls away. The trees dissolve into stars. The air collapses like breath held too long.

I wake with a gasp, sitting bolt upright, the cold stone beneath me unfamiliar and unwelcoming. My skin is damp. My heart pounds. I'm back in Ileyana's keep. The others are still asleep, but I'm not the same girl who closed her eyes a few hours ago. I remember, not everything, but enough.

Enough to know that the peace I saw was real. That it once existed. Elves and dragons, united…not by dominance or fear, but by purpose, and I was a part of it. Not just a witness. A centerpiece. A fire meant to illuminate, not destroy. I don't know how long I sit there before dawn, but when the first light creeps through the cracks in the stone, I know one thing for certain: the memory wasn't just a dream. It was a warning, and a promise.

Morning comes slowly, stretching gold across the sky like a promise not yet spoken. The others stir around me, limbs tangled in cloaks, breaths slow from sleep, unaware of how different the world feels to me now. I haven't moved. I can't. That dream…memory…whatever it was… it lives in me now, rooted deeper than anything I've known. It hums beneath my ribs, echoing in every slow heartbeat, in every breath.

I watch the sun rise in silence, then finally stand, my legs stiff, my chest tight with all the things I don't yet know how to say, but someone needs to hear them. Sera crouched near the edge of a stream, filling her flask, her wild curls still half-tamed from sleep. She startles a little when she hears me approach but then smiles. Not her usual teasing one, but softer. Like she sees the shift in me even before I open my mouth. "Couldn't sleep?" she asks. "Didn't want to," I say. "I had a dream." That's all it takes.

Her whole posture shifts, her focus turning inward, the way it always does when she knows something matters. "What kind of dream?" she asks, careful not to crowd me. I sit beside her, watching the water slip past stones smoothed by centuries. "It was… old. Not like a story. Like a life I forgot. Elves and dragons, living together, not hiding, not hunting. Just existing. Together."

"There was music. Peace…and me…or someone who I think was me…laughing like I had no idea the world could burn." I hesitate, heart thudding. "I saw her. She knew I was there. She looked right at me and said, 'You're not ready yet.'" Sera doesn't speak at first. Just reaches out and rests a hand on mine, warm and steady. "Then maybe that's what we're going to Orion and Ileyana for. So, you *can* be."

We leave again before midday; the sun is already high and glaring against the stone. The narrow mountain passes winds like a thread along the ridgeline, clinging to the rock as if afraid to let go. The air changes as we climb…thinner, colder, edged with a dry sharpness that prickles the inside of my nose. It smells of sun-scorched stone, brittle dust, and something faintly acrid, like dried venom or old bones baking beneath the surface. There's a silence here that feels older than anything I've known. It presses close, heavy, as though the mountains are listening.

Kaelen moves at the front with quiet urgency, scanning the ground and horizon in equal measure. The others follow suit, subdued. Tamsin still hums, but it's softer now, like a lullaby meant to ward off whatever ghosts linger in the rocks. Bennick keeps glancing up, squinting at the sky as if he's expecting something to fall out of it. I lag a little, my thoughts snagged on the memory of that crack…the one in the dream.

The one in the sky. I don't know what it means yet, but I know it means something. My boots scuff against loose gravel, and I drift toward a pale rise of sand nestled in the stone. It seems to shimmer faintly, the way heat does, and I take a step closer. A hand clamps around my arm and yanks me back. Kaelen's grip is iron. "Don't move," he growls, low and sharp. His eyes are locked on the spot where I was about to step.

At first, I don't see it. Then the sand shifts…just slightly…and I catch the faint gleam of scales beneath it. Not gold or brown, but a muted blend of both, the exact color of the desert around us. A snake, long and coiled tight, its body almost invisible against the sand. Its tongue flicks out once, tasting the air. "Dustscale," Kaelen mutters, easing me away with care. "They burrow just beneath the surface. Wait for heat and movement."

"Their venom acts fast…drops a traveler in minutes." The wind stirs, and with it comes a bitter, dry scent, like scorched earth and old copper. I realize it's coming from the creature, its body giving off a faint, sour musk that lingers in the back of my throat. Kaelen keeps his body between me and the serpent until we're clear. Only then does he let go, though his eyes still flick back once, just to be sure.

"Watch your footing," he says, quieter now. "This land doesn't offer second chances." With that, we move on, the mountain watching in silence. The path ends at a set of ancient stone gates, half-covered in vines and carved with symbols that feel more familiar than they should. Kaelen steps forward, places a hand against the center stone.

It pulses with faint gold light, and the gates open with a sigh like a breath released after ages of holding still. Inside, it's not what I expect. Ileyana and Orion's sanctuary isn't some towering fortress or grand throne hall. It's a garden carved into the mountain itself, half-wild and breathtaking. Water cascades down stone walls. Trees grow sideways from cliffs, their roots winding like veins.

Homes are built into the rock, glowing with soft amber light. The air smells like sage and pine, and magic. *Old* magic.

We're not ten steps in before they appear. Orion emerges first…towering, solid, his presence like a thundercloud at rest. In his normal form, he commands attention, striking in that quietly dangerous way, a blend of power and restraint. His deep brown skin is lit with ember-burnished undertones, glowing faintly in the dim light, while his honey-gold eyes flicker, settling on each of us with a quiet intensity.

His dark hair is streaked with flame-red, wild, and wind-tossed, as if he's just returned from the sky itself. His clothes are worn, edges scorched, the gauntlets hanging from his belt like trophies of battle. Every inch of him speaks of fire, of conflict, and the weight of experience, but there's a calm behind his eyes that softens the edge…like he's a storm waiting to break yet holding himself steady.

It's the scent that comes with him that catches my breath. It's sharp, like charred wood and the burn of iron, tinged with something darker, a subtle undertone of something primal…like the air just before a lightning strike. It isn't overwhelming, but it's *there*, lingering, the faintest trace of smoke that clings to him like a second skin. Beneath it, though, is something more…something *intriguing*, almost sweet, like the earth after rain, or the warmth of a fire that hasn't quite burned out.

It tugs at something inside me, pulling me deeper into the moment as he steps closer. He nods once at Kaelen, acknowledging him without a word, but then his gaze lands on me, and holds. There's something in that look, something searching, like he's looking for something he never expected to find, something that wasn't meant to be there.

Then Ileyana steps into view, and the world seems to hush around her. She is radiant, almost otherworldly. Her silver-blonde hair cascades in gentle waves down her back, braided through with wildflowers that glow faintly in the dim light, casting tiny sparks like stars caught in the twilight. Her robe is moss-green, trimmed in delicate gold thread, with tiny stones sewn into the fabric that glint with faint enchantment, as if the very threads are alive with magic…but it's not just her appearance that catches my breath…it's the scent that fills the air with her arrival.

It's subtle but undeniable…a mix of fresh earth, wildflowers, and something else, something familiar, almost forgotten. A smell that tugs at the edges of my memory, like the faintest trace of something I once knew but can't quite place. There's a softness to it, like morning dew on leaves or the air after a spring rain, and yet beneath it, there's a deeper, older scent…like a memory that has been buried for years, only now starting to resurface. I know I've smelled it before, but from where? When?

It was then that I realized. She is the woman from my dream…older, but her skin still holds that soft elven luminescence, like moonlight caught in motion, flickering with life. Her green eyes pierce through the space between us, and when they meet mine, they widen in shock. She freezes, her hand trembling as it lifts to her mouth, and then...she starts to cry. Not loud, not dramatic, but silent tears, falling one after the other, down cheeks that rarely seem touched by sorrow.

The weight of it hangs heavy in the air, and everyone around us seems to stiffen, caught in the quiet moment. Kaelen mentioned that Ileyana is full of joy, sharp wit, and clever taunts, she's the first to laugh, the last to leave the fire. Though, now she stands still, barely breathing, tears running freely, and all her strength seems to vanish in the weight of her knowing. Orion moves to her side, one large hand resting at her back.

He doesn't ask what's wrong. He doesn't need to. His eyes, too, are locked on me. Something flickers in them, recognition, and awe, and maybe even fear. Not *of* me. *For* me. Kaelen steps forward slowly, voice low and reverent. "This is Haji," he says. "She is the one I told you about. She shifted." Ileyana doesn't speak. She just walks toward me, slow and cautious, like I might vanish if she blinks too hard.

When she finally reaches me, her hand brushes against my cheek, soft and shaking. "It's true," she whispers. "You came back." I swallow hard. "Do I know you?" She smiles through her tears, and it breaks something in me. "Not yet," she says. "But you *will*." Orion steps closer, arms folded, that ember-glow behind his eyes flickering higher. "Do you remember the name?" he asks. "The name beneath yours?" I shake my head. "Only pieces."

"That's more than most ever get," he murmurs, eyes searching mine like they hold constellations. "We have much to tell you. Much you were never meant to forget." Just like that, I feel it again…that shimmering weight from the dream. The peace. The unity. The crack. It's all connected. I'm standing in the middle of it now, no longer alone. The myth is waking, and I'm not the only one who remembers.

CHAPTER 14: WHO I WAS AND WHO I AM TO BE

They don't tell me outright. Not at first. Ileyana, once the kind of woman who'd pull you into a story with nothing but a glance, now walks softly around me…like she's afraid one wrong word might shatter something delicate.

Orion watches in silence most of the time, arms folded, brow furrowed like he's holding a piece of a puzzle no one else has seen. They don't speak of my dream. They don't mention the shimmer on my scales, the fire in my veins. Though at night, when the fire is low and the others are asleep or pretending to be, they start telling stories. They never use my name. Not the one I know. They use another: Elara. The name hangs in the air like a hymn wrapped in thunder, sharp with memory and glowing with something I can't yet touch.

Ileyana speaks first, voice hushed but steady. "She was more than a queen," she says, tracing the rim of her mug with a fingertip. "More than royalty. She was the bond that held the races together. Elves and dragons…two peoples so different, so

314

proud…trusted her. They loved her. Not because she ruled. Because she understood." Her eyes flick to me for just a moment, then away again, as if the weight of her gaze might press too hard. "She spoke to the wild magic like it was language. Shaped storms with her hands. Bent time when the world needed mercy. I've never seen power like that. Not before and not since."

Orion shifts then, the fire catching the gold in his eyes, and when he speaks, it's quiet thunder. "Elara could pull magic from the air like breath. Build sanctuaries out of starlight. Break barriers that stood for centuries. She wasn't just a sorceress. She was…" he exhales, searching. "She was the balance. When elves feared dragons, she stood between. When dragons raged, she soothed them. When the world bent too far toward war, she held it steady." His jaw tightens. "And for that, *they* turned on her."

That part hits harder than it should. Like it's been waiting beneath my ribs, buried beneath smoke and blood and the ache of not knowing who I am. I don't speak. I can't. Ileyana leans back, eyes distant now. "Betrayal from within. They say someone close…someone she trusted…took her memory. Put her into sleep so deep the world forgot her name. It's been over five hundred years, and still, when the wind shifts and the fires burn strange, there are whispers of her. The Black Flame Queen. The last true sovereign. The one who'll rise when the world fractures again."

There's silence for a while after that. Kaelen stares into the fire like he's memorizing the shape of the flame. Tamsin has stopped humming. Sera sits across from me, eyes wide and glassy, mouth parted like she wants to speak but doesn't dare. I don't ask the questions burning in my throat. I already know the answers are waiting…but they're not ready. I'm not ready.

The name Elara pulses in my mind like a heartbeat out of time. A truth that lives just out of reach, waiting to be remembered. Orion stands slowly, stretching, and begins to walk toward the ledge of the sanctuary, overlooking a steep cliff off of the mountain side. I follow him without thinking. When I reach him, he doesn't look at me, just out across the night. "Do you know what it means," he says, "When a dragon is born with the gold shimmer?" I shake my head.

"It means their magic runs older than the world. It means they are not born…they return. Carriers of something ancient.

Something the world tried to forget." He finally turns, and in his eyes I see it…not fear, but awe, and sorrow. "There's a reason we don't speak Elara's name lightly, because those who still remember her…" he pauses, then finishes, voice cracking just slightly, "…we've been waiting." The word lands like a drumbeat through my bones. Waiting. For what, I don't fully know. For who…I'm starting to. The air seems to tighten, charged with the unsaid, but then Orion smiles, soft and weary, and nods toward the horizon where first light spills over jagged peaks. "Come. You need to see something."

We walk in silence until we reach the stone ledge overlooking the valley. Then, without warning, he shifts. One moment, man. The next, dragon. It is not a quiet thing. His body expands with a rush of molten heat, bones cracking, wings snapping open like thunder through the air. His scales gleam black as polished obsidian, but as the dawn hits them…gold. Not a flicker. A blaze.

The shimmer runs across his body like sunlight through water, alive and breathtaking. His wings stretch out, vast and shadowed, and the earth trembles beneath his feet. He turns his massive head toward me, and I feel the fire of his gaze settle like truth on my shoulders. I am no longer staring at a creature. I am standing before a memory made flesh. The wind rises. The mountains echo.

Deep within me, something answers. Not in words, but in certainty. Elara. The name hums louder now, threading through every breath. Maybe I was her. Maybe I still am. I don't know what that means. I don't know what comes next, but as Orion's wings catch the sun and Ileyana steps beside me with tears still drying on her cheeks, I feel…for the first time in a long, long while…like I am not alone. I am not lost. I am becoming.

We stay in the sanctuary for three days. Maybe four. Time slips differently here, soft at the edges, hard at the core. I feel it like a slow turning beneath my skin. Every hour, something else begins to stir. The ache behind my eyes when I walk near the oldest stones. The way my magic pulses without my asking, responding to sounds, to emotions, to presence.

I dream more. Not always clearly, not always kindly. Faces blur. Voices rise and fall like tides, carrying names I almost remember. Sometimes I wake up crying and don't know why.

Sometimes I wake up burning, fists clenched, with my jaw locked in a scream I never let loose. I don't ask the others if they notice. I know they do. Orion and Ileyana don't press me. They just wait.

Like the stone waits for rain. Like fire waits for air, but I see it in them…the way they glance toward me when they think I'm not looking. The way Ileyana's voice sometimes trembles on the edge of a name. The way Orion stands when I walk past, as if bracing against a memory too powerful to name.

They don't say it, but I'm not stupid. They think I'm her. Elara. What's worse? A part of me thinks they might be right. It's not a title. It's not even a memory yet. It's a weight. A pull. I don't remember ruling anyone. I don't remember wielding mystic energy like breath or stitching the world back together with will alone, but something inside me does.

There's a quiet command in the way I walk now, a stillness in my voice that I didn't have before. My magic…when I let it rise…doesn't lash out anymore. It listens. It follows. I can feel its shape now, like light pressed into my bones, old and aching and mine. I still burn when I try to push too hard, still lose control if I let

fear get a foothold. However, there are moments, brief and sharp, where it all fits. Where I stop trying to use it and just am.

They tell stories when the nights are still and the wind turns cold. Ileyana's voice carries like song, soft and rich with memory, threading the past through every flicker of the fire. "Elara wasn't just a queen," she says one night, the others all drifting in and out of sleep around us. "She was a storm given form. She could command the sky to kneel. She once stitched the soul of a dying forest back together using nothing but starlight and will…and yet…" Ileyana pauses, stirring the embers.

Her eyes gleam green in the firelight. "She never once raised her hand unless the world gave her no choice. Her first instinct was always to protect. She would fight the gods themselves to spare her people pain." "She did," Orion says, his voice low. His massive frame is half-shadowed, lounging near the edge of the ledge, but his gaze is fixed on the flames. "More than once."

"What happened to her?" I ask, my voice quieter than I mean it to be. Orion's eyes shift toward me, heavy with things unspoken. "She trusted the wrong hearts. A council sworn to serve her. A commander, who called her sister. A mage who claimed to

love her." He shakes his head. "They feared her power. Her choices.

Her peace. So, they took her memory. Sealed her away before she

could finish what she began. A spell older than anything I've seen."

"To protect her, or to erase her. Maybe both," He finishes.

"And the world forgot," Ileyana whispers. "But not all of us." I

don't speak after that. I stare at the fire and try to make sense of the

storm building in my chest. The story doesn't feel like someone

else's. It fits into the cracks of my thoughts too perfectly.

The compassion they speak of? I feel it. I look at Sera

when she sleeps and know I would burn a kingdom to protect her. I

watch Tamsin and Kaelen bicker and catch myself strategizing like a

general, without even thinking about it. I track Bennick's shifts in

posture and movement like a commander reading a battlefield. I

plan. I protect. I don't mean to. It's just… there.

Deeper still, there's the grief. The betrayal. That part

doesn't come in stories. That part comes in silence. In dreams. In

sudden, sharp pangs of pain in my ribs, my throat, my chest, when I

hear certain tones or see certain looks pass between others. I don't remember names, but I remember what it felt like…having someone stand beside you with a hand on your shoulder and a dagger hidden behind their back.

That ache lives in me like an old scar. Quiet, but not healed. The more they speak, the more the name Elara echoes inside me. Not like a trophy. Not like someone else. Like a part of me remembering itself. She was regal, they say. A force of nature. Magic moved for her…not because she bent it with force, but because she was it.

She bent space, time, the very threads of the world, and yet, her greatest strength was not in breaking things…but in healing them. In making the shattered whole. They speak of her standing between armies, hands raised not in fire, but in peace. Of how she walked among the wounded after battle, how she never let rank separate her from the people she served.

They speak of her as someone who could not be swayed by flattery or fear, but who listened deeply to those she trusted. A ruler who made no decision lightly but made every decision with heart and fire. They say she laughed often, even through exhaustion. That she carried the world and still found time to plant gardens. All I can think, again and again, is…how could someone like that fall? How could a force so steady, so rooted in love and loyalty, be undone by those she called her own? I don't say it aloud, but I already know the answer. Because trust is the sharpest blade, and because people don't fear power. They fear what they can't control.

I am not her. Not yet, but I feel her rising in me like a tide. Her instincts. Her grief. Her fire. I don't know what I'll do when the memories fully return…what kind of pain they'll bring. Now, I do know this: I will not run from them. Not anymore. I'm not a girl lost in a clearing. I'm not a weapon trying not to break. I am something older.

Something stronger, and if I am Elara…if that fire truly belongs to me…then the world will remember who I was, and who I'm becoming. You think you know someone by the stories told around them…the songs, the titles, the way the world speaks their name like it's part of a myth rather than a life. Though the longer we stay here, the more those myths start to bleed into something real.

Orion isn't what I expected. None of them are. When Kaelen first mentioned his name, it was laced with a reverence that made me expect some unshakeable warlord with fire for blood and no time for anyone beneath his station. However, the man who greets us each morning is usually half-dressed, grease on his hands, squinting into the guts of some half-finished portal frame while cursing like he's negotiating with demons.

He mutters constantly to himself, to his tools, to the portal stones, occasionally throwing in a crude joke so sharp it could flay skin. One morning, as Kaelen and I walk past his workshop, we catch him yelling, "No, you little shit…I said *invert* the polarity, not combust the damn node!" Followed by the sound of something exploding and Orion emerging with a new singe mark on his eyebrow, grinning like he just solved an ancient riddle.

Kaelen just sighs and mutters, "He hasn't changed." Orion smirks, throws an arm around Kaelen's shoulder, and says, "You wound me. I'm the very picture of maturity and grace." Then adds, "Also, I made a fire-breathing toaster. Wanna see?" Nevertheless, beneath the sarcasm and unapologetically inappropriate commentary, I start to see the truth of him…especially in the way his eyes linger on Ileyana when he thinks no one's watching.

There's a softness there, an ache that speaks of more lifetimes than I can imagine. He jokes because silence hurts more. He builds because destruction was never his goal. He's the kind of man who would rather show you his heart through invention than words. When he speaks of Elara, it's never in public, never to a crowd. It's quiet. Honest. Like a prayer he's not sure he has a right to say anymore.

Ileyana, on the other hand, moves like wind through old trees…graceful, grounded, but with strength behind every motion. She doesn't command a room; she *settles* it. Her presence is peace wrapped in steel. She's quieter than Orion, but when she speaks, it's always with purpose. When I train near the stone gardens she tends, I watch her move through the space like she's listening to the land breathe.

She hums to the roots. Whispers to the wind. There's something about her that makes even the most stubborn trees lean just slightly in her direction. One evening, when Kaelen and I stay

behind after dinner, Ileyana shares stories, not of war or power, but of trivial things.

Of Orion getting stuck in one of his own portals for two days because he forgot to mark the exit rune. Of the first time they fought together and she ended up throwing a boulder at a dragon because he got too cocky mid-air and forgot to dodge. Orion chimes in from the other side of the fire, half-laughing, "She *says* she aimed for the dragon." "I did," Ileyana replies with perfect calm, sipping her tea. "You were just in the way."

The more time I spend with them, the more I understand that what binds them isn't just magic or duty. It's love. Quiet, enduring, unshakable. A bond that's lasted longer than most kingdoms. There are nights when I see them standing together just before dawn, foreheads touching, not speaking. Just breathing together. Existing. It's something so sacred it almost feels wrong to watch, but I do.

Because a part of me aches to remember if I ever had something like that. If Elara ever stood the same way with someone at her side. If there's a piece of me that once knew what it was to be so wholly seen. Kaelen watches them too. He's more comfortable around Orion, their banter easy, old, but even he grows quiet when Ileyana speaks of the old days.

When she mentions the war halls of Elara's court, the way the Queen used to walk into a room and silence it…not with fear, but with *presence.* "She was fire and mercy," Ileyana says once. "A storm when we needed it and a shelter when we didn't know we needed anything at all." Her voice softens. "It took them lifetimes to break her and still they didn't win. Not truly."

Later that night, I sit on the stone steps beneath the stars, Kaelen beside me, both of us nursing silence like an old wound. "Do you think I'm her?" I ask finally. The question sounds small in my throat, like I'm afraid of the answer. Kaelen doesn't look at me, just rests his arms on his knees. "I think," he says, "You're something more dangerous than that." He glances over. "You're her… and you're you. You've got her fire, but your own shape. That's what scares them." I let that sit.

Let the stars crawl slowly across the sky. Orion and Ileyana aren't just legends. They're *survivors.* Carriers of a world that should've died but didn't, and maybe, just maybe, I'm a piece of that world too. A piece waking up, learning to breathe again. The thought should terrify me. It doesn't. Not anymore.

Training with Ileyana feels like trying to hold a river still with bare hands. She doesn't bark orders or push me into drills. Instead, she waits for me to listen. She takes me out past the boundary stones, where the forest fades into the cliffs and the sky yawns wide overhead. "The earth remembers," she says one morning, pressing a stone into my palm. "So must you."

We start slowly. Grounding. Breathing. She teaches me to listen, not just to my heartbeat, but to the life around me. I thought magic was force. Fire. Fury. Ileyana shows me how it's also rhythm. Patience. Intention. She walks barefoot across mossy stone, murmuring in Elvish, and when I copy her steps, my skin hums. Like something ancient has begun to recognize me. When she isn't training me, she sits with Sera, showing her how to spin her magic into something more.

It's Orion who teaches me how to burn. He waits until the second week to step in, probably because he knows his version of training is more... explosive. I find him one morning at the edge of the crater field, sleeves rolled, wings half-unfurled in the rising light. "Ready for the fun part?" he grins, tossing me a pair of flameproof gauntlets that still smell faintly scorched. "Time to stop tiptoeing around what you are." Orion doesn't believe in control the way Ileyana does. He believes in immersion. Fire, he says, doesn't ask to be controlled…it demands to be understood. "You're trying to keep it in a cage," he tells me, circling as I try again to shift. "That's not how this works. You are the fire. It doesn't live inside you like some parasite…it is you."

It's the most painful lesson I've had so far. Shifting still isn't easy. It hurts. It tears. It stretches and burns and remakes me cell by cell. Though, Orion's presence steadies me in ways I didn't expect. He shifts with me…sometimes just partially, his skin darkening to obsidian, his eyes glowing amber as he shows me how to lean in instead of brace against it.

"The pain?" he says, voice rough with memory, "It stops mattering when the fear dies." There's one day I lose control entirely. Fire erupts from my back in violent arcs, wings too big for my body slamming into the trees around us. I'm roaring, I'm breaking, I'm failing. Orion steps forward, unflinching, his own wings cracking the sky open as he meets me mid-burn.

"Breathe," he growls, pressing his forehead to mine in dragon form. "Don't run from it. Ride it." I do. For the first time, I shift without collapse. It's not perfect. I'm still shaking. My wings are jagged at the edges, but I hold, and when I look up, Orion is grinning like a proud, slightly unhinged older brother. "Now that is a damn dragon."

The days that follow are split between the two of them. Mornings with Ileyana, where I learn to root magic into the earth, to weave life with intention, to pull light from the air and form it into threads I can feel. Afternoons with Orion, where I'm pushed to my physical edge, forced to fight mid-shift, learn to fly, to burn, to call flame like breath. They're nothing alike in method, but the balance between them is everything. Ileyana reminds me who I am. Orion shows me what I'm becoming.

One evening, after a long flight with Orion through the upper canyons, we land on the high ridge. Our wings fold slowly.

He lights a cigar with the flick of a claw, then offers me one, which I refuse with a glare. He just chuckles. "Suit yourself. Dragon lungs can take it." The smoke trails between us as the stars start to press into the sky. We're quiet a long time before he speaks again. "You remind me of her, you know." I don't have to ask who he means.

"But also not," he adds, flicking ash into the wind. "You've got her fire, sure. The spine. The stare that could drop a warlord to his knees, but you've got something she didn't have yet back then. Choice. You're waking up in a world that's already broken. She built it, and they tore it down around her. You… you get to decide if it's worth rebuilding."

I swallow. My throat's tight. He sighs, leaning back. "Don't carry her story like a cage, kid. She's not your prison. She's your echo. Let her teach you, yes, but don't forget…you're writing your own damn myth now." For a moment, I see something crack in him. Not fire. Not steel. Just… memory. The kind that doesn't go away.

He loved her deeply, I realize. Not romantically, but fully. Devoutly. Like a knight who never put down his sword, even after the war was lost. Later, I find Ileyana tending a patch of glowing

root vine along the path to the lower spring. She smiles as I approach, handing me a smooth stone humming with energy. "You did well today." I nod, fingers closing around it.

"He said I remind him of her," I squeak out. Ileyana's smile softens. "You do, but you're not just a mirror. Elara's strength came from her love for this world. Yours will come from the choice to love it again. Even after what it took from you." I stare at the stone. It thrums in my hand, alive and quiet. Like the land itself is listening. She brushes a strand of hair behind my ear like I'm still a child.

"We don't serve you because of who you were, Haji. We follow because of who you are, and what you're becoming." I carry her words with me as we return to the keep, my wings aching, my hands still buzzing with power. I am fire. I am root. I am memory awakening, and choice unfolding, and I'm not afraid anymore.

That night, I find Kaelen waiting for me in the garden alcove just off the east wall, where the moonlight slips like silver threads between the curling vines. He's seated on the low stone bench with his boots off, legs stretched out, toes in the cool moss.

His eyes are half-closed like he's been waiting a while, but the way he looks up when I step near…Mother Above, that look…it's like watching a flame remember how to burn.

I try to stay in a constant state of being half shifted. I sink down beside him, and for a moment we don't speak. The silence isn't heavy anymore, not like it used to be. It breathes with us, soft and still. He reaches out, almost hesitant, brushing his fingers over mine. I let him. I turn my hand, so our palms meet, and the moment they do, I feel it…that steady pulse, that quiet knowing. Not a rush, not a firestorm. Just warmth. Just him.

He tilts his head, studying me, and in his gaze I see all the storms we've weathered…every doubt, every fight, every word left unsaid, but also every time he chose to stay. Every time I did. As we begin to speak, we stand and walk back to his room. "You're different," He whispers, not like a judgment, but like a vow. He opens the door and ushers me in. He then continues… "I've watched you change, watched you fight it, watched you rise…and I…" He falters, swallows, tries again. "I kept waiting for the part of me that wanted to run, but it never came."

I breathe out slowly, my fingers tightening around his.
"Maybe we're both tired of running." I say and he smiles at that,
soft and rare and just for me. "Then stay…Just…stay." So, I do. I
lean in, my forehead resting against his, my wings brushing as they
fold close, shifting back into my elven form, breath mingling
between us. I can smell the wild mint on his skin, the sun still
clinging to him. I felt it as he grew near, that low hum beneath my
skin. The one that only answered to him. True mate. The words used
to make me ache, now they made me burn.

He didn't speak as he stepped closer, didn't push. Just
waited…eyes dark, jaw tight…as if he felt the storm in me too. I
should have run, but when his fingers grazed mine, the jolt wasn't
pain. It was permission, and Mother Above help me…I didn't want
him to stop. I felt him before our bodies touched. That familiar hum
sparked under my skin, quiet at first, then roaring to life the closer
he came.

I hated how much I craved it. How much I craved him. I
wasn't ready. I hadn't been ready since the moment the world broke
open and left me bleeding, but when our fingers brushed, something

in me snapped loose. My breath caught. Not from fear. From the way my body leaned toward his like it remembered something I hadn't given it permission to want.

He moved slowly, careful like I might shatter. I hated that too…because I already had. His hand slid to my waist; I didn't flinch. I felt. Fire, heat, hunger…things I thought were buried with everything I'd lost. When he whispered, "Say stop," my throat went tight because I could have. I should have, but the words never came. Instead, I looked at him and saw something that scared me even more than grief. Hope.

I whispered, "…Please." He paused, leaned in, and he kissed me. Not soft. Not safe. It was all tongue, heat, and everything I swore I'd never feel again. I kissed him back like I'd been starving and didn't care if it burned, and maybe I didn't. Maybe I wanted to burn. Maybe I needed to know I could still feel anything, but Mother Above it wasn't just anything. It was him, and I knew, even before I pulled him closer, that I wouldn't be able to let go.

His hands didn't rush. They searched. Like he was trying to memorize me through touch alone. My skin burned where he held me…waist, hip, thigh…like every inch of me had just remembered what it was made for. I arched into him without meaning to, and he growled low in his throat, the sound vibrating against my chest like a promise…or a threat.

I wasn't sure which I wanted more. His mouth left mine only long enough to drag across my jaw, my neck, leaving heat behind like a trail of sparks. My breath came in shudders. I should have felt overwhelmed, but all I felt was awake. Like I'd been walking half-dead for months and he was the only thing that could drag me back into my body.

"You don't have to do this," he murmured against my skin, voice rough, reverent. That undid me more than anything else. That he gave me the choice. That even as his hands roamed my body like I was sacred, he'd still stop if I asked, but I didn't want him to stop. I tangled my fingers in his shirt, yanked him closer, and whispered, "Please…Don't stop." He lifted me like I weighed nothing…like need had made me weightless, and I wrapped around him like I'd been built to fit. His lips found mine again, and this time there was no hesitation. No grief. No fear. Just fire.

We moved like the bond was pulling strings we couldn't see, couldn't fight. Most of our clothes slipped away, time disappeared, and all that remained was the press of skin and the kind of hunger that came from soul-deep longing. He touched me like he wanted to erase every memory of pain and replace it with this…with us. Mother Above, I let him, because I wasn't broken. Not anymore. Not with him, in that moment nothing else mattered.

He placed me on his bed and leaned back. My eyes found his and I saw the animal hiding behind them. As his eyes danced across my body covered by a sheer sheet, his jaw clenched again. I licked my bottom lip and that seemed to undo him. He ripped the sheet in a single second and pressed his chest against mine. His hand gripped the back of my neck, while the other explored areas, where no other has touched before.

Again, his lips pressed deep against mine and my legs began to shake. This pulled a smirk across his mouth, his hips now grinding against mine. The only cloth between us was his pants which were still on, and did little to hide the bulge, begging to be released. I traced my finger across his chest, which pulled a deep

shudder from him. I could see that even now he was holding back. I didn't want him to, I wanted all of him…now. My hand continued lower, to his waist, his hips, and to the top of his pants. His body tensed as I gripped what was hiding beneath. His head kicked back and a low rumble came deep from his chest. As he was unraveling, I began to move and gripped him tighter. "Fuck…Haji…" He moaned, looking back into my eyes.

He took both of my hands with one hand and held them above my head, I was trapped. With the other hand he gripped my waist, and I let out a small whimper as I saw him in all of his glory. My hips grinded against him, almost pleading for him to move faster. He smiled again, this time darker, his eyes lowered and his jaw tensed. He released my wrists and let his hands explore me further. As he reached my core, my body tensed. This feeling. I couldn't hold it in anymore, "Kaelen…Please…"

He glanced up at me, gripping one of my thighs and pushing it to the side. His fingers slid from my thigh closer to my center. He smelled like smoke and storm…like something wild that shouldn't be tamed. There was heat to it, sharp and clean, like the first crackle of firewood catching flame. Beneath that, something

darker. Spiced leather, a whisper of cedar, and the faintest trace of

metal, like a blade worn too close to the skin for too long, but there

was something else, too. Something that wrapped around me like

memory and magic. I didn't have a name for it…only that it was his,

and the second it hit me, my legs began to shake again and my body

went weak.

It wasn't just how he smelled. It was what it did to me. My

pulse responded before I even understood it. That scent filled my

lungs and made my bones ache, like my body had been waiting for

it. For him. My body tightened as he slid his fingers closer, sliding

through my wetness. I groaned and it made his body tense. He

looked me in my eyes and there was a quiet understanding that

danced between us, it was something that we both craved.

He began with circular motions near my clit, slowly, then

stroking motions up and down, then back down and with one last

look at me, slowly inserted a finger. It was slow and deep. It didn't

hurt, though it was my first time doing something like this. I tossed

back my head in pure ecstasy and let out a small moan. He growled, gripped my thigh with his other hand, and slowly repositioned

himself, but not in the way I thought, he placed my leg above his

shoulder.

His fingers didn't leave me, but I looked down to try to see

what was going on. I saw his eyes peaking at me right as he kissed

my stomach lower and lower. Mother Above, he was watching me

unravel. My body shivered…what was he doing to me? He traced

his tongue lower and lower down my hips. Finaly, he reached his

destination and placed his mouth near my lips and slid his tongue

through the slickness.

His tongue was soft and flat as it slid down me, and I began

to lose my breath. I found my hand on the back of his head, now

gripping his hair. "Kaelen…Wait…Something…" As if he

understood what I meant he quickly picked up speed. Between the

motions of his fingers sliding in and out of me and his mouth

exploring my clit. My back arched; my body began shaking. I was

tense and I completely lost control. "That's it…" He whispered, "Let

go."

With a rush of euphoria, I let out a loud moan that I couldn't keep in. He slowed his movements and waited for me to ride the waves pulsing through my body before pulling back. His lips sheen with moisture cracked into a monstrous smile, he came next to me and placed a kiss on my lips. It almost undid me again. My body was exhausted.

"Kaelen," I murmur, and it's a prayer, a promise, a thousand unspoken things finally given shape. He kisses me again…not like the world's ending, but like it's just beginning. Like he's saying, we get to build it different this time. I melt into him, into that slow, certain heat, and for once, there's no fire behind my ribs, no weight dragging me down.

Just the softness of his hand against my jaw, the safety in his touch, the way he holds me like I'm not broken, just beloved. I think, maybe love like this is what Elara never had time for. Maybe this is the myth I get to write…one not made from war or sacrifice, but from tenderness, from survival, from the quiet joy of being chosen, again and again. He reached for the blanket and covered our bodies, repositioning himself behind me. He pulled me close and nestled his face in my neck. My breathing slow and evened out with his. This calm. This feeling was new. I just needed him and only him.

The room was quiet now, except for the slowing rhythm of our breaths. The fire between us had burned through everything…grief, fear, the walls I thought I'd never let fall, and now there was only stillness. His hand slid across my back, warm and steady, fingertips tracing the shape of my spine like he wasn't done learning me yet. I didn't move. I didn't want to break the silence that felt more sacred than any prayer. He pulled me in, slow, careful, like he thought I might vanish, and Mother Above, I almost did. Not from fear this time, but from the way it felt to be held like that. Not claimed. Not possessed. Just held. Safe.

I let myself sink into him, resting my head against the place where his heart beat strong and sure. That scent…smoke and storm and something I could never name…wrapped around me again, and I breathed it in like it was the only thing keeping me grounded. His thumb brushed slow circles against my shoulder, and when he spoke, it was barely a whisper. "You don't have to run anymore."

For the first time in so long, I believed it. I closed my eyes, not because I was tired, but because I felt peaceful. Whole, in a way I hadn't since the world cracked open.

I stay with him until the stars blink out one by one, and even then, I don't move. I just breathe him in and think: If this is what it means to love in a broken world, then maybe the world's not so broken after all. He was still holding me when sleep pulled me under…arms like armor, breath steady against my hair…and the last thing I felt was warmth, deep and soul heavy. Like maybe I'd finally come home.

CHAPTER 15: EMOTIONS LAID BARE

The moon is still high when I wake, tangled in the soft remains of Kaelen's warmth. I don't move. His hand is draped over my waist, thumb grazing lazy circles against my side like he's still dreaming of me. My breath stays slow, even, as I watch the silver light drift across the garden wall through the open window, chasing shadows through the curling vines.

There's a peace in this moment I don't quite know how to hold yet. Like I've found something fragile and real in the ash of everything else. For the first time in longer than I can name, I don't feel like I'm running from the past or toward some future I can't see. I'm just here. With him. Kaelen shifts slightly, pulling me closer, and I let my eyes close again. Just for a little while. Just until the morning finds us.

When I wake next, the light has turned gold and soft, and his lips are at my temple, whispering something I can't quite catch. Maybe my name. Maybe a spell. Maybe both. I don't ask. I don't need to. Because this…this is mine. Not stolen, not survival. Just something soft, something earned. The comfort of home, falling asleep with no fear, just comfort and warmth.

It was the first night that I shared with him alone and I felt safe, like nothing could harm me. His fingers move first, brushing the hair from my cheek like he's afraid to wake me, but already knows I'm not really asleep. I keep my eyes closed anyway, just for a moment longer, letting myself sink into the way he touches me…like I'm precious, not powerful. Like I'm something he's still learning how to hold.

Eventually, I open my eyes. He's already watching me. No walls, no shields, just that clear, steady gaze that always feels like it sees more of me than I mean to give. "Hey," he says, voice low and rasped with sleep. It's ridiculous how much that single word makes my chest ache. I breathe in slowly and reply just as softly, "Hey."

He smiles, faint but full of something unspoken, and shifts to sit up, one knee drawn, arms resting across it. I follow, pulling my knees to my chest, the moss cool beneath us, the world quiet like it knows not to intrude. For a long time we just sit there, side by side, not touching, but not apart. The silence is deep, not empty. Full of breath and unspoken questions.

"You ever think about what comes after?" he asks finally, not looking at me. "After the fighting. After the storm." I do. More than I admit. "All the time," I answer. He exhales, nodding like he expected that, then laughs under his breath. "I don't know if I ever thought I'd survive long enough to find out." There's a crack in that laugh. A quiet grief, and Mother Above, I know it. I know the way it sits in your bones. "Me either," I say, "But you're here."

He looks at me then, really looks, and says, "And so are you." That shouldn't feel like a miracle, but it does. I press my forehead to my knees for a second, grounding myself. "Sometimes I feel like I'm holding all these pieces of other people's stories," I admit. "Elara. The realm. My bloodline. The war…and I don't know how to tell where they end and I begin."

Kaelen reaches out, fingers curling gently around mine. "Maybe you don't have to yet," he says. "Maybe it's enough to know the pieces are real. That you get to choose what shape they take now." I look up at him, and there's no hesitation in his gaze.

Just truth. Just Kaelen. "What if I don't know how to be anything but broken?" I ask. The words come out quiet, raw. "Then we make something from the breaks," he replies. "Gold in the cracks. Isn't that how the old potters used to do it? They didn't hide the damage. They made it beautiful." I let the silence settle between us again, but this time I lean into him, let my shoulder press against his.

"I don't know what the end of this looks like," I whisper. "But I know I don't want to face it alone." He doesn't flinch. Doesn't falter. "Then don't," he says simply. "You've got me. For whatever comes next." It's that…those four quiet words…that undo something in me. Because they're not grand. Not poetic. Just true.

I nod once, unable to speak, and he presses a kiss to my temple like a seal, a vow. The sun climbs higher, casting golden light through the vines, and for the first time in forever, I let myself hope…not for a war won or a prophecy fulfilled, but for a life built, one moment at a time, beside someone who sees me not for what I carry, but for who I am when the burden's put down.

We stay like that for a while, letting the morning spill over us in warmth and gold. Eventually, Kaelen brushes a thumb along my cheek and murmurs, "We should probably get moving before Orion comes looking and pretends it was an accident when he drops a boulder on my head." I huff a quiet laugh and roll my eyes, but there's a blush already creeping up my neck, heat blooming under my skin before I can stop it. I glance away, fingers fidgeting with the edge of my sleeve, and Kaelen sees it. Of course he sees it. His grin is slow, smug, and so stupidly pretty it should be illegal. "Is that a blush, Haji?" he teases, voice low and warm.

I shove his shoulder with just enough force to make him rock back on his heels, but not enough to hide the way my ears are burning. "Shut up." He just laughs, easy and full, and it echoes softly through the garden like something sacred. I can't help it…I smile too. It's ridiculous how light I feel. Like I'm learning my body all over again, not just as a weapon or a vessel for power, but as something that can feel this…tenderness, joy, affection so fierce it softens me.

We wash at the spring…quick, cold, and quiet…and dress in the shade of the outer trees, where the morning breeze carries the scent of moss and blooming night flowers. Kaelen laces up his tunic beside me, but his hand keeps brushing mine, knuckles grazing knuckles like he's not quite ready to break the contact we held all night. I don't pull away. I don't want to. We walk back together, our steps in sync, not speaking but not needing to. There's something easy between us now. Natural. Like we've finally stepped into the same rhythm after all this time spent circling each other in shadows and silence.

The others are already gathered near the main training clearing when we arrive, Orion is sparring with a young shifter from the northern camps, flames licking up his arms as he grins through the fight like it's a game. Ileyana stands just beyond them, directing another small group weaving root spells into the ground to reinforce the perimeter.

She glances up as we approach, and her gaze catches on me first…then flicks to Kaelen, then back again. There's the faintest arch of one brow, not unkind, just knowing. I feel the flush rise again, traitorous, and immediate, and try extremely hard to pretend I'm entirely normal and not glowing like a damn lantern. Kaelen smirks, completely unhelpful.

We slip into the group like nothing's changed, but everything has. I can feel it in the way Kaelen stays closer than usual, the way his hand brushes my lower back as we pass through the crowd, subtle but steady. In the way our eyes meet without flinching. It's not dramatic. Not loud. Just…real, and I think the others feel it too, even if no one says anything.

Orion pauses mid-duel to throw me a look…half grin, half appraisal. "Someone's walking like she just figured out she can fly," he calls, loud enough for half the clearing to hear. I shoot him a glare, but my lips twitch despite myself. "Maybe I did." He whistles low and wide-eyed. "Mother Above help us all." Ileyana's laugh is quiet but bright, and she only shakes her head like she's been waiting for this since the beginning, and me?

I stand a little straighter, the burn in my cheeks fading into something steadier. Something sure because I'm not alone anymore. Whatever comes next, we'll face it together…with fire in our blood, roots in our bones, and hearts that know how to stay. The teasing fades eventually.

The morning hum settles into routine...spell work, drills, laughter tucked beneath effort, but I can feel the shift before it happens. The air tightens like a held breath. Orion's smile dims first. Not gone, just...shelved. I catch him and Ileyana exchanging a glance across the clearing, the kind that carries more weight than words. Something old, familiar, dangerous. Kaelen notices too.

His hand finds the hilt at his side out of habit, fingers flexing once, twice. When Orion finally calls us in, it's with a tone I haven't heard from him since the first time I nearly burned down the south ridge...it was serious, prepared, and laced with something sharp beneath the surface.

"We've been waiting," he starts, voice low, eyes on me. "Not because we doubted you, but because you weren't ready yet." I don't flinch. Not anymore. "Ready for what?" I ask, already knowing the answer won't come easy. Ileyana steps forward, her presence steady and calm, but there's tension in the way she clasps her hands. "There's a place in the mountains," she says, and even her voice seems quieter, more careful. "High in the mist line, beyond the glacier fields. Old as the first flames."

"Elara found it once. Said it showed her things no one else could." I stare at her, something stirring low in my chest. A memory not yet fully formed. "You think it could help me," I say. Not a question. A truth already forming. Orion nods. "There's magic in those peaks…wild and ancient. It doesn't follow the same rules. Time bends there. Memory bleeds through. If your past is buried somewhere in this world, that place might unearth it."

My throat goes dry. "What's the catch?" I ask. Ileyana hesitates, then answers quietly, "The mountains are cursed. At least…that's what the stories say." Orion's jaw tightens. "Not just stories. Whispers. Murmurs from scouts who got too close. Screams in the snow. Fire that doesn't burn clean. Some say there are dragons up there…what's left of them. Twisted. Lost."

My pulse kicks up. "Cursed dragons?" He nods grimly. "They weren't like you. Not reborn. Not chosen. Left behind after the Sundering. Half soul, half rage. They've forgotten what it means to be alive, and now they guard that place like it's their tomb." A silence settles over us. Even the wind seems to hold its breath.

I glance at Kaelen. His face is unreadable, but his hand brushes mine again, grounding. Real. I turn back to Orion and Ileyana. "And you want me to go there," I say. Not accusing. Just steady. Ileyana steps closer. "We won't make you," she says. "But if there's a chance it could help…if you feel called…" Her words fade, but I already know. I do feel it. That pull. Deep and aching. Like a thread tugging somewhere in the hollow between my ribs.

I look at the mountains far beyond the ridge. Snow-kissed and shadowed. Waiting. "Then I go," I say, and my voice doesn't shake. Orion crosses his arms, fire flickering briefly along his shoulders like approval. "You won't go alone." I don't look at Kaelen, but I feel the way his presence shifts closer, like the promise has already been made. Like he'll follow me anywhere. I take one breath, then another. Memory or not, cursed dragons or not, whatever waits in those peaks…I'm not the same girl who once ran from fire. I'll walk into it now, eyes open.

We don't leave right away. The next day is spent in motion…packing supplies, binding spell scrolls, reforging blades dulled from training. I spend the morning with Ileyana, learning how to anchor protective wards to physical objects: stones, bone fragments, strands of root vine woven like thread. She braids one into my hair before I go, her hands careful, eyes distant. "For clarity," she murmurs. "And for courage."

I don't ask which she thinks I'll need more. Orion gives me a new cloak before we part…dark leather lined with dragon-scale, light but strong, and warmer than it has any right to be. He claps me on the shoulder, the way someone might a fellow soldier about to cross a battlefield. "You come back with truth," he says, "or with more questions. Either way, don't come back empty."

Kaelen doesn't leave my side. He moves through the preparations like a quiet flame, steady, constant. When our eyes meet, it's like speaking a language we didn't know we shared until now. It's near dusk when I find Sera alone, sitting on the edge of the north terrace with her feet dangling over the ledge like she's tempting fate. The wind picks at her hair, wild and dark, tangling it across her face, but she doesn't push it away. She just stares out toward the horizon like she's trying to find something in the falling light. A way out, maybe. A way in.

I almost leave her there, thinking she wants the solitude, but something in the set of her shoulders stops me. Not tension… but something hollower. So, I step forward and ease down beside her. She doesn't look at me. Just keeps flipping a small, cracked crystal between her fingers, catching bits of sunlight in its fractured surface.

"So," she says, voice too light, too practiced, "You and Kaelen, huh?" I glance at her, cautious, and ask, "Is that your way of saying congratulations?" She snorts, but there's no real humor in it. "It's my way of saying I noticed." She finally turns her head, meets my eyes, and there's something raw in her gaze. "You've got that look. Like someone kissed the war out of you and made you think maybe there's still something left worth hoping for." I feel heat rise in my cheeks…part surprise, part shame that I didn't see what she was carrying sooner. "Sera…" I start, but she cuts me off, sharp but not cruel. "Don't. I don't need you to explain it. I'm not mad." Her voice cracks just a little. "I'm just…tired."

We sit in silence for a moment. Below us, the wind rustles through the stone garden. "You ever feel like the world handed

everyone else a story and forgot to write yours in?" she asks suddenly. "Like you're just…background. Everyone around you is chosen, or powerful, or tragic in some way that makes them the center of something, and you're just the one who survives it all, again and again, until even that stops feeling like anything special." Her words hit something deep in me because I've felt that before…when I was nothing but fire and fear, when I was living in someone else's legend. "Yeah," I say quietly. "I know that feeling." She swallows.

Her hand tightens around the crystal. "I thought maybe, just maybe, if I gave enough, fought hard enough, stayed long enough…someone would see me. Not just my usefulness. Me…and I don't mean I want what you have with Kaelen…Mother Above, not exactly…but I want something like it. Someone to look at me and not flinch. Someone who chooses me, even when I'm a mess. Especially when I'm a mess." Her breath catches. "But every time I get close, it slips away. I'm either too loud, too clumsy, too sharp, too much…or I'm not enough to matter."

"Sera…" I whisper as I reach out, brushing my fingers against hers. She lets me. Barely. Her voice is lower now, ragged. "It hurts, Haji. Watching people fall into something soft while I keep getting handed the sharp edges. I'm happy for you, I swear I am, but it feels like the gods keep forgetting I'm still here. That I'm still waiting, and I don't know how many more "almost" I can take before I stop believing love's even real for people like me." Her words gut me. Because she means every one of them, and because I don't know how to fix it. I squeeze her hand tighter, my own voice shaking.

I begin, "You are not too much. You are not invisible, and if the gods have been overlooking you, then they're fools. You love harder than anyone I've ever met. You stay, even when no one asks you to. You fight for people who don't always deserve it. That is not nothing, Sera. That's everything." She looks at me, and her eyes are wet, but no tears fall. She's too used to holding them back. "Then why does it still feel like I'm alone in a room full of people?" she whispers.

"Why do I feel like I keep showing up for everyone, but no one ever shows up for me?" She continues and I don't have a perfect answer, but I don't lie. "I don't know," I admit. "But I swear to you…one day, someone will. They'll show up. They'll see you. All of you…and they'll stay." She doesn't respond right away, but she leans into me, lets her head rest against my shoulder. "And if they don't?" she asks softly. "Then I'll keep showing up," I say. "Until they do. Until it's your turn."

We sit like that for a long time. The last of the sun bleeding into the sky, the cold creeping into our bones, but neither of us moving. Just two souls holding each other steady against the ache of being too much and not enough all at once. When I finally rise, she grabs my hand…not to stop me, but to anchor herself for just a second longer. "Come back with something," she says, voice low and tired. "I don't care if it's a memory or a miracle. Just don't come back empty."

I squeeze her fingers, fierce and sure. "I won't…and Sera?" I wait until she looks up. "You're not empty either. Not even close. You may not think so, but you're coming with. I need you with me.

We may not have known each other long, but you have become
irreplaceable in my life." Her lip trembles, and then she nods. "Are
you sure? I will only get in the way." I respond almost immediately,
"Of course I am sure, what would happen if we didn't have our
trusty healer with us?" She smiles and nods again.

I leave her sitting there, bathed in the bruised light of dusk,
and I carry the weight of her words with me as we all set out the
next morning. The truth is, not all the broken things in this world are
cursed. Some of them are just waiting for someone to see them
clearly enough to say: you're still worth loving. Maybe the hardest
thing of all…is believing it yourself.

The morning we leave, the world feels quieter than usual.
Not in that peaceful way, but in the way that happens just before
something important breaks open. There's a hush over the courtyard,
even as boots scrape against stone and packs are checked and
rechecked, even as Orion barks out last-minute warnings about
frostbite and ancient deathwards like we're just going for a weekend
hike.

I see Ileyana near the south wall, speaking softly to the wind again, her eyes closed, palms lifted, as if she's asking the mountain to make room for us. Maybe she is. Maybe she knows more than she's letting on. She always does. Sera stands near the supply cart, tightening the straps of her pack with short, sharp tugs like she's daring the leather to argue. She's wearing her traveling leathers…dark green, with the reinforced sleeves she stitched herself…and there's a fresh braid in her hair, a sprig of thorned clover tucked just above her ear. Protection charm. Luck, maybe.

She doesn't look at me right away, but I can feel the shift in her. The hurt is still there, but it's tucked beneath a layer of resolve now. Like she's not sure she believes she belongs here, but she's coming anyway… and Mother Above, that's courage too. I approach her slowly, not wanting to jolt the fragile calm she's wrapped around herself. "Hey," I say. She glances up, eyes still a little red, but clear. Steady. She replies, "Hey." There's a pause, the kind that used to be awkward between us, but now just feels honest. I reach for her pack, tightening one of the straps she missed. "Still think you'll get in the way?"

I murmur. She gives a breath of a laugh, dry and crooked. "Only emotionally." I smile and respond, "That's fine. We could use a little emotional chaos." I straighten and look her in the eye. "But for the record, I meant what I said last night. I need you with me, Sera. Not just as our healer, but as you. The person who tells me the truth even when I don't want to hear it. The one who reminds me what it means to stay soft in the middle of all this steel and fire. I don't want to face whatever's in those mountains without you."

She swallows hard, and for a second, I think she might break again…but she just nods, once, fiercely. "Then I'm coming. Even if the cursed dragons eat us both." I chuckle. "Especially if they do. Someone's got to stitch me back together after." She snorts, wiping a bit of dust from her coat. "Don't make a habit of needing that. You're already exhausting to heal." I start to reply, but Kaelen appears behind me, his shadow long in the morning light. He doesn't interrupt, just nods at Sera with that quiet respect he always gives when he knows someone's fighting a battle he can't see. She nods back, and something passes between them, unspoken but solid. Then she steps aside, giving us space.

Kaelen doesn't say anything right away, just slides his hand into mine. It fits easily now. Like we've stopped pretending we don't know how. I look out toward the trail ahead, already winding its way into mist and shadow, and I think of what Sera said…about always showing up, even when no one else does. About being seen, and I think…maybe that's all any of us really want. To be known, not just for our strength, or what we can offer, but for the messy, hurting, holy chaos of who we are underneath it all.

We set out together, the six of us…Kaelen at my side, Sera just behind, her hands already glowing faintly with ward light. The wind howls once through the high ridges, and somewhere far above us, something answers it. A roar, faint but undeniable. The cursed dragons are real. The mountain is waiting, but so are we, we are not walking into that storm alone.

CHAPTER 16: THE JOURNEY TO THE MOUNTAIN

The road to the mountains is quiet in that ancient way…the kind of silence that feels thick with things watching from the trees. Not dangerous, not yet. Just…aware. Like the land remembers what it used to be, and it's holding its breath to see what we'll make of it now. We travel light, but not unguarded.

Ileyana warded our packs before we left, her fingers tracing protective sigils over leather and canvas. Orion gave us a rune-flare that's only to be used if things go so sideways that fire is the only answer. I tucked it into my satchel beside a blade I rarely use anymore, and a smooth piece of root stone Sera slipped into my palm the morning we left, no explanation, just a look that said *I know what it's like to need something to hold on to.*

The first two days pass gently…rolling forests bathed in pale light, meadows stretched wide and quiet beneath a thin frost. The air is crisp, clean, tinged with the scent of cold pine and distant snow. There's a sweetness beneath it, subtle but constant, like the lingering trace of winter blossoms or the breath of something old and wild moving just beyond sight. As we climb higher, the trees begin to thin, their limbs creaking in the wind, and the sharpness in the air deepens. It bites at our cheeks, and fills our lungs with something that feels almost sacred...cold stone, running water, and the faint musk of fur carried on the breeze.

The group settles into a rhythm without speaking much of it. Sera hums when the silence stretches too long, her voice soft and steady. Ileyana walks just ahead of us all, her eyes scanning the horizon, as if she's listening to something woven into the wind. Kaelen stays close. Always. Our fingers brush often, casual, quiet, like a heartbeat I don't notice anymore. It's just there. Like breath. Like choosing him again and again.

By the third night, we make camp near a frozen stream, its surface crusted with ice that glitters like crushed glass. Our fire crackles low, ringed by old stones worn smooth by time, the kind that feel like they were placed with intention. That same scent lingers in the air...earthy and cold, but with an edge of wildness now, something more alive.

Then I hear it…just beyond the tree line, a low, melodic howl that raises the hairs along my arms. Eyes gleam in the dark. Not threatening. Watching. "They're Lunaris wolves," Ileyana says quietly from her place by the fire. "They're guardians of these paths. Silver-furred, moon-eyed, and older than any of our songs. They don't approach unless they sense peace in you. Or purpose."

I stare into the trees, and for a breath, I see them…massive and silent, their coats catching the moonlight like snow-dusted steel. Their glowing eyes hold no malice. Only awareness. They vanish between the trees as quickly as they appeared, like shadows stitched into the forest. "Their scent is part of what you're smelling now," Ileyana adds. "Like cold fur and night air. You'll start to recognize it. They never wander far from the sacred places." I glance at the stones around our fire, then back at the fading glint of silver in the woods, and something in me settles. Not in certainty…but in understanding. Some places don't need answers to be real.

Sera's curled up with a heating charm pressed to her ribs, already half-asleep, and Ileyana's off mapping runes into the dirt with one hand while she drinks tea with the other. Kaelen stokes the fire, slow and thoughtful, then glances at me with a small smile. "You want to hear something strange?" he asks, voice soft like it's meant for me alone. I nod, tucking my cloak tighter around my shoulders.

"Stonehide Golems," he begins, shifting so his boots rest near mine, "They were built by the Ancients to guard places of power. Temples, vaults, sometimes whole cities carved into the cliffs. The name makes them sound like big dumb brutes, but they weren't just muscle. They were *made* from the land. Each one anchored to the place it was born. Enchanted stone, fused with sigils and sacred metals. Some of them were stories in themselves…carvings that wrapped around their limbs like prayers. They moved slow, yes, but they didn't need speed. One hit from a golem could level a Arach'naara., and if you managed to break them? They'd just rebuild. Stone doesn't bleed."

"Arach'naara?" I asked puzzling on the word. He chuckles, "They are the things of nightmares. Towering arachnids native to the dense forests of Sylvaris, Legends speak of their ability to weave webs that resonate with the melodies of the forest, creating harmonious sounds that can soothe or ensnare the unwary. These creatures are both revered and feared, often serving as guardians of ancient groves." My breath hitches as I begin to imagine a spider of that size. A shiver runs through my body. I continue to listen, leaning in without meaning to.

"Did you ever see one?" I ask. He shakes his head, gaze far away. "No, but my father swore he did. Said when he was young, his unit stumbled into a ruin near the edge of the Skyreach cliffs…old, cracked open by time. They thought it was abandoned. Then the ground moved. Said it rose from the rubble like the mountain had grown a spine. Half its face was missing, but it didn't matter. It still came for them. Not fast. Just relentless."

He taps the hilt of his dagger once, absently. "They ran. Most of them made it out. One didn't." "What happened?" I ask. His eyes flick to me, and there's something solemn in them. "The golem didn't kill him. Just…stood over him. Then it stopped. Like it realized he didn't belong there, or maybe it recognized something in him. My father never figured it out. Just said the golem turned its head, like it was *listening*, and then sank back into the rock." He's

quiet for a beat. "I think it was waiting for someone." I feel a shiver work its way up my spine that has nothing to do with the cold. I glance toward the ridge above us, where the mountains loom darker now, touched with snow and shadow.

"You think there'll be golems where we're going?" I ask. Kaelen shrugs, then smiles faintly. "Wouldn't be much of an ancient ruin without something trying to crush us, would it?" I laugh…quiet, breathy…but the sound eases something tight in my chest. The fire pops, and Kaelen reaches out to brush a strand of hair from my cheek without thinking, like it's just a thing he gets to do now.

I let him. I want him to. I lean into the warmth, both his and the flames, and close my eyes for a moment, letting the quiet wrap around us like a promise. Tomorrow, the climb begins. Two more days until the ruins. Until the ghosts in the stone, but tonight…tonight, I let myself be here. In the hush of the wild, with stories in the firelight and someone beside me who remembers how to stay.

The fourth day is harder. The air grows thinner as we climb, the trees turning to twisted, wind-scoured shapes that lean away from the path like they know what waits above and want no part of it. The sky hangs heavy, gray, and low, and the sun becomes a pale blur through the clouds. We move single file now, Kaelen at the front, Ileyana behind him, guiding with soft murmurs to the wind spirits that still linger in these parts.

I take the middle, flanked by Sera, who is unusually quiet. Bennick, and Thorne at the rear…Orion would not let us leave without him. "He knows the mountains more than anyone I know, if Ileyana goes, so does he," Orion said. Thorne is ever watchful, his blade never far from his hand. The tension is low, but it's there, curled beneath our ribs like a second heartbeat.

Sera stumbles once on a patch of ice, and I reach back without thinking, catching her arm. She steadies, breathless, mutters, "Thanks," but doesn't meet my eyes. Her silence worries me more than anything. She's always been the voice when things get heavy…the one who cracks a joke too loud just to remind us we're still alive.

Though today… she carries something quieter. I don't press. We all carry things differently. The climb steepens around midday. Snow begins to fall…not a storm, just a steady drift that veils the trail and makes the world feel like it's slowly forgetting its own shape. Ileyana says little, but I catch her glancing upward often, as though measuring some invisible thread strung between us and whatever waits at the summit.

Kaelen checks the map, then the horizon, then me. "We're close," he says under his breath. "Tomorrow, if the weather holds." I nod, though the truth is, my legs ache and my wings…half-shifted for warmth…twitch with something restless I can't name. Anticipation. Dread. Maybe both. That night, we make camp beneath a stone outcropping, half-sheltered from the wind.

The mountains rise like broken teeth around us, and I can feel the pressure building in the air. Not magical, exactly. Just old. Heavy. Like this place remembers more than it should. Ileyana draws a protective circle around our camp with powdered iron and ash. Sera helps her, silent but focused, hands steady even when her face is drawn tight with exhaustion.

Thorne sharpens his blade, the rasp of stone on steel steady, familiar. Kaelen lights the fire. It takes longer here…the wood damp, the wind stubborn…but he gets it going. He always does. Bennick sits toward the edge of camp, quiet as normal. We eat in relative silence. The heat is welcome, but no one lingers close. I think we all feel it: the shift. Like we've passed some invisible threshold.

The world has grown quieter, and in that quiet, there are eyes. Not near, not yet, but watching. Waiting. Afterward, Kaelen joins me at the edge of the firelight. I sit with my knees drawn to my chest, cloak pulled tight. He doesn't speak right away. Just lowers himself beside me, close but not crowding.

Finally, he says, "You ever think about turning back?" I glance at him, surprised. "No," I say, without hesitation. Then softer, "But I think about what's waiting…and whether I'm ready to face it." He nods slowly, staring into the dark beyond the fire's reach. "I think we're never really ready. Not for the big things. Not for the truth."

His eyes flick to mine. "But you're not the same person you were when we started this. You're stronger. Not just in magic. In the places that matter more." His words settle into me like warmth.

Like weight. I don't know how to answer that, so I just lean my head against his shoulder, and he lets me. We sit like that, silent, until the fire dies low and the others begin to drift into restless sleep.

Tomorrow, we will reach the ruins. Whatever truths lie buried there…whatever memories, or monsters, or echoes of what I once was…I'll face them. With Kaelen at my side. With Sera behind me. With fire in my chest and something steadier in my spine. We came for answers. I only hope we're ready for what they cost.

The next day, the air is sharp with cold, and the wind has picked up, slicing through our cloaks as we push forward. The journey has become more difficult, the path narrowing and the terrain rougher. The higher we climb, the more the mountains seem to close in around us, the weight of the rock and snow pressing down like an unspoken warning.

We move cautiously, eyes scanning the cliffs, the air thick with something *off*. Ileyana is the first to pause, her head tilting as if listening to something in the wind. Her hand goes up, signaling us to stop. We fall into stillness, and the world around us seems to go quiet, unnaturally so. Not a bird, not a sound from the earth, just the faintest shift in the air. "There's something wrong," she whispers, her voice barely audible. "Can you feel it?" At first, I don't. It's subtle, like the world is holding its breath. No wind. No wildlife. The weight of silence presses in, thick and oppressive. Kaelen's brow furrows as he scans the horizon, his gaze narrowing as he takes a step forward.

"Keep your eyes open," he says, his voice low. We move cautiously, staying close, each of us becoming more aware of the unnatural stillness that has settled over the land. It doesn't take long before we see it…a vast, sunken basin nestled between the jagged cliffs ahead, like a scar in the landscape. The ground below us is littered with bones…ribs the size of wagons, wings torn to shreds, blackened, twisted remains scattered across the snow.

They're dragon bones, or what used to be dragons. Their twisted bodies are half-buried in the snow, corrupted and scarred beyond recognition, their wings frayed and burned. Ileyana's voice barely breaks the silence as she speaks again, her words almost reverent. "Cursed dragons."

There's nothing majestic about them now. They look wrong…twisted, like something that was once grand but is now lost to rot. Their scales are cracked, darkened with decay, and the air around them smells *sickening*. The scent is heavy on the wind, a nauseating mix of spoiled meat, burnt flesh, and something sour, like old blood congealed in the bones.

It clings to everything, thick and choking, making it hard to breathe without tasting it in the back of my throat. Their eyes... their eyes are hollow, burning with an unnatural fire, the kind that comes from a magic twisted beyond recognition. The magic that once gave them life has turned against them, corrupted, festering in their decaying forms. It's like they're no longer creatures of this world, but something else…something monstrous that's been left to rot in its own hatred.

They don't even seem to see us at first, their heads lying low, half-buried in the rock and snow, their bodies still in a half-sleep. Their breathing is shallow, but it doesn't matter. The smell lingers in the air, too thick, too wrong. I crouch low behind the rocks, every breath too loud in the stillness, my heart thudding in my chest as the oppressive scent of the cursed dragons wraps around me. "We can't fight them," I whisper, the truth heavy and sinking like a stone. "Not all of them." Kaelen nods, his jaw tightening, the lines of his face sharp with determination. "Then we go around."

We move quickly, making our way along a narrow ledge above the basin. It's treacherous, but we move with purpose, keeping our heads down and our steps as silent as possible. Ileyana wards our boots with magic, muting the sound of our footsteps, and I watch as Kaelen's eyes dart around, alert for any signs that we've been spotted.

For a while, it works. We stay out of sight, moving with quiet precision, but then, the wind shifts. A cold gust blows through the basin, carrying with it the scent of decay, of death, of something wrong. One of the dragons…*no*, not dragons. *Cursed things…*lifts its head, the broken skull shifting toward us, the hollowed eyes locking onto our position.

It snarls, a guttural sound that echoes through the empty basin. The rest of them stir. Heads rise from the snow and the rock, their twisted forms lurching into motion, drawn toward us with a hunger that isn't just physical. They sense us, and they're coming. "We need to move!" Kaelen snaps, already turning toward the path ahead, but there's nowhere to go. The ledge is too narrow, too exposed.

Behind us, a rumbling sound shakes the ground, and I know before I even turn that they're coming. All of them. We don't have time to make it to safety. I don't think. I just act. "Run!" Kaelen yells, and we take off. The ground behind us shatters as the cursed dragons leap, their wings broken and frayed but still deadly. They scramble up the rocks, claws digging into the stone as they chase us with terrifying speed. The sound of their pursuit is deafening, a terrible screeching, clawing, growling noise that sends a shiver through my bones.

I can't look back. I don't dare, but then, I do. I glance over my shoulder, just for a second, and I see one of them. Its face is half-melted, its eyes burning with black fire as it closes the distance between us. I feel the panic rise in my chest, my heart racing in time with my feet. We need to get away, but the ledge is narrowing, the path falling away into the dark snow below.

There's no room to run, and that's when I stop. Kaelen

yells my name, but I don't hear him. I raise my hands, and the fire

bursts from me before I even realize I've called it. A blast of heat

and flame erupts from my chest, swallowing the cursed dragon

whole, its shriek cut short as it's consumed by the fire, but it doesn't

stop. It doesn't even flinch. It keeps coming, dragging itself toward

us like the very earth is trying to tear itself apart to let it through.

"*Haji*!" Kaelen roars, his voice panicked as he grabs my

arm, pulling me back, but there's no time to think. I don't even look

back. We both leap, and for one terrifying moment, I feel the ground

give way beneath us. We tumble down a short embankment, the

snow giving way as we crash to the earth. My body aches from the

impact, but I scramble to my feet as Kaelen pulls me up.

The others are already moving, Thorne cursing and

drawing his blade as he looks back at us. "We need to go!" he yells.

"Now!" I don't look back at the cursed dragons. I don't need to. The

howls are still echoing through the mountains, the sound of hunger

and fury so close it feels like they're in my bones, but we're alive.

For now. "We need to get to the ruins," Kaelen says, his voice harsh, urgent, and with that, we're moving again, running, not stopping until the echoes of those monsters are nothing but distant memories in the wind.

Soon, we'll reach the ruins and whatever answers they hold, we'll face them. Right now, all I want is to survive. To make it to that place of ancient stone and hope there's something waiting there that can stop what's hunting us. I know one thing for certain…we're not alone on this mountain. Whatever lies ahead, I'm not sure we're ready for it.

We don't stop running until we reach the cover of the next ridge, our breath coming in sharp, ragged bursts, each inhale a painful reminder of how close we came to being consumed by the cursed dragons. The wind howls through the narrow canyon, chilling us to the bone as we crouch behind the jagged rocks, just out of sight of the basin we fled from. The snow beneath us is already stained red from the chaos of our escape. I begin to question my powers, why didn't I hurt the cursed dragon? Am I still not enough? I just don't get it.

I shake the thought away and I glance around at the others, each of us shaken in our own way, but still standing. Kaelen's hand is gripping his sword tightly, the hilt slick with his sweat, his eyes scanning the cliffs above us like they might come alive at any moment. Ileyana is already pulling at the stone beneath her feet, drawing up the magic to steady us. Thorne's jaw is set, his breath coming out in slow, controlled puffs, though his eyes betray the tension that's rooted deep in him. Sera is the quietest, her face pale, but she doesn't show fear. Not aloud, at least.

We all know how close we came to losing everything in that basin, how we almost didn't make it out. The weight of it settles around me like an oppressive fog, suffocating in its intensity. "We can't stay here long," Kaelen mutters, his voice hoarse, low. "They'll be coming for us soon enough." I nod, my thoughts a chaotic whirl as I try to steady my breathing.

The fear is still there, gnawing at my insides, but there's something else now too. The fire from earlier, the heat that came from me without warning, it still burns in my chest. Not just from the magic I called…no, something deeper. A flicker of strength. I'm

only beginning to understand the power, but the sense of urgency that's flooding through me now is stronger. We need to move.

I push the thoughts away, focusing on the immediate need to survive. The ruins are close. They're still ahead of us. We just have to get there. "We need to keep moving," I say, my voice shaking slightly, but there's no turning back now. Not after what we just faced. "If we can make it to the ruins, we can regroup. We'll be safer there."

Sera steps forward then, her gaze fixed on the snow beneath her feet. She's quieter than usual, her eyes shadowed with something I can't quite place. She's holding her breath, holding herself together, but I can see the cracks in her composure. "You really think the ruins will be safe?" Her voice is soft, almost distant. "We're running blind. What if there's nothing there for us but more danger?"

I can't blame her for the doubt in her voice. We're walking into unknown territory, and the promise of safety feels fragile at best, but I don't have a better answer. I don't have the luxury of doubt. "I don't know, Sera," I admit, my voice softer than I intend.

"But I have to believe there's something there. Something worth fighting for."

She looks up at me, her eyes tired but steady, and for a moment, I see the weight of her struggles in the depth of that gaze. She opens her mouth to say something but then stops herself. Her shoulders slump, the tension in her posture giving way to a vulnerability I didn't expect. "You have something in you, Haji," she says quietly, her voice barely audible over the wind.

"Something... stronger than I think I'll ever have, and I hate it. I hate that I can't seem to find it in myself, not the way you have. I don't know why. Why I keep fighting, why I keep pushing people away, but I can't seem to stop." Her words hit me harder than I expected, sinking deep into the quiet space between us.

She's not just questioning herself…she's *doubting* herself, doubting the very strength that has kept her alive, kept her moving all this time. There's an ache in my chest at the rawness of her pain, and I wish I could offer something more than just empty words. "You're stronger than you think," I say, though I'm not sure I even believe it. "You've kept all of us alive. You've kept me alive. We wouldn't be here without you, Sera. Don't let yourself forget that."

She doesn't respond right away. Her gaze flickers briefly toward Kaelen, who's standing a little further off, his back to us as he surveys the surrounding landscape. For a long moment, it's just the two of us, standing in the silence of the mountains. "I want to believe that," she murmurs. "But I'm tired of believing in things that don't ever come true." I reach out without thinking, placing a hand on her shoulder, a steadying touch, like I can anchor her just for a moment. She doesn't flinch, but her eyes close briefly, like she's accepting the weight of everything I'm not saying. The truth I don't have the words for.

"We're all tired, Sera," I say softly. "But we're still here. We're still fighting, and we're going to keep fighting until we find what we're looking for." She nods, but there's something broken in the way she holds herself, the way she looks away from me as though she's afraid of what she might say next. I pull my hand back slowly, giving her the space she needs, but the ache of her words stays with me, gnawing at the edges of my resolve.

I don't have answers. I don't have the right words for her pain. I don't know how to fix the cracks in her spirit, in all of us…but I know this much: whatever comes next, we'll face it together. We have no choice but to. "We'll leave at first light," Kaelen calls, his voice cutting through the tension in the air. "The ruins aren't far, and we need to get there before nightfall." I nod, but my thoughts are still with Sera, with the weight of the journey we've only just begun.

As we prepare to move again, I can't shake the feeling that the hardest part of this trek isn't the cursed dragons, the mountain's unforgiving terrain, or even the mysteries of the ruins ahead. It's the broken pieces we carry with us…pieces of ourselves, of each other…that we can't seem to fix. Not yet, but we have to. Because if we don't, we'll never make it out of this mountain alive.

The wind howls against us as we make our way through the final stretch of the mountain pass, the cold biting into every exposed part of my skin. We've been traveling for hours, the climb growing steeper as we push forward, the pressure of the mountain pressing down like an unspoken promise. The ruins are close now, just beyond a thin veil of mist clinging to the jagged rocks.

The wind, cold and biting, howled through the mountain pass, but it did little to ease the heavy weight that hung in the air. The path before us, winding through snow and ice, seemed to stretch endlessly toward the looming dark silhouette of the cave entrance.

The sun hung low in the sky, dipping beneath the horizon and casting long, stretched shadows that seemed to grow with every step we took. The landscape was frozen in time…an ancient, desolate place where the very ground felt like it had not stirred for centuries. The air was thick with the scent of stone, damp earth, and something else... something older, as if the land itself were breathing in the forgotten remnants of ages past.

CHAPTER 17: THE HEART OF THE MOUNTAIN

There was an unmistakable eeriness to this place. An unsettling quiet that made the hairs on the back of my neck stand on end. It was as though something unseen was watching, waiting. Despite the unease creeping through me, I knew there was no turning back.

This was the path we had chosen…the one that had led us through cursed dragons, biting winds, and the weight of fears we had each carried in silence. We had come too far, passed too many trials, to stop now. Whatever darkness lay ahead in the belly of this mountain, we would face it, together. Just as I was about to speak, to try and shake the heavy feeling that was settling in my chest, the ground trembled beneath our feet.

A deep, rumbling sound echoed from the mountainside, vibrating through the frozen air, and the earth seemed to shift as if alive. My pulse quickened, the hairs on my skin standing on end, and then, from the very stone of the mountain walls, they appeared. The Stonehide Golems. Constructed from ancient, enchanted stone, these creatures were gargantuan, their hulking forms made from

massive slabs of rock bound together by magic that pulsed with an otherworldly energy. They were slow-moving, but each movement carried the weight of an immovable force, as though they were the mountain itself brought to life. Their stone faces were blank, expressionless, but their eyes…those deep, hollowed sockets…seemed to gleam with an inner fire.

It was clear these golems were not just statues; they were protectors, guardians of something long forgotten. They were a force to be reckoned with, their very presence filling the narrow mountain path with an overwhelming sense of power. The golems lumbered forward, blocking our way, and for a moment, panic spread like wildfire through our group.

The sheer size of them was enough to steal the breath from our lungs. Each golem towered over us, their massive bodies creating an imposing wall of stone. The ground trembled with each step they took, and the air itself seemed to vibrate with the power they radiated. There was no room to move past them, no way to continue.

In that moment, fear gripped me, as I realized just how easily they could crush us underfoot. My wings fluttered slightly in instinct, their tips brushing against the cold stone walls of the narrow path, but it didn't help ease the sense of being trapped. Then, something I couldn't have anticipated happened. The three golems, with their immense forms and unyielding presence, paused. Their stony eyes turned toward me, all at once.

Just as slowly and deliberately as they had emerged, they knelt. Their heavy stone limbs creaked under the weight, and with a sound that echoed like distant thunder, they bowed before me. It wasn't an act of aggression or intimidation; it was something else. It was as if they were acknowledging something they had sensed…something ancient and powerful.

For a moment, the weight of their gaze was overwhelming, and I felt a strange connection, an invisible thread that tied me to them. Before I could fully grasp what had happened, the golems stood once more, their massive forms shifting as though the ground itself had accepted them. With a low, rumbling noise, they meld back into the stone walls of the mountain, as if they had never been there at all.

The path was clear again, but the air was still thick with the remnants of their presence. Ileyana, who had been watching the entire exchange with quiet intensity, was the first to speak, her voice barely above a whisper. "They only act like that in front of power," she said, her tone carrying a weight of understanding. "Old power. Power that has been forgotten by most."

I stood frozen, her words sinking into me like stones into water. It was an unsettling thought. I didn't fully understand what the golems had seen in me or why they had bowed, but I knew that whatever ancient force they had recognized was a force I had yet to fully grasp. My heart pounded in my chest, and a mix of curiosity and unease twisted in my gut.

Was this power truly mine? Or was it something far older, far more dangerous than I could comprehend? Ileyana seemed to sense my unease, but she offered no further explanation. Instead, she turned toward the entrance of the cave, her hands glowing faintly with the soft, green light of her magic. The light was enough to illuminate the path ahead, casting long shadows on the walls as we stepped forward into the dark cavern that awaited us.

The air inside the cave was thick with cold and damp, the stone walls pressing in around us. My wings unfurled slightly, brushing against the tight spaces as we moved deeper into the belly of the mountain. The oppressive silence of the cave enveloped us, broken only by the sound of our footsteps and the distant drip of water from somewhere far above.

We were no longer just travelers on a journey; we had crossed some invisible threshold, and now we were moving into the unknown, into a place where time and memory seemed to blend and twist. Whatever waited for us here, we would face it as one, each step forward bringing us closer to the answers we had come to find or to whatever darkness the mountain held within.

The cave system is vast, twisting passages, sharp turns, and lofty ceilings that echo with the sound of our footsteps. It's clear that no one has been here for a long time. We stop after what feels like hours of winding through the caves, the air cool and damp against my face. The flickering glow from Ileyana's magic catches on something ahead, something that stands out in the dimness of the cave. It's a wall, covered in markings. Cave drawings, smeared and faded with age but still unmistakable. I take a hesitant step forward, my heart pounding in my chest. Something about these markings calls to me, like they hold a part of a story I'm only beginning to understand. As I move closer, I see them clearly for the first time.

They're crude, but the images are unmistakable: dragons, battles, figures of warriors standing tall in the face of an encroaching darkness, and then there is her…Elara. The drawings depict her as a towering figure, standing proud and fierce, her wings outstretched, flames licking the air around her. In one of the images, she's wielding a sword, her posture resolute, eyes burning with defiance. She is unyielding, her form immortalized in the stone itself.

I swallow hard, the weight of the images sinking deep into my chest. Elara, the warrior I've been told about, the legacy that has shaped everything I've known. Though these pictures… they tell a different story than the one I've heard. "She was here," I murmur, my voice thick with awe.

"In these caves." Kaelen steps up beside me, his eyes

scanning the wall, his face thoughtful. "She was. These look ancient.

Whoever made these... they knew her." He pauses, his fingers

brushing against the stone. "But what are they saying about her?" I

stare at the drawings, tracing the figures with my eyes. The images

are too much to decipher all at once, but there's one that stands out

more than the others.

It's a depiction of Elara standing in the middle of a battle,

but she's not fighting alone. Around her, figures gather, each of them

with wings, each marked by symbols I recognize from our travels:

Ileyana's roots, Kaelen's fire, Thorne's weaponry. They are

surrounded by overwhelming darkness, a shadow that seems to

creep toward them like a living thing, blotting out everything in its

path.

"What does this mean?" Sera asks, her voice quiet,

hesitant. "What's the darkness? Why is she surrounded by it?" "I

don't know," I reply, my voice strained. "But it looks like she wasn't

alone. Like she had... companions. People who fought with her."

"But where are they now?" Sera murmurs, almost to herself. Ileyana steps forward, kneeling beside me, her hand gently grazing the stone. "There's more," she says softly. "This isn't the end of the story." I look at her, confusion creeping into my expression. She motions for us to follow as she steps further into the cave, where more drawings appear along the walls, more images of Elara. However, now, the stories are changing.

In some of the newer images, Elara does not stand proud. Instead, she is kneeling, her hand on the ground. A dark figure looms above her, its wings stretched wide, its features indistinct, a twisted reflection of her own form. I stare at the new images closely. They're harder to read, the lines jagged, the symbols more foreign. There is one thing I can make out clearly: Elara's face. It's not defiant anymore. It's tired, worn, and in the last image, the one that's almost entirely worn away by time, I can see something else…the faintest hint of tears in her eyes, like she's seen something no one should ever have to see. Something too painful to forget.

Ileyana stands back, her eyes distant. "This part of the story... it's not the one we know. The one the legends told." "Then what happened to her?" I ask, my voice barely a whisper. "She... she made a choice," Ileyana says, her voice quiet but filled with certainty. "A choice that cost her…and in the end, that choice brought about the breaking of everything she built. The darkness that followed her... it was meant to destroy what she fought for."

"And what was that choice?" Kaelen asks, stepping closer, his voice tinged with urgency. Ileyana looks back at the wall, her expression unreadable. "I don't know, but I think we're about to find out."

The words hang in the air, a chilling reminder that the past isn't as simple as it seems. Elara's legacy is not just one of victory, but of loss, of choices made in the shadow of a world already broken. Now, it seems that the broken pieces of that past are reaching for us. We stand there for a long time, staring at the cave drawings, at the story they tell. A story of power, of love, of sacrifice, and of something darker, something that might just be waiting for us in the depths of this mountain. I take a deep breath, my heart pounding in my chest, and turn to the others. "We need to keep going," I say, my voice steadier now, despite the fear that's starting to claw at the edges of my resolve. "There's more here…and I think we're meant to find it."

The cave system ahead is vast, twisting into labyrinthine depths. We move cautiously, our footsteps echoing in the silence, until we come across a strange sight. At first, I think I'm seeing things…a glimmer, like the shine of gems reflected by the faint light from Ileyana's magic. I stop. "What is that?" Kaelen looks down at the ground. "It's... ants."

A wave of translucent, gem-like ants scuttles across the stone floor, their bodies glinting like shards of crystal. The Crystal Ants. I remember hearing stories of them from Kaelen many moons ago. They are ancient creatures found in the crystalline caves of Luminara, known to create tunnels that refract light and lead those who follow them to hidden treasures…or forgotten knowledge.

"Their tunnels," Ileyana says softly, "They refract light. They create paths. If we follow them... they'll show us the way." For a moment, we all hesitate, but then we see the ants moving in intricate patterns, weaving their way through the cavern, guiding us deeper into the cave.

Their tiny bodies create trails of shimmering light, like a constellation of living gems, guiding us through the dark. We follow them in silence, the clicking of their delicate legs against the stone filling the air. As we continue down the winding passages, the walls begin to shift. The drawings from earlier fade into the background as we are led toward something new…a hidden room, deep within the mountain.

At the center of the chamber, bathed in the soft, eerie light refracted by the ants' movement, we see something incredible. Ancient stone pillars line the walls, covered in faint etchings, and at the far end of the room, there is a pedestal. On it rests a small, ornate box…covered in the same patterns that are scattered throughout the cave drawings. This, I realize, is what we've been brought here to find. The treasure.

The knowledge. Elara's final message, sealed away for all these years. I step forward, my breath catching in my throat. The Crystal Ants continue to scuttle along the walls, their journey guiding us here, and as I reach for the box, I feel the weight of the past, and the promise of the future, pressing in around me. The world is waiting for the truth to be uncovered, and I think we're about to find it.

The moment my fingers brush against the ornate box, a pulse of energy surges through the air, electric and thick with the weight of ages. The Crystal Ants scatter, retreating into the shadows as if sensing the shift in the atmosphere. The air grows colder, charged with an ancient presence, and for a moment, I hesitate, uncertainty rising in my chest, but I don't pull away. I can't. With a deep breath, I lift the box from its pedestal, feeling the tremor of something greater than myself stir within it. The weight of the object is heavier than it should be, like it holds a piece of the mountain itself, or perhaps a fragment of Elara's soul.

I open it slowly, cautiously, as though the very act of unsealing it might disturb the fragile balance of this forgotten place. Inside the box lies a scroll, wrapped in a cloth that shimmers like the surface of a still lake, reflecting the faint light from Ileyana's magic. My heart pounds in my chest, my pulse quickening. I look back at the others, but no one moves. They, too, feel the gravity of this moment. I gently unroll the scroll, its brittle edges crinkling under my touch. The markings on the scroll are familiar…symbols, like those etched into the walls of the cave, but these are more precise, more deliberate. As my eyes trace the script, I feel a whisper of understanding, like the words are meant to be heard, not just read.

"It's a map," I mutter under my breath. "A map of the mountain…but... this... this isn't just any map." Ileyana steps closer, squinting at the symbols. "It's more than that. These markings... they're connected to the magic of this place. The power that was sealed away with Elara." Kaelen leans in, his hand resting on the stone pillar beside him, his gaze intense. "What's it leading to?"

I study the map, feeling a strange pull, a magnetic force that draws me in as I read the hidden path laid out before me. The map doesn't just show the mountain's physical layout. It hints at something deeper, an energy source, buried deep beneath the earth, where Elara's legacy still lives in the stones themselves. "It's leading to the heart of the mountain," I say quietly. "Where Elara's final stand was. The place she made her choice."

The weight of those words hangs in the air, heavy with the implications of what we might find there. "There's more," Ileyana adds, her voice tight with anticipation. "Look at this." She points to a series of symbols near the end of the map. "These… these aren't

just directions. They're a warning." I look closer, my brow furrowing as I decipher the symbols.

It's clear now: *Do not disturb the heart. The darkness will awaken.* The words are not written in any language I recognize, but the meaning is unmistakable. This place, this heart of the mountain, is not just a repository of Elara's power. It is the source of the power she carried with her, the thing that destroyed all she had built.

I feel a chill run through me as the weight of the truth settles in. We are standing on the precipice of something dangerous, something that could tip the balance of this world if we're not careful. Elara's legacy is not one of victory, it is one of sacrifice, of a woman who gave up everything to protect what little was left.

The power, the darkness that followed her, still lingers here, waiting. "We need to move carefully," I say, my voice steady, though the uncertainty gnaws at me. "The heart of the mountain… it's more than just a place. It's a power, and if we disturb it…" Kaelen's gaze hardens. "We'll face the consequences." I nod, feeling the weight of his words.

This isn't just about uncovering Elara's past. It's about preventing that past from consuming us, too. With a sigh, I carefully roll the map back up and place it back in the box. I lock the box with a heavy heart, the decisions growing heavier the longer we stand in the glow of the Crystal Ants' light. We've come this far, but now, I realize, the real test has only just begun. I glance at the others, Sera, Thorne, Ileyana, Kaelen, and Bennick. I find their eyes on me, waiting, steady.

We've been through so much already, but I know this will be different. This will be the moment that defines everything. "We need to keep going," I say, my voice firm now, despite the doubts that linger like ghosts in the air. "But we do it together. No one goes ahead. No one strays from the path, and we stay focused. This isn't just about uncovering the truth of Elara's story anymore. It's about making sure we don't become part of it." Kaelen gives me a sharp nod, his usual smirk replaced by a seriousness I've rarely seen. "Lead the way."

Ileyana steps up, her hands glowing again as she scans the map. "We're going deeper. We'll need to be ready for whatever comes next." Sera squeezes my hand, her eyes softer now, but the pain of her earlier words still lingers in the silence between us. "We'll get through it," she whispers, as if to remind herself as much as me.

Thorne, ever stoic, places a hand on his sword, his eyes unwavering. "Whatever it is, we'll face it. Together." Together. I hold onto that word because it's the only thing that makes sense now. We continue down the path, following the faint glow of the Crystal Ants as they lead us deeper into the heart of the mountain.

The further we go, the more the air thickens, the more the weight of the past bears down on us. Each step brings us closer to the truth…closer to the heart of the darkness that has haunted Elara's legacy. Though as we walk, I can't shake the feeling that something is watching us, waiting. The mountain is alive with memories, with power, and with danger.

We are nearing the point of no return, and I can only hope that whatever Elara did, whatever sacrifice she made, will be enough to guide us through the storm that's coming. We moved in silence, our footsteps echoing off the damp stone as the tunnel curved deeper into the earth. The glow of the Crystal Ants shimmered along the cavern walls like a river of starlight, their soft blue light casting our shadows, long and flickering.

The further we went, the more the mountain seemed to close around us, stone pressing in from every side, the air thickening with the scent of age and the tang of something arcane. My breath came slower, heavier, like even the air had to be pulled from the grip of time. It wasn't just the depth that made it harder to breathe. It was the pressure.

The weight of something waiting, buried beneath centuries of silence. There was a hum now, just at the edge of hearing…a vibration through the soles of my boots, in the marrow of my bones. The mountain wasn't sleeping…it was stirring. I could feel it, and I knew, somehow, that it could feel me too.

Then we reached it. The tunnel opened into a vast cavern carved not by tools or mortal hands, but by ancient forces older than language. At its center stood a pedestal…smooth, elegant, and pulsing with pale golden light. Veins of magic coursed through its surface like lightning frozen in crystal, and I knew before I even moved that it was calling to me. My feet moved before I could think, drawn forward by a force I couldn't name. I heard Ileyana's sharp breath behind me, felt Kaelen's tension like a blade in the air, but none of it stopped me. The pedestal pulled at something buried deep inside me, and I couldn't resist.

My hand stretched forward, trembling, and the moment my fingers brushed the surface, everything exploded. A surge of power erupted from the stone…raw, ancient, electric. It slammed through me, around me, into the very air. The cavern shook violently as dust and shards of stone fell from above, a deep rumble echoing in the bones of the mountain. I staggered, gasping, my vision consumed by blinding light and unfamiliar symbols, but I couldn't pull away.

The magic wasn't trying to hurt me…it was recognizing me. Unlocking something. I saw shapes, lines, paths winding through the stone like veins. A map carved into my mind. A sudden stillness stole the breath from the air. Light drained from the cavern until only the faintest glow from the Crystal Ants remained. Then, like a tide pulling back from shore, the world around me dissolved.

I was standing alone. The mountain was gone. The cold,

the stone, the weight of earth…all of it replaced by a vast sky of

swirling stars, suspended over a mirrored surface like glass. In the

distance, fire burned on the horizon, and wind moved with the sound

of wings. I turned, slowly, as a figure emerged from the dark. Elara.

She walked like someone who belonged to every corner of

the world, each step echoing with the memory of ancient halls and

forgotten battles. Her hair shimmered like starlight, long and

unbound, and her armor…etched with draconic sigils and elven

latticework…glowed with soft, pale light. Wings of translucent

flame arched behind her shoulders, not fully there, not fully gone.

Her eyes, Mother Above, her eyes…held the weight of centuries.

She looked at me like she had known me forever. "…You

go by Hajira now," she said, her voice a low, resonant chord that

wrapped around my name like a prayer and a command. I tried to

speak, but no words came. She stepped closer. "You touched the

heart," she said, not accusing, but acknowledging. "And now, it

touches you." The air around her shimmered with magic…ancient

magic, high magic. The kind I'd only ever read about in forbidden

texts and ancient ruins. It coiled around her like a living thing, responding to her every breath. "You feel it now, don't you?" she said, tilting her head. "The weight. The pull. The hunger. It is not evil, only old. Only powerful. You have inherited what was once mine."

The mirror-like ground began to ripple beneath my feet as her aura grew stronger. Majesty rolled off her like heat from a forge, pressing into my chest, my mind, demanding I kneel…yet offering protection all the same. I stood still, trembling, not from fear but awe. Her presence was enough to bend the very air around her, and I realized that she wasn't just a queen in name.

She was a force…of dragons, of elves, of ancient balance itself. "You carry it now," she said. "The *Aura of Majesty*. With it, others will feel your presence before they see you. They will obey, or they will fear. You will shield those who walk beside you, even as you push your enemies to their knees, but be warned, Hajira, it does not care for morality. It only amplifies what is within."

Elara raises a hand, and pure arcane light bloomed between her fingers, swirling and folding in on itself in delicate spirals. "And this," she continued, "this is your birthright, too. *Mystic Energy Manipulation.* You will feel the magic in the air, in the earth, in the bones of your enemies and the dreams of your allies. You will bend it to your will. Barriers will rise, spells will fall. You will learn to *consume* the spells cast against you and *turn them into strength.*"

I watched in stunned silence as she summoned a storm of light and shadow with a flick of her wrist. "Your mind will stretch," she said, her eyes never leaving mine. "You will come to understand spells before they are finished being spoken. You will move through space, vanish from one point to the next. *Spellcasting Mastery…*it is yours, now, but it is a gift that sharpens into a blade the moment it is wielded without purpose."

The stars brightened above her, and a rush of wind coiled around us both like a serpent. "You are not Elara," she said, her voice softer now. "You are not bound by my choices, by my sacrifice, but the mountain knows you. The power knows you and now it is part of you. What you become… will depend on whether you lead with your heart or let the shadows take its place." I opened my mouth to speak, to ask her what I was supposed to *do* with all this, but she was already fading, her image dissolving into starlight. "Restore the balance," she whispered. "Or break it. That is the choice." The vision snapped away like a breath extinguished. I staggered back into myself, into the stone chamber.

The others surrounded me, worry etched on their faces, Ileyana already reaching out with her magic to steady me. My breath came ragged, the pedestal's glow now nothing but a memory behind my eyes…but the power? That hadn't gone anywhere. It was still with me. Inside me. Waiting. I stepped back, the echo of the pedestal's power still thrumming in my veins.

"We're standing on the edge of something dangerous," I said. "This place... it's not just a tomb. It's a vault. A prison, and we've just opened it." Kaelen's jaw tightened. "We keep moving, we have to leave… now" I said, louder now, meeting the eyes of each of my companions. Ileyana's worry burned behind her steady gaze, Kaelen's usual smirk was gone, replaced by something grim and resolute. Sera took my hand, a silent reassurance in her touch, though I could still feel the ache of her doubts.

Thorne said nothing, but his fingers curled slightly around the hilt of his blade. Bennick, simply nodded and adjusted the straps of his pack. Together, we turned from the pedestal and stepped into the tunnel beyond, leaving its golden glow behind. The path sloped downward, deeper into the mountain's gut. With each step, the air grew heavier, the silence more complete. The Crystal Ants continued to light our way, casting a ghostly shimmer over the ancient stone.

The mountain was awake now. Elara's legacy, her sacrifice, her buried truth… it waited for us in the dark. The further we walked, the more the weight of the pedestal's magic settled into my bones. I could still feel its pulse under my skin, as though something had been left behind, something ancient and alive now coursing through me. My steps grew heavier, not from exhaustion but from the weight of awareness. My fingertips tingled. My thoughts swam in unfamiliar patterns. The air thickened, humming with energy, until it became hard to tell if I was hearing my companions speak or if the mountain itself was whispering to me. Then, just as the tunnel widened into a chamber wreathed in shadows, everything stopped.

CHAPTER 18: OUR OBSIDIAN SAVIOR

The cold hit my face like a slap, sharp and sudden. It should have startled me, pulled me fully back into the moment…but it didn't. Not yet. I was still floating, somewhere between the mountain and the memory, between the woman I'd been and whatever I was becoming.

The cave's mouth opened behind us like a gaping wound in the cliffside, the path we'd just walked swallowed up in a curtain of shadows. I was aware of the others stepping out before me, their figures framed in the dying light…Kaelen with his hand still hovering near the hilt of his sword, Ileyana's cloak tugged by the wind, Thorne bringing up the rear with his usual quiet watchfulness. Bennick glanced back, his eyes narrowed.

Me…I was there. Walking. Breathing. Moving with them, but for the last stretch of that descent, I hadn't spoken a word. Hadn't responded. Not really. I'd followed the group like a ghost tethered to its old life, present in body but distant in soul. My feet had carried me, yes. I had navigated the stone paths, avoided the loose gravel, ducked beneath the low-hanging crystal growth without pause. However, none of that had come from conscious thought. It was instinct, muscle memory pushed forward by something primal. A sliver of willpower keeping me upright while the rest of me was trapped deep inside. It wasn't sleep.

It wasn't unconsciousness. I *knew* I was there, I saw the way the light shifted on the cavern walls, heard the quiet rustle of Thorne's armor, the way Bennick hummed under his breath to calm himself. I felt Sera reach for me once, her hand brushing mine, lingering for a second too long. I felt everything.

That was the worst part. Every sound, every heartbeat, every breath of wind brushing the stone halls felt amplified, but I couldn't respond. Couldn't speak. It was like being buried under a thin sheet of glass, able to see the world, to hear it, even to feel it…but unable to *touch* it. I was walking… but not present. Being… but not *being.*

Inside, I was stuck in the echo of her voice. Elara. The vision. The *knowing.* Her words had hollowed out a part of me and replaced it with something else…something vast, ancient, and alive. *"You go by Hajira now,"* she had said, her voice like thunder

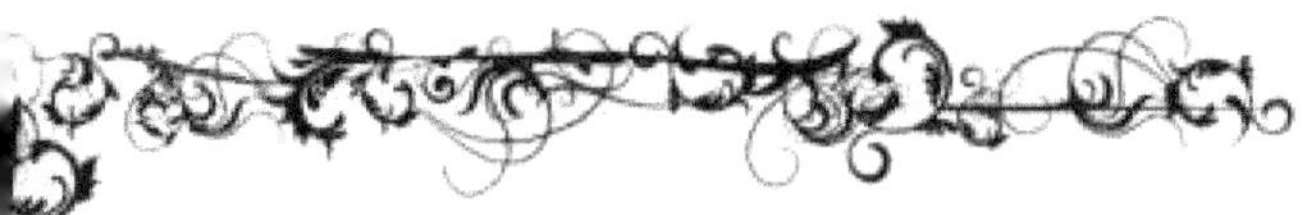

wrapped in silk. She'd said it like it mattered. Like it was a truth the

world had forgotten and she was reminding it. That name hadn't left

me. It had carved itself into my bones.

The power still churned inside me like a storm waiting for

release. It wasn't loud. It didn't scream. It *watched.* It *listened.* It

breathed in time with mine. I could feel it coiling through my veins,

brushing up against the edges of thought, reshaping how I

understood the world. What did she mean? Who was I before?

Magic wasn't just something I wielded now…it was something I

was.

My body felt like a container too small to hold what had

been poured into it, and still the mountain had chosen me. Or

maybe… recognized me. By the time I finally came back, truly

came back, we were standing on the snow-dusted slope just outside

the cave's entrance. The last fingers of sunlight were clawing across

the frozen peaks, setting the sky ablaze in hues of crimson and

indigo. The wind was bitter but clean, carrying the scent of ice and

pine.

I could hear the faint crackle of frost under our boots, the rhythmic flutter of Sera's cloak, and Kaelen's low mutter as he scanned the horizon for threats that hadn't yet come. The quiet felt wrong. Too fragile. Like the world itself was holding its breath. I exhaled, long and slow. My legs trembled. My hands, when I looked down at them, were clenched into fists without me realizing. My nails had drawn faint crescent moons into my palms.

Sera turned toward me, her features drawn with concern, her eyes searching mine like she was trying to find something she'd lost. "You're back," she whispered, cautious. Hopeful. Like she wasn't sure if she believed it. I blinked at her, trying to focus on her face. On the realness of her. The weight of the world outside the vision. "I never left," I murmured, but my voice didn't sound like my own.

It was too hollow, too far away. "Not really." I responded, but it was a lie, or maybe not a lie, just not the whole truth, because the part of me that had stood before Elara, who had heard her voice and felt the shape of her legacy settling into my bones… that part

was still there, buried deeper now, quiet and watching. Waiting. I didn't know what it would become, only that it had awakened.

The power she spoke of…the *Aura of Majesty*, the *Mystic Energy*, the *Spellcasting Mastery*, they weren't just words anymore. They were truths etched into my soul. I could feel them humming beneath my skin, shaping my breath, influencing the way my thoughts unfolded. I wasn't who I'd been when we entered that mountain. Though I didn't know yet if that should terrify me…or everyone else. The silence didn't last long. We began our descent just as twilight surrendered to full night, the last hints of sun vanishing behind the cragged peaks like a secret slipping out of reach.

The sky stretched wide above us, crisp and endless, littered with cold, unblinking stars. Below, the path carved its way down the mountain in narrow ribbons of frost and stone, winding through jagged outcroppings and sheer cliffs slick with patches of ice. Each step felt precarious, a negotiation between gravity and will. Kaelen took the lead, sharp-eyed and tense, scanning both the terrain and the sky. Ileyana kept to my side, silent but steady, her magic simmering beneath the surface like a tether to keep me grounded. The others said little, and I couldn't blame them. Maybe they were waiting for me to fall apart again. Maybe they already sensed that I hadn't truly put myself back together.

The wind sharpened as we descended, picking up speed and teeth. It howled through the narrow gaps in the rocks and tore at our cloaks with impatient hands. I pulled mine tighter around my shoulders, though the cold barely touched me anymore. The power in me, whatever it was, pulsed with a low, steady heat…unearthly and constant. It didn't match my heartbeat. It wasn't tied to breath or movement. It lived in me now, independent and watching. Sera moved just behind me. She hadn't spoken since we left the cave, but she didn't drift far. Her presence was a silent question that hovered in the space between us, unanswered and aching.

It was Bennick who first faltered, his boots grinding to a halt against the gravel. "Wait," he said, low and uneasy. His head tilted, eyes narrowing toward the peaks above. "Do you hear that?" We all stopped. The wind filled the space. Then…something more. A sound that prickled the skin along my arms, ancient and wrong.

Not wings exactly, not the natural kind. A heavy, stuttering rhythm that pulsed through the dark, like bones moving long after death. Kaelen's curse cut the air. "Not again. These fucking cursed dragons" The sky answered him. A shriek tore across the stars, high and unnatural, followed by the beating of monstrous wings.

Shapes emerged from the clouds…twisted, grotesque, massive. Smoke trailing from their scaled forms, their eyes twin embers of corrupted hunger. The cursed dragons. The same ones we had narrowly escaped before, their broken magic clinging to them like rot. They flew not with grace but with fury, not with purpose but with vengeance, and they had found us again.

"Down!" Kaelen barked, already in motion. "Get to cover…now!" We scattered just as the first one dove. A column of acidic smoke roared from its throat, striking the rocks behind us in a sickly burst of green fire. Stone exploded outward in shards and smoke. I reacted on instinct…there was no time to think. My magic surged forward, unbidden, a reflex made of fire and will.

A shield shimmered to life in front of me, casting violet and emerald light into the shadows, the force of the impact slamming against it like a wave against the cliff. It held, but the impact rippled through my entire body, leaving my arm aching from wrist to shoulder. We dove beneath an outcropping, the stone cold and jagged beneath us. The ledge offered scant protection, but it was enough for now.

Ileyana was already kneeling, weaving wards into the rock with whispered spells and glowing fingertips. Sera crouched beside me, arrow loaded, her hands trembling but her aim steady. Thorne vanished into the dark, the hilt of his sword the only gleam as he melted into shadow, already setting himself in position for a strike. Bennick stood close to Ileyana, his staff aglow with heat, a quiet fury on his face. "They shouldn't be here," I said, voice raw. "Not this far north. Not this close." "They followed us," Ileyana said without looking at me. "Or they followed *you*."

My heart skipped, then settled into a deeper, heavier rhythm. I didn't argue. She was right. Another shriek cut through the sky, and one of the creatures dipped lower, casting a massive shadow over the ridge. I felt its gaze brush across my mind…a scraping, icy pressure that wasn't just sensing… it was

remembering. Me. Or the magic inside me. Elara's magic. Her legacy. Her burden. Now, her weapon. It knew what I carried, and it hated me for it.

I rose slowly, wind snapping at my cloak, power coiling in my chest like a storm gathering behind dammed walls. I could feel the ancient weight of what Elara had passed to me pulsing just beneath the surface, begging for release. The dragon shrieked again and dove. My pulse didn't spike. My breath didn't hitch. Not this time. "Stay behind me," I said. It wasn't a command. It was a vow.

Then I stepped forward and released the storm. The magic poured out of me in a torrent…bright, searing, impossibly vast. It struck the beast mid-descent, and the air shattered with the sound of it. Light and force crackled together, bending the dragon's charge and sending it careening off-course into the cliffs with a scream of fury. The mountain shook. Stones tumbled. Snow spilled like broken glass down the slope.

The others pressed in tighter beneath the ledge, sheltering against the debris and the power pulsing from me in waves. Though, even as the creature fell back into the clouds, even as my breath came sharp and my hands still glowed with residual energy…I felt it. Not victory. Not triumph. Just the emptiness that came after. The ache. My limbs trembled. My knees buckled slightly, and I caught myself against the wall with a hand that no longer felt steady.

My vision blurred at the edges, and every breath burned a little colder. The magic that had felt limitless now settled heavy in my bones like molten iron. The mountain had taken more than I realized. I wasn't just tired. I was drained…used up. Even with all the power I carried, even with the magic still pulsing under my skin… I was weak. The mountain had given me something vast, but it had also taken something I might never get back.

The battle with the cursed dragons had reached its peak, the night air crackling with the fury of our struggle. The cursed dragons attacked relentlessly, their bodies undulating through the air like specters of death. Their eyes, burning red with malice, glowed in the shadows, and their jaws snapped with the hunger of a thousand years. They clawed at us, their wings creating gales that threatened to knock us from our feet. We fought back with everything we had, but the cursed dragons were relentless.

Kaelen's sword flashed in the dim light, striking with precision, but it was as though their scales were forged from something darker than steel. Ileyana's magic bent the wind, trying to push them away, but they came in wave after wave, each one more vicious than the last. Sera's arrows pierced their hide, but they didn't falter. Bennick's fireball flared against one of them, but it barely made a dent. Each moment was a struggle to stay alive, to push back against the encroaching darkness.

I could feel the power within me, the magic of Elara's legacy, pulsing through my veins. It surged with every breath, but it was a distant, aching force, an unfamiliar weight that was becoming harder to bear. My body was heavy, my limbs unsteady, and the more I called upon the power within, the more it felt as though I was unraveling, slipping into something else. However, still, I fought, not for myself, but for those around me. For us all. Just as the tide seemed to be turning against us, a roar split the night.

A deep, thunderous bellow that shook the earth beneath our feet. From the shadows of the mountain, something massive emerged…a dragon, but unlike any we had seen before. Its scales were black as obsidian, shadowed by the darkness that had now surrounded, and its eyes burned with an inner fire that blazed through the night like the heart of a star.

The air around it seemed to crackle with raw power, and its wings beat like thunder, propelling it downward toward the cursed dragons. The cursed dragons faltered, hesitation creeping into their attack. The obsidian dragon was a force of nature, and it showed them no mercy. With a roar, it unleashed a burst of flame so intense it scorched the very air, sending one of the cursed dragons plummeting to the ground in a shower of sparks and charred remains.

Another dragon was hit with a blast of molten rock from its maw, falling to the ground, lifeless before it could even scream. The battle shifted. The cursed dragons, no longer the apex predators of the night, were now retreating, scrambling to escape the might of the obsidian dragon.

Kaelen took his cue, rallying us to press forward, and for the first time since the battle began, I felt like we had a chance to win. We fought as one…Sera's bow finding its mark, Bennick's staff glowing with the heat of fire magic, Thorne moving with deadly precision in the shadows. Slowly but surely, we pushed the cursed dragons back, the tide of battle turning in our favor, but just as it seemed like victory was within our grasp, the obsidian dragon let out a terrible screech.

One of the cursed dragons had managed to recover, circling back for a final strike. It plunged downward, slashing at the obsidian dragon's wings with brutal force. The obsidian dragon barely managed to twist in time, but the damage was done. Its wing was torn open, dark blood staining the night air. With a roar, the obsidian dragon attempted to retaliate, but the strike had taken too much out of it.

Its movements slowed, its wings faltering as it was struck again, this time by another of the cursed dragons. The mighty beast, which had come to our rescue, was faltering. Blood poured from the gaping wound in its side, dark and viscous like tar. The obsidian dragon's strength was fading, and I watched helplessly as it crashed to the ground, its massive form hitting the earth with a thunderous thud. The cursed dragons, now littering the grounds around us.

Some torn to pieces, some burned to ashes. I bellowed and with the last of my power shot a firestorm toward the remaining cursed dragons. The last one seeing that it was now alone, began to run into the darkness.

The night seemed to close in around us, and for a moment, it felt as though we would all be consumed by the darkness. Then, a soft voice cut through the tension. "We're not leaving him," Sera said, her voice steady despite the fear in her eyes. Kaelen turned sharply, his face a mask of concern. "Sera, it's dangerous. We don't know what it is. It could be cursed. It might be the reason the dragons came after us in the first place."

Sera's gaze hardened; her lips pressed into a thin line. "No. If it were cursed, it wouldn't have saved us. It fought with us. We owe it this. I owe it this." "Ileyana's right," Kaelen insisted, his voice low. "We need to move now. We've lost too much time already." Sera shook her head, determination burning in her eyes. "If it were truly cursed, it would have let us die. It saved us. It deserves more than to be left to die alone."

The others exchanged looks, but none of them argued.
They knew Sera. Knew the fire in her heart that couldn't be easily
extinguished. Ileyana hesitated, then stepped forward. "She's right,"
she murmured, more to herself than anyone else. "If it wanted us
dead, we wouldn't still be standing." I looked down at the obsidian
dragon, my heart heavy with a strange sense of gratitude.

The creature had come to our aid in our darkest moment,
risking its life to protect us. Now it was gravely wounded…barely
clinging to life, its black scales dulled, and its breath shallow. Sera
didn't wait for another word. She approached the dragon slowly, her
hands trembling but her gaze steady. The power she carried surged
within her as she knelt beside the beast, pressing her palm against
the obsidian scales, murmuring soft words of healing.

The air around us seemed to shift, as though the mountain
itself were holding its breath. I watched as Sera's magic intertwined
with the dragon's essence, the soft glow of her power lighting up the
black scales. It was slow at first, the magic barely making a dent, but
then, gradually, the wounds on the dragon's side began to close, the
bleeding slowing.

The faintest stir of life returned to its chest as it inhaled deeply, its obsidian eyes flicking open just enough to meet Sera's gaze. Her breath hitched in relief. The group stood still, wary, unsure. Sera's unwavering confidence in her magic, in her belief that the obsidian dragon wasn't cursed, spoke louder than any words could. It had saved us, and now she was trying to return the favor. "I told you," Sera whispered, her voice breaking the tense silence. "It's not cursed."

The air was thick with the scent of magic and the weight of the night settling around us. The mountain itself seemed to hold its breath, watching, waiting. I couldn't shake the feeling that we were being drawn into something far bigger than any of us could comprehend. I glanced at the others, their faces shadowed, their eyes betraying a mixture of awe and fear.

The dragon laid still, its dark scales gleaming faintly under Sera's hands, as though her healing magic was bringing it back from the brink of death. My thoughts swirled, a storm of conflicting emotions. I knew Sera had always had a deep connection to her magic, but this? This was something else entirely.

The urge to walk over to her gnawed at me, to see for myself what was happening between her and the dragon. Something in the way she knelt beside it, her voice soft as she spoke her healing incantations, made me uneasy, though I couldn't fully understand why. Her connection to the dragon was undeniable. It was as if something invisible tethered them together. I didn't know whether to be concerned or relieved.

After a long moment of silence, I found myself moving toward her, my boots crunching softly on the rough ground. She didn't notice me at first, her eyes locked on the dragon, her hands steady and sure. I waited until I was just a few paces away before speaking. "Sera," I said quietly, careful not to disturb her concentration. "Are you sure about this? You're... too close to it." She didn't immediately respond, her focus unwavering, but I could see her lips twitch.

When she finally turned her head to face me, her eyes were dark, and there was something in them I couldn't quite place…something unyielding. "I can't leave it," she said simply, as if the answer was already written in the stars. Her voice, though soft, was firm, unwavering. "There's a pull inside me, Haji. It's… it's like I'm bound to it." I frowned, stepping closer, my gaze flickering between her and the dragon. "A pull? What do you mean?" She hesitated for a moment, as if unsure of how to explain the inexplicable. Her eyes dropped to the dragon, her expression softening. "I don't know. It's like... I was meant to be here, meant to help it." Her hand trembled slightly as she spoke, but her resolve didn't waver.

"It saved us, Haji. I owe it this. I can't just turn my back on it now, not after everything it's done for us." I looked at the dragon again, really looked at it this time, its massive form lying helpless, vulnerable. I couldn't deny the sense of gratitude that I felt for the creature. It had fought by our side when we had no hope left, and now it was clinging to life, relying on Sera's magic to keep it from slipping away entirely, but there was something else there too. Something I couldn't place.

"Are you sure you're not... too attached to this?" I asked, my voice quieter, a flicker of concern rising in me. "What if it's not just the magic pulling you in? What if it's something else?" Sera looked at me, and for a moment, I saw the same doubt in her eyes that I had felt stirring in my own heart.

She bit her lip, as if wrestling with a part of herself she wasn't fully ready to confront. When she spoke again, her voice was steady. "I can't explain it, Haji, but I know this…if I leave it now, it would feel like abandoning it and that would make me no better than the ones who would have let it die."

Her gaze shifted back to the dragon, her hands still glowing faintly with the power she was channeling into it. "I don't know what this is, or what it means, but I can't turn away from him." I stood there, silent for a long moment, absorbing her words. "Him…?" I reply. Sera straightened her back and said quietly, "I think it is a him."

The wind howled around us, distant and mournful, but Sera remained undeterred, her eyes locked on the dragon. I didn't understand it, not fully. However, I knew her well enough to recognize the fire in her heart. When she made up her mind, there was no changing it. "Alright," I said, my voice heavy with reluctant acceptance.

"I trust you, Sera. Just... be careful." She nodded, her face softening, and for a moment, I could see the gratitude in her eyes. "Thank you, Haji." I stayed beside her for a while longer, watching as the night deepened around us, the shadows stretching long and dark. I could feel the weight of it all pressing in the unknown, the danger, the promise of what lay ahead. For now, we were here, and we would stay. The world could wait, but the dragon and Sera could not.

The night stretched on in an uneasy silence, broken only by the soft, rhythmic hum of Sera's healing magic as it continued to flow into the dragon. I sat in the shadows, my thoughts scattered like leaves in the wind. I couldn't fully comprehend what had transpired between Sera and the creature, but a strange sense of peace had settled over the camp.

The others eventually found their rest, some close to the warmth of the fire, others beneath the canopy of stars, but I stayed near Sera, my eyes flickering between the dragon and the stars above. The darkness pressed against the mountain like a living thing, but within our little camp, we were safe.

Eventually, exhaustion won, and I slipped into a fitful sleep, the weight of everything pressing down on me like an invisible hand. It was the pull of the morning that stirred me first. The sky was still dark, but a faint light was creeping over the horizon when I awoke. My muscles ached, and my mind was foggy, but there was something strange in the air.

Something that made me open my eyes more slowly than usual. I blinked into the dim light, and my gaze immediately shifted to Sera. My breath caught in my throat. There she was, nestled within the wings of the obsidian dragon, her body curled against the warmth of its massive frame. The dragon's wings were spread slightly, encircling her in a protective cocoon.

I could see the faint rise and fall of its chest, the deep, almost imperceptible shift of its breathing. Its obsidian eyes were locked onto her…unwavering, unblinking. There was a bond there, undeniable, and ancient. I froze, heart pounding in my chest. I had never seen the dragon so still, so... aware. Its gaze didn't leave Sera, and it felt as if the entire world had fallen away, leaving only the two of them in this intimate, surreal moment.

I held my breath, afraid to move, afraid to disturb whatever was between them, but then, in that heavy silence, the dragon shifted slightly, its massive form stirring as it noticed me watching. Its dark eyes…still gleaming like polished stone…turned toward me, and I felt a chill run through my spine.

The air around us seemed to crackle with tension, the silence stretching, thickening like a storm about to break. Then, inside my mind…clear and sharp…came a voice. It wasn't a sound in the air, but something deeper, woven into the very fabric of my thoughts. "Do not be afraid. I mean no harm." My breath caught in my throat, and my pulse quickened as the words echoed through my head. I hadn't heard that voice before, but there was no mistaking it. It was the dragon. It spoke to me without moving its lips, without any sound passing through the air.

The scent of it hit me next…a heavy, acrid tang that flooded the space, like brimstone and smoldering embers, thick and unmistakable. It wasn't the putrid stench of decay, but something sharper, older, the scent of power bound to fire and ash. Beneath that, though, was something more…an undercurrent of something

intriguing, like fresh earth after a storm, or the faintest trace of something alive hidden in the smoke.

It was a scent that didn't just fill the air but *settled* inside me, like it had always belonged. "You are Haji, yes?" the dragon asked, its voice deep and resonant, vibrating through the core of my being. The presence of it pressed against my thoughts, not invasive, but undeniable, like a weight I couldn't escape. "I sense your hesitation. I do not wish to cause you fear, only to explain. She told me stories of you. What is her name?"

I swallowed hard, unsure how to respond at first, my thoughts tangled in disbelief…but then the words came, rising up as if they'd been waiting all along. "You can... speak to me?" The dragon let out a low, almost gruff sound…something close to a sigh, though quiet enough not to wake Sera sleeping nearby. "I can," it said, voice steady and deep within my mind. "I choose to, but only when it is necessary."

There was another pause, the kind that felt weighted, intentional. A soft breeze stirred the air between us, carrying with it the gentle scent of lavender. The dragon's head tilted slightly as it glanced toward Sera, then spoke again…quieter now, almost reverent. "She smells of lavender… please… her name?" I shifted, careful not to disturb the others, rising slowly to a crouch.

My gaze stayed locked on the dragon's glowing eyes, searching for something…answers, understanding, maybe even reassurance…but I wasn't sure what I expected to find. Everything still felt unreal. Sera's magic, the dragon's sudden appearance, and now this strange, undeniable connection between us. It was all unraveling in ways I didn't yet understand, but somehow, none of it felt like a coincidence.

I could feel it, faintly…an energy that thrummed just beneath the surface of my skin. "Her name is Seraphina, we call her Sera…What are you?" I asked, voice a little more cautious than I intended. "You're not like the others…" The dragon seemed to consider my question for a long moment before replying, its tone now tinged with something like sorrow…or perhaps resignation.

"I am of your kind, Haji. I have been hiding from the world for long years, but I am bound by a different path than yours. A path that, it seems, has led me to this moment. I can feel that we are of the same. I was sure that I was alone in this world." My heart skipped in my chest. "My kind?" I echoed, my mind racing. "But… how? What do you mean?"

The dragon's voice lowered, rough and resonant like thunder muffled by distance, but each word landed with the precision of a blade. "You are a child of the fire, are you not? One of the Forgotten. You are not alone, Haji." The moment the words touched my mind, a chill unfurled down my spine, cold and deep despite the warmth of the dragon's breath nearby.

I froze, unable to speak. Child of the fire? Forgotten? The terms stirred something ancient inside me, like a lock clicking open somewhere deep beneath bone and blood. I could almost smell it…like the faintest trace of smoke from an old hearth long extinguished, mixed with scorched pine, sun-warmed stone, and the sweet burn of distant wildflowers crushed underfoot. The very air around us seemed thick with memory, tinged with a metallic edge like iron in the back of my throat, and beneath it all, a subtle pull of brimstone…sharp, clean, and strangely comforting.

Beside the dragon, Sera shifted in her sleep, her brows tightening as though reacting to the invisible shift in the world around us. The lavender that always clung to her skin, soft and grounding, stirred with the cool night breeze. The sky above was clear, but the air held that heavy stillness that comes before a storm…not of weather, but of change.

My voice came out hoarse, uncertain. "Why me?" I asked, eyes still locked on the dragons. "Why now? Why say this now?" The dragon's eyes narrowed…not in anger, but in solemn thought. "Because the world turns faster than you know. The threads that bind past to present are unraveling, and the Forgotten must remember, or all will be lost."

He paused, the silence that followed stretching thick between us. "You carry fire in your blood, whether you want it or not. The time for silence has passed." Something caught the light then…just beneath the cracked black scales of his chest…a faint shimmer, like golden embers pulsing from deep within. Not a reflection, not a trick of flame or shadow. It was alive. I leaned forward, my breath catching.

It wasn't just magic. It was memory. Essence. History. The dragon noticed. His voice softened. "You see it, don't you? That shimmer. That pulse. It is the same that stirs inside you." My heart began to beat faster, pounding against my ribs. "I've felt it before… but I thought I imagined it. Dreams. Fire in the sky. Voices I couldn't understand." I muttered, not loud enough for anyone to hear or so I thought. "Not imagined," the dragon replied gently. "Buried. Forgotten. You were not ready…until now."

The pieces were falling into place too fast for me to catch them all, but the shape of the truth was beginning to take form. "You're one of them, too. One of the Forgotten," I whispered, trembling as the words passed my lips. "Just like me." The dragon dipped his massive head slightly, the gesture slow, reverent. "Yes, Haji. My name is Aeris'Kal Nyrathos. We are of the same blood, born of the same flame. Now, the path opens again…but it must be walked together."

Before I could answer, a faint rustle broke the stillness. Sera stirred, her eyes fluttering open, gaze dazed before it found mine…then the dragon. Her mouth parted slightly, confusion flashing across her features. She glanced between us, the silence thick with unspoken truths, but I saw it then: understanding dawning behind her eyes, slow and heavy like the rising moon. The others would wake soon. The wind carried the scent of change…wild, sharp, alive…and the world, as I had known it, was already gone.

CHAPTER 19: THE UNSPOKEN BOND THAT TIES US ALL

Sera bolted upright with a sharp inhale, her eyes wide and alert before her body had even fully caught up. Her gaze flicked to me for half a second, then locked onto the dragon. In one smooth movement, she was on her feet, rushing to his side. The scent of crushed lavender and fresh morning dew followed her, softening the air around us.

Her fingers moved over Aeris'Kal's massive flank with surprising gentleness, brushing along the edges of his scales, checking for any signs of tearing, or swelling. "You shouldn't be up," she murmured, more to herself than to him. "Not after what you did." The dragon did not speak…at least, not aloud…but he watched her with an intensity that pulled at something deep in my chest.

There was curiosity in his gaze. No, more than that. Interest. Though Sera… she didn't sense it yet, but I could feel it in the space between them. He was drawn to her. I stood slowly, brushing the sleep from my limbs, and joined her, watching as her hands hovered near a burn that had already begun to fade.

The scent of the campsite around us mixed with the chill of early morning…ashes from the night's fire, damp earth, pine smoke carried on the breeze. "He's healing faster than I expected," Sera said quietly, awe creeping into her voice. "Almost like…" She trailed off, her brow furrowed in thought. "Like something ancient is waking up inside him," I finished, and she looked at me sharply.

I hesitated, then nodded toward the edge of the clearing. "Come. We should start preparing for the day." She hesitated a moment longer, then followed, glancing back at the dragon once before falling in step beside me. We walked in silence through the thin veil of mist clinging to the grass, the sun just beginning to pull light over the tops of the trees.

The quiet was peaceful, but I could feel her waiting. "His name is Aeris'Kal Nyrathos," I said softly. "He told me himself." Sera blinked at me. "He spoke to you?" Her voice was hushed, not out of disbelief, but reverence. I nodded, the memory still echoing in my chest like a drumbeat. "Not aloud. Not like we're speaking now. It's… in the mind. Deeper than words. Like he reached into something ancient inside me and woke it up."

I paused, drawing in a breath thick with pine and something faintly sweet from the nearby wildflowers. "We can communicate. He said I'm one of the Forgotten… like him. A child of the fire." Sera didn't speak at first. I could see the questions racing behind her eyes, but she didn't ask them. Instead, she whispered, "You believe him?" "I know it," I said, a tremor of truth in my voice I couldn't hide.

"There's something between us. It's more than a connection. It's like… we've been waiting for each other, and…" I glanced at her, hesitant. "He feels something when he looks at you. I can sense it. Intrigue. Recognition, maybe. You stir something in him, Sera." She didn't answer. She just stared back toward the dragon in the clearing, the wind catching her hair.

She didn't answer right away. Her eyes stayed fixed on the dragon curled in the clearing, his obsidian-scaled form half-shrouded in the morning mist. Her face was unreadable, but I could see the subtle tension in her shoulders, the way her fingers fidgeted at her sides like they were reaching for something just out of reach. The breeze stirred again, gentle but charged, lifting strands of her hair and wrapping the scent of crushed herbs, smoke, and damp earth around us.

I stepped closer, watching the way her breath caught in her throat, her body still as stone. "He's not just curious," I said softly. "He watches you the way people look at stars they haven't seen in a long time…like something lost has been found again." I hadn't meant to say it that way, hadn't planned to lay that much truth between us, but I couldn't help it. The words came out raw, honest, and heavy with meaning.

Sera turned toward me slowly, her expression cautious. "Haji… why aren't you afraid of him?" she asked, barely above a whisper. "Even now. After everything. I look at him and I feel… pulled. Like there's something there, something I don't understand…but you… you walk toward him like he belongs to you." I hesitated, unsure of how to explain what I didn't fully understand myself.

There *was* fear. It lived in the same place as the wonder, the ache, the strange calm that wrapped around my chest when he said my name. "Because I think I've known him longer than I've known

myself," I said finally. "Because when he looks at me, it's like all the things I never understood about myself start to make sense. Like I've been half-asleep, and he's the thing that woke me up."

She looked away then, back toward the dragon, her eyes narrowing slightly as if she were trying to see him differently. "And you think… I matter to him, too?" she asked. There was a fragile note in her voice, something tender she rarely let show. I didn't hesitate this time. "I *know* you do," I said. "Not the same way I do, but something about you speaks to him. I felt it the moment your scent hit the air. He noticed you. Not just with his eyes…with something deeper." I paused, letting that settle before continuing. "You've always carried something different in you, Sera. Something strong. Maybe he sees it more clearly than the rest of us ever could."

The camp behind us remained still, the others still tucked in sleep or drifting toward it, unaware of how close everything was to changing. Only the dying fire crackled softly, and even the wind seemed to hold its breath. Sera exhaled slowly, like she was letting go of something long-held. "Then maybe it's time I stopped being afraid of what I don't understand," she whispered. Her voice had shifted…softer, but steadier.

She turned to me again, a quiet kind of resolve building in her eyes. "You said we're walking the path together. Does that mean he's coming with us?" I nodded once, firm. "He *has* to. He's part of it now. Just like you. Just like me." I glanced back toward Aeris'Kal, his body still and vast, the glow of gold beneath his scales barely visible through the fading mist. "The world is changing, Sera. I can feel it, and I think this… this is only the beginning."

The stillness didn't last much longer. One by one, the others began to stir, the rhythm of the camp shifting like a tide coming in. First Kaelen, always the lightest sleeper, pushed off his bedroll with a groan and ran a hand through his tousled hair. His eyes found me immediately, then drifted past to the dragon in the clearing.

He stilled, shoulders tensing…not with fear, but that silent readiness he always carried, like a blade never fully sheathed. Tamsin woke next, stretching with a loud yawn and smacking her lips as if sleep had left a bad taste. Her gaze landed on the dragon, and her brows arched up. "Well," she muttered, "That's a way to start the morning."

Ileyana and Bennick emerged from their tents nearly at the same time. Ileyana's cloak was wrapped tight around her, her silver-blonde hair braided back, and her eyes narrowed with caution the second they landed on Aeris'Kal. Bennick stayed quiet, but his hand hovered near the hilt of his blade. Thorne, last to rise, barely concealed his scowl, muttering something about "waking up to monsters" under his breath. The change in the camp's mood was immediate…a low hum of tension threaded through every movement, every glance toward the dragon. Aeris'Kal noticed. Of course he did.

He stood slowly, stretching his great wings just enough to show the span of them, a clear display of both strength and warning. He didn't roar or bare his teeth, but his posture shifted subtly…head raised, body angled away from the group but ready to defend if needed. I could feel his wariness pulse in my mind, not sharp, but steady, guarded. He began, "They do not know me. They will not trust easily, nor I them." "They will," I thought back. "Just… give them time."

The scent of breakfast slowly began to wrap around the morning chill…smoke and sizzling meat, the rich, earthy aroma of roasted roots, and something sweet wafting from a pot that Tamsin had set near the coals, likely honey and dried fruit warmed into oats. It softened the air, chased off some of the tension. Hunger, at least, was a language we all still spoke. "I assume we're not staying long," Kaelen said, stepping beside me, his voice low and even.

"No," I replied. "We need to get back to Ileyana's land. If what Aeris said is true, and the Forgotten really are tied to what's coming… then her people need to know." I glanced over to Ileyana, who had crouched near the fire, her fingers absently toying with a stone in the ashes. Her expression was thoughtful, distant, but I saw the flicker of something there…recognition. Maybe even fear. "And the dragon?" Kaelen asked. I met his gaze. "He's coming with us." I responded almost too quickly.

Kaelen didn't argue. He just looked at Aeris again, long, and slow. "Then let's hope your fire-born friend knows how to fly

quiet." I glanced toward the dragon once more. He stood apart,
silent and immense, golden light still flickering faintly beneath his
dark scales. I could feel him watching…not just me, but all of them,
measuring, waiting, and though he said nothing aloud, his thoughts
brushed mine again, steady, and clear.

"They are yours, Haji, and for now, that is enough." He
stated, frankly. I only nodded, the scent of charred wood and spiced
meat thick in the morning air, the promise of another long journey
settling over our shoulders like a second skin. The wind carried the
scent of the mountains ahead…cold, sharp, and clean. It was time to
move.

We ate in a strange sort of silence, the kind that hums
beneath the surface when too much has changed too quickly. The
food helped…it always did. Tamsin handed out portions with a half-
hearted grin, trying to pull the edge off the morning, but even she
didn't crack a joke. The smell of roasted meat, thyme, and sage
drifted in warm ribbons through the camp, layered with the sweet
tang of cooked berries and oats. It grounded us, gave us something
familiar to hold onto as we sat in the shadow of a creature that

belonged to legends. No one asked questions yet. Not aloud, but the glances…sharp, lingering, uncertain…spoke volumes.

Aeris'Kal kept his distance, standing like a statue at the far edge of the clearing, the mist curling around his legs, his wings half-furled. He was watching them all, not with threat, but with that quiet intensity of someone who knows they're being judged and chooses stillness over defense. His golden eyes caught the light, slivers of sunlight threading through the trees and glinting off his scales. I could sense the tension in him…not fear, but restraint.

He didn't want to frighten them. Not more than he already had. Bennick, chewing methodically on a hunk of bread, finally broke the quiet. "So," he said, eyes flicking between me and the dragon, "He's not going to eat us, then?" "He would've done it already," I replied flatly, and beside me, Kaelen snorted softly. "That's comforting," Bennick muttered, but didn't press further.

Ileyana hadn't touched her food. She sat cross-legged near the fire, her hands resting on her knees, her eyes locked on Aeris as if reading a language only she could see. Eventually, she spoke without looking away. "He carries ancient magic," she said, her

voice calm, reverent. "Something older than even the First Trees. I can feel it pulsing beneath his skin."

She turned her head then, and her gaze found mine. "He's tied to you, isn't he? He reminds me of you and Orion…" "Yes," I said simply because it was the only answer that mattered. Thorne gave a low grunt from where he leaned against a stone. "We're bringing that thing *with us* into my homeland?" He asked, as if he already knew the answer but needed to object anyway.

"It's not a thing," Sera said, sharper than usual. "And he saved us. Saved *me.* He could've destroyed everything back at the ruins, but he didn't." Her voice was low, but steady, and when she spoke, I saw Aeris turn his head just slightly toward her, the motion subtle, but unmistakably attentive. My chest tightened. He *was* watching her. Not the way he watched the others. There was something else in it…curiosity, yes, but something deeper. A recognition he didn't fully understand yet.

"We leave within the hour," Ileyana said, rising with that smooth, fluid grace of hers, her cloak catching the wind like it had a mind of its own. "The path back into my lands is narrow and steep.

446

It will not welcome a creature of his size easily, but I'll send word ahead to the outer guards. They'll stand down once they know it's me." Kaelen stepped closer to me, his voice low enough only I could hear. "Are you sure about this?" I looked at him, really looked, and then nodded. "He's not what we were taught to fear and neither am I."

The air shifted then, the scents of breakfast fading into the cooler sharpness of the mountains above. Pine, snow, and stone. The path ahead was steep, but not nearly as steep as the one unfolding within each of us. We were no longer the same people who had started this journey…and the road home would demand more than we had ever given before.

The journey stretched on beneath a sky that shifted from slate gray to brilliant blue and back again. Each day brought us deeper into the edges of Ileyana's territory, the wild borderlands where the forest gave way to jagged stone and ancient paths worn smooth by time and elemental wind. The scent of pine remained thick in the air, but now it mingled with the sharp tang of ice forming on shaded rocks and the mineral-rich breath of mountain

springs. Smoke and char from our night fires clung to our cloaks, a reminder of the cold that crept in stronger each night.

The landscape felt older here, steeped in forgotten power that whispered through the trees like distant voices carried on the wind. Though we all moved with purpose, a quiet reverence began to settle over the group…especially around Aeris. He remained a towering presence, his massive form always just a few paces removed from the rest of us.

He never intruded but never strayed too far either, a silent sentinel watching the edges of our path. His scent was impossible to ignore. It was of fire and something ancient buried deep beneath it, like the inside of a storm about to break. It lingered in the air behind him, not unpleasant…more like brimstone wrapped in the memory of sun-warmed stone and distant lightning.

Sera, more than any of us, stayed close to him. What began as hesitant curiosity bloomed quickly into something warmer, a thread of trust that strengthened with every passing day. She spoke to him often, her voice carrying softly across the path as she recounted our strange and winding adventures.

She told him about the wild creature that had mistaken Thorne for a mate, the enchanted forest that had tried to barter Kaelen for a song, and the night she and Tamsin accidentally released glowing bees in a market square. Sometimes she laughed while telling them; other times, her voice dropped into something more thoughtful, quieter, like she was trying to understand her own memories even as she shared them.

Aeris listened. Always. He never spoke aloud, but his attention never wavered. His massive head would tilt slightly. He would adjust his pace to keep her close, gently sweeping his tail to the side when branches hung too low or the path narrowed. I'd never seen a dragon move with such deliberate care.

It was on the fifth day, after a stretch of narrow trail carved into the mountainside, that Sera stumbled. Her boot caught a loose stone and she pitched forward with a gasp, barely catching herself. In an instant, Aeris was there. He moved with surprising speed for something so large, stepping in front of her and lowering his head slowly, carefully, his neck curving like a bridge to meet the earth. Sera stared at him, eyes wide, breath shallow. "You… you want me

to get on?" she asked, blinking in disbelief. Aeris didn't answer with words, but his stillness said enough. His eyes, molten gold in the morning light, never left her face.

With a hesitant hand, she touched the curve of his scaled neck, fingers brushing over the faint lines of glowing gold that pulsed beneath the dark obsidian. Aeris tensed as her hand brushed his form. "Are you sure?" she whispered. He didn't move…just waited, patient as the earth itself.

She climbed slowly, gripping his ridges for balance. When she was finally settled, he rose in one smooth motion, steady and unshaken, and she clutched his neck with both arms, her cheek pressed to the warm, living stone of his scales. "Thank you," she murmured, and though the wind nearly took the words, I felt them just the same.

I watched it all from a few steps back, my chest tight with a strange mix of awe and certainty. There was something between them…something old and profound. A connection deeper than simple trust. They moved now with a shared rhythm, like two beings bound by something more instinctive than language. I'd heard of it before. In old stories. In half-whispered bedtime myths. *Soulbonded.*

That night, beneath a cloudless sky dusted with stars and the scent of roasted herbs and mountain ash curling up from the fire, I sat close to Kaelen. The warmth of him was steadying. He hadn't asked about Aeris and Sera, but I could feel the question in his silence. "They might be mates," I said softly, watching the way Sera curled against Aeris' side, his wing curved protectively around her. "There's something in the way he watches her. It's not just caring. It's recognition."

Kaelen glanced at them, then at me. "Like the way I see you?" I looked up at him, my heart catching. "Yes," I whispered. "Just like that." The wind shifted, rustling the trees overhead, and with it came the scent of snow and something older…change. It settled over the camp like a promise. We were nearly there, and the world we walked into would not be the one we left behind.

The final stretch of our journey seemed to stretch on endlessly, each step bringing us closer to a place that felt as though it had been waiting for us all along. The landscape shifted once

again, becoming more familiar, yet still foreign in its own right. As we crossed the last hill, the view before us opened up into a valley that led to Ileyana's land. The ground beneath our feet became softer, more forgiving, and the distant cliffs that framed the valley felt like silent sentinels, their jagged faces carved by centuries of wind and time.

The air here carried the scent of dew-laden grass, freshly turned soil, and something sweeter still, as though the earth itself had been softened by the soft whisper of spring. The breeze, fresh and cool, carried the subtle fragrance of flowers just beginning to bloom, mingling with the sharp scent of pine and the lingering tang of the ozone from distant thunder clouds. I couldn't help but feel a strange calm settle over me as the land seemed to breathe in rhythm with our steps, as though it was alive and aware of our presence.

The rhythm of our journey had been steady and almost peaceful, but now that we were nearing the final destination, I could feel a subtle shift in the air. The quiet of the land deepened, the forest holding its breath as though the world itself was pausing in anticipation. I glanced over at Sera, who had been speaking softly to Aeris for the past few hours.

Her voice was light, almost musical, and Aeris was always attentive, his golden eyes following every movement of her lips with the sort of intent focus that seemed so natural, so profound, that it made my heart stutter unexpectedly. He was not merely listening to her words…he was absorbing them, his connection to her deepening with each shared moment. As the journey went on, I began to see the way Sera seemed to glow in the dragon's presence, a spark in her that had not been there before. It wasn't just magic…they had something more, something unspoken but undeniable.

The path before us began to narrow as we neared the entrance to Ileyana's land, the trees thinning and giving way from the soft golden-green of the meadow to the more dry, tan landscape. The warmth of the day lingered in the air, but the gentle breeze had a bite to it now, carrying with it the promise of something new...something that had not been part of our world before.

It felt like the beginning of a change, a shift that had been set in motion long before any of us had known it. Just as I felt the breath of that change, I heard it. A rumble. Low at first, barely

noticeable, but it grew louder with each passing moment. It wasn't

thunder…it was something else, something that echoed from deep

within the earth itself. The trees ahead seemed to part for an unseen

force, and from within the forest, a figure emerged…a shadow

against the dimming light. It was Orion.

His presence filled the air before he even appeared, and as

he stepped into view, it felt as if the very land itself bowed to him.

His towering frame moved with a quiet grace, each step measured

and heavy with purpose. The deep brown of his skin was lit by the

golden flame-red streaks in his hair, which ruffled in the wind like

embers caught in a gale. His honey-gold eyes swept across the

landscape before settling on us, his gaze sharp, almost as if he could

see straight through to the very heart of us. There was power in him,

ancient and unyielding, and it was evident in every fiber of his

being.

Yet, in that moment, I saw something else…something that

made the hairs on the back of my neck stand up in recognition: a

quiet acknowledgment. A calm strength that spoke of both mastery and restraint. Orion's gaze shifted then, landing on Aeris. The dragon's massive body tensed for a split second before he took a step forward, a low rumble issuing from deep within him. In that instant, something incredible happened. The air between them seemed to crackle, charged with power, an almost tangible energy. There was no grand announcement, no fanfare, just the subtle hum of power connecting the two dragons. Then, they both did the same thing at once. They bowed their heads.

It wasn't the simple dip of a creature's head; it was more than that. Their movements were deliberate, reverent, and the world seemed to shift with them. The earth trembled slightly, as if in response to the weight of their acknowledgment, as if it recognized that two beings of immeasurable power were standing before it. The energy that passed between the dragons was not just physical. It was a pulse, a vibration that ran deep into the earth itself, an unspoken bond, a recognition of something ancient and sacred. I felt it then.

The power that surged between them, a spark that jumped from their connection and into the very marrow of my bones. It was like I was witnessing the return of something that had been forgotten, a force long buried under the weight of time. It wasn't just magic…it was memory. History. It was the stuff of legends, the kind of power that could shape worlds.

The moment between them stretched on, but it felt timeless, suspended outside the boundaries of time and space. I watched in awe as the two dragons stood in mutual respect, their energy merging in a way that felt like the completion of a long-forgotten ritual. For a brief moment, everything else seemed to fade away. It was just us, standing there, in the presence of something far greater than any of us could comprehend.

Finally, as if some unseen signal had passed between them, the moment broke, and the energy between us all seemed to settle. Aeris lifted his head, and Orion did the same. The connection, though still palpable, was no longer as intense, but the respect between them was undeniable, and it lingered in the air like the lingering heat of a flame that had just been extinguished.

I couldn't help but feel the weight of it…the sense that something had shifted, that the world had been set into motion again. Ileyana's land, once a quiet and untouched space, now felt as though it too had become a part of something much larger than any of us could utterly understand. Then as the three of us…Aeris, Orion, and I…stood there together, the power that connected us felt both overwhelming and comforting, as though it had always been meant to be this way. The path ahead, though uncertain, felt clearer now, and whatever came next, I knew one thing for certain: we would walk it together.

CHAPTER 20: OUR DEPARTURE

It happened all at once. Orion's eyes locked on the group cresting the rise behind us, and before I even had time to register who had emerged from the trees, he was already moving. There was no hesitation…no words, no command…just motion. His body responded to something older than thought, as if some part of him had already known she was coming.

Ileyana stepped out from the cluster of our returning group, her boots sinking softly into the dew-kissed earth, shoulders squared against the last stretch of the trail. Dust clung to her skin like a memory, and though her posture was steady, I could see the wear behind her eyes. Still, she was radiant in a way that had nothing to do with light and everything to do with presence. She didn't just enter a space…she filled it…and when Orion saw her, the storm inside him, the tightly held fury, grief, and fear, quieted all at once.

He didn't run, but there was an urgency to his steps, a gravity. As if the entire world tilted forward, drawing him to her. She saw him, too. Her lips parted slightly, but she didn't speak. Her pace slowed, then stopped altogether as he closed the distance. Without a word, he reached her. The camp seemed to vanish around them.

Orion cupped the side of her face with one calloused hand and pressed his forehead gently to hers. The contact was soft, reverent, a breath held between two storms. Ileyana closed her eyes, and her shoulders dropped the weight they'd been carrying. Her fingers curled lightly around the edge of his shirt, anchoring herself to something only they could understand. They stood like that for a long moment, the kind that stretches so wide it forgets how to end.

The others around us slowed to a halt, silent, respectful. Even the wind bent gently around them. I saw in that quiet something sacred, not a reunion, not even relief. It was recognition. A returning. The way fire remembers the shape of the hearth. When Orion finally pulled back, he said something only she could hear. She smiled…not with her lips, but with her entire body. Then she turned and walked toward the tents, her fingers brushing briefly along his arm before letting go.

Orion stood where she left him for several breaths, eyes closed. When he opened them again, something had changed. The weight hadn't disappeared, but he carried it differently now…shoulders squared, back straight, heart steadier. We gathered near the edge of the valley just as the last light of dusk poured gold across the hills. The land around us seemed to exhale. The breeze that passed over us smelled of warm stone, pine, and something aged still…like the bones of the earth had stirred beneath our feet.

Aeris joined us silently, his steps near soundless despite the weight of his frame. He came to stand beside Orion and me, his golden eyes scanning the horizon as if trying to see something hidden just beyond the edge of sight. When his gaze met Orion's, something invisible passed between them. No words were spoken, but both men inclined their heads to each other with the exact same motion. Simultaneous. Purposeful. Just like before, the ground itself seemed to recognize them.

I felt it again then, just as I had the first time in the clearing…the deep, humming resonance that came not from above or below, but from within. It wasn't magic. Not exactly. It was older than that. More primal. It was blood calling to blood. "Aeris, this is Orion. I know we all felt it," I said quietly, my eyes fixed on the distant cliffs that framed the valley. "The stirring. The fire. The memory."

Orion turned slightly toward me. Mentally he replied, "And the recognition. You felt it when we crossed into this place." I nodded. "Like we were being drawn here." "It's not just the land," Aeris said, in my mind his voice was low and even. "It's us. Together. The blood remembers when we stand side by side." I looked between them.

The three of us…each touched by the old flame in different ways yet undeniably linked by it. I'd known it in battle, when fire had poured through my veins and the shape of something ancient had nearly taken form in my shadow. I'd seen it in Orion's gaze when he shifted, when the lines between dragon and man blurred into one sovereign truth. I'd seen it most of all in Aeris…who bore the weight of his lineage like a crown of smoke and flame.

"We're echoes of something larger," I said. "Fragments of an old-world bleeding into this one." "And it's waking," Orion murmured. "Not just in us. In others, too." "You felt that when you met me," Aeris added. "And I felt it when I met Haji. A resonance. Like a string pulled tight." I drew a slow breath. "So, what does that make us now?" Orion looked past me, toward the path Ileyana had disappeared down.

"The beginning," he said simply. "The first of a forgotten order. Not chosen, but remembered." For a while, we stood in silence. The wind rolled through the grass at our feet, and the stars began to pierce through the thinning clouds above. The firelight from camp flickered behind us, but none of us moved to return just yet.

Here, in the cradle of Ileyana's land, something had aligned. Not fate. Not prophecy. Something quieter. Deeper. Like the earth itself had turned to welcome us home, and whatever waited beyond that moment…whatever shadows still hunted our steps…we would face them with the fire of a legacy that refused to be forgotten. Together.

A long silence stretched between us, but it wasn't uncomfortable. It was the kind of silence that came after a truth had been spoken…something raw and grounding, almost sacred. The breeze brushed past us, tugging gently at the edges of our cloaks, and from somewhere beyond the hills, the soft murmur of water reached our ears…the sound of the river winding through Ileyana's valley. It felt like the land was exhaling, welcoming us not as strangers or warriors, but as something else entirely. Aeris shifted beside me, arms crossed, gaze fixed on the horizon though his thoughts were clearly elsewhere.

"I'm not used to this," he said finally, his voice low, a little quieter than usual. I glanced at him and asked, "You've traveled alone for a long time?" He nodded, a single, slow movement and replied, "Always. It was easier that way. Safer. Not for me…for them." His jaw tightened slightly, and I recognized the weight behind those words. "Most people see the dragon and nothing else. They don't see the man beneath the fire. Just something to be wary of, something they can't control."

Orion gave a short grunt, not unkind, just knowing. "They fear what they don't understand…and they destroy what they fear." Aeris gave a small, wry smile, but it didn't reach his eyes. "Exactly.

So, I kept my distance. I told myself I didn't need to belong to anything. That I was meant to walk alone…but that wasn't truth. That was survival."

He looked at me then, really looked. "Now, with the two of you, I feel it. That pull. Like I'm not just surviving anymore. Like I've been circling something all my life and I'm finally stepping into it." His voice had gone softer, more vulnerable, but it didn't waver. I felt the truth in it…familiar and heavy. "Legacy," I said. "It's not about pride or status. It's about not being the last in a long line. About being the bridge instead of the end." Orion spoke without lifting his gaze from the hills.

"It's about what we do with the fire we carry. Whether we burn or build." We stood in silence after that, but this time it felt different. We were no longer just three powerful beings sharing a moment. We were three branches of the same flame, realizing, finally, that we belonged to something older and more profound than war.

Footsteps in the grass pulled me from the moment. I turned to see Kaelen and Sera approaching from the southern slope, their shadows long in the golden light. Kaelen's steps were confident as ever, his expression unreadable but alert. Sera moved beside him like she always did…with quiet grace and eyes that saw more than she ever said. "You three look like statues," she teased as they drew near, her smile soft and a little curious. "Have you been standing here all this time?" Kaelen gave a low chuckle, a spark of humor in his voice. "Probably brooding. Orion's specialty."

Orion didn't react, but I saw a flicker of amusement in the corners of his mouth. I answered, "We were speaking of blood…and of what connects us beneath it." Sera's expression shifted slightly, her eyes narrowing in thought. "I feel it too. When the three of you are close, it changes the air. It's like the earth itself leans in to listen." Kaelen tilted his head. "Poetic and accurate."

He stepped beside Orion, watching him closely. "I've seen it since you arrived. The way your power echoes one another. It's not just strength. It's harmony. Like you were never meant to move alone." Orion looked at him, his golden eyes unreadable. "Then maybe we're not just remnants. Maybe we're the beginning of something that was lost." Kaelen nodded slowly. "The world's

changing. I can feel it, cracks beneath the surface. Something's waking. Whatever it is, it's going to take all of us to face it." Sera came closer, gazing toward the hills. "This land feels it too. It's listening. I think it's been waiting for you… for this moment… longer than we can possibly understand."

I looked at each of them…Orion, Aeris, Kaelen, and Sera…and something deep inside me stirred. For the first time in a long while, I didn't feel like a blade waiting to be drawn. I felt like a piece of something whole and above us, as the last of the daylight slipped away, the stars began to bloom…slowly, silently…like ancient eyes watching us take our first step into a world we were always meant to claim. Then, quietly, Kaelen took my hand, pulling me gently away from the group.

A knowing glance passed between us…something that needed no words. I stepped beside him, feeling the warmth of his presence as we walked together in silence. The land seemed to open up before us, the steady rhythm of our footsteps the only sound for a while. Eventually, we moved farther away, out of sight and sound of the others, until it was just the two of us beneath the growing stars.

"Do you ever feel like everything's shifting?" Kaelen's voice was soft, but there was weight behind the words.

I looked up at him, meeting his gaze. His eyes were filled with something more than just the world around us…something more profound. "Yes," I said, the word escaping me before I even realized how much truth lay in it. "I feel it too. Like the earth itself is changing." Kaelen stopped walking and turned to face me, his hand still holding mine. He looked at me for a long moment, his expression shifting from unreadable to something softer…something I hadn't seen before.

"You've become so much more than you were. All of us have." His thumb brushed gently over the back of my hand, sending a shiver through me. "But you... I can feel it in you. You've become something that this world desperately needs, Haji. I've seen your strength, your power, but it's your heart that I admire most."

My breath caught in my throat at the quiet sincerity in his voice, and the tension I hadn't realized was there eased between us. "I never thought I could be something more than the fight," I admitted, feeling the weight of my own words. "But now, with you... with all of this... I know there's something bigger waiting for me. For us." Kaelen took a step closer, his gaze softening further. "We've always been part of something bigger. You've always been part of it."

I didn't have the words to say what I was feeling…not in that moment…but I didn't need them. Kaelen closed the distance between us, his lips brushing softly against mine. The kiss was tender, quiet, filled with all the things neither of us could put into words. The world seemed to still around us, and in that silence, I felt the truth of everything that had been building between us…the years, the loss, the fears, the long roads we had walked alone, now converging into something more.

When we pulled away, neither of us spoke at first. There was no need. Kaelen finally whispered, his voice thick with emotion, "I'm not sure what this is, or what it will become, but I know I don't want to face it without you." I rested my forehead against his, my heart pounding in my chest. "You won't have to," I murmured, and with that, we stood there in the quiet, our hearts beating in time with the land that surrounded us, knowing we were no longer alone. I glanced back to where Orion, Sera, and Aeris stood. I saw Ileyana approaching with her quiet grace, her steps light yet purposeful.

She was drawn to Orion, and as their eyes met, an unspoken understanding seemed to pass between them. She pulled him gently to the side, leaving Sera and Aeris standing alone in the growing silence. Sera's gaze followed Ileyana and Orion for a moment, her expression unreadable, before she turned her focus back to the land around us. Aeris, too, seemed lost in thought, his usual quietness amplifying the stillness between them.

Without a word, Kaelen's presence beside me seemed to anchor me further to this moment. His hand, still in mine, gave a gentle squeeze, and for a heartbeat, we both stood there, taking in the scene. The soft murmur of the wind played in our ears, the sounds of the valley stretching out before us, but there was something deeper at play, something that neither of us could fully explain. "Do you ever think about how we got here?" Kaelen's voice broke the silence; his words slow and deliberate.

I turned to face him, brushing our shoulders as I did. His eyes were a little darker in the fading light, but they held the same warmth I had come to rely on, the kind of warmth that made the cold nights feel bearable. "All the time," I answered, the truth simple but layered. "But I think I'm just starting to understand what it all means. What it's all leading to."

Kaelen's gaze softened, his thumb brushing lightly over my skin as he stepped closer. "I used to think this was all just a series of battles, one after the other," he said, his voice lowering as though sharing a secret, "But now, I see it's more than that. It's the path we're meant to walk. Together." His words, simple as they were, settled into me like a seed taking root, and I felt my chest tighten slightly.

There was so much I hadn't known about myself…about us…until this journey had started. "Together," I echoed, the weight of the word hanging between us. "It's strange, isn't it? How much I fought against it before. I never thought I needed anyone, but now…" My voice trailed off as I searched his gaze, feeling something shifting inside me. Kaelen didn't rush to fill the silence.

Instead, he let the space between us stretch as he studied me, the quiet words unspoken but clear in his eyes. "You don't have to fight it anymore, Haji. You've become something more than you ever thought you could be…and I'm here, with you, for all of it."

A lump formed in my throat, and I bit my lip, fighting the urge to let it all spill out. I wasn't sure how to articulate the way I felt…how everything I'd ever known seemed to be rearranged in that moment, as if the world had turned on its axis and made room for something new. Kaelen stepped forward again, his hand lifting to cup my face gently. He leaned closely, his breath warm against my skin as his lips met mine, slow and tender.

It wasn't a kiss of passion, but of understanding, of shared space in a world that had suddenly become so much larger than the two of us. When we pulled away, the silence between us felt sacred. Kaelen's forehead rested against mine, and we stood there for a long moment, as though we were both allowing the weight of our shared connection to sink in. "We're not alone anymore," I whispered, the words slipping out without thought, but they held truth…deep and undeniable. Kaelen's fingers traced the line of my jaw, and he nodded.

"No, we're not." His voice was thick with emotion, and for the first time, I felt like we had both crossed a threshold, one that hadn't been there before. Behind us, I heard the soft sound of Sera's voice, though it wasn't directed at us. It was low, murmuring something to Aeris, but there was a distant quality to her tone.

Her words floated over to us, soft and murmuring like the wind, and though I couldn't catch the meaning of them, there was a sense of weight in her voice. It wasn't like the lighthearted conversations I had heard earlier…it was something deeper, more reflective. Aeris stood still, his golden eyes fixed on her, listening intently, absorbing every word as though he too felt the gravity of the moment.

Kaelen must have heard the shift in her tone as well because his expression softened, and his hand lingered on mine. "She's telling him a story," he murmured, glancing over his shoulder at the pair. "About her past, maybe. Or something about him." I nodded, though I couldn't make out what she was saying either, but there was something in the air…something that shifted, something ancient and familiar.

It was like the earth was remembering something long forgotten, and for a brief moment, I felt that connection stretch between all of us. Each of us carrying something older than time itself, bound together by fate or destiny or some force greater than us all, and though I couldn't understand it fully, I knew we were standing at the cusp of something monumental.

Turning back to Kaelen, I gave his hand one last squeeze before we began to walk once more, the distance between us and the others growing as we moved further into the valley. The night stretched before us, the stars beginning to twinkle in the deepening sky like the flicker of memories long lost. In the quiet, I felt that pull again…the same one Aeris had spoken of, but now, it wasn't just survival. It was purpose. It was belonging.

Kaelen spoke again, his voice almost a whisper as we continued to walk. "This is just the beginning, Haji. I can feel it. There's more to us, to all of this, than we realize, and I'm going to be right here with you, every step of the way." I squeezed his hand tighter, my heart swelling with a mixture of awe and love. "I know," I whispered back. "I know." Together, we walked into the night, toward a future neither of us could yet comprehend, but one we would face together.

The scent of roasted game, wild herbs, and fresh bread filled Ileyana's home, wrapping around us like a memory of peace we hadn't yet earned. The flickering hearth cast dancing shadows across the stone walls, its warmth mingling with the low hum of conversation and the clinking of plates.

The long wooden table was heavy with food…glazed birds with crisp skin glistened beside bowls of seasoned root vegetables, dark-crusted bread still steaming from the oven, and pitchers of honeyed wine that caught the firelight like amber. It should have felt like comfort, but beneath the ease of food and shelter, something restless stirred in all of us. This was the calm before a tide we couldn't turn back.

As we sat together…Bennick, Tamsin, Aeris, Sera, Kaelen, Sylas, and me…there was a quiet understanding that what lay ahead would demand more of us than we had ever given. Orion, standing at the head of the table, waited until our hunger had softened into stillness before he spoke. "The path to the Elven Kingdom begins tomorrow," he said, his voice low and steady. "I can open the way, but the rest will be yours to walk. Ileyana and I will remain behind. The journey from here is no longer ours to shape…it belongs to you."

His words hit with a finality I hadn't expected, and when I looked at Ileyana, her gaze was calm, certain, as if she'd known all along we would leave without them. "The elves do not welcome strangers lightly," she said. "But the forest listens to intent. If you walk with truth in your heart, it will guide you. If you do not… it will swallow you whole."

Bennick asked the question we were all thinking. "How does the portal work? And how can we trust it won't break apart the moment we step through?" Orion rose, moving to a carved niche in the stone wall and retrieving a smooth, dark stone veined with glowing gold. He held it in one hand, and with the other traced a symbol in the air.

The runes on the stone began to glow, pulsing in time with the beat of something older than language. "The portals are tied to the ley lines, anchored with runes I forged from my own fire. They are not wild, like the ones the world once feared. They are bridges…strong and true…but they require your will to guide them. If your heart is uncertain, the path will resist you. You must step forward with intent."

He laid the stone on the table, and a map unfurled beneath it, glowing faintly with a soft internal light. "This one will place you within a day's ride of the outer forest. From there, the land is no longer mine to shape. It will be your choices that carry you forward." Ileyana's eyes met mine then, and for a heartbeat I felt her strength reach me across the firelight. "Trust in each other," she said. "Trust that you were chosen for a reason."

We finished the meal in silence, the gravity of what came next settling around us like the weight of ancient snow. Afterward, we gathered our things, taking only what could be carried swiftly: weapons, provisions, and the talismans we had earned or inherited. By dawn, the whole of us stood before the portal, an arched gate of obsidian stone, etched with runes that shimmered like liquid gold. The clearing beyond Ileyana's home was quiet, wrapped in mist and dew, the trees watching like guards. Orion stepped forward, placing the key-stone into a carved recess at the top of the arch.

A deep hum resonated through the ground as the center of the portal shimmered, then burst into light…a swirling vortex of flame, not burning but alive, like memory made motion. "Step through with purpose," Orion said. "The portal bends space to will and flame. Fear will only make the journey longer. Please take this…" I reached out to grab a second keystone offered by Orion.

He continued, "This will allow you to use any of the many portals I have built across the lands." My voiced cracked as I realized the gravity of what was happening, "You trust me to have this?" Ileyana was the one to respond, "My child, we would not be here without you. You will soon know what I mean. So, until then, yes, we would trust you with this, with our home and hopes, with our lives." Tears began to stream down my face as I embraced them one last time.

One by one, we moved toward the portal, the silence between us louder than any farewell. Kaelen went first, his jaw set, shoulders square, stepping into the swirling firelight without a glance back. There was no hesitation in him, just the quiet certainty of a man who had already chosen his path. Then came Sera and Aeris, moving side by side.

They didn't speak, didn't need to…there was something unspoken between them now, something solid and unshakable. Together, they vanished into the golden light. Tamsin followed, calm as ever, her braid swinging behind her. Bennick went next with a grim nod, and Sylas last, his expression unreadable, already halfway to wherever the future would carry us. One by one, they disappeared in brief flashes of light, swallowed by the portal's living flame.

I lingered a moment longer, heart thudding in my chest. The archway pulsed with heat, the runes along its edges flickering like breath drawn in and out. The portal shimmered like molten glass, a liquid veil of fire that bent light and air alike. The smell of it reached me fully now…metallic and sharp, like hot iron scraped across stone.

Beneath that, there was sulfur and scorched earth, and something older still: petrichor laced with smoke, as if the storm-washed bones of the world had been ground down and fed into its heart. It was a scent I'd never forget, ancient, unclean, and alive. I turned once, one last time. Orion stood still, arms crossed, a towering figure of fire-forged strength.

His golden eyes watched me…steady, unblinking, the way a mountain might watch the sky. Ileyana stood beside him, arms folded across her chest, her silver-threaded cloak stirring in the wind. Her gaze was softer, but no less fierce. She didn't speak, only nodded once. There was something in her eyes I didn't yet have words for. Not goodbye. Not pride. Something deeper. Something I might one day understand.

This was their place, I realized. Here, at the edge of the known world, where ancient power still curled beneath the earth like sleeping roots. They weren't meant to follow. They were guardians, keepers of what had come before. We were the ones meant to walk into what came next. I took a breath, stepped forward. The fire

curled around me, not burning but alive, brushing over my skin like wind off a forge.

The heat clung to me, heavy and clean, and the scent hit all at once…char, lightning, and the crisp edge of something wild and eternal. It filled my lungs, lodged in my throat, and for a breathless heartbeat, I felt as though I had stepped into the pulse of the world itself. Then the flame closed behind me, the heat dissolved into nothing, and the world…everything I had known…fell away.

CHAPTER 21: SYLVARIS: LAND OF THE ELVEN

The world reassembled itself in fragments of light and sound. Heat gave way to cold, the scent of char and lightning dissolved into damp moss and the sweetness of decaying leaves. My feet touched down on soft earth, and for a moment, my senses struggled to adjust.

We had emerged in a wide glade surrounded by towering trees, their bark silver-gray and glowing faintly in the gloom of the canopy above. Mist clung low to the ground like breath frozen in time, and shafts of pale, unnatural light filtered down through the leaves, illuminating the forest in eerie hues of blue and green. The air was cool but not lifeless there was still magic here, though it clung to the bones of the world like a dying ember refusing to go out.

Ahead of me, the others had already gathered, Kaelen standing a few paces forward, his posture still, his gaze stretched out over the forest. I stepped up beside him, watching the strange stillness of the land unfold: vines that moved like slow breath, trees

that stood too quiet, and a silence that ran deeper than the absence of sound. It was the silence of memory, of loss.

"This is Sylvaris," Kaelen said, and though his voice was even, I heard the ache buried beneath it. "My homeland." We all turned to him. His eyes were distant, his shoulders squared as if holding the weight of centuries. "I haven't been back in over two years…It wasn't always like this," he said.

We settled into an old, abandoned building, its walls cracked and its foundation crumbling under the weight of time. The structure, though still standing, seemed barely able to hold itself together. I could hear the faint groan of wood and stone settling, the occasional rustle of something small skittering through the debris. I glanced at Kaelen, who studied the building with a mixture of nostalgia and wariness. It was clear that he had been here before, and the sight of it now, in such a fragile state, seemed to tug at something deep within him.

"This place... it was once full of life," he murmured, his eyes scanning the room like he was expecting to find traces of the past hidden in the dust. "But now... it's barely holding on." A soft sigh escaped him as he took a seat by the cracked fireplace, his fingers brushing the remnants of what had once been a beautiful mural on the wall…a depiction of elves and dragons soaring through a vibrant sky. It was almost too painful to look at. His gaze hardened, but his voice remained steady as he spoke again.

"Once, this land sang with life. Old stories told tales of how the elves lived within the great trees and beneath crystal canopies woven of magic and light. The dragons soared above the forests and rested in sanctuaries built in the cliffs. We didn't just coexist… we were bound. Elves and dragons were two halves of a sacred whole, but then came the war, or the Sundering, as Ileyana and Orion call it." I watched him closely, feeling the weight of his words. This wasn't a tale Kaelen had ever chosen to tell before. His usual stoic demeanor softened, the edges of his voice trembling with something I couldn't quite place. I leaned in, eager to hear more.

"There was this curse," he continued, his voice heavy with the sorrow of generations. "A deep magic, twisted from within. No one knew its source… some say it came from betrayal, others from something older, something buried, but it tore the bond apart. In

time, it was uncovered that only those who misuse dark or blood magic catch the disease. However, before this was discovered, the dragons fled. The forests began to rot from the inside out. The rivers dried, the roots went silent, and the elves… we scattered. Isolated ourselves. Clan from clan. City from city. Some gave up their magic. Others vanished into the deep woods, never to return."

I let my gaze drift across the glade, the sight of it leaving a hollow feeling in my chest. What should have been a place of vibrant life now held only the faded ghosts of it. The trees stood gnarled and splintering, their branches reaching like skeletal hands towards a sky that no longer cared to shine. A once-grand stone arch, half-swallowed by ivy, marked the remnants of a road that had not been walked in years. The beauty was undeniable, but it was broken, lost to time. A land that remembered what it was, and mourned what it had lost.

"We're close to the outer borders of what was once the capital," Kaelen said, his voice quiet, as if speaking too loudly might break the fragile stillness that hung in the air. "Ael'thara. We'll ride there in the morning if the road hasn't crumbled completely. I don't know what we'll find, but for now, we camp…" His voice trailed off, and I could hear the weight of the unsaid words hanging between us. He was trying to remain hopeful, but the past was a heavy thing to carry.

Then, his voice grew firmer, a spark of determination returning to his violet eyes. "This isn't just about finding answers. It's about healing something that should never have been broken." Behind us, the portal shimmered once more before fading, the runes dimming to ash. Whatever lay behind was gone now, closed. The hum of magic that had accompanied us through our journey had faded, leaving nothing but silence in its wake. Before us stood the ruins of a kingdom, a land starving for magic, for purpose, for hope. We were the first breath it had drawn in a long, long time.

While Kaelen began to prepare a meal over the crackling fire, a quiet murmur reached my ears, and I glanced over to find that Aeris had slipped away unnoticed by all but me. He moved with the ease of someone who had done this countless times, a predator in his own right. His wings seemed to ripple in the air, and for a moment, I wondered where he was going, but then, with a knowing glance

shared between us, I understood. Aeris needed space…time to think, to breathe, away from the growing tensions of the group. Kaelen, Tamsin, and the others focused on the task of preparing lunch, but I couldn't shake the feeling that something had shifted, even if it was just the quiet departure of one among us. I didn't know where Aeris had gone, but I knew he would return when he was ready.

As the smell of roasted meat filled the air, mingling with the scent of smoke from the fire, I couldn't help but wonder what the future held for us. This place, this land that had once thrived, seemed to whisper of possibilities and secrets long buried. We weren't just here to uncover answers about the curse, about the dragons or the elves.

We were here to understand the very heart of Sylvaris…and perhaps, in doing so, heal it. The warmth from the fire flickered softly around us when a strange sound began to fill the air…a distant, steady roar. At first, it was subtle, almost like the rumble of thunder far off on the horizon, but it grew louder with every passing minute. The sound of rushing water.

I glanced at Kaelen, who had already noticed it, his brow furrowing slightly as he scanned the surroundings, trying to locate the source. "That's the sound of the waterfalls," he explained calmly, as though it was nothing out of the ordinary. Kaelen turned toward me; his voice was steady but filled with a touch of sadness.

"This region is known for its many waterfalls," he began, gesturing toward the distant sound of rushing water. "They run through the forest, hidden within the folds of the land. Some are small, others large, but they've always been a part of Sylvaris. The water used to flow like the lifeblood of the land, filling the rivers and nourishing the trees. Now, it's the only thing that still seems to have some strength left."

As Kaelen finished speaking, the sound of rushing water grew louder, pulling his attention toward the distant waterfall. I was sitting off to the side and focusing more on the food being prepared, but looked up at the mention of waterfalls, clearly not understanding. "Waterfalls?" I asked, a pure picture of confusion. "You've never seen one?" he asked. "Well, imagine a river or stream falling from a height, crashing down into a pool below."

The force creates a roar, the sound of the water striking the rocks below. In Sylvaris, many of them are sacred…places where elves used to go for meditation or where dragons would rest during the warmer months." I nod in understanding, though my expression suggested that I still didn't fully grasp the concept, which I didn't. The idea of such a natural phenomenon seemed foreign to me.

He paused for a moment, allowing the sound to fill the air before continuing. "There are creatures that live in these waters, some tied to the old magic of this land. The Koi of Serenity, for example. In the tranquil ponds near Ael'thara, they're revered for their graceful movements and vibrant colors. Some legends say they can grow to immense sizes, their scales reflecting the stars. Gazing upon them is said to bring visions of the future, a symbol of perseverance and transformation." Kaelen's eyes lit up as he spoke, clearly passionate about the creatures of his homeland. "And then there are the Lumina Minnows. Delicate fish with translucent scales that glow in dimly lit waters. They're believed to guide lost travelers, representing hope and safety in times of need."

He smiled at the thought before continuing, "In the shallow pools, you'll find Emberfin Gobies. They're small but lively, with orange and red hues like flickering flames. They're playful, always leaping over obstacles in the water as if daring the currents to catch them." My brow furrowed in curiosity, but Kaelen didn't seem to notice as he pressed on, describing the Whispering Catfish. "They're silver fish, small but known for the gentle, melodic sounds they produce by vibrating their swim bladders. It's said that the whispers they create carry messages from the spirit world, making them sacred to many cultures here."

Sera, who had been listening intently, seemed captivated. "And the Veilfin Bettas?" she asked, her voice soft with intrigue. Kaelen's smile deepened. "Yes, the Veilfin Bettas. Their flowing fins trail behind them like veils, and they come in an assortment of colors. They're admired for their beauty, often kept in ornate glass tanks as living art." "And the Crystal Shrimp?" Sera added, already imagining the delicate creatures.

Kaelen nodded, his eyes reflecting a sense of reverence. "The Crystal Shrimp are small and translucent, their bodies

shimmering in the light. They scuttle along the riverbeds, creating a mesmerizing display with every movement." He sighed, his gaze drifting over the land, almost lost in thought. "These creatures, these symbols of the land's vitality, were once what Sylvaris thrived on. Now they serve as reminders of what has been lost."

As Kaelen continued speaking about the history of the land, my attention started to drift, and a sense of unease began to settle in. The sound of rushing water grew louder, more insistent, as though something inside the land was stirring. I felt a sudden shift in the air, an almost imperceptible change, and then it hit me, I remembered that Aeris was still gone. I scanned the room, looking for his familiar form, but there was no sign of the dragon. It was as though he had slipped away without a sound. Panic washed over me.

I stood quickly, casting a glance at Sera, who was distracted by the food. I muttered his name softly, my heart beginning to race. "Aeris…" I murmured under my breath, but there was no sign of him. Sera, now realizing what was wrong, turned toward the open door, feeling the absence of his presence keenly. The sound of rushing water had grown louder, pulling at her, beckoning her toward it like a call from deep within the land itself. Sera slipped through the broken doorway and into the open air.

Following Sera's Point of View

The wind was cool, fragrant with earth and moss, and it carried the sound of the waterfall more clearly now, calling me further into the forest. There was something in the air, and the pull of it was undeniable. I stopped for a moment at the edge of the ruin, the overgrown landscape stretching out before me. The sound of the water roared like a heartbeat, and I couldn't help but feel that Aeris was somewhere ahead, drawn to it just as I was.

He had slipped away without anyone noticing. I think he may have needed a little time to himself, but I could feel this…pull toward him. It was like I knew exactly where he was. At this point my interest in him was more than just curiosity; it was an instinct to reconnect with him, to stay near him at all times.

I turned back just in time to see Haji glance up. Before she could speak, I was already gone, drawn toward the rushing water and the magic that seemed to vibrate just beneath the surface. I was certain that whatever was waiting for us at the source of the water would reveal something significant…something waiting for us to uncover it.

The air around me was thick with the scent of damp earth and moss, the cool breeze carrying the distant roar of the waterfall like a beckoning call. My heart quickened, an inexplicable pull urging me forward. Each step felt deliberate, as if the forest itself guided me toward something…or someone…unknown.

The underbrush thickened, and the path narrowed, but I pressed on, driven by an instinct I couldn't name. As I neared the source of the sound, the trees parted, revealing a hidden glade bathed in the soft light filtering through the canopy. The waterfall cascaded down a jagged cliff, its waters crashing into a pool below, sending mist into the air. The scene was serene, almost otherworldly, and at its center stood a figure…a man, tall and imposing, standing in the shallows of the pool.

He was unlike anyone I had ever seen. His height was striking…easily taller than six feet and his physique was lean yet muscular, the kind that spoke of both strength and agility. His skin was pale, almost luminous, with a subtle shimmer that hinted at something uncanny. His hair was dark, streaked with gold that caught the light, but it was his eyes that captivated me…amber, molten, burning with an inner fire that seemed to pierce through the very fabric of reality.

He stood there, unaware of my presence. His movements were fluid, graceful, as he bathed in the cool waters, the golden embroidery on his dark clothing catching the sunlight. He exuded a regal aura, a presence that demanded attention even in his solitude. I felt rooted to the spot, my breath caught in my throat. There was an undeniable pull toward him, a magnetic force that drew me in, compelling me to approach.

I took a tentative step forward, my footfall muffled by the soft earth. The sound seemed to reach him, for he froze, his posture stiffening as if sensing something…or someone…was near. Slowly, he turned, and our gazes met. His amber eyes locked onto mine, and for a moment, time seemed to stand still.

The world around us faded, leaving only the two of us in that suspended reality. His expression was unreadable, a mask of

calm that betrayed nothing, but beneath it, I sensed a storm…a turmoil that mirrored the tempest within me. My heart raced, my pulse quickened, and warmth spread through me, not from the sun, but from something deeper, something primal. I felt exposed, vulnerable, yet strangely safe. I was exactly where I was meant to be. I opened my mouth to speak, to call out to him, but no words came. The connection between us was so intense, so consuming, that language seemed inadequate.

Instead, I took another step forward, my body moving of its own accord, drawn to him by forces I couldn't comprehend. He remained still, watching me, his gaze unwavering. The tension between us was palpable, thickening the air, making it hard to breathe. I didn't know what to expect, what would happen next, but in that moment, I knew one thing for certain: I was no longer just an observer in this world.

I was part of it, intertwined with him, bound by fate or magic or something beyond understanding. As I closed the distance between us, I realized that it was Aeris…it had to be… and whatever lay ahead, I was ready to face it…together with him. "…Sera…"

The sound of my name, spoken in his voice, hit me like a wave crashing against the shore…soft, yet powerful enough to knock the breath from my lungs. It was the first time I had heard him say it, and it carried a weight that rooted me to the earth.

His voice was deep, but not harsh…a smooth, molten tone that rolled over me like warm smoke, curling into the hidden spaces of my chest and setting something alight. There was surprise in it, yes, but also a quiet reverence, as if he hadn't expected me to find him, or perhaps hadn't wanted me to, but was no longer certain which he preferred.

My name on his lips felt intimate, sacred in a way I wasn't prepared for. It wasn't just the way he said it…it was how it lingered afterward, like a whispered promise carried on the mist. Something in my chest tightened. I hadn't realized how much I needed to hear it, how much I had yearned to be seen by him…not just looked at, but truly seen, known.

His gaze held mine, and in it I saw the echo of the dragon…ancient, proud, powerful…but there was something else too. Vulnerability. It flickered in the gold of his irises like firelight across polished stone, subtle and fleeting. His bare chest rose and fell with the rhythm of his breath, droplets of water tracing down his skin, catching the light. His expression was unreadable, but his eyes… his eyes betrayed everything.

I stepped closer, only several feet now between us, and I felt my pulse in my throat. My heart ached with the silence; swollen with emotions I couldn't name. I didn't know what he saw in me at that moment, or if he could sense the way my thoughts scattered like leaves in the wind, but something told me he did. I had felt drawn to him from the very beginning, but this was different.

This was no longer curiosity…it was gravity. It was destiny, and now, he had spoken my name like it meant something. I swallowed hard, my voice caught somewhere between breath and hope. "Aeris…I was worried," I whispered, the words sounding insignificant compared to the roar of the waterfall, yet somehow I knew he heard them. Every part of him seemed attuned, like a creature of instinct and old magic. He didn't move, but the way his eyes softened ever so slightly told me he understood.

Aeris took a slow step toward me, water rippling around his legs as he moved through the shallows. His presence was commanding…not in the way of a warrior or a king, but in something far older, elemental, like the wind shifting the course of birds or the tide pulling the ocean's edge. His movements felt guided by some ancient rhythm, each one echoing inside me as though we were tethered to the same pulse. "I didn't mean to be gone long," he said, his voice gentle and resonant, like the wind whispering through high branches. "The water called to me… I needed to remember something of what I am. Of what I was. I haven't taken this form in so long,"

His gaze dropped to the pool, the golden light of his eyes flickering across the surface like twin suns. "It's easy to forget when I'm always surrounded by war, by ruin." There was something fragile in his words, and the vulnerability in his tone sent a shiver through me. I had never heard Aeris speak… it was soft, unguarded, stripped of the mystery he usually cloaked himself in. The roar of the waterfall, the mist curling between us, all of it faded beneath the weight of his truth. He continued, "I wanted to show you who I was…who I am…I was scared you would reject me like so many others…”

I took a step closer, the moss beneath my boots damp and pliant, the air thick with the scent of water and stone. “You don’t have to explain,” I whispered, my voice barely more than breath. “But I felt it too… the pull. Like I had to find you.” His head lifted, and something flickered across his expression…surprise, disbelief, hope. “You feel it too?” he asked, as if daring to believe it.

I nodded, unable to find words to describe the ache that had drawn me here or the strange rightness of standing in this moment with him. He stepped from the water, the light catching on the golden streaks in his hair, droplets glistening against his luminous skin like starlight on marble. Though he towered over me, I didn’t feel small. I felt grounded, anchored in the way his gaze held mine, in the way his presence filled the air between us.

“I’ve never… felt this with anyone before,” he said quietly. “I can’t explain it. It’s like if I lost you, then I would lose a part of myself, and I know that’s a lot, you don’t know me…” The silence that followed was full…not empty, but rich with the weight of things unsaid questions, longing, the hum of something new taking shape. I didn't speak. I didn't need to. The forest itself seemed to hold its breath with me, as though it, too, recognized the shift. Whatever tomorrow held…ruins, danger, answers…I knew this much in my bones: I wasn't alone anymore, and neither was he.

Aeris, now in water to his thighs, stood there, just watching. I took a deep breath and stepped into the water. His body became more tense with every step. As I grew near, he just stood and watched me with those golden eyes. The water was cold at first…sharp and startling…but it quickly warmed where it lapped against my legs.

Each step I took stirred up soft clouds of silt beneath the surface, and the sound of the falls seemed to dull, like the world was growing quieter just for us. I kept my eyes on Aeris, watching the rise and fall of his chest, the tight line of his shoulders, the subtle tremor in his hands as I drew near.

He wasn't just watching me; he was absorbing everything…my hesitation, my heartbeat, the way my breath caught in my throat. The shimmer of his skin under the misted light, the

glowing strands of gold threaded through his dark, tousled hair…it all pulled at something deep and instinctual inside me. It was his scent that truly unraveled me: warm and wild, like sunlit cedarwood and storm-kissed air, edged with the faint, smoky trace of something ancient…something draconic.

It was wrapped around me, subtle and magnetic, awakening a part of me I hadn't known was waiting for him. I stopped when I was only a few feet away, the water reaching just above my knees now, and for a moment we simply stood there, suspended between breath and decision, the space between us thrumming with unspoken gravity.

His voice came again, lower this time, almost reverent. "I didn't expect you to come after me." His gaze flicked over my face, lingering at my mouth, my eyes. "Most people… they walk away once they see what I really am. Once they feel what I carry." There was something ancient behind his words, an ache shaped over centuries.

I wanted to speak, to tell him I wasn't like them…but the words didn't come. Instead, I reached out, slowly, carefully, letting

500

my fingers hover just inches from his. The air between us sparked faintly, like the edge of a storm just beginning to stir. "I don't want to walk away," I said. "I don't think I could, even if I tried."

Aeris's lips parted, just barely. That single breath between us was heavier than anything I'd ever known. His golden eyes flickered…shifting, deepening…like twin hearths burning in the shadows. "You feel it too," he whispered again, not as a question this time, but a truth he was only just allowing himself to believe, and I did. It wasn't something I could explain. It wasn't rational or even entirely safe, but it was real…raw and overwhelming and utterly undeniable.

He slowly closed the space between us, the tips of his fingers brushing against mine. It wasn't a grand gesture, but something quiet and sacred, like the beginning of a vow neither of us had spoken aloud. The contact sent a jolt through me…not painful, not frightening, but electric. Like something waking up inside me that had been waiting for this exact moment.

For a long time, we just stood there, skin to skin, hands half-entwined, eyes locked. Around us, the mist curled like smoke, the water moved in slow currents, and the earth beneath our feet hummed softly with approval, as though the land itself remembered the bond that once was. I had come here thinking I'd lost him. That I might find a dragon broken by a cursed world, but instead, I'd found a man standing at the edge of something he didn't fully understand…and offering me a place beside him.

When he finally spoke again, his voice was barely audible over the waterfall. "Stay." One word. One plea. Not a demand, not a command…just a hope. I stepped in closer, until the space between us was gone, until I could feel his breath on my skin, and I whispered back, "Always."

CHAPTER 22: ÆRIS'S TRUTH

We were all sitting by the fire when Sera and Aeris came back, but they didn't come back with the typical thuds of his heavy steps in dragon form. Instead, it was quiet…and that's when we saw him for the first time. At first, none of us spoke.

The crackling fire was the only sound as he stepped into the firelight. For a moment, we didn't even recognize him. The towering figure that emerged beside Sera wasn't the massive, scaled beast we had grown used to, but a man…though even calling him that felt too ordinary. He moved with a quiet, unnerving grace, like a predator used to the weight of his own power but choosing restraint.

His black hair, streaked with glints of gold, caught the firelight in such a way that it looked like it was burning from within. The golden embroidery on his cloak shimmered faintly, echoing the same regal bearing he carried even in his true form. However, those eyes…Mother Above, those eyes. Even without his dragon visage, they held the same intensity, the same ancient, molten fire.

Tamsin was the first to speak, her voice barely above a whisper. "Aeris…?" He gave a small nod, and something in that simple gesture, quiet and solemn, confirmed what our eyes were still struggling to accept. He was beautiful in a way that felt otherworldly, terrible, and divine all at once.

Bennick stood, perhaps to get a better look…or maybe to brace himself. He finally pushed out, "So this… this is what you really are." "No," Aeris said, his voice deep, resonant, and unmistakably familiar. "This is only part of me, but it's the part I've hidden the longest." Silence stretched again. We weren't just seeing him…we were witnessing a revelation.

For the first time, the veil between dragon and man had lifted, and in its place stood a figure that belonged to both worlds and yet neither. Tamsin's breath caught in her throat. She'd always been the most empathetic among us, the one who spoke to Aeris not just as a dragon but as a person beneath the scales. Still, seeing him like this…beautiful, human, and undeniably regal…shook her.

Her eyes glistened with awe, maybe even sadness, like she was seeing the ghost of someone she'd always sensed but never truly met. "You look like the stories," she murmured. "The ones about the golden kings of old." Bennick, ever the skeptic and soldier, kept his arms crossed, jaw tight. He didn't trust easily, and change unsettled him more than he liked to admit. "So, what now?" he asked, tone clipped. "You going to start sitting on a throne and giving us orders?" Beneath the sarcasm was something else…uncertainty. The power Aeris radiated, even as a man, made it clear: he was not just a companion on the road. He was something ancient, something sovereign.

Kaelen, who had been quietly sharpening his blade moments earlier, now held it still in his hand. His eyes scanned him like he would a puzzle…an enemy or an artifact. "You've been hiding this the whole time?" he asked, voice calm but probing. "Why show us now?" His hand didn't move toward his weapon, and his gaze lingered longer than he probably realized.

Sylas, gaped openly. His eyes went wide, darting from Aeris' eyes to the gold-stitched cloak, to the way the light seemed to ripple against his skin. "You're like a hero from a song," he blurted, then immediately looked mortified. "I mean…not that you weren't

cool before, but this is… wow." Sera stood silently beside him, unreadable as always, but her posture was relaxed, protective even. She had known, of course.

Her eyes scanned the group, wary not of Aeris, but of our reactions. She took a small step closer to him, as if to say: *He's still ours. Don't forget that.* Then there was me. I didn't speak at first. I was still trying to match this tall, gleaming figure with the dragon I'd silently spoke to through storms, whose roars had split mountains, whose silence sometimes spoke louder than our words.

Even so, he *was* still Aeris. The way he held his shoulders, the quiet watchfulness, the weight of his presence…it was all still there. Just… distilled into a different shape. "You've always been more than you let on," I finally said. "But I didn't realize how much you were carrying." He met my eyes, and for the first time, I saw not just power in that molten gaze…but vulnerability. "I wasn't sure if you'd still see *me,*" he said, and just like that, the firelight didn't seem so warm anymore…because we all understood that this wasn't just a reveal. It was a risk. A plea, and maybe, a beginning.

For a long moment, none of us said anything. The fire crackled in the center of our circle, throwing shadows against the trees, but it might as well have been silent for how still everything became. I could feel the shift, not just in the air, but in the weight of what we were seeing. Aeris stood before us, not as the dragon we'd known, not quite as the man he rarely chose to be, but as something in between. Something raw. Something real.

Bennick rose slowly, his movements stiff, like he couldn't decide whether to draw his blade or just steady himself. It wasn't silence that followed. Not really. It was more like a collective breath held too long. Like we were all afraid to move, afraid that if we spoke too quickly, the truth would vanish into smoke. I couldn't stop staring at him. Aeris…no, Aeris'Kal. Regal and sharp-edged in a way that didn't belong to either man or dragon. Just… him. Beside me, Tamsin's breath caught again, even she looked shaken. Her eyes were wide with something like awe, and maybe grief too.

Then Tamsin, ever unafraid to cut through the quiet, leaned forward, her tone low but clear. "So," she asked, "Why now? What changed?" Aeris' gaze lifted to her, then drifted across each of us.

He didn't answer right away, and when he did, it wasn't with the voice of a dragon…it was softer, uncertain. "For a long time," he began, "I thought being what I am would only ever make me more alone." He stepped toward the fire, and its light played across the sharp angles of his face, catching the gold in his eyes like a buried sun. "I was born into a lineage older than this continent…dragons of red and fire, sworn to keep balance. Revered. However, when I came into this world, I bore not the blazing red of my ancestors… but black scales. A mark of ruin, they called it. A curse."

Even Bennick, who lived with doubt sharpened into instinct, softened at that. Aeris didn't stop. "They cast me out before I ever spoke my name. My own kin saw me as an omen. The elves…more cautious still…feared what I might become. So, I wandered. Alone. For centuries. I survived off instinct, off silence. I trained not to prove my worth, but because I had no one to guard me. I carried the name Aeris'Kal because no one else would give me one." His hand rose to the pendant at his throat…the one we'd all noticed, all ignored. "I mastered old magics, ancient paths. Not because I wanted acceptance. Because it was the only way to keep going."

Then, quietly, almost like a confession, he said, "Until Sera." He didn't need to look at her. We all felt the shift, the center of his gravity pulling subtly toward where she stood. "She saw me. Not the exile, not the dragon, just… me. She stayed even when I didn't want her to. When I snarled, when I shut her out…she stayed." His voice faltered for a breath, then steadied. "She reminded me that I didn't have to be what they feared. That maybe, just maybe, I could be more." His eyes swept over us again, that molten gold softened now with something close to vulnerability.

"I wore masks for centuries. I was too much for dragons, too much dragon for elves. Even among you all, I never believed I could show you both. I thought you only accepted the beast… not the man I might be underneath." His gaze met mine then, and I felt something in my chest crack open, something I hadn't realized I'd been holding back. "But Sera showed me that hiding wasn't protection. It was distance, and when you trust someone enough to bleed beside them, to fight with them… you owe them the truth of who you are."

Sera's voice came then, soft but firm. "He used to think hiding kept us safe, but a mask can become a cage if you wear it too long." Kaelen broke the silence next, his brows drawn together. "But weren't you scared?" he asked. "That we'd see you differently?" Aeris nodded once. "I was scared. Still am, but fear doesn't have to mean retreat. Sera reminded me that fear is only weakness when it stops us from choosing honesty, and I was tired of being afraid of myself."

Sylas let out a breath like he'd been holding it the whole time and muttered, "Well, now I get why you always looked at Sera like she was the stars." Sylas smiled faintly. "You found it in her…Strength." I glanced at Aeris just in time to see him look at Sera again, his eyes holding a warmth I hadn't seen there before. He didn't have to say anything. We all understood.

Tamsin stepped closer, her voice thick. "You've already done what most of us never could. You chose to become whole. That matters more than gold or prophecy." Bennick gave a short nod. Not

510

full agreement, but something close. "You've bled beside us," he said. "That's more real than lineage." Finally, Sera…still and unwavering…spoke again, this time to all of us. "He's not asking us to follow him. He's showing us the man who stayed when he had every reason to fly."

I… I couldn't speak at first. I kept thinking about all the nights I'd sat beside him in silence. Yet here he was…not just a beast or a legend, not even the warrior we'd relied on…but the soul that had never been allowed to be whole. In that moment, I understood something I hadn't before. This wasn't the end of a secret. It was the beginning of belonging.

The tension didn't disappear, not really, but it changed, settled into something gentler, like steam rolling off sun-warmed stone after a hard rain. We didn't speak about what had just happened. Not directly. Instead, we passed food around the fire in quiet solidarity. Tamsin handed out roasted roots she'd cooked earlier, and Bennick, still visibly chewing on his thoughts, shared what remained of the salted elk.

No one said it, but the act of eating together felt like a line in the sand…one we had all silently chosen not to cross alone. Aeris remained quiet, seated beside Sera with a gravity that felt ancient. Even in his human form, he radiated something that felt larger than the body he wore. Regal without meaning to be. His eyes flicked between the flames and us, thoughtful, perhaps still unsure if the fragile thread of trust he'd offered would hold.

Kaelen cleared his throat after a while, breaking the stillness. "We're still heading for Ael'thara tomorrow." His voice was steady, but I knew him too well not to notice the undercurrent beneath. Not nerves, exactly…more like the long breath before diving beneath freezing water. The thought of returning home after so long…was a wound I could still feel pulsing in him. I nodded from across the fire, my hand finding his beneath the blanket and squeezing once.

"We should reach the outer forest by noon, if we don't dawdle." I tried to say it lightly, but the weight of what waited in the Elven Kingdom pressed against the edge of my voice. His parents.

The court. Everything he'd walked away from more than two years ago.

Sylas was the first to cut the mood with something like humor. "Can't wait to see their faces," he said, voice too bright. "Nothing like storming into a royal palace with two extra dragons and a band of semi-reformed miscreants." Tamsin gave a dry chuckle. "You forgot 'bard with a mouth too big for his boots.'"

"Excuse you," Sylas said with mock offense. "My boots are perfectly sized for my lyrical genius."

Bennick, who'd stayed mostly silent, glanced Kaelen's way. "They'll hear you out," he said. It was the closest he came to offering comfort, but Kaelen gave a faint nod, like it was enough. Aeris finally spoke, his voice low but firm. "You won't be walking in alone." His gaze swept over all of us…not demanding, just certain. "We've faced worse things than elven courts, and we faced them together."

Tamsin stirred the fire with a stick, sending sparks into the dark. "Let's just hope they're more reasonable than your average flesh-devouring dragon." One by one, we drifted into our quiet

rituals. Tamsin took first watch, as usual. Bennick checked the perimeter. Sera and Aeris stayed by the embers, speaking softly, shadows wrapping around them like a cloak.

Kaelen leaned against me, his hand still wrapped in mine. I could feel his heartbeat, steady but tense. He didn't say much…he didn't have to. I knew what it cost him to go back. When I finally lay down, the stars overhead shimmered clearer than I remembered. Maybe it was the clarity that comes after breaking a silence. Maybe it was that, for the first time in a long time, there were no more masks between us.

Morning broke pale and quiet. Mist curled through the trees, and the ground was still damp with dew. We moved through our routines in a kind of half-silence, but it wasn't tension…it was focus. Bennick packed the tents with efficient precision, while Sylas hummed something tuneless as he double-checked his satchel for ink and paper. Kaelen stood at the edge of the clearing, staring toward the trees that marked the edge of Ael'thara's borders. I joined him there, brushing a lock of hair from his cheek, and he leaned into the touch like a man holding onto something solid.

Aeris remained in human form, his cloak trailing behind him, dark fabric glinting with the subtle gold of his lineage. Sera walked at his side, her armor already donned, calm as ever…but her eyes stayed sharp, scanning the trees like she could already feel the weight of court scrutiny. No one had to say it. We all knew what today was. Not just another leg of our journey…but the one where history might come calling. For the first time, we were ready to answer.

The towering gates of Ael'thara rose before us like a wall of starlight, etched with runes older than memory and bound in silvery vines that pulsed faintly with magic. Sunlight filtered through the trees in shafts of gold, painting the forest path in otherworldly hues as we approached the elven capital. Even from here, we could feel the hum of the wards woven into the air…ancient protections that had guarded the kingdom for thousands of years.

A dozen elven guards stood at attention beneath the arched threshold, clad in living armor that shimmered like layered leaves, their expressions unreadable as we approached. Without hesitation,

two stepped forward and crossed their halberds, blocking the path with a snap of steel. "Halt," one commanded, his voice clipped and formal. "State your names and purpose in Ael'thara."

Kaelen stood beside me, silent, still wrapped in his dark cloak, the hood shadowing most of his face. He had barely spoken during the last stretch of the journey, a tension building in him the closer we got to home. Now, he stepped forward without a word. He reached up slowly, pushed back the hood, and revealed the truth he had worn in silence. Silver hair, sun-touched and windblown, spilled around his shoulders. A circlet of silver and midnight opal caught the light beneath his cloak.

His eyes…icy violet and unmistakably royal…met the captains with quiet power. "Kaelen of House Arathiel," he said, his voice carrying the calm strength of a name that had not been spoken here in two years. "Second born of King Valorian Arathiel and Queen Miraelen Arathiel. I return from my passage."

The silence that followed struck like a bell through glass. The guards stared, stunned. Then the captain dropped to one knee, helm pressed to his chest, eyes wide in awe. "My prince," he whispered. One by one, the others followed, kneeling in perfect synchronicity as the weight of Kaelen's identity settled over them like falling snow. Behind us, Sylas let out a low, breathless whistle. "Well. That's one way to knock." Tamsin arched an eyebrow, murmuring under her breath, "They weren't expecting this." Kaelen remained still, watching the guards with a detached calm. "They weren't expecting me so soon," he said quietly, as though answering a question we hadn't asked.

The great gates of Ael'thara opened with a soft groan, vines unraveling from their sacred wards, the runes glowing faintly as they withdrew. We stepped into the elven capital not as wanderers or strangers, but as something more dangerous…changed. The city bloomed before us in sweeping spires of white and silver, trees with trunks wide as towers twisting upward into the sky. Songbirds scattered in the canopy overhead, and magic shimmered faintly in the air, a symphony of ancient life.

The streets curved gently beneath our feet, paved in silver stone, each step echoing with memories Kaelen had left behind. He walked ahead now, shoulders straight, his hand finding mine in the

quiet, holding fast. "I'm home," he whispered, but not to me…only to himself. There was something in the way he said it that made me tighten my grip.

The scent of Ael'thara was unlike anywhere else in the world. It hung thick in the air…fresh rain on ancient bark, crushed herbs underfoot, and the sweet floral perfume of moon vine blossoms that bloomed only under elven light. Beneath it all was something older, earthier…the musk of magic too old to name. Every inhale stirred something deep in the chest, like memory and prophecy intertwined. Kaelen led us down the broad arching path just inside the gates, the hush that followed our entry interrupted only by the shift of armor and the soft whisper of leaves.

The captain stood quickly, breath caught in his throat and turned to his men. "Alert the palace," he barked, voice ringing sharp and urgent. "Send word to the King and Queen…their son has returned. Now!" Two of the younger soldiers, still wide-eyed, broke formation at once and sprinted down the silver stone causeway that arched over the flowing river.

Even at a distance, I could hear the echo of their boots on the bridge as they vanished beneath the lattice of ivy-wrapped arches that led deeper into the heart of the city. The remaining guards stood straighter, reverence etched into every movement, their hands pressed over their hearts in salute as we passed.

Around us, the elven capital unfolded like a living dream. Buildings rose with organic elegance, carved from pale stone and woven seamlessly into the trees. Balconies bloomed like petals from spiraling towers, trailing silk banners embroidered with stars and constellations. Light flickered across crystal lanterns, casting faint reflections of sky and leaves along the curved walkways.

Children paused in their games, ears twitching at the disturbance, and shopkeepers stilled in the middle of tending their wares, eyes widening as they caught sight of Kaelen. Somewhere to our left, the scent of honey-bread and steamed root wine drifted from an open-air café, blending with the sharp tang of juniper from a nearby apothecary.

It was beautiful…achingly so…and every step deeper into the city made Kaelen's fingers tighten around mine. Sylas was quiet,

his usual mischief softened by the awe that filled the air like golden dust. Tamsin walked beside him, her sharp eyes scanning the balconies and rooftops, not out of caution…but reverence. Bennick's hand hovered near his blade, but his posture was relaxed, not defensive; he knew we were safe here, even if his instincts didn't.

Ahead, the palace came into view, half-grown, half-carved from the trunk of the oldest tree in the kingdom…the World Tree, as Kaelen explained the night before. Its canopy vanished into the heavens, and its base was as wide as a castle. Vines of silver-threaded blossom wound along the carved stairs, and a soft blue glow emanated from the arched windows high above.

Kaelen slowed as we reached the base of the great stair. The guards here did not move…did not challenge us…for word had clearly already reached them. They parted in silence, heads bowed, and the great double doors of the palace began to open of their own accord, creaking outward like a heartbeat. There, framed in the arch of living stone and glowing wood, stood the King and Queen of Ael'thara.

CHAPTER 23: THE ROYAL REUNION

The moment the palace doors opened, the world seemed to still. Light spilled out like molten silver, catching on the pristine marble floor and the shimmering arcane sigils embedded within it. At the top of the wide, sweeping staircase that led into the heart of the palace stood two figures who could have stepped from the pages of a myth.

Queen Miraelen was ethereal, haunting in her beauty…waist-length black hair cascading like midnight silk down her back, piercing blue eyes dimmed by years of worry and quiet sorrow. Her pale skin was touched by moonlight, and she wore layered robes of deep blue and ash-grey, adorned with delicate, arcane embroidery that whispered of long-forgotten magic.

Many of the threads had faded with time, their brilliance dulled but not diminished. She looked more like a statue carved to honor a goddess than a woman of flesh and blood…regal, distant, a presence that lingered with the weight of remembrance. When her eyes found Kaelen, that statuesque calm shattered.

Her lips parted, trembling, and a breath escaped her that sounded more like prayer than speech. Without waiting for decorum or formality, she moved, the elegance of her every step folding into something raw and maternal as she ran…truly ran…down the stairs, her layered robes whispering around her like falling leaves.

"Kaelen…" She gasped, his name a fragile shard of sound wrapped in wonder, grief, and joy, and then she was in his arms, clutching him with all the desperation of a mother who had counted every day of her child's absence. Her fingers fisted into the fabric of his cloak, her shoulders wracked with sobs that pulled from a place deeper than memory, as though in holding him, she was trying to erase the ache of the years he had been gone.

Kaelen held her just as tightly, his face buried in her shoulder, his body rigid from the force of emotion too long restrained. He said nothing, only let her cry, only held on. At the top of the steps, King Valorian watched in silence. His tall, broad frame was wrapped in regal robes of forest green and silver, elegant yet practical, each fold adorned with symbols representing the kingdom he ruled, the people he governed, and the many sacrifices he had made.

His long silver hair, streaked with white, fell loose across his back like threads of starlight. His face was a map of responsibility, carved with the sharp lines of time and burden. His violet eyes…piercing and solemn…remained fixed on his son. He didn't move. He didn't speak, but a single tear slid down his cheek, unbidden, cutting through the composure like a crack in polished stone.

As Queen Miraelen pulled away from Kaelen just enough to cup his face, brushing silver strands from his brow, her hands trembled. "Your light," she whispered through a watery smile. "It's stronger. You've grown into it. You shine like your father once did." Kaelen's voice was quiet, steady. "I've come back changed."

He looked past her then, toward where I stood at the base of the stairs, just behind him. His fingers found mine, and the weight of his gaze shifted everything in the air. The King followed his son's eyes and found me in the crowd, his attention sharpening in an

instant. The faint energy of the courtyard stirred, as if recognizing something sacred.

"Her aura," he said suddenly, his voice calm but resonant, as though announcing a prophecy. "Miraelen…do you see it?" The Queen turned, still catching her breath, and her gaze landed on me. Her lips parted again, this time not in grief, but in wonder. The grief in her eyes cracked into something else…recognition, hope, joy. "Oh… Kaelen…" she whispered, stepping back to look at him again, searching his face. "Is it true?"

Kaelen squeezed my hand, then turned fully to face his parents, standing straighter now, no longer just the returning son…but something more. "This is Haji," he said, reverently. "My mate. My heart. The one the stars chose for me…and the one I would have chosen even if they hadn't."

The Queen let out a soft cry and stepped toward me, her fingers now trembling for an entirely different reason. She took my hands in hers, warm and shaking with emotion. Her gaze never left mine. "You've walked beside him. Through fire, through silence, through change. I see it in you…how he leans into your presence without even thinking. How your magic bends toward his like gravity." I tried to speak, but my voice caught in my throat, so I simply nodded. "He carries the weight of the crown," I finally managed. "But he never asked me to carry it with him. I chose to." Miraelen's eyes filled again, and she leaned forward to rest her forehead gently against mine in an old elven gesture of welcome and blessing. "Then you are ours now," she whispered, "As he is."

When she stepped back, King Valorian took a slow step forward, the silent power of his presence shifting the very air. "You're not merely his equal," he said to me. "You are his balance." Kaelen looked to his father, something soft and searching in his expression. "She is the reason I could return at all. She reminded me who I was before the silence." A deep silence followed…not strained, but solemn, reverent. Around us, the elven guards who had once stood so rigidly now bowed their heads. This was no mere reunion. It was a restoration. A prince returned, a soul mended, a bond formed under starlight.

As we stepped deeper into the radiant marble halls of Ael'thara, the weight of Kaelen's return still rippling through the air like a pebble dropped into a still pool, the King's gaze shifted again. It moved past Kaelen and me, catching on another figure standing just behind us…Aeris. Even amid the grandeur and layered enchantments of the elven capital, Aeris held his own presence like a storm held behind still skies. His golden eyes, calm but never dull, met King Valorian's with the quiet poise of something ancient, something watched but never caged.

His hand remained clasped in Sera's, a tether of subtle intimacy that didn't waver. There was a moment…a heartbeat…when Valorian's entire posture changed. Not openly, but in the way a predator notices another in its domain. He stilled, sharp violet eyes narrowing slightly, not in threat, but in silent calculation. It wasn't hostility, but something far older: the instinct of a ruler sensing power that had not bowed to him.

Aeris didn't move. His stance was neither submissive nor defiant. He simply stood as he was, shaped by exile and flame, wearing nothing but truth. It was Sera who stepped forward first, slipping her hand from Aeris's with a brush of her fingers, and without hesitation, dropped to one knee before the throne.

Her silver-threaded cloak pooled around her like moonlight, and her voice, when it came, rang with calm reverence. "My King. My Queen," she said, bowing her head low. "I am Seraphine of the Crown's Guard, daughter of none but the duty I was raised to uphold. I come before you as a loyal servant of Ael'thara… and to present my mate, Aeris'Kal Nyrathos of the Flameborn." Silence settled like mist.

The very air shifted. Even the palace itself, so thick with the presence of old magics, seemed to pause. Sera remained perfectly still, head bowed not in fear, but in earned humility. It was Queen Miraelen who stirred first. Her expression…beautiful and solemn, her face ageless beneath cascades of midnight-black hair…softened.

Her pale skin caught the light of the stained-glass windows, casting faint colors across her arcane-embroidered robes. She stepped down from the dais with slow, graceful movements, as though drawn by something larger than protocol. Her vivid blue eyes widened as they rested on Aeris, her voice hushed with awe.

"The Flameborn… I thought your kind was lost to ash and memory." Her gaze swept across his form, not with suspicion, but with a fragile wonder. "No written record has spoken your name in generations, not since we found Sylas. Yet, here you stand, not as a beast, but as a man." Aeris bowed his head slightly. "I hid because I had to, but I am here now…because Sera believed I belonged and I chose to believe her."

The queen's breath caught faintly, her hand rising to touch her chest. "And you are bonded," she murmured, glancing to Sera. "It is in your aura. You are not just lovers, but life-bound." It was then the King stepped forward. His bearing was unmistakable…tall and broad, his long silver hair sweeping behind him like a mantle of snow and time. The symbols on his regal robes shimmered faintly, marks of war and peace both.

He regarded Aeris carefully, deeply, his voice quiet but ironclad. "You walk with a power few still remember. You could tear down walls with a thought… yet you choose her." "I do," Aeris replied. "I would again." The King's gaze lingered on him for a long, unreadable moment, before he finally nodded once. "Then you are known to us now, Aeris'Kal Nyrathos of the Flameborn and are

accepted." His attention turned to Sera, still kneeling. "Rise,

Seraphine. You have always served this kingdom with honor… now

you return not just as its sword, but as its future."

Sera stood, a quiet breath leaving her as though she'd been

holding it for far too long. She returned to Aeris's side without

hesitation, and when their fingers brushed again, it was with a

familiarity born not just of love, but of survival. Queen Miraelen's

eyes glistened with unshed tears as she took in the sight of them,

then turned her gaze to Kaelen, her voice warm and bittersweet.

"You bring us more than your return, my son. You bring us

a future shaped not only by blood, but by choice. Though neither of

you have completed the ceremony, you both come mated." King

Valorian's gaze, sharp and ever-observant, swept over the remainder

of our group…and landed squarely on the trio lingering a few

respectful paces behind us.

Tamsin, Sylas, and Bennick stood shoulder to shoulder,

trying…mostly unsuccessfully…to appear regal. Tamsin offered a

practiced bow, though the impish glint in her eye betrayed her

amusement. Sylas gave a flamboyant, sweeping gesture more suited for a stage than a throne room, and Bennick simply grunted and gave a two-fingered salute, already looking vaguely uncomfortable in the gilded quiet of the palace. A long pause followed, until Queen Miraelen's lips curved faintly, and she murmured, "Ah… the infamous three." Valorian's mouth twitched in what might have passed for a smile…at least by royal standards.

"I've heard stories from the border patrol captains," he said. "Tales of three wild-hearted companions who survived ambushes, negotiated with smugglers, and turned a village festival into a three-day tavern brawl… all before breakfast." "I object," Sylas said, raising a hand with mock solemnity. "It was two days, and the brawl technically started after breakfast." "Because you stole the town lord's wine cask," Tamsin added helpfully.

"He said it was ceremonial!" Sylas retorted, like that explained everything. Queen Miraelen let out a soft, melodic laugh that echoed gently through the high-arched chamber, more musical than mocking. "They remind me of the old court adventurers," she said fondly. "Those who brought chaos… and kept the court from growing too cold." Valorian nodded. "A kingdom needs its warriors, its seers… and its scoundrels."

He inclined his head to the three of them, something almost warm flickering in his gaze. "You have our gratitude for standing beside our son. Whatever you did to survive… you did well." Bennick raised an eyebrow. "Is this the part where you offer us medals?" "No," the king replied dryly. "This is the part where we let the kitchens know to triple the mead supply." Tamsin whooped, throwing her arms around Sylas and Bennick both. "I knew I liked this place!" The tension in the air, the weight of reunions and legacy and ancient magic, eased like snow melting beneath spring sun.

Laughter stirred among us, small but real, and the immense halls of Ael'thara, so solemn moments before, felt just a little less cold. Kaelen's hand found mine again, grounding me in the warmth of the moment. Around us, we were no longer wanderers or warriors or ghosts of old bloodlines…we were something simpler, something brighter. A family, mismatched and a little scarred, but bound together by choice. For the first time in what felt like ages, I looked around and saw not uncertainty, but promise. The storm was behind us…for now…and the future, strange and wild as it might be, waited just ahead, and for this night, at least, we would rest in peace.

The Queen took Kaelen's face in her hands again, tears flowing anew. "You've come home," she said, as if still needing to convince herself it was real. Kaelen, his voice quiet and sure, replied, "I never stopped carrying it with me." The King turned toward the open doors, and his voice was low, steady. "Come. Let the halls of Ael'thara welcome you both. The kingdom will want to see what its future truly looks like."

Kaelen's fingers tightened around mine as he led me forward, and in that moment, I knew nothing would ever be the same again. So, we stepped forward into the heart of the elven capital…Kaelen, the prince returned; I, the bond he had chosen; Aeris, a relic of fire and myth reborn; and Sera, once a servant, now something far greater. We entered not only as those who had survived the road, but as the heralds of what the next age might yet become.

King Valorian turned slightly, his deep voice rising to command the chamber with ease and strength. "Tonight," He said,

"We cast aside the burdens of war, journey, and pain. Tonight, we welcome our son, our prince, and those who have walked beside him through fire and shadow. Let there be a feast that rivals the Solstice Flame." Queen Miraelen raised her hands, the runes on her sleeves shimmering like starlight as she echoed, "Let the halls of Ael'thara be filled with music and warmth. Let the hearths be stoked and the tables overflow. Let the city know…our son has returned."

The doors to the grand hall opened wide, revealing the preparation already underway as elven attendants moved with graceful urgency. Word had clearly traveled fast, and the palace staff had wasted no time turning tradition into celebration. We were guided down a corridor of marble and moon stone, the walls aglow with enchanted lanterns, until we stepped into a chamber large enough to house a battleship.

The banquet hall was a vision out of legend…long tables of carved crystal wood lined with cascading greenery and glowing blossoms. Chandeliers of woven silver branches held orbs of soft light that hovered like floating stars. Every surface shimmered, and yet it was not cold…it felt alive, like the forest had grown its way into the palace and agreed, just for tonight, to dance.

The smell of roasted fruits, spiced root vegetables, honey-glazed meats, and the unmistakable sharp sweetness of elven wine filled the air. My stomach growled before I could stop it, and beside me, Sylas actually groaned with pleasure. "If this is what diplomacy tastes like," he muttered, "I take back every complaint I ever made." Tamsin elbowed him in the ribs, grinning. "You never complained about the food. Just the politics."

"Fair," He admitted, eyes already locked on a platter of flame-seared stag garnished with moon berries and herbs I couldn't name. Music began to rise, light and airy, played by a group of elven musicians whose instruments shimmered with enchantment. The songs were old…Kaelen told me once that many of them were older than the first stone laid in the palace…and yet they felt timeless. Some guests began to dance in swirling, graceful steps, while others gathered in quiet groups or took their places at the feast.

Kaelen and I were guided to seats at the high table, just beside the king and queen. Sera stood close, her hand still clasped in

Aeris's. Though his golden eyes remained alert, there was something easier in his shoulders now, some of the tension melted in the warmth of acceptance. Even Bennick, who usually hovered at the edge of any gathering, was laughing with a servant who offered him what looked like a whole leg of something roasted and glistening.

Queen Miraelen leaned toward me slightly, her blue eyes no longer dimmed but softly alight. "You've done well," she said quietly, not just to me, I think, but to all of us. "You've returned him not just alive… but whole." Kaelen glanced over, hearing it, and for the first time since we'd crossed into Ael'thara, the guarded look in his eyes faded completely. He looked like the boy he must have been once…lighter, rooted, home.

The evening had settled into a soft hum of warmth and joy, the grand hall glowing under the delicate spill of starlight and lantern fire. The scent of roasted herbs and spiced meats lingered in the air, mingling with the sweetness of honeyed fruit and fresh loaves still steaming from the ovens. Laughter floated like ribbons through the space, winding between nobles and warriors alike, and

the music…light, lilting strings, and the subtle pulse of hand-

drums…shifted to something gentler, something made for

memories. I was cradling a glass of plum flower wine, watching the

dancers begin to circle across the polished stone floor, when

Kaelen's hand found mine.

His touch, familiar and warm, sent a quiet jolt through

me…soothing and electric all at once. I turned to find him already

watching me, a soft smile curving his lips, his violet eyes catching

the light in that way that made them look like amethysts kissed by

flame. He didn't speak right away. He didn't need to. Then, with a

voice barely above the music, he asked, "May I have this dance?"

The breath caught in my chest, stupid and fluttering, but I

managed a nod, setting the wine aside and letting him lead me

forward. We stepped into the open space, his fingers twining with

mine like they'd done a hundred times before, and yet this time felt

different…heavier with meaning, lighter with joy.

He pulled me close, one hand settling at the small of my

back, the other clasping my fingers. My free hand pressed gently to

his chest, right over the steady thrum of his heartbeat. We moved slowly at first, learning the shape of each other again through motion. His steps were sure, practiced, but never forceful, guiding me more than leading me, like we were partners in something deeper than just a dance. It didn't take long for the rhythm to settle into something natural…like remembering a dream you used to live inside. "You remember how to dance?" I teased under my breath, tilting my head just enough to see the glint in his eye.

His grin bloomed, and the quiet sound of his laugh…deep, warm, unguarded…wrapped around me like a favorite song. "You think I could forget?" he murmured. "Not with you trying to lead half the time." I laughed, the sound catching somewhere in my chest, and I leaned in closer, the scent of him…cedar and clean smoke and something uniquely him…filling my senses.

"I've always been obsessed with your laugh," I admitted softly, cheeks warming. "Back at camp when it was quiet and the fire burned low… I used to think about it. Even when everything else was falling apart, I'd remember that sound." His arms tightened around me slightly, pulling me a little closer. He didn't hesitate. "I thought about you every night," he said, and his voice, though quiet, carried more than words.

"The sound of your voice. The way you looked at me like I wasn't just a prince, or a soldier, or some symbol of what might break. You saw me." He leaned his forehead against mine, breath mingling with mine. "I never stopped feeling the spark, Haji. Not for a moment." I swallowed hard, the room blurring for just a second, the sting of tears barely held back. "Neither did I," I whispered.

We danced like we were the only two people in that room. The celebration swirled around us, voices rising in joy, feet stomping to faster rhythms elsewhere, but here…in this small piece of time carved out of gold and memory…there was only Kaelen and me. The fire that had once ignited between us hadn't dimmed. If anything, it had deepened, strengthened, becoming something truer, steadier.

The music eventually slowed, shifting into something even softer, and as it ended, I rested my head briefly against his shoulder, content in a way I hadn't been in a long time. He looked down at me, his smile gentle, eyes dancing with starlight and emotion, and I knew without needing to speak that whatever storms might come, this was home. Maybe, just maybe, I'd get to hear that laugh every day for the rest of my life.

Cups were raised, toasts made, and as the first stars rose outside the vine-laced windows, laughter mingled with music, and the warmth of the room wrapped around us like a memory we never wanted to end. We had survived too many nights thinking we might not see another. Tonight, we celebrated because we could…because we were still standing, side by side, and because in this place of ancient wonder, we were finally allowed to be more than just what we'd endured. We were family. We were home.

CHAPTER 24: THE MATE BOND

The celebration still hummed in the halls behind us, muffled now by the long corridor's velvet quiet. The lantern light softened the edges of the stone as we walked, Kaelen's hand firm around mine, his thumb grazing my knuckles in rhythmic reassurance.

The air grew cooler, more intimate, as we left the heart of the palace behind and moved deeper into the private wings. Every step carried a weight of anticipation, drawn tight between us like a string ready to hum. When we reached the door to his chambers, carved from deep obsidian wood and inlaid with delicate silver filigree in the shape of crescent moons and runes of protection, he paused...not out of hesitation, but reverence.

He looked at me, and I felt the question in his gaze before he asked it aloud. I gave a quiet nod, and with a whisper of old hinges and magic, the door opened. The room was immense...easily the size of a small ballroom...with ceilings that arched high above, carved with constellations that glimmered faintly even without light.

Shadows moved gently along the walls, not ominous but velvet-soft, wrapping the space in a hush that felt sacred. Almost everything was black, or near enough…deep obsidian furnishings, raven wood shelves lined with old tomes, midnight blue tapestries embroidered with starlight threads. A massive hearth crackled with quiet flame to our right, its glow casting warm golden light across the polished onyx floors.

At the room's center stood the bed…no, not a bed, a monument. Large enough to hold a family of six with space to spare, its posts carved from ancient raven wood and draped with heavy velvet curtains the color of storm clouds. The sheets were ink-dark silk, the kind that shimmered with subtle hints of blue and silver when the firelight caught them.

Kaelen let go of my hand only to close the door behind us, the click echoing like a heartbeat. His eyes never left me. He moved through the space like it belonged to him…which it did…but there was nothing arrogant in it. Just calm, certain gravity, like the pull of the moon on the tide. He shrugged off his formal jacket, revealing the soft shirt beneath that clung to the lines of his chest and

shoulders, and crossed the room to where the fire burned low and steady.

"I haven't been here in two years," he said softly, like a secret. "I used to think it would feel empty coming back, but it doesn't. Not with you here." I stepped deeper into the room, my fingers grazing the edges of a dark shelf, the smoothness of the carved headboard as I passed. Every surface seemed to breathe with a quiet kind of power…elegant, restrained, but undeniably Kaelen.

He sat at the edge of his bed as I wandered around his room taking in every detail. Finally, I approached him where he was sitting. Kaelen's hand brushed the small of my back as he rose from the bed, the firelight casting golden hues across the sharp lines of his chest. His voice, low and velvet-smooth, carried the warmth of all we'd shared.

"There's a bath drawn for you," he murmured, his thumb grazing my jaw with gentle reverence. "You've journeyed long, and you deserve more than rest. Let me give you peace." He stepped away, disappearing through an arched doorway off to the left of the hearth, and returned moments later, holding out one of his robes…a

542

silken thing in rich black, embroidered subtly with silver thread that shimmered like starlight, and a matching towel. As I grabbed the two items, he guided me with a touch toward the open door, his voice softer now, more intimate. "Go on. It's all yours."

I stepped into the bathing chamber and froze, wonder blooming in my chest like light through fog. The space was more sanctuary than room, carved of pale moonstone and obsidian veined with silver. Hundreds of tiny, star-shaped crystals glittered across the ceiling, casting a soft, celestial glow over everything. The air was thick with warmth and fragrant with lavender, cedarwood, and the delicate sweetness of night-blooming jasmine.

In the center of the chamber sat the bath…no ordinary tub, but a sunken pool of dark marble, its edges inscribed with glowing runes, the water itself steaming gently, scattered with violet and pale blue petals. The surface shimmered like liquid starlight.

Shelves carved from crystal wood lined one wall, holding elegant glass jars filled with oils and salts, folded towels of the softest fabric, and combs carved from bone and gold wood. A faint melody played in the air, lilting and distant, as though the room

itself sang in welcome. I stepped to the water's edge, heart caught between awe and disbelief. This wasn't just luxury…it was magic, crafted for serenity and grace.

I slipped from my clothes and eased into the water, gasping softly as warmth kissed every aching inch of me. I sank deeper, letting the petals swirl around me, the enchanted stillness pressing against my skin like a second breath. I lay back, my head resting on the smooth stone lip, eyes drifting shut as my body surrendered completely. Every sense was alive…the floral scents, the glow of the runes, the velvet water that cradled me as though the very room recognized my weariness and chose to love it away.

Time passed slowly, the kind of slowness that feels sacred. When I finally rose from the water, skin flushed and limbs loose with peace, I dried myself with the towel and then wrapped myself in the robe that smelled faintly of sun-dried linen. When I turned to leave, I found Kaelen standing just outside the doorway. Bare-chested, his silver hair loose down his back, he watched me with that familiar quiet hunger that never quite left his eyes when he looked at me.

A soft smile tugged at his lips, and when I stepped into the warmth of his gaze, he reached out, brushing a damp strand of hair from my cheek. "Was it to your liking?" he asked, voice dipped in amusement. I exhaled a laugh, half-dazed. "It was like walking into a dream." His smile deepened, full of that maddening charm only he could wield so effortlessly. He leaned in, brushing his lips across my temple. "Good," he whispered. "Wait here for me, my love. It's my turn now."

He wasn't gone long, but when he emerged from his bath, he pushed open the doors and steam circled his body. When I looked up at him, his gaze had deepened, violet eyes darkened by firelight and something older, more primal. He took a step toward me, then another, until there was barely space for breath between us.

His hand rose to touch my jaw, feather-light, as though asking permission without words. I leaned into it, and the slow smile that curved his lips was both gentle and devastating. "I've dreamed of you in this room," he whispered, voice husky, brushing against my lips. "But not like this. Not just want. Not just memory. You… here. Now."

He kissed me then…not rushed or hungry, but deep and searching. A kiss that said we had all night, that we didn't need to rush toward anything because we had already arrived. My hands slid up into his hair, soft and silken as the robe around him, and I felt the past months fall away between us like ash. When he pulled me onto the bed, it wasn't desperate…it was worshipful.

Every movement deliberate, every touch speaking volume: I missed you. I see you. You're mine, and I'm yours. The silk beneath us was cool, but his skin was fire against mine, and the way he looked at me…like I was moonlight and salvation all in one…made it hard to breathe. In that vast, dark room…wrapped in velvet and shadow and the quiet glow of a flame meant only for us…we forgot the world outside.

There was only the two of us, the space between heartbeats, and the heat of a promise rekindled in the hush of Kaelen's long-awaited home. He moved with reverence, as though memorizing me all over again, tracing lines down my spine like a sacred scripture, and I responded with the same hunger, the same worship. Our whispers tangled with the rustle of sheets and the soft creak of the mattress beneath us, a rhythm of rediscovery unfolding with every shared breath.

Time slipped its hold on us completely…we were suspended in a moment that stretched endlessly, a slow-burning star between two souls who had finally found their way back to each other. When the world eventually stilled, when our limbs curled into one another and the silence settled around us like silk, Kaelen pulled me closer, burying his face in the curve of my neck.

His voice was low, hushed against my skin, reverent and raw. "You make this place feel like home," he whispered. "Not the marble or the walls… just you." I closed my eyes, heart thudding with the soft weight of everything we'd become, and held him tighter, knowing with every breath that I had never been more certain of anything. He slowly leaned in and nuzzled my neck. I opened for him and with a growl he began kissing my neck down to my chest.

Our hands continued to explore each other's bodies and something between us lit on fire. I pulled him toward me, and in response he rolled on top of me. He pulled my robe off in a swift

motion and I his. For the first time, I saw him, all of him. Something like a small moan escaped my lips as he leaned over me and I saw his muscles contract.

Our hands darted around endlessly as he began kissing me again. His hand slipped lower down me and slowly gripped one of my breasts. The feeling of this seemed to set my soul on fire. I slid my hand from his face down his shoulders and to his waist. He pulled his lips from mine and looked into my eyes. His violet eyes darkened as he rolled his hips toward my core. Kaelen smiled breathlessly and began kissing my shoulder as his hand moved lower until it slipped down past my hips.

He growled again as he began circling my clit. This feeling I had only felt once weeks ago, seemed to undo me all over again. I threw my head back with a quick moan as he slid his fingers deep within me. I gripped his shoulders, my nails causing crescent moon shapes along them. His kisses were no longer soft or sweet, but more ravenous. His intensity as he kissed me made my legs weak. I reached down to grab him and this time he let me.

My hand could barely close around him and only covered less than half of his length. I began moving my hand up his erection and back down slowly. Kaelen threw his head back with a deep snarl. He looked back at me and with a husky voice said, "If we continue like this, I don't think I will be able to stop." I let out a soft purr and replied, "Then don't." He paused, his eyes lowered and pulled his fingers from within me. It was almost as if he wasn't expecting my response.

"Are you sure?" He whispered back. "Yes," I whispered back. With no other words needed, he grabbed my leg, moved it to the side to make room for him, and lowered his head. He moved my other leg above his shoulder and his tongue trailed down my ankle to my leg. He peppered it with kisses all the way to my thigh. My breath caught in my throat with this movement.

He continued lower and lower until his tongue flicked across my clit. He began licking all around my center and slid his finger back in me. At this point, I let out a loud moan and my vision was clouded with stars shooting through the room. He didn't say down long before he removed his mouth and hand from me.

I whimpered as this loss of sensation, and moaned out in frustration, "Please… don't stop again…" He let out a low sultry chuckle and brought his face to mine. "Oh…I won't be stopping until were both unable to move…" he responded and pressed his lips onto mine again. This sentence was the start of my undoing.

His hips began grinding against mine and I knew in that moment that I would do anything for him. He aligned his erection with me and slowly rubbed it around the opening. The sensation was torturous, and I felt myself grinding my hips toward his. This was something that I needed now. The only thing that could quell the desire blooming in my chest.

With one last circle, he roared deeply as he pushed in slowly, not to cause me any pain. I tossed my head back against the bed beneath me and finally let out a deep breath. He entered with short slow strokes, until he felt me loosen around him. "Kaelen…" I breathlessly moaned. I glanced at him, and his eyes were already on me. As soon as our eyes locked, he slid in deep with one slow push. We both let out a deep breath and he growled as he pulled out, all the way to the tip before pushing back in.

I felt my body slowly lose control as he repeated this motion. He leaned down and pressed his lips against mine. As our bodies were entangled, his movements began to pick up speed. No longer slow with compassion, but quick and deep with desire. I was in a complete state of bliss. Everything inside me awakened and I felt a tingling sensation along my chest. I opened my eyes, something on his chest caught my attention.

The moment the mark appeared on Kaelen's chest, time seemed to slow. I was watching him…his breath still uneven, his skin flushed and glowing from the bond we'd just completed…when a shimmer of silver light began to spread just over his heart. It caught my eye immediately. At first, I thought it was a trick of the moonlight, but then it pulsed…gently, deliberately…and I knew.

My breath caught in my throat. The symbol took shape slowly, like it was being drawn onto him by some unseen hand, curving with perfect grace across his chest. It glowed softly, not like fire, but like starlight…quiet, sacred, eternal. It was a slender elven vine curling around a coiled dragon, forming an infinity heart.

Kaelen gasped, one hand flying to the spot as though he could feel the change happening from the inside out. I reached for him instinctively, fingers brushing over the mark as it settled into his skin. "It's beautiful," I whispered, and it was…not just the way it looked, but what it *meant*. My fingers lingered over the glowing curve, and I felt something under my skin thrum in response, a call and answer between the mark on his body and the one now glowing softly on mine.

Kaelen didn't speak at first. He just looked at me, eyes wide and full of something raw…awe, maybe, or disbelief. I could feel his thoughts skimming the edges of mine even before he found his voice. "It's you," he finally said, and his voice was thick with something unspoken. "You live here now." The words hit me like a wave. My throat tightened, and I blinked against the sudden sting of tears. I knew exactly what he meant.

The mark wasn't just a symbol. It was proof…that we were no longer two separate souls. That we had been rewritten, stitched together by something older than blood, older than time. I placed my hand fully over the symbol, feeling the warmth of it, the steady thrum of our bond underneath. "And you live in me," I whispered back, knowing he didn't need to hear it aloud to understand. He could already feel it.

The symbol glowed once more between us, a shared light…not a brand, but a promise. One we hadn't spoken but had written to each other all the same. He reached down and traced something on my chest where I just felt that tingle. "It's true…It's not a myth." He whispered, "My mate, my love." He leaned down and kissed me, but, before I could realize what was happening, he drove back inside me, this time more feral than before. Something changed between us.

What once felt like an electric charge, quickly changed to a burning flame. I felt something building deep within me. I looked up at Kaelen, his body dripping with sweat, and reached for the symbol again. My touch seemed to unravel something within him and he threw his head back and let out a deep growl.

With every push in me, I came closer and closer to losing all sense. My back arched into him in pleasure. His movement became quicker, his breaths shorter. My body erupted in euphoria,

and I let out a moan louder than intended, but in this moment, I could care less if the entire kingdom heard me. At the same time, Kaelen's hips stuttered, and he groaned, his seed filling me deeply. He soon slowed to a standstill and looked down at me.

When we finally caught our breath, I let out a deep breath, as if all of my tension and fear from the past months were escaping my body. He pulled from inside me, leaned down to kiss me, and moved to grab the towel from his earlier bath. He slowly began wiping the evidence of what we had done from my thighs and slowly cleaned me as I lay there. After, he wiped himself down and rejoined me in bed.

The room was quiet, the kind of quiet that only comes after something sacred has passed between two people. The air was warm around us, the sheets tangled and soft beneath my skin, Kaelen's body pressed close to mine like he belonged there. Like he always had. Moonlight spilled across his back, silver and serene, casting a gentle glow over the shape of him…strong, steady, real. My fingers moved across his shoulder without thought, tracing slow circles, memorizing the feel of him again and again, just to make sure this wasn't a dream. I could still feel the heat of where we'd touched…not just skin to skin, but soul to soul…and my chest ached in the most beautiful way.

The mark between my collarbones pulsed softly. The symbol…delicate and radiant…shimmered like a quiet promise. I shifted my hand lower, brushing against Kaelen's chest where the same mark lived over his heart. The bond had sealed. We weren't just lovers now. We were mates. "It's real now," he whispered, his voice a low breath against my hair. "All of it. You feel it too… don't you?" I nodded into him, my cheek against the warm skin over his chest. "It appeared when we came together," I murmured. "When everything aligned. It doesn't just mark us. It binds us."

"But what is this symbol?" I asked He didn't respond right away. I felt his arm tighten around me slightly, the smallest tremor beneath his stillness. Then, with quiet vulnerability, he said, "I am not sure…I never believed in this kind of fate…but now I'd believe in anything, if it meant you were mine." Something in my heart turned over at those words, and I smiled softly. "You always were," I whispered. "Even before we knew."

He then went quiet. Not the kind of quiet that needed filling, but something deeper, like he was standing still on the edge of a cliff inside himself. I felt the shift. The way his heartbeat slowed. The way his breath stilled for just a moment, and then something came through…not words, not exactly…but a feeling, blazing and fierce. *"I would burn the world for you."* I gasped.

The words weren't spoken aloud, but I heard them…clearly, powerfully, as if they were carved into my bones. My head shot up and I met his eyes, wide and stunned. "Kaelen…" I whispered. "I heard that." His brows pulled together slightly, confused, and intense all at once. "You didn't speak," I said. "But I still heard you." He lifted a hand and touched the mark on his chest, like it might explain what had just passed between us. "The bond…"

"We're mind-linked," I said, breath catching. "It's not just instinct or emotion. It's *everything*. I don't need to hear your voice to know what's in your heart." He looked at me then…really looked…like I was the answer to every question he'd never dared ask. *"Then you know,"* came his thought, deliberate, sent to me. I nodded, feeling my chest swell. "I know you'd set the sky on fire for

me," I said, eyes burning. "But I don't want fire. I just want you."
His arms wrapped around me tighter, pulling me to him like he
couldn't stand even an inch of space between us.

No more words passed between us after that. We didn't
need them. The silence became a shared language. I could feel his
thoughts brushing mine, gentle like hands, and I offered mine back
just as freely. *"You are my everything,"* I told him, mind to mind,
heart to heart. *"And you are mine,"* he answered, and I knew it
wasn't a claim, but a truth. Eternal. Unshakable. We stayed like that,
wrapped in each other beneath the glow of the moon, our crescent
marks pulsing in perfect harmony.

The bond was more than I'd imagined. It wasn't a chain or
a duty. It was a becoming. A fusion of souls. Where he ended, I
began…no longer two voices, but one quiet, boundless echo of love.
Our thoughts moved between us like ripples on still water…subtle,
soothing, constant. I could feel the warmth of his affection pressing
gently into the corners of my mind, like hands cupping my face
without ever touching me. I let my eyes fall closed, listening not to
his breath or heartbeat, but to the quiet presence of him within me

now, an echo that would never fade. I let my thoughts drift, slow and drowsy.

I remembered the way he looked at me earlier, like I was the only thing that mattered. I remembered the way his hands had held me, not with hunger, but with reverence. I remembered every broken moment of my life before him, and how none of it seemed to matter anymore…Because now there was only this. Him. Us. Always. *"I'll never leave you,"* I thought, not even fully awake anymore, but I knew he heard me.

I felt the quiet hum of reassurance rise from him in return, a warmth that settled over my skin like a blanket. *"I wouldn't let you,"* his thoughts whispered, laced with something like a smile. His fingers threaded through mine, and I pressed myself closer until I was tucked beneath his chin, his body curved protectively around me.

The weight of the day, of the bond, of everything we had just become…it should have overwhelmed me, but it didn't. It felt right. Like coming home. The night air drifted in, cool and quiet, and our breathing slowed together again, like twin tides pulled by

the same moon. My last waking thought was of his arms around me and the certainty that I had never been safer, and as we drifted into sleep, our minds still touching, still wrapped around each other in silence and certainty, I felt it: that unbreakable thread between us, glowing quietly in the dark. Bound. Whole. Loved.

CHAPTER 25: THE DRAVELYN KNOT

The morning found us before the sun did. I woke to the soft rhythm of his heartbeat against my cheek, steady and slow, like it had been waiting for me to match it again. The world hadn't changed, not really…there were still battles to face, truths to uncover, and the weight of what we were becoming pressing in at the edges…but for the first time in what felt like forever, I didn't wake with fear.

His eyes were already open when I looked up, the barest hint of a smile tugging at his lips, though he said nothing. He didn't have to. There was something in the quiet between us, something that spoke louder than words ever could. A shared breath. A shared promise.

I slid my fingers across his chest, tracing the line where warmth met skin, and he caught my hand, holding it there like it anchored him. Maybe it did. Maybe we anchored each other now. "We should go," I murmured, though I made no move to get up. "We will," he said, voice rough with sleep, but still threaded with that ever-present certainty. "Just not yet."

Yes, not yet. The world could wait a little longer. The war outside these walls, the uncertainty of the future, the echoes of pain and past lives…it could all wait. Because here, in this single, fleeting moment, we were still just two people holding onto each other like gravity itself had shifted to pull us closer.

Eventually, we did move. Together. The cold found us quickly once we left the warmth of the blankets, but his hand never let go of mine. The sky outside was a pale blue bruised by the fading shadows of night, and everything was hushed, like the earth was still holding its breath. Waiting. I dressed quickly, feeling the familiar prickle of anticipation crawling up my spine. Something was coming. I didn't know what yet, but it tugged at me, quiet and insistent. A ripple beneath still water.

He watched me from across the room, eyes sharp now, awake in a different way. Ready. "We're not the same," I said, fastening the last clasp of my coat. "No," he agreed. "We're more." We were. As we stepped out into the morning, hand in hand, I knew it wasn't just a new day. It was the beginning. Of something bigger. Of something that would change everything.

The grand hall glowed with morning light as we stepped inside, the scent of warm bread, spiced tea, and roasted fruit rising like a gentle welcome. Despite the lingering hum of the bond still thrumming between Kaelen and me, there was something grounding about the clatter of silverware and the soft rustle of silk robes. At the far end of the long stone table sat the king and queen, regal in deep emerald and silver, their crowns catching the light with quiet authority. Their eyes found us instantly…not with judgment, but with the heavy weight of knowing. "Ah," the king said, rising to his feet. "You've come at last…and I see you bring more than just yourselves."

His gaze dropped to our joined hands and glanced to our open chests, where the mark shimmered faintly across our skin…an intricate knot of light and shadow woven together in a shape that felt ancient and alive all at once. The queen's eyes widened, her breath catching softly. The king stepped forward, not touching, but close enough that I could feel the energy shift around us.

"That," he said slowly, "…It's the Dravelyn Knot." Kaelen frowned. "The what?" "The Dravelyn Knot," the king repeated, voice quiet, almost reverent. "It's a symbol that hasn't been seen in this realm for an age. It signifies more than a bond between two souls…it's the mark of a union forged between dragon and elf. A connection powerful enough to shape kingdoms."

He looked past us then, eyes distant, like he was chasing the memory through time. "It first appeared in the age of Queen Elara. She bore the mark on her armor when she united our peoples…elves and dragons…under a single banner. Her reign brought peace across the lands, a golden era that lasted nearly a century. The stories say the Dravelyn Knot was etched into her very soul."

I felt Kaelen tense beside me, and I knew his thoughts mirrored mine. The queen stepped forward, voice soft but unshakable. "And now, it reappears… on you." Her gaze pierced through the moment, through us. "This means your destiny is written in the stars. The return of this mark signals momentous change." The king nodded slowly. "I remember reading about the knot in the old texts, but I saw it once with my own eyes…carved into the walls of the ancient ruins beyond the Veiled Forest. I was

only a child. Something about the place called to me. I didn't understand it then, only that I had to see it for myself, but the golems that stood guard chased me off before I could step inside."

"Elara," Kaelen said suddenly, his voice tight, alert. "Did you say Queen Elara?" The queen's eyes narrowed slightly, curious. "You know the name?" "Orion and Ileyana," I said quickly. "They told us about her. They said she was the key. That the past and present are bound through her...and that the ruins hold answers." The king's eyes sharpened. "You've spoken with Orion and Ileyana? Then the threads of fate are already moving. Faster than we'd hoped."

"Where exactly are the ruins?" Kaelen asked, stepping forward. "Southeast," the king said, turning toward the distant windows. "Past the Veiled Forest, along the cliffs where the sky meets the stone. Hidden, unless you know how to look. The golems still guard the place…unchanged, unmoved. They do not recognize me as king."

He turned back to us, his face solemn. "Go. The mark has returned for a reason. If the truth of Elara lies buried there, then it's time it was unearthed. Whatever sleeps beneath those stones, it's calling to you now." The queen placed her hand gently on his arm. "This is only the beginning. You were not chosen by chance. You were chosen by fate. Written in the stars long before this life began."

A shiver ran through me, not of fear but of something deeper…like the world itself had turned its gaze upon us. Kaelen's fingers tightened around mine, the marks between us glowing faintly. *"Whatever waits in those ruins… we face it together,"* Kaelen said to me through our mind-link. *"Always,"* I echoed back, and in the silence that followed, I felt the future rising to meet us.

The days that followed passed like a dream wrapped in motion…slow and fast all at once, each moment a brushstroke painting the edges of something vast and unseen. Preparations began immediately after the audience with the king and queen. Word traveled quickly through the halls of the citadel, carried on whispers and wary glances, and though no one said it outright, we could feel the shift…the sense that the court, the city, perhaps even the realm itself, was holding its breath.

We trained each morning in the royal gardens, Kaelen and I, side by side, blades moving in rhythm, his fire, and my focus dancing together like old companions. Aeris circled above during sparring, his sharp eyes always watching, always scanning the horizon like he expected danger to arrive before we left. At night, Kaelen and I studied the old maps the king had unearthed from the library vaults…fragments of parchment that smelled of dust and memory, ink faded by time, but still readable enough to trace a path to the ruins.

In quiet hours, I wandered the citadel's oldest halls, letting my fingers glide along the stone walls as if they could tell me what was coming. Sometimes I would feel the pull of the bond, Kaelen's presence flickering at the edge of my awareness like a second heartbeat. He always found me before I called for him. The queen summoned her personal seers to speak with us once, reading the stars and the shifting energy in the wind. "The world tilts," one of them whispered, his eyes clouded with starlight. "And you are its axis now." I didn't know whether to feel honored or terrified. Maybe both.

We gathered supplies…more than we could carry, it seemed…rations and salves, enchanted cloaks woven with protective sigils, and an obsidian compass that only pointed toward the ruins when held between both our hands. A relic, the queen said, from Elara's time. "It answers to blood and bond," she told us, watching the needle twitch as we stood together.

The nights were quieter. Kaelen and I often found ourselves on the eastern terrace, looking toward the mountains that we would soon cross. He would wrap his arms around me from behind, his chin resting lightly atop my head, and we would stand in silence, watching the stars shift overhead like threads weaving themselves into new constellations. One night, I whispered, "Do you think we're ready?" He didn't answer with words. He just turned me in his arms, pressed his forehead to mine, and let the mark between us pulse once with soft light. That was enough.

The morning of our departure came with a sky streaked in rose and gold. The king and queen met us at the citadel gates, dressed not in royal finery but in travel-worn cloaks. The queen handed me a small leather-bound book…thin, worn, but intact.

"This belonged to Elara," she said. "Her last journal. It was recovered from the ruins once… before they closed themselves. Perhaps it will open again… for you."

The weight of it in my hands felt heavier than paper. Kaelen took my hand. Our blades were strapped to our backs, the obsidian compass secured between us. We did not look back. As the gates opened and the world beyond spilled out before us…untamed, wild, full of shadows and truth…I felt the bond hum once more, steady, and sure. The wind curled around us like a whisper, and in the distance, the mountains waited. We were ready, or we would be.

We didn't travel alone. Not entirely. As the final preparations were checked and the gates creaked open, two familiar figures stepped from the shadows…Sera and Aeris, already dressed for the road, silent and resolute. Sera, in worn leather with her braid slung over one shoulder, had the look of someone who'd already made peace with whatever lay ahead. Her staff strapped across her back, the crystal at its tip pulsing with quiet anticipation.

Aeris stood beside her, cloaked in storm gray. "We're coming," Sera said, no hesitation in her voice. "We wouldn't let you do this alone," Aeris added, his gaze steady. "You might not return the same people. Someone should be there to remember who you were…and remind you, if needed."

Kaelen gave a single nod, and that was all the answer they needed. We left as the sun crowned the eastern peaks, casting the land in gold. Behind us, the citadel shrank into the morning mist; before us, the world opened wide and wild. We followed the winding path through the outer forests, where the air smelled of moss and old magic, and the light filtered down like whispers through the leaves.

Aeris moved ahead like a phantom, blades at the ready, eyes always watching. Sera walked quietly beside me, occasionally murmuring spells beneath her breath…wards, protections, quiet shields of energy against the things that lurked beyond sight. Kaelen never strayed far from my side, his presence like a second heartbeat. The bond between us pulsed with every step, not overwhelming, but constant, like a magnet pulling us toward something we hadn't yet named.

That first night, we camped beyond the forest's edge, where hills rolled into the foothills of the Veiled Mountains. The stars stretched brighter overhead, like they were leaning closer to watch. Around a low fire, we shared silence, warmth, and fragments of thought. "The Dravelyn Knot," Sera murmured, her voice soft but sure, "Do you feel different since it appeared?"

Kaelen glanced at me, then answered, "Yes. Not in power. In purpose." I nodded, feeling the truth settle in my chest. "It's like the questions I've always carried finally have somewhere to go…even if I don't have the answers yet." Aeris stirred the fire, his gaze distant. "Elara, the ruins, your bond… they're not just stories anymore. They're a map, and you two…you're the key." None of us spoke after that. The fire crackled. Thunder rumbled faintly on the horizon, though the skies were clear. It sounded like a warning…or a call.

Sera left the fire without a word, her boots whispering over the frost-bitten grass as she moved toward the edge of the tree line. I followed, wings folding as I touched down beside her in my smaller form, shifting with ease into something more human, more companion than creature. She didn't look at me right away, just stared out toward the horizon like it might answer a question she hadn't asked aloud.

"You've been quiet," I said, keeping my voice soft. "More than usual. Something on your mind?" She exhaled slowly, a breath that curled into the frigid air. "You already know, don't you?" Her fingers brushed the edge of her collar, revealing the soft glow of silver beneath…the crescent moon etched just below her collarbone, delicate but unmistakable.

"The bond completed itself," I said, not a question. She nodded. "Last night. I didn't mean for it to happen, but it did. It was fireworks and thunder, but it was also… stillness. Like I'd been holding my breath for years, and I finally let it go." There was something awed in her tone, like she hadn't expected the moment to be so quiet, so certain. "The Crescent Moon," I said. "Rare. Older than most know."

She glanced at me then, her expression unguarded. "It felt old. Like I was stepping into a story that had been waiting for me. Aeris…he never rushed me. He just… knew." I sat on a stone

nearby, wings tucked behind me, watching her the way I always did…like I could see the edges of the flame she kept hidden. "You don't need courage to love," I said gently. "Just the willingness to be seen." She laughed then, short, and dry, but not without warmth. "Well, he definitely sees everything. Even the parts I'd rather leave buried."

She looked toward the trail where the others had remained near the fire, their figures half-faded in mist. "I don't know how he puts up with me," She stated. I smiled. "Patience is its own form of faith. He waited because he believed in you. Not just in the bond…but in what it would mean when you were ready to meet it." Her grin came back then, crooked, and full of mischief. "Okay, but it is kind of hot. We found out how connected we were when I heard his thoughts for the first time. Haji, with what he said, something melted in my soul."

"The matching symbols. Not that I'll tell him that. At least not directly." I raised a brow. "So, no starry-eyed confessions? No soul-bearing monologues under the moon?" "Mother Above, no," she said with a mock shudder. "But I'll let him think I'm impressed when he broods a little. Maybe throw him a look." We both laughed, the sound light and real, a welcome relief from the tension that had been knotting tighter around all of us. Then her smile faded, replaced by something thoughtful.

"It's strange though, isn't it? Two bonds, two ancient marks appearing back-to-back. The Dravelyn Knot. Now the Crescent Moon. You feel it too, don't you? Like something's aligning?" I nodded slowly. "Threads pulling tight. It's not coincidence. It's convergence." She touched the mark again, fingers trailing lightly over it. "A warning… or a promise." "Maybe both," I said, standing, stretching my wings out behind me.

"Come on. The ruins won't wait, and if Aeris starts waxing poetic about the stars again, we'll lose half a day just trying to translate him back to reality." That drew a proper laugh from her, and she fell into step beside me again, the silver crescent at her collarbone glowing faintly as the sun broke over the hills, casting long shadows toward the mountains that waited ahead.

Later that night, sleep came only in fragments, filled with dreams of stone doors and glowing symbols, of voices speaking languages I didn't know but somehow understood. When dawn came cold and gray, we rose together, our footsteps quiet but sure. By midday, we would reach the cliffs. By nightfall, the ruins, and whatever waited beyond those crumbling stones…memory, monsters, prophecy, or truth…we would face it as one.

The weight of it pressed against the edges of my mind…not fear, exactly, but a deep sense of inevitability, like the turning of a page we had always been meant to reach. The air grew thinner as we climbed, laced with the scent of stone and something older, something waiting. With every step closer, the bond between us all seemed to tighten, not just the magic between mates, but the unspoken tether forged in fire, in loyalty, in choice. Whatever we found in those ruins, whatever the past had buried and the stars had marked…it would not break us. It would define us.

The next morning broke sharper than the last, the wind biting against our cloaks as we pressed higher into the ridgelands. Mist clung low to the ground, curling around our boots like grasping fingers, and the path grew narrower, choked by old roots and stones cracked with frost. None of us spoke much…the quiet was purposeful now, ears tuned to the strange hush that blanketed the land like something holding its breath. It wasn't long before we saw them. They emerged from the mist like broken statues, thin-limbed and gaunt-eyed, their skin gray-washed and veined with flickers of shadow. Elves…but not living in the way we understood.

Their armor was rusted through, mottled with moss and bone-dry blood, and their eyes... hollow, like pits carved into ash. Cursed. Bound to something ancient and cruel, left wandering the edges of memory. Sera saw them first, a low curse hissing from her lips as her Staff was drawn in a blink. "Five," she muttered, stepping forward to block the narrow path. "Maybe six. No words…just motion." Aeris's power was already humming, he half shifted, wings extended behind him. I moved to the side, wings half-extended, ready to shift if needed. Kaelen glanced at me, then at Aeris, and nodded once.

The first one lunged without a sound, blade raised in a wild arc. Kaelen met it cleanly, steel-on-steel ringing out into the fog. Another came from the right, and he intercepted it with a brutal parry, his own sword driving into the creature's chest…but it didn't

fall. It hissed like something unearthly, smoke leaking from the wound instead of blood.

"They don't die easy!" he called. "Strike deep…heart or head!" I shot forward in dragon form, large, but fast, knocking one off its feet with a blast of wind from my wings. Sera raised her staff and shouted a phrase in the old tongue; lightning crackled out and arced through two of the cursed elves at once, their forms seizing with violent energy before crumpling into heaps of ash.

Aeris danced through the melee with lethal grace, his claws flashing in a blur of silver and black blood. One of the cursed elves nearly caught him off-guard, but I threw myself between them, catching its blade with the armored ridge of my wing. He nodded, never slowing. "Owe you one." "Add it to the list," I shot back.

The last of them shrieked…a sound that didn't belong in this world…before Kaelen drove his blade through its eye, the body spasming once, then stilling. Silence followed, sharp and immediate. The mist seemed to thin then, as if the cursed things had carried it with them, and now, with their defeat, it was bleeding back into the shadows.

We stood among the ruins of the brief skirmish, breathing heavy, blood…some ours, most not…dotting the frost-covered stones. Sera lowered her staff, her voice quiet. "They were guardians once. Bound to these lands by honor. Twisted by something darker." Kaelen wiped his blades clean with a grim expression. "Then whatever cursed them might be close. They should not be this close to the capital. Let's go, we're not far from the ruins." I looked toward the ridge ahead, where the mountains sloped down into shadowed valleys choked with fog and time-worn stone. The ruins waited, and whatever lay within them, it had already begun reaching for us.

The path narrowed as we pressed onward, silence settling again in the wake of the cursed elves, but it wasn't peace. It was that watchful silence, thick and expectant. The terrain grew jagged, sheer walls of rock hemming us in until we were forced into single file. Then, as we crested the final ridge, the ruins came into view…carved into the mountainside like they'd always been there, untouched by time or storm. Towering spires, half-buried and broken by age, jutted from the earth like ribs of some ancient beast.

Their surfaces shimmered faintly with runes beneath layers of moss and dust, and the air changed, dense with power and memory. On the walls outside the cave, was the Dravelyn Knot.

We weren't alone. They moved before we saw them…massive figures peeling away from the cliffs themselves, stepping free from the stone with grinding weight. Stonehide Golems. Constructed of ancient, rune-bound rock, they were towers of strength, each movement slow but deliberate, like the shifting of mountains.

Their eyes glowed dimly at first, a dull ember deep within their helmed visages, but as we approached, they flared brighter, and one stepped forward. Aeris's claws were drawn and Sera stepped forward, but I held out my arm, halting them. I knew that feeling…deep in my bones, in the humming thread of the bond that tugged at the space between the ruins and my blood.

The golems paused. Then, like the first time, they bowed. One by one, each construct dipped its massive form to the ground, kneeling before me, lowering those stone-etched faces in solemn recognition. Not to the group. To *me*. The same way they had bowed at the ruins before. Around us, the glyphs along the archways and broken pillars brightened with a steady pulse. The others watched, silent, the weight of it falling around us like gravity.

I stepped forward, the earth beneath my feet humming in response, and the golems parted, slow and reverent, forming a clear path into the heart of the ruins. "They remember," Aeris murmured. "Or maybe they were waiting." Sera nodded beside him, eyes narrowed but curious. "Whatever it is, they know who you are, just like last time."

I didn't answer. I wasn't sure I could. The truth of it lived in the thrum of the stone, in the flicker of memory that wasn't entirely my own. The ruins were awake now, and they had opened their gates…for me. As I stepped through the threshold, the last of the warmth from the glowing runes pulsing gently beneath my feet, the Stonehide Golems began to move again…not toward us, but away.

One by one, they rose from their kneeling positions with the slow, deliberate grace of beings who had waited centuries just to perform that motion. Their eyes dimmed, that molten amber fading

to a dull glow as they turned back to the cliffside. Then, without a

sound, they began to sink. Stone shifted to stone…shoulders

merging with rock, limbs folding seamlessly into the jagged face of

the mountain until they were indistinguishable from the stone that

birthed them. In mere moments, they were gone. Only the faint

shimmer of residual magic remained in the air, like a breath held too

long.

Sera came up beside me, her voice low but sharp with awe.

"That's twice now they've bowed to you. Do you understand why?"

I kept my eyes on the place where the last golem had vanished, the

answer rising from deep within, like something I didn't remember

learning but had always known. "Not completely," I admitted. "But

I think... I'm part of whatever this place is, or maybe it's part of me.

They're not just guardians…they're memory, written into

stone…and something in them remembers me, or what I'm

becoming." Aeris and Kaelen lingered just behind us, quiet in the

aftermath. No one argued. No one doubted. There was no need.

The entrance to the ruins yawned ahead, framed by

towering stone pillars etched with symbols that pulsed gently in time with my breath, like a heartbeat beneath the earth. The air that drifted out was cold, but not lifeless. It was waiting. I looked back once, at the narrow path we'd taken, at the empty mountainside now free of the golems' towering forms, and then forward, to what waited in the dark.

Without a word, I stepped across the threshold. The others followed, the sound of our footsteps swallowed by the stone as we descended into the silence of the ruins. The past was buried here…written on the walls, in symbols, in memory…and we were walking straight into it.

CHAPTER 26: THE JOURNEY OF A LIFETIME

The darkness didn't swallow us all at once. It folded over us in layers…first the light of the sky, then the sound of the wind, and finally the pulse of the world outside. Step by step, it all receded behind us, until the only rhythm left was the hush of our breathing and the faint hum that vibrated through the stone beneath my boots.

Not quite sound. Not quite sensation. More like... recognition. The path sloped downward, cut with uncanny precision through rock that bore no chisel marks. The walls around us glowed faintly, the same sigils from the pillars outside etched deep into the stone, each one pulsing with that quiet, patient light. It was more than just illumination…it was a language. I didn't know the words, but I could feel them pressing gently against my skin, like someone tracing the shape of old memories across my bones.

Sera walked beside me, her torch held high though we didn't need it. Her eyes kept darting to the walls, the floor, the ceiling…trying to take everything in at once. "I thought it would feel colder," she said softly. "It is cold," Kaelen muttered from behind. "No," she said. "I mean…it should feel… empty. Like ruins usually do, but it doesn't. It feels like someone's still here. Watching." I didn't say anything, but I felt it too. Not malevolent. Not exactly. Just present. Alive. Aeris didn't speak at all. He'd gone very still the moment we crossed the threshold, his usual sharp glances replaced by something more distant…like he was trying to listen for a voice only he could hear. I wondered, not for the first time, what exactly he saw in places like this.

The path curved left, then right, then widened into a vast chamber that opened above us like the inside of a mountain's heart. My breath caught. Here, the carvings weren't just sigils. They were scenes. Whole stories, laid out in spirals across the walls and domed ceiling. Battles. Pilgrimages. A line of figures kneeling before a flame that burned in the air itself….and in the center of it all…a figure that made my stomach twist with recognition.

It was me. Not exactly. Not in face or detail, but the shape, the posture, the way the figure's hand reached out to the flame…that was me. I'd done that exact motion at the first gate, without

knowing why. It had felt instinctive, necessary. Sera saw it too.

"Haji..." "I know," I whispered.

I stepped forward. The moment my boot touched the central stone, something deep in the ground shifted. A tremor…not violent, but aware. The torches on the walls flared to life, one by one, in concentric rings of golden-blue fire. Light danced across the carvings, and suddenly, I could read them. Not in words. In memory. Each image became a sensation…a thought not my own, threading through the marrow of my bones. I saw the first flame bearer walking the same path, heard the chants of stone-bound guardians as they raised this temple from living rock. I felt their hope, their fear, their purpose…and the choice that had to be made, again and again.

The chamber grew warmer. My breath steamed in front of me, but I didn't shiver. Instead, something inside me aligned…like all this time I'd been walking slightly out of step with the world, and only now had I found the right rhythm. I turned slowly, and the others were staring…not at the chamber, but at me. "Your eyes," Kaelen said quietly. "They're glowing." I raised my hand to my face, half-expecting pain, but there was none. Just warmth. A faint, golden light at the edges of my vision, like the last sliver of sun on the horizon.

Aeris took a step forward, voice low. "This place remembers you, but more than that... it's preparing you." "For what?" Sera asked, barely above a whisper. I looked at the far wall. Another path led out from the chamber, narrower, its mouth framed by two statues whose faces had been worn smooth by time. Though even without features, I knew they were watching. I didn't know what lay beyond that threshold. Whatever it was, it was meant for me. "Not for what," I said. "For who I have to become..." and then, heart steady, I walked toward the next gate.

The passage narrowed the deeper we went, the air thickening with the scent of mineral dust and something faintly sweet...like the memory of lightning just before it strikes. The walls began to change. The clean, chiseled stone gave way to a more natural shimmer, subtle at first, then impossible to miss: veins of crystal laced through the rock, catching the torchlight and scattering it in all directions. I reached out and ran my fingers along the

surface. The light didn't just reflect…it *bent*, casting strange, deliberate patterns on the floor that shifted when I moved.

"They're here," Aeris said behind me, his voice low and certain. He didn't need to explain. I have already seen them. Crystal Ants: small, luminous creatures with gem-like exoskeletons. They moved in silent processions across the walls and ceiling, their translucent bodies catching the light like stained glass. They worked tirelessly, carving and reinforcing a network of tunnels within the crystal. The paths they left behind refracted light into shifting geometric patterns that felt too intentional to be random.

Kaelen let out a soft breath and stepped up beside me, eyes scanning the glowing tracery overhead. "You remember the first ruins near Ileyana's Keep?" he asked. "The ants showed us the way there, too. We just didn't realize it until after." He was right. I hadn't made the connection until now. The light trails, the shifting reflections, the way they led us to the sealed chamber beneath the collapsed ruins…it had all been them.

"They're not just workers," I said. "They're archivists. Guiding us through memory." I stepped closer to the wall, watching as one of the ants paused, antennae twitching, then resumed its path along a crystalline ridge. The refraction around it shifted again…rearranging itself until the shapes formed a corridor I hadn't seen before, half-hidden in shadow, its entrance curved like the inside of a polished geode.

"They want us to see it," I murmured. "Or they want us to follow," Kaelen added. "Not always the same thing." Still, none of us hesitated as we moved toward the revealed path. The air grew colder again, sharper, but laced with something different…music.

The tunnel opened into a cavern so vast it felt like stepping into the belly of night itself. The ceiling was lost in darkness, but movement drifted through the air above…soft, weightless, celestial. "Echo Moths…" Kaelen murmured. They glided silently through the open space, wings like slices of sky dusted with starlight. Each flap released a delicate hum, barely louder than a breath, but resonant. The tones layered across one another in slow, looping harmonies that made the very stone feel like it was singing.

Aeris stepped forward, his face tilted slightly upward, gaze following the slow drift of a moth above him. "They're not just flying," he said. "They're listening. To each other. To us." "To *something*," Sera added. "They don't sound like insects…they sound like... music trying to remember itself." One of the moths broke from the cluster above and spiraled toward me. Its wings caught the crystal glow, the pattern across them resembling constellations I didn't recognize…older, maybe. Forgotten. As it passed near my shoulder, a note pulsed through my chest. Not sound. Not quite. It was feeling, carried like a whisper on the wind.

A path. A question. A warning. "They're guiding us too," I said, voice hushed. "But not the way the ants do. This is about what we're *meant* to hear. If we're willing." Aeris nodded slowly. "Some truths are carried by stone," he said. "Others ride the wind." Above, the moths sang on. Below, the Crystal Ants continued their work in perfect silence.

Between them, a path unfolded…woven from light and sound, memory and meaning. Whatever waited ahead wasn't just hidden in the dark. It was being *offered*, by the creatures who remembered when the world itself was young. I stepped forward, each footfall echoed by the moths' song, the crystal refracting my way. Behind me, the others followed, and somewhere in the wind, I thought I heard the past begin to speak.

The path narrowed again, funneling us deeper into the crystalline caverns, where silence pressed in more tightly with every step. Even the hum of the Echo Moths faded behind us, replaced by a solemn stillness that felt reverent…sacred. The glow from the Crystal Ants continued, a soft, steady guide leading us into a new chamber. When we stepped through the threshold, I stopped short.

The walls here weren't just carved or etched. They *breathed* with story. Images bloomed across the stone…murals of such impossible detail they seemed to shimmer with life. Not paint. Not ink. The stone itself had been coaxed into shape, each scene fused from crystal and memory, refracting torchlight into layered, moving tableaus. As I moved closer, they shifted subtly, aligning with the rhythm of my breath, the pulse in my veins.

She stood at the center of it all…tall, commanding, her silver hair braided with strands of firelight, her eyes aglow with ancient knowing. A crown of golden woven branches and dragon bone rested on her brow. Dragons soared above her, wings

outstretched in trust, while elves stood at her feet with heads bowed and weapons sheathed. Peace radiated from her…not passive, but *earned*. "Elara," I whispered, the name rising from somewhere deep inside, uncalled but utterly certain. Sera stepped beside me. "You've seen her before?" "Not exactly," I said, my voice thin. "I think... I *was* her."

Even saying the words felt impossible…and yet, the moment I spoke them, something shifted inside me. Like a door unlatched, a breath finally taken. The mural rippled faintly, the crystal catching light in a new way.

Another scene unfurled before me…Elara standing at the edge of a cliff, the wind pulling at her cloak, two figures behind her. One held a blade, the other a vial of something dark and dangerous. They didn't strike openly. The betrayal was quiet, patient. A final conversation. A promise turned poison. I took a step back, and then the visions struck.

FLASH.

Wings thundered above me. Screams. The smell of burning cedar and hot metal. I stood in a war council, voice raised...not in anger, but command. I remembered the weight of a crown on my head, not as ornament, but as burden. A hand...scaled, warm...clasped mine. A voice, deep and trembling, saying goodbye.

FLASH.

My body suspended in a lattice of magic, runes coiling around my limbs like vines. The world receded. A name...mine...whispered one last time before silence took me. The murals continued, the narrative now unmistakable. Elara, her crown fallen, placed in crystalline sleep by those who once loved her. Dragons and elves alike weeping as they sealed her away.

Then the split...two diverging paths. One showed her reborn in a quiet forest cottage, cloaked in forgetfulness, a girl named Hajira chasing fireflies along the riverbank. The other showed the world unraveling: kingdoms crumbling, dragons and elves hunted, the land sick with imbalance.

Kaelen's voice broke through the rising noise in my head. "Haji. You're pale. What is it?" I looked at him, blinking against the blur of memory and light. "I think..." My throat felt dry, too small for the words. "I *was* her. Elara. Not just a piece of her. Not some echo. Me." Silence followed. Not disbelief…just the weight of the moment settling around us.

I stepped forward again, my legs were unsteady, and I placed my palm against the next image. My skin tingled. The mural shifted beneath my touch. A new figure appeared…faceless, shadowed…standing at a crossroads between fire and rebirth. Runes began to glow around her feet, and in the center, a sun cradled by a dragon's wing.

Aeris came to stand beside me, his voice lower than before. "You said this place remembered you. Maybe you're not just waking Elara up." He met my eyes. "Maybe you *are* her waking up." I couldn't deny it anymore. The way the magic responded to me. The way the golems had bowed. The way the murals flowed with my breath, my heartbeat. These weren't someone else's memories…they were *mine*.

Forgotten, buried, stolen...but mine. Sera exhaled softly.

"So...what does that mean now?" I turned toward the next passage, where the Crystal Ants were already lighting the path, their glow pulsing with the rhythm of something ancient returning. "It means I was never meant to sleep forever," I said. "And it's time I remember why I was put to rest at all."

The air thickened as we stepped away from the murals, the faint glow of the crystal walls now tinged with something sharper...a current just beneath the surface, like static before a storm. The Crystal Ants scurried ahead, guiding us deeper through a narrow arch veined with pulsing light.

My thoughts churned with the weight of everything I'd just seen, the pressure of recognition pressing harder against the edges of my mind. Each step forward pulled more from me...memories I didn't know I had, names I hadn't spoken in lifetimes. My breath caught as another flash pierced my vision.

FLASH.

A garden beneath twin moons. Elven banners fluttering. A dragon circling high above. My laughter…Elara's laughter…echoing off stone, ringing clear before it turned to a scream. I stumbled. Kaelen was beside me in an instant, his hand at my elbow, steadying me before I hit the ground. "Careful," he said, but there was something more in his voice…not just concern, but *certainty.* "You saw something again."

I nodded, swallowing hard. "They're getting stronger. It's like the walls are peeling away, and what's underneath… it's all still alive." I looked up at him. "*She's* still alive. Inside me. I don't know where she ends and I begin." Kaelen didn't let go. His voice dropped, just for me. "Maybe that's the wrong question."

"What do you mean?" I finally got out. "You're not two people, Haji. Not a girl pretending to be a queen, or a queen lost in someone else's life. You *are* her. Just… not all at once. You're remembering who you were, and you're still becoming who you're meant to be."

His words were solid ground in a world turning fluid around me. I hadn't realized how much I needed to hear someone say that. I looked at his hand…still steady, still warm…and didn't pull away. The next chamber opened around us like a wound. Dark, vast, and silent.

At its center stood a great circular dais, ringed with twelve crystalline pillars, each etched with unfamiliar sigils and one much more familiar…The Dravelyn Knot. The air vibrated faintly, like the echo of a voice that hadn't spoken in centuries. In the center of the dais was a pedestal…and on it, a circlet of gold and red stones. A crown laid next to a massive bow and arrow. My breath hitched.

"I know that," I said, voice barely audible. "I wore that. I fought with that…" My feet moved before I could stop them, drawn toward the center like the world itself had tilted. The closer I came, the louder the silence grew, until it was pressing against my ears like the weight of deep water. Behind me, I heard Sera whisper a ward, felt Aeris draw his sword…not in threat, but instinct. Kaelen didn't move. He stayed close. When I reached the pedestal, I stared down

at the forgotten items. They weren't gleaming. They didn't shine. They *waited.*

A voice…half memory, half presence…spoke from nowhere and everywhere at once. *"You are remembered."* The chamber trembled. Dust fell from above. The sigils on the twelve pillars sparked, one by one, flaring to life like stars reigniting after a long darkness. The temperature dropped sharply. Frost traced across the edges of the pedestal. "Step back," Aeris warned, but Kaelen didn't. "I think she's past the point of stepping away," he said, his voice fierce now. "Whatever this is…it's part of her. Let her *face it.*"

I reached out, fingers hovering just above the crown. My heart thundered so loudly I felt it in my teeth. The magic in the room had changed. It wasn't passive anymore. It *watched.* It *waited,* and I knew…if I touched the crown, I would see everything. Not flashes. Not fragments. The whole of her life. My life. Kaelen stepped even closer. His voice, suddenly soft again, came just behind me. "You don't have to do this alone."

I turned slightly, just enough to meet his eyes. "I don't think I ever was," I told him, and then, with a breath that felt like

596

diving into the deep end of the world, I touched the crown. The moment my fingers brushed the crown, the world fractured. Not in sound or sight, but in sensation…like my body was still standing on the pedestal, yet every part of me was being pulled backward, inward, downward. The chamber faded. My breath caught. Heat surged behind my eyes, and suddenly…

FLASH.

I stood in a great hall of woven roots and living stone, a dragon's head bowed before me. Its breath was warm against my skin, eyes ancient and sorrowful. "We are bound, Elara," it said, its voice like thunder filtered through velvet. "Your word is fire and sky." I reached forward and touched its brow, feeling the magic pulse between us…deep, eternal. That moment burned like truth.

FLASH.

I was on a battlefield, the sky torn by arcane storms. My armor was scorched. My arms ached from wielding too much magic for too long. Elven blades and dragon fire carved through waves of corrupted beasts. I shouted commands through the roar, my voice

597

hoarse and bloodied, but unyielding. My people moved with me...not behind, but beside me. I gripped my bow and arrow. I was not just their queen. I was their shield. I was their sword.

Pain spiked through my temples. My knees buckled, but Kaelen caught me before I fell, his arm wrapping firmly around my waist. "Haji...Haji, look at me," he said, his voice urgent but steady. I couldn't. Not yet.

FLASH.

A throne room. My throne room. Silent and still. A man...one of my council...kneeling at my feet, his hand trembling as he held a scroll. "They've turned on us, Elara. The accords have been broken. The dragons are retreating to the high sanctuaries. The elves are fracturing into factions." My heart clenched. I remembered that feeling...the unbearable knowledge that peace was slipping through my fingers, and I couldn't hold it together anymore.

The weight of the crown grew heavier. My fingers curled tightly around it now, not by choice but necessity. If I let go, I felt like I'd be ripped in two. We moved forward, slowly...Kaelen guiding me, one step at a time toward the center of the dais. Sera and Aeris kept a careful distance, their weapons lowered but ready, their eyes wide with unspoken understanding. I wasn't just remembering…I was *becoming*.

FLASH.

The betrayal. The worst one. The council chamber in flickering torchlight. My most trusted friend…her voice cracking, eyes shining with unshed tears…whispering the words of the sealing rite. Magic twisted around me, not cruelly, but desperately. I begged her. I begged her not to do it. "You don't understand," I cried. "If I sleep, the balance will break. The world will suffer." But she couldn't bear to see me wield that power again. Not after what it cost. "You're too close to the fire, Elara," she said. "We're saving you from it."

A noise tore from my throat…half gasp, half sob. Kaelen stopped, pulling me into him, shielding me from the weight of the moment. I pressed my forehead to his shoulder, eyes shut tight. "They took everything," I whispered. "They buried me in silence.

They called it mercy." "You didn't deserve that," he said, voice close to breaking. "You *didn't*." …But I wasn't finished.

FLASH.

A child. My niece. Silver-eyed, laughing in a sun-dappled glade. I reached out to lift them, and the world shifted again…fire, screaming, the child ripped from my arms by unseen hands. I chased, I screamed, I called out their name…but I couldn't find them. That wound opened fresh and raw across my soul.

I collapsed to my knees at the heart of the dais. The crown trembled in my hands. All twelve crystal pillars were burning now, pulsing in rhythm with my heartbeat, with the memories pouring back into me like floodwaters through a broken dam. Kaelen knelt beside me, his hand firm on my back. "Haji," he said, softer now. "*Elara*. If this is you…if this is who you were…then take it. Take her. All of her. You don't have to fight it anymore." Tears blurred my vision, but I didn't look away from the crown.

I sobbed louder, "It hurts." "I know," He said, and I believed him. "But pain means it's real. You're not lost. You're

remembering." The crown no longer felt like a relic. It felt like a part of me…something returned after ages apart. My grip steadied. The trembling stopped, and for the first time, I spoke with a voice that wasn't just mine…it was hers too. "I remember." The chamber pulsed. The crystal glowed brighter. Something ancient stirred beneath us, something bound to my name, waiting to rise again, and this time, I would not sleep.

The moment the words left my mouth, it was as though the very walls of the chamber trembled with a sudden, undeniable force. My heart pounded in my chest, a sound that matched the wild, thunderous beat of the world as everything around me shifted, warping and stretching. Memories, long buried, exploded to the surface. It was no longer flashes or moments…it was an ocean, crashing into me, overwhelming my senses.

FLASH.

I stood in the heart of a great battlefield, the sky split by storms and dragon fire. The air was thick with blood and magic. I raised my arms, summoning the winds to my will, calling the

dragons down from the heavens. They answered…screaming in defiance as they tore through the ranks of our enemies, their flames burning so bright I could feel the heat on my skin. The land itself shuddered, bending to my will.

FLASH.

My heart clenched as I looked into the eyes of the one I had trusted most. She…my second most beloved confidante…stood before me, offering me the dagger. "This is for your own good, Elara," she whispered, her hands shaking as she pressed it into my palm. I took it, unwilling to question her, and as the blade sank into my side, the pain was almost a relief. She had not betrayed me out of malice. She had done it out of fear. Fear of what I had become. Fear of what I could do. Together with him…the monster who caused all of this. He stood behind her, a sickening smile plastered across his face…

FLASH.

The crown was in my hands again, my fingers trembling as I placed it upon my head for the last time. The voices of the people I had loved…the elves, the dragons, all of them…echoed in the back of my mind. They had begged me to stop. To let go, but I could not. The weight of the crown, of my purpose, was too heavy. The magic that coursed through my veins was too powerful, too consuming. In my heart, I knew. I knew that if I let go, I would lose everything. I would lose them all.

FLASH.

My body was suspended in crystal. The runes had bound me, placed me in a deep, magical sleep to protect me from myself, from the terrible power I had wielded. I had fought against it. I had screamed. I had begged them to release me, but it was no use. My memories were taken. My purpose erased. I was cast aside, hidden away like a forgotten relic. Every single moment of my past…every victory, every loss…came crashing down at once. The love. The betrayal. The power. The fear. The pain. It was too much, too raw, too real.

The crown burned in my hands, and I felt it…the surge of magic, of pure, unadulterated power, coursing through me once again. It was not a whisper now, not a faint echo. It was a roar, a hurricane of flame, ice, and stone. I could feel the earth tremble beneath me. The world was shaking, and it was *my* awakening that had caused it. I took a shuddering breath, my voice a raw whisper.

"The betrayal that bound me to slumber was but a shadow. I am no longer its prisoner. I will rise from the ashes, and the world will tremble before me." The words resonated deep within me, igniting a fire in my chest. I rose slowly, unwilling to let the power take me all at once, but knowing that I was no longer in control of how quickly the flood would come.

It built, higher and higher, until I felt as though the very air around me would tear apart. My body hummed with the magic of the dragons, the magic of the elves, the magic of the world itself. I was no longer the quiet girl named Hajira. I was *Elara*, the queen who had once brought balance to all things. I had slept, yes, but I would sleep no longer.

FLASH.

I was standing in the center of a city, the crown upon my brow, the land before me stretched in all its glory. The dragons circled overhead, their wings vast and mighty, while the elves bowed before me, offering me their fealty. There, in the distance, the first of the dark forces that sought to undo everything I had built rose from the shadows. I raised my hand, the winds answering my call. The ground beneath me cracked open as the earth itself bent to my will. The air thickened with magic as I stepped forward.

FLASH.

I was on the edge of a precipice. Below me, the world was burning...my people, my kingdom, my dragons...all torn apart by the very power I had sought to protect them with. The guilt, the sorrow, it was suffocating. I had been forced into a prison, a sleep, to keep that power from destroying everything...But no longer. I was awake, and I was whole.

I opened my eyes, and the world around me shifted again. Kaelen was there, his eyes wide with a mixture of fear and awe. He

had been there for me, helping me rise from the ruins, but even he could not fully understand what was unfolding. Sera and Aeris watched from a distance, their faces pale, unsure of what they were witnessing. I didn't need their understanding. I was Elara, and the world would soon feel the weight of that name.

The ground beneath us trembled. The pillars of crystal flared with blinding light. The dragons stirred far in the distance, sensing the awakening of the power that had once ruled them. I lifted my gaze, feeling the magic surge within me, flooding every fiber of my being. The world would *tremble*. I placed the crown on top of my head. I reached for my beloved bow and arrow.

I straightened my back, remembering my prowl and grace, once long forgotten. "I have slept for centuries, hidden in the shadows of forgotten legends," I said, the power in my voice shaking the very air. "But now I awaken, and the world will know that I am not a myth…I am the nightmare that comes for all who dare to challenge me."

To be continued…

ABOUT THE AUTHOR

Hi there! I'm Sarah Jackson, Co-CEO of DragonShrimp Publishing LLC, author, dreamer, and lifelong lover of fantasy. With a Master's in Business Administration and a background in public service, I have spent years working in local government before answering the creative call I could no longer ignore.

Books have always been my escape, a place where magic is real and the impossible becomes possible. As a kid, the fantasy genre offered me solace from a tough reality and planted the seeds of storytelling in my heart. I've been writing in one form or another ever since, from heartfelt poetry scribbled in high school journals to the sprawling, imaginative worlds I bring to life today.

I share this adventure with my amazing husband and fellow Co-CEO, Damian Jackson. Together we run DragonShrimp Publishing LLC from our cozy home in Southwest Florida, where we're supervised by our spirited boxer, Thor McBacon Bits (yes, that's really his name).

Thank you for taking the time to read my book and supporting this wild, wonderful journey of words and worlds. I'm so glad you're here.